Also by Martha Wells

Martha Wells

WITCH KING

TOR PUBLISHING GROUP

NEW YORK

WITCH KING

Copyright © 2023 by Martha Wells

Map by Rhys Davies

A Tordotcom Book
Published by Tom Doherty Associates / Tor Publishing Group
120 Broadway
New York, NY 10271

www.tor.com

Tor® is a registered trademark of Macmillan Publishing Group, LLC.

The Library of Congress Cataloging-in-Publication Data is available upon request.

ISBN 978-1-250-82679-4 (hardback)
ISBN 978-1-250-82680-0 (ebook)

Our books may be purchased in bulk for promotional, educational, or business use. Please contact your local bookseller or the Macmillan Corporate and Premium Sales Department at 1-800-221-7945, extension 5442, or by email at MacmillanSpecialMarkets@macmillan.com.

First Edition: 2023

Printed in the United States of America

0 9 8 7 6 5 4 3 2 1

To Felicia

DRAMATIS PERSONAE

KAIISTERON: Prince of the Fourth House of the underearth (called Witch King)

ZIEDE DAIYAHAH: High Teacher in the Mountain Cloisters of the Khalin Islands (called the Scourge of the Temple Halls)

TAHREN STARGARD: an Immortal Marshall of the Blessed Lands (called the Fallen)

DAHIN: Tahren's Lesser Blessed sibling

GRANDMOTHER: An ancestor of the Saredi of the grassplains, once a Captain of scouts, who negotiated a treaty with the forces of the underearth and married a demon prince

The Present

SANJA: a street child of the Mouth of Flowers

TENES: a Witch of unknown origin, captured as a familiar by Aclines

BASHAT BAR CALIS: Current Prince-heir of Benais-arik, foremost of the Rising World Coalition Council, soon to be Emperor

RAMAD: personal vanguarder to Prince-heir Bashat

ASHEM: a cohort leader for the Rising World, stationed in the Arkai

MENLAS: an unfortunately ambitious expositor

ACLINES: an expositor of great power

SAFRESES AND KINLAT: lords of the court of Nient-arik

SAADRIN: an Immortal Marshall of the Stargard line, estranged from Tahren

FAHARIN: an Immortal Blessed

NARREIN AND SHIREN: Lesser Blessed of Faharin's House

KAVINEN: Lesser Blessed of the Stargard line

TANIS: eldest daughter of Ziede Daiyahah

The Past

BASHASA CALIS: the Prince-heir of Benais-arik, sent to the Summer Halls as a hostage for his city's good behavior (called the Great)

ADENI, VARRA, AND ILUDI: cousins to Enna, of the Kentdessa Saredi

CANTENIOS: an expositor of the Hierarchs' court at the Summer Halls

ARN-NEFA: a demon of the Kanavesi Saredi

TALAMINES: a High Expositor of the Hierarchs' court at the Summer Halls, originally conscripted from Irekan

HIERARCH'S VOICE RAIHANKANA: the servant-noble charged with speaking the Hierarchs' will to those too low to listen to the Sacred Voice

ARSHA, TELARE, NIRANA, HARTEL, CERALA: Ariki soldiers who followed Bashasa to the Hostage Courts of the Summer Halls, later seconded to Kaiisteron Fourth Prince

ARAVA, VASHAR, TRENAL: Ariki soldiers of Bashasa Calis' personal cadre

SALATEL: Second Shield Bearer to Prince-heir Bashasa, later leader of the cadre assigned to the Fourth Prince

THE TESCAI-LIN: Great Sage of Enalin and Light of the Hundred Coronels

LAHSHAR CALIS: maternal cousin to Prince-heir Bashasa of Benais-arik

DASARA: the son and heir of Lahshar Calis

HIRANAN: First Daughter of the Prince-heir of Seidel-arik

VRIM: Second Son of the Prince-heir of Descar-arik

ASARA: Second Daughter of the Prince-heir of Bardes-arik

STAMASH: maternal uncle of the Prince-heir of Renitl-arik

KARANIS CALIS: paternal cousin to Prince-heir Bashasa, who was selected by the Hierarchs to usurp the rule of Benais-arik

ONE

Waking was floating to the surface of a soft world of water, not what Kai had expected. Reaching out in that darkness, he found a cold, black sea ebbing and flowing, dropping away like a tide rolling out. Something was wrong with his body, everything was impossibly distant. He stretched out a thought and called, *Ziede?*

She was slow to answer, her voice low and strange. He couldn't see her. She whispered, *I'm sleeping, Kai.*

You're not sleeping, you're talking to me. He should know where she was, he always knew where she was, she had a drop of his blood hardened into a red pearl buried in her heart.

I told you not to wake... She stopped. Her languid voice turned alert and urgent. *Kai. Where am I? I can't move.*

None of this made sense. He reached out as far as he could stretch, searching for something, anything solid. He made his inner voice sound calm, though a sinking sensation told him he wouldn't like the answers to any of his questions. *I'm not sure where I am, either,* he told Ziede. Some terrible revelation loomed but he kept it at bay; better to just focus on finding her. He pulled in the parts of himself that drifted in the dark water that perhaps wasn't water, to concentrate his being back into his own body. Except his body wasn't there.

Kai squelched a spike of panic. Panic had to be postponed.

Her mental voice astringent, Ziede said, *Take your time, Kai. Wherever I am, I can't see, I can't move. I'm breathing, but I can't feel*... *I can't feel my chest move.* He could hear the suppressed fear as she added, *I can't find Tahren, she doesn't answer.*

Something had cut them off from the outside world. He told

her, *Don't try to move. Just wait.* If Kai could think, he wasn't help-less.

He pulled all his focus in until the black sea yielded and re-solved into dark stone walls, a large circular chamber, water run-ning down from the upper shadows. Mossy weeds furred the gaps between the stones, light crept in from somewhere behind him. He needed to move, but swimming around in the air as an amor-phous cloud was new and deeply disconcerting. He imagined his body around him, pulled his arms in, and spun himself to look down.

At his own body.

It lay on a raised plinth in a glass coffin box. His face was vis-ible, the rest wrapped in dark fabric. His cheeks, the flesh below his eyes, were drawn and sunken but still recognizable. *It's been months . . . maybe a year?* If someone had done this to him, what had they done to Ziede?

Ziede, you said you can't move, can't see. In this terrifying, un-familiar place, there was no other box, nothing large enough to conceal her. The water drained away through diagonal vents in the floor. Water. It must have filled the chamber to keep Kai in-side his inert body. When the level dropped he had been able to drift out and wake. Insubstantial, he had no sense of motion, so was the chamber lifting up out of the water? And what did it matter when Ziede might be entombed alive and he had no way to release her. He groped for some way to get more information. *What do you smell?*

Nothing but fabric . . . Like old silk? She added, *Kai, what is this? Where are we?*

I don't know. She was sealed inside something, possibly a silk-lined casket. He would have closed his eyes in despair if his eyes hadn't been rotting in the glass coffin below. *Ziede, I'm afraid we're . . .* He hesitated. Something had caused the water to run out of this bizarre burial chamber.

Something was coming.

Soundless, the curved wall across from the plinth split, allowing in a narrow column of muted blue light. Figures spilled through, dim and distant. It was hard to focus in this insubstantial form. Five human shapes, who dragged two bundles—bodies—behind them.

They dumped their burdens on the floor near the curved wall. The smaller body kicked, struggled, was kicked back, and subsided to huddle against the wall. The other lay in a still heap.

Kai scented death on that limp form. He thought of Ziede, trapped and helpless unless he could find her, and the pain of it gave him a spark of power.

The body was empty, the occupant flown, but warmth still radiated from the flesh. Just enough. Kai spun again, concentrated his whole being inward, and fell through the void toward that warmth.

Sound, color, and sensation roared back in a wave, aching joints, the grind of a bone in the wrong place, raw and burning throat, damp fabric clinging to long awkward limbs. But the pain generated a restorative well of power that burst through this new flesh.

Kai pushed himself up on his hands and lifted his head, dragged in a stabbing breath. Dark curls hung past his shoulders, tangled in a heavy veil of metal and fabric. The skin on his hands was a familiar warm brown. He wore a long dark skirt and tunic, a common variation on traditional eastern clothing. But there was nothing under it, and it was stained with blood and worse. He gasped in another lungful of air, damp, stale with mold and rot. He had lost his sense of Ziede, but that should be temporary. He hoped it was temporary, but the way this day was going so far he wouldn't count on it.

The mortals examined the glass coffin. One prodded at the lid. Kai hadn't completely settled into his new brain yet and he couldn't understand their speech.

Four wore clothing like the mariners along the southeastern

archipelagoes, wide cotton pants gathered at the ankles, short open jackets, and broad leather belts. Two also wore the long knee-length shirts more common to women of that area. Their skin was pale under the weathering and their light-colored hair was straight and long, pinned or tied back. The fifth person had the same looks but was older, and wore richer garments, a red knee-length coat over a long dark tunic and skirt, the glitter of silver chains and onyx ornaments hanging from his belt. Kai smelled an expositor, and the man's complacent and predatory demeanor confirmed it.

Words started to make sense again. The person huddled next to Kai was whispering, "You were dead."

His new body's memories were patchy and staccato, fading fast, but one whispered, *A little girl, too young to be here.* With the painful weight of the metal veil tugging at his head, Kai had to crane his neck to see her. She was small, dressed in a ragged filthy shirt and pants cropped at the knee, too light for the dank chill in the room. Tight curls were hacked off close to her head, and her skin was a dark brown. Eastern coast, maybe. She had spoken in Imperial Arike, which as the dominant trade language didn't narrow it down, and he didn't recognize her accent.

The temporary power well created by Kai's own pain restored his new body: bones knit and shifted back into place, a burst organ pulled itself together, the broken nose clicked into alignment, splintered pieces of jawbone grew into new teeth with a jabbing burst of pain that almost collapsed him to the floor. He breathed through it until his blood stopped bubbling, then shoved his jaw back until it clicked and held. He whispered, "Do we know each other?"

She flinched like she would have recoiled, if she wasn't more afraid of attracting attention. Wide-eyed, she shook her head. "Not . . . Not really. Your eyes . . ."

Kai dragged the veil forward, just enough to conceal the top half of his face. "It's for the best. He's—She? They? Aren't here anymore."

The girl's breath hitched. She understood, but she didn't want to. "I thought . . . but they beat you . . . him to death."

From the other side of the room, the expositor said, "Get the girl."

A mariner turned and strode toward them. He leaned down to grab for the girl, saying, "Guess you get to go first."

Kai lunged. The man grabbed him instead and dragged him to his feet. Once he was holding Kai up he stared, startled. A woman mariner protested, "No, not that one! The other."

"I thought he was dead," someone else said.

They were speaking Imperial Arike, too; the expositor correctly and the mariners with a thick accent and slurred vowels. Kai said, "Oh, please, take me! I want to go first." He wrenched out of the man's grip and staggered on unsteady legs toward his coffin. Catching himself on the corner of the plinth, he leaned back against it, facing this very unlucky group of tomb-pillagers. "To bring him back, right?" He jerked his head toward his old body, wincing as the heavy veil yanked at his scalp. "I don't have a lot of time, so let's just get this over with."

Another mariner laughed and drew a long knife. He said, "He'll be dead enough now." He had a shallow prettiness that didn't reach past his tawny skin. A name came to Kai, a fragment of memory engraved into this brain in agony, reluctant to fade. This mariner was Tarrow, who had pretended to be kind at first so his betrayal would hurt more.

Between the shadowy room and the veil, the mortals couldn't see Kai's face clearly. But the expositor stared, his gaze sharpening into the edge of horrified realization. He said, "Wait."

But Tarrow was eager to cause more hurt. He stepped forward and stabbed Kai through the chest. Kai fell back against the plinth. The pain blacked out his vision, the steel cleaving already abused flesh.

As Tarrow moved away, Kai grabbed the blade. The edge cut into his fingers as he pulled it out. He tossed it aside, ignoring the brief gush of blood down his chest as his flesh wove itself back together. The new power well blossoming under his skin pulsed like a second heart. "Now," Kai said, grinning as he shoved the veil aside. "Which one of you wants to go first?"

No one was laughing now. The chamber was utterly still except for the drip and gurgle of draining water.

"Come here, Tarrow," Kai said, focusing his will, his smile pulling at tendon and bone that was still tender after its restoration. Caught like a petal in amber, Tarrow took stiff steps toward him, resisting with all his mental strength, which sadly for him was not nearly adequate. Kai brought him close enough that he could easily grip his throat. He said, "Tell me, did you know his name? This one's name, that you brought here to die?"

Tarrow made a choking noise. The expositor tried to cast an intention, something to bind Kai's new body. But the pain of being stabbed had filled Kai with terrible power and he caught the intention as it formed. He turned it back, spending most of his temporary strength to trap the expositor and the other mariners where they stood. They struggled uselessly, unable to move their feet or draw weapons. One whimpered, which almost made Kai crush Tarrow's throat in reflex before he was ready, which would have been a waste. With an edge of panic, another said, "Menlas, you said you could master him—"

"Shut up!" Fighting to move, his voice rough with shock and desperation, the expositor Menlas said, "We brought you offerings! We appeal to—"

"You brought me a child and a youth so close to death he didn't last a heartbeat past the threshold of this room. Did you think to coax me into a weak, helpless body so I'd be your slave?" Kai laughed, a raspy sound hampered by his still regrowing lung tissue. From the expression on Menlas' face, Kai knew he was close to the truth. "That isn't how this works, expositor." Then he peeled Tarrow's soul from his body and ate his life.

A heartbeat later Kai let the withered husk drop to the floor.

The others broke like twigs. The screaming and pleading was noisy and irritating, more so from mortals who had not bothered to listen to the screaming and pleading of their own captives. Kai took the first two quickly, to replenish the power he had spent to trap them. Then he let the expositor and the last mariner loose to try to run, just because Kai found himself still surprisingly angry and he wanted to let it all out before he had to be rational again. The heavy veil, still stuck in his hair and torturing his scalp, wasn't helping.

When the last mariner was a dry heap of desiccated flesh and Kai was sitting on the expositor's chest, he asked, "Who put me here?"

Menlas shook his head wildly, gasping.

Maybe Kai had phrased the question badly. "Who did this to me? Who put me in this tomb? And how did you know I was here?"

"I can't—The stories said—I—" And then the idiot's heart started to seize up.

Exasperated, Kai drained his life before the man expired and wasted it.

He pushed to his feet, briskly shaking out his skirt. "All done," he told the girl. She was shivering, still huddled against the wall, but she had watched every moment. He kicked the nearest woman's body over and stripped the long shirt off it. He tossed it to her. "Put that on and get up. I'm not going to eat you, we're friends."

She caught the shirt, then dragged it on over her head. She stumbled to her feet, which were bare, dirty, and marked with cuts and mottled bruises. "What . . . What are you going to—"

"I have to find someone." Kai leaned over another desiccated body, tore open the laces of its wrap boots and dragged them off, then tossed them to the girl. His sense of Ziede's presence grew at the edge of his awareness. But it was still hard to tell her direction. "Was there another coffin? Did you see one?"

The girl picked up the boots, trailing after him to the doorway, unsteady and still trembling. She answered, "No. I just saw the stairwell."

Kai stepped through the opening in the wall. It led to a passage, blue light coming from polished stones set in the rounded ceiling. The powerful web of intentions that had gone into constructing this place was written into every handspan of rock. Someone had taken an already existing structure and modified it for their purpose. The passage curved around a solid column and turned into a set of upward stairs, water still running down over worn white stone. The girl said, "Do you have to do that to people to live?"

"No," Kai told her. "I did it because I wanted to. And bad people taste better than good ones." He held out his hand.

She looked up at him, brown eyes wide in the dim light, bruised and sunken from hunger. Then she took his hand. Her skin was cold with shock.

Tugging her along after him, he climbed the spiral of steps up until the well opened into a broad hall, the high ceiling dotted with more of the blue glowstones. At the end was a clear curved bubble of crystal, looking out into dull gray-green water.

From the fish swimming by, this place stood in a large body of water, and now that Kai had a working nose, he could smell salt, as if over years it had seeped into the seals between the stones. Someone had gone to a lot of trouble to make certain he wouldn't wake enough to escape his corpse. The other walls were set with large square carvings, like decorative frames around doorways, but the plaques in the center were empty. He led the girl around the central pillar to see the stairs curved up the far side. "What is this place?" he asked.

"An island, but like a tower, all made of stone," the girl said. She rubbed at her bloody nose and winced. "They brought us in through the top. What are—"

Kai held up a finger for silence. His sense of Ziede was stronger here, on this end of the hall. He focused on the slender thread that tied him to the pearl in her heart. *Ziede?*

Still here. Her voice was bleak, under tight control.

He let go of the girl's hand and went methodically along the wall. Each carved panel was part of the intention woven through this place. Nothing lived behind them, but there was a sensation of a cavity or hidden chamber in the stone. Empty cavities, with nothing stored inside, not even decaying bodies. *She has to be here.*

Then on the far side of the chamber, he felt an occupied void, the weight of something large and heavy filling the space. He could get through the thin layer of polished stone with a heavy tool if he could find one, but first he tried the easy way. He felt along the carvings of shellfish and water snakes for a catch or a seam. Crouching to run his fingers along the lower edge, Kai found a small depression; when he pushed it, a dull thump sounded from inside.

Kai stood and backed away, almost stepping on the girl, who had been hovering close behind him. It said interesting things about her character, or maybe her recent past, that she found him less terrifying than anything else that might be in this place.

The panel cracked and crumbled and the plaster clattered to the floor. Resting inside the cavity was a dark marbled coffin box on a smooth stone bed. Kai grabbed the curved end and pulled. A clanking counterweight caught and the whole slid out of the sepulcher. There was no glass lid, the top was rounded carved stone. Kai found the seam and shoved with almost all his strength. The lid flew off and hit the floor with an ear-shattering crack.

Ziede lay inside.

Her eyes were closed. He put his hand on her forehead. She was alive, warm and alive. She hadn't aged or altered in any way he could see; she had the same deep brown skin, high forehead, and long straight nose, her dark hair drawn back in dozens of braided rows the way she preferred to wear it. She was dressed for a ceremony or a celebration, in red the color of arterial blood, a draped tunic of close-fitting silk. Kai found the shape of the intention that held her life in suspension; a gentle twist snapped it.

Her chest moved as she drew a sharp breath. He slid his arms under her and lifted her free of the box. Her eyes fluttered open and she grabbed his shoulders, nails digging into his neck. He was almost choking with relief and it made his voice thick. "You're safe, Ziede."

She blinked, startled to be looking at an unfamiliar face. As awareness came into her gaze, Kai slowly set her on her feet, keeping hold of her arms to steady her.

They were the same height now. His old body had been shorter, and he was used to tilting his head to look up at her. She touched his cheek. "Is that you in there?" Then she answered her own question. "Yes, that's you. Did they kill you?"

"Somebody did." He was still so relieved it was hard to think. He tapped the edge of Ziede's stone bier. "They put me into one of these."

Ziede looked at the niche where she had been entombed alive and her shoulders hunched. "I don't remember how we got here." She frowned down at herself. "I don't remember owning these clothes."

"I don't remember how we got here either." Kai rubbed her arms. "Are you all right?"

"Yes." She steadied herself and took a deep breath. "So we have no idea how long . . . ?"

"I looked like I'd been dead around a year." He turned to the girl. He and Ziede had been speaking in Saredi, the first mortal tongue Kai had ever learned, and he switched to Imperial Arike so the girl could understand. "Is Bashat bar Calis of Benais-arik still leader of the Rising World?"

"I guess?" she said. She had seated herself on the floor to pull the boots on, biting her lip as she wrapped the leather flaps over bruises and broken toes. "That's the name on the coins?"

Not helpful. Kai persisted, "Do you know the month in Imperial reckoning?"

Her forehead furrowed in thought. "It was the end of the third solar month. Almost the end. They hadn't changed the marker on the calendar tower. And it took about five days to get here."

"Close enough." Reassured, Kai turned back to Ziede. "Can you get this out of my head?" He pointed to the tangle of fabric and gem-bedecked chains stuck in his hair. Giving her something constructive to do would help ground her, and also he really needed to get rid of the awful thing.

Ziede turned him around and prodded the lump where the veil was wound up. "Is it embedded in your skull?" She had followed his lead, speaking in Imperial Arike.

"It feels like it." The pull on his scalp made him want to kill at least ten more mariners and expositors together, possibly by skinning them alive, if he couldn't think of anything worse.

"It's just a chain veil," the girl said, pulling at her boot laces to make them fit.

"Who is this?" Ziede asked him, exasperated as her fingernails picked at the tiny tangled chains.

"She's new." He wanted to relax into Ziede's careful touch as she unwound his hair from the decorative torture device, but there was still no time.

"I'm Sanja," the girl said, getting to her feet. "I don't want to be here."

"She's Sanja," he explained to Ziede. "They brought her as a sacrifice." Probably Menlas had meant to kill her to power whatever intention he planned to use to bind Kai. Menlas had apparently known just enough to be dangerous, mostly to himself.

"Hello, Sanja. Do either of us look like we want to be here?" Ziede asked her.

"No." Sanja lifted her chin defiantly, but there was a little tremble in her voice. "Did you bring me for her? If she needed a new body?"

Ziede's laugh was harsh. "I can't step into a new body, alive or dead. That's Kai's trick."

Kai told her, "That's why we had to find Ziede while she was still breathing." Sanja still seemed too much in shock to look relieved, she just breathed out a little and fiddled with the sleeve of her new shirt. Kai continued, "You said you couldn't reach Tahren."

"I've been trying this whole time." Ziede's voice sounded calm and sure, unless you knew her well enough to hear the emotion underneath. Tahren had a heart pearl from Ziede, and even if they were too far apart to use them to speak, she should have some sense of her presence.

If Tahren had also been attacked, their situation was even worse than it looked. Kai said, "Tahren's not here, no one else is here."

Her hands stilled for a moment, then continued to unwind the chains. "If Tahren was free, she would have come for us. She would tear the world apart to find us. Dahin . . . Dahin wouldn't just leave us either."

Kai's throat went tight. Dahin might be estranged from Tahren, but he wasn't from Kai and Ziede. And no matter how much he and Tahren might argue, Dahin would still protect her, and Tahren would still destroy anything that tried to hurt him. But that didn't mean they were dead. "All we know is that they aren't here. Something could be obscuring Tahren's pearl. She could be looking for us, she could be protecting the others at home. We won't know until we can get some idea of what happened."

With that false calm, Ziede said, "If they've touched one hair on Tahren's stubborn head, I will slaughter them." With one more tug, the chain veil came free. Ziede tossed it to the floor and ran her fingers through Kai's loose curls, shaking the tangles out.

"We'll slaughter them." Kai rubbed his aching head, already feeling the tension in his back and neck ease. "Where do you come from, Sanja?"

"The Mouth of the Sea of Flowers. They bought us both." She hesitated. She was hugging herself, but her trembling had eased. "Why didn't you ask me my name before?"

"I didn't want it until you were ready to give it to me." At least Kai knew where the Sea of Flowers was, just not in relation to where they were now. The Mouth was a free city outside the Rising World's reach, the last surviving fragment of the lands of the Nehush. It had been resettled by sea raiders after the war had left it nearly deserted, but now it was a well-traveled port again. It was still an ideal place for an expositor to hide. "They came here from the Mouth in a boat?"

"In a shell-whale." Sanja shrugged thin shoulders. "I'd never seen one close-up before."

"Huh. So Menlas the expositor must have been a powerful sorcerer."

"I guess he thought he was," Sanja said, a trace of dryness in her tone.

Scratching his liberated scalp vigorously, Kai said, "You two wait here. I'm going back to search the bodies. Ziede, I'll get you some clothes."

As he started away, Ziede said, "Kai. You should check your heart for a pearl."

He hesitated and shook his head. "It's not there, Ziede."

"Prove that to me, Kai," she persisted as he walked away. "Prove it."

TWO

The best thing about draining the life from the mariners was that they had all died without soiling their clothes. Kai searched all five, took some of their clothing for Ziede, and set out the weapons and other objects they had carried with them for closer examination. There was no food, so hopefully the crew had brought plenty of supplies on their craft. Kai didn't need to eat very often but Ziede got cranky when she didn't and Sanja looked underfed.

Kai's new body was short on clothing and the tunic was badly stained. He took the skirt and the close-fitting leggings that the expositor Menlas had worn, and the fine long-sleeved tunic that came down to his knees. He cinched it with a mariner's leather belt and had to bind the overlong sleeves up so they wouldn't fall over his hands, but otherwise it was comfortable. He took a braided silk cord that probably had some great significance to Menlas' family or culture and used it to tie back the section of his hair that most wanted to fall forward into his face.

Then he gathered everything useful or pretty out of the pile of belongings and scooped it all into an empty bag one of the women had brought, obviously hoping for loot. He should have taken it and gone back to Ziede and Sanja, but he found himself standing there. Facing his body.

Ziede's wrong, he thought. *There's no pearl in my heart. I don't have to look.* And they didn't have time. A tomb so carefully constructed undoubtedly had alarms attached to it. Someone would know they were free.

But he went to the glass box and, with a little tendril of power, broke the design that sealed it. Trapped foul air hissed out as he lifted the lid.

It was strange, and not pleasant, to see himself this way. He hadn't been born into this body, but he had been in it for a long time, so long he had almost forgotten what it was to be anything else. Like Ziede, he didn't recognize the clothes he was wearing, the coarse gauzy fabric of the shroud, the plain dark coat beneath. He had been entombed with no jewelry, nothing that should accompany an Arike noble's grave.

He took the knife that Tarrow had stabbed him with and used it to cut through the shroud and coat, then the skin of his chest, and the rotting flesh beneath.

There, in the center of his heart, was a silver-white pearl.

———∞———

When Kai returned, Sanja was explaining about Menlas and telling Ziede what had happened in the tomb below. "He said he was going to enslave a great demon, make him a familiar."

"Yes, that's what all the idiots think," Ziede told her.

"I brought clothes." Kai dropped them on Ziede's slab and pushed a pile toward Sanja. "Pick out what you want."

Ziede tugged at the waist of her draped tunic in frustration. "I don't know how to get out of this thing. I think I'm sewn into it."

Sanja took a half step toward her, meaning to help, but Kai just handed her the knife. Ziede took it and started methodically hacking the clothing off her body. She clearly needed to hack at something for a while to retain her composure.

Watching her, Kai said, "Ziede, you were right."

Distracted, she sliced the tunic up the front. "I usually am. What is it this time?"

"I looked. The pearl was there."

He expected her to say some variation on *I knew it was there, I told you it was there.* But she went still, staring at him, her gaze troubled. "I thought . . . I thought you would come back and tell me I was wrong." Her mouth went thin, holding back emotion, and she took the knife to her tunic again. "I wanted to be wrong."

Kai looked at the floor, not wanting to see her expression, especially if it was sympathetic. Sanja had pulled on a pair of mariner's pants under the shirt he had given her earlier. Watching them with wary confusion, she said, "How can you have something in your heart and not die?"

Kai sighed. He felt like an idiot, a betrayed idiot. There was an answering flash of memory from what was left of his body's previous occupant, and an image of the pretty Tarrow. "That's a good question. A better one is 'How could I have a pearl in my heart and not know.'"

"I have one," Ziede told Sanja. The tunic finally came off and she dropped the remnants to the floor and kicked it away as if it were a vicious snake. "From Kai, for protection. He gave it to me and I swallowed it."

Kai told her, "Put clothes on, you'll get chilled." He pulled out another pair of pants, a tunic, and Menlas' red coat to hand to her.

"Who put the pearl there?" Sanja asked. She had rolled up the pant legs to fit and looked even more like the child she was.

Ziede was methodically dressing. Her voice was hard. "Someone we thought was a friend."

There were no lights in the upper part of the curving stone stairwell, so Kai called an imp the size of a dragonfly and they followed its darting glow upward. The higher they climbed, the more the air had the faint scent of fresh salt wind. Behind him, Ziede was interrogating Sanja.

"When we got here it was night, but they waited until morning." Sanja huffed critically. "I guess they thought it was safer."

Ziede asked, "How did this Menlas get in? Was there a key of some sort?"

"If there was, I didn't see." Sanja took a sharp breath. She had been veering between tough ageless street rat and badly scarred child. Her voice wavered. "They were hitting . . . him."

Kai paused and looked down at her. The flitting imp's white light washed the color out of her face. It would make it impossible to see his expression. "What was his name?"

She bit her lip. "I never knew. They gave us poppy, I think. It made me sick and they got angry because I kept throwing up. They kept taking him away, I guess he was trying to fight them? We never had a chance to say much to each other."

Kai turned back to the climb. Now that the body's memories had faded, he would never know anything more about the former occupant. Of all the things he had to be angry about at this moment, it should be a minor consideration. But it wasn't.

Maybe because he had been in his last body so long. He had taken it from an enemy, not been forced to accept an unwilling sacrifice. He could have taken longer to kill Menlas and his hirelings, but it wasn't like punishment ever fixed anything. Kai had been punished by eager experts, and it had just made him more determined. "Did the mariners say much about the expositor? Did they know him well?"

"Maybe? We were down in the bottom of the shell, and he never came in there with them, so I didn't see them talk to each other." After a moment of consideration, Sanja added, "But I think they didn't like him much. Maybe they thought they were going to steal whatever he found and then kill him. Maybe he was going to kill them, once he didn't need them anymore."

"Probably," Kai said absently. He thought she was getting away from the facts of what she had seen and heard and into made-up stories about her captors' motivations; it wouldn't help to question her further unless she remembered something specific. Even if her stories might be close to the truth, since expositors didn't get to be powerful without standing atop a large pile of victims and betrayed subordinates.

Still focused on the mechanics of the tomb's construction, Ziede asked, "How did the water drain from the lower part of the tower?"

Sanja said, "I didn't see. We were in the stairwell, then Menlas told them to bring us in, and the water was running everywhere." She hesitated, then asked, "Why was the water there? He was dead in the glass box. Sort of dead?"

"Do you know who I am, Sanja?" Kai asked. From what she had said, Menlas hadn't been free with his plans, at least not where his victims could hear.

"No . . . Not . . . No," Sanja admitted. "I don't really know what a demon is. You're like an expositor?"

"Just tell her, Kai," Ziede said, then was too impatient to wait. "He's Kaiisteron, the Witch King."

There was a scuffle behind him as Sanja missed a step and was caught, steadied, and pushed into motion again by Ziede. "But that's a story," Sanja protested. "From the Arike, the Rising World. Like the Hierarchs."

"The Hierarchs aren't a story either," Ziede said grimly. "The murderous shits were hard enough to kill."

The next turn of the stairwell opened up into bright sunlight and a wash of cool salt-tinged air. Kai ran up the last few steps to the wide top of a cylindrical tower. The mid-morning sky was bright blue, dotted with clouds, though heavier gray bands to the west promised rain. Kai flung out his arms and twirled, taking a deep breath of wind with a hint of storm rain to it. He hadn't realized how the weight of the surrounding water and the enclosed space had worn on him until now. The only sign of land was far to the south, smudges on the horizon that would be low-lying islands.

He released the light imp with a wave. It sped away so fast it winked out of sight. Imps weren't keen on water and enclosed spaces either.

Despite the wind, the air was warmer out here, though if that far-off storm came this way, the temperature would drop. After the chill below, Kai wanted to lie down on the paving and soak in the sun.

A deep echoing groan and a slosh of water against the tower's side sent him to the balustrade. The shell-whale Sanja had promised was docked below, a huge, partially submerged shape washed by the waves lapping against the tower wall. Its skin was a deep dark blue blending into red along its flanks. A brown and ivory striped nautilus shell attached to its back sat high above the water, as large as a substantial house, an indication of Menlas' power. The curving mouth of it faced upward, the stairs inside spiraling down out of sight.

"The stone's weathered for years, this place has been here for a long time," Ziede said behind him. She was examining the top of the tower with a critical eye. "It might be an old sea people's tomb. It wasn't built for us."

Kai agreed. Building something like this would have taken the resources of a minor city-state at least; it was more likely their enemy had spent their time looking for a deserted ruin that could be made to serve their purpose once it was altered with the right designs and intentions. "It still means there was a lot of advance planning, but then, they'd need that to catch us both. Sanja, how did Menlas get you all up here?"

Sanja leaned over the balustrade beside him. "There was a thing, like a block and tackle with a platform for him and the crew. They hauled us up in a net . . ." She pointed. "There it is!"

A bundle of wood and rope debris floated near the dome of the shell-whale's head. The net was caught on the barnacles below the tower's waterline, trailing away under the water. The expositor would have used a minor intention to suspend the structure from the tower's balustrade; when Kai killed him it had collapsed. "Are we going to haul it back up here?" Sanja asked doubtfully.

"We won't need it." Kai glanced at Ziede, who was studying the paving thoughtfully, the wind-devils plucking playfully at her clothes and hair. "Ziede, where are we?"

She lifted a hand, tasting the air currents with her fingertips. "We're east of the Mouth of Flowers," she said. She nodded toward the distant smudge of land to the south. "That's one of the islands in the Eligoes."

Now Kai knew where they needed to go. "We need to move."

Ziede scuffed at the paving one last time and then came to the balustrade. She put her hand on Kai's shoulder to steady herself and stepped up onto the low wall. Kai pulled his skirt out of the way and scrambled up beside her. Ziede reached down and Sanja, eyes wide, took her hand and let herself be pulled up. "Uh." She looked at Kai, and then at the long way down to the water. "Can you fly?"

"No, but Ziede can," he said, as Ziede stepped into the wind-devil that opened like a flower for her. Sanja made a choked noise of dismay as Ziede drew her and Kai off the wall into empty space.

The wind-devil dropped like a fallen leaf, swaying and twirling them, until it reached the shell mouth. Ziede pulled them out of the devil's grip and onto the first steps of the shell. "It's not flying, it's entity manipulation," Ziede corrected in annoyance.

Kai went down the spiral steps into the shell's pearly interior. The air was close and it smelled dank and fishy; he winced. Close to the water wasn't the way he preferred to travel but it wasn't as if they had a choice.

The steps led to the shell's uppermost chamber, a serpentine space where curves and cavities in the interior had been used to store a set of small decorated chests, like those for writing or medical instruments, and other supplies. One large cubby was lined with heavy quilts and cushions, probably the spot where Menlas had made his bed. Kai took the narrow passage down into the lower part of the shell, finding a smaller chamber holding net bags of fruit and gourds, waterskins, and clay pots. Other chambers held hammocks with rougher blankets where the crew must have slept, cubbies and shelves storing spare weapons, personal possessions. At the bottom, next to the whale's skin, he found the stinking chamber with its ropes and chains, where Sanja and her dead companion had been held, which had apparently also been the craft's latrine.

He climbed back up, where Ziede and Sanja waited. Sanja held tightly to Ziede's hand. Understandable, Kai didn't like revisiting places where he had been tortured, either. Prowling along the wall, checking all the cubbies more closely, he said, "No one else is aboard. We need to get away from here."

Ziede lifted her brows in acknowledgment. "Do you know how to make this thing go?"

"No, but if an expositor can do it, how hard could it be?" He found a small nacreous shelf near the front where some ingredients had been set out. Salts and powders in tiny polished cups of shell, a few bits of wood splinter darkened with blood, a diagram etched on a faded scrap of cloth. *This . . . is not it.* Menlas hadn't been working on intentions here, he had been trying to duplicate Witch's work. From the sparks of intention still clinging to the pieces, whatever it was had been successful. *I wonder if this is how he found us?*

The expositors originally conscripted and trained for the Hierarchs' use had survived long enough to pass their knowledge along to apprentices. Whoever had taught Menlas had let him think he was powerful enough to enter a sealed tomb meant as a trap for the immortal Witch King. Possibly it had been meant as an elaborate method of murder.

Kai continued to poke around the shelves, aware of Ziede going below and bringing up a couple of bags and pots. "Is he your husband?" Sanja asked her in a whisper.

"Devils of the Four Winds, no," Ziede answered in a normal tone. "We're old friends."

Kai found an elaborate metal compass, with a piece of something that looked like whalebone mounted in the center. Menlas probably had another way to access the threads of connection embedded in it, but Kai just touched it. He felt the whale's mind, old and patient and simmering with a slow fury at its captivity. He wove his way inside and told it, *I want to ride you even less than you want to carry me. If you take us for a time to the southeast, first to the fire-under-water and then to a mortal port, I'll break the chains that hold this thing atop you and send you on your way.*

The whale considered in a deep silence that seemed to stretch for a long suspended heartbeat. Kai wasn't impatient, because being impatient with a creature this old and with this much weight to its deliberations was pointless. It was easy and restful to just float in that silence, waiting.

The answer came back on an eddy in the current: *Why should I trust?*

Always a good question. Kai replied, *I wore chains once, too.* He sent the whale an image, a memory, of the old Cageling Demon Court in the Summer Halls of the Hierarchs, how he had huddled there with the diamond chains around his throat and wrists, the perpetual rain soaking his ragged clothes, searing his skin.

The whale took in the memory and the song flowed on.

Then the mental current and the physical shell swayed together as the whale turned from the tower. Its tail lifted and dropped to propel it away and across the open sea. Kai came back to himself and realized he had been kneeling on the floor, head down in communion with the whale. His new body still ached in odd places, a side effect of the sudden restoration and the nearness of the smothering water. He pushed to his feet with a groan. The shell rocked in long slow swells with the whale's motion. Whatever mortal thought this was a good way to travel was a masochist, as well as uncaring of the captive whale's pain.

Kai had been dimly conscious of Ziede and Sanja in the rear portion of the chamber. They had eaten some fruit and pickled water chestnuts, and what looked like very dry grainy cakes. Then

Ziede had stuffed some of the expositor's bedding into another cubby, where Sanja was now curled up with a blanket pulled over her head. Ziede herself was sitting in the expositor's bed, leaning back in the nest of cushions against the pearl-coated wall, watching Kai worriedly.

Kai squeezed in next to her so they sat shoulder to shoulder. It was still a relief to feel that she was warm and alive, to be warm and alive next to her. "I told it to take us to the Gad-dazara first." It was one of the mortal names for the place so many languages called fire-under-water. "It's close, and there's a conduit there that will let me talk to Grandmother. She should be able to help me see home, to see if Tahren's there, and to see if anything happened in Benais-arik that might have ended with both of us dead. Or mostly dead."

"A good plan," Ziede said. She took his hand between both of hers and said, "Well, this is all very distressing."

Kai made a noise of displeasure at this massive understatement and slumped down so he could put his head on her shoulder. They had known it might be unwise to go to court in the year of the Rising World coalition renewal, but it would have been equally unwise not to appear in answer to Bashat's summons. "And things were going so well."

"Were they?" Ziede sounded unconvinced, but didn't press the point. "Do you remember anything of where you were when this happened?"

Kai had been racking his memory. He knew that he and Ziede had been in the old palace at Benais-arik. That Tahren hadn't been with them. She had been cagey about what she meant to do, though Ziede might know. But the last images from his old body remained confused and elusive. "The summer pavilion. Night. That big pool with the water lilies."

"In it?" Ziede asked, baffled. "Why?"

"No, beside it," he said in exasperation. "On a couch. With Bashat."

Ziede sighed. "And here we are."

"You don't know that." *You don't know it was him who did this to us.* He wasn't going to argue with her now, he was too tired. And too uncertain, whether he wanted to admit it or not. "Where were you?"

"In our rooms in Benais House, I think." She shook her head, her braids soft against his cheek. "The planning, the time, to do this . . . Unless they had some way to hold you in suspension, when they struck, they must have been ready . . ."

Kai couldn't stop thinking about the lily pond, the pearl in his heart, his last memory. Lounging on the silken cushions under a star-filled sky, the lamplight glittering on the most beautiful court of the most celebrated palace at the new center of the world. Bashat's smile, as he handed Kai a cup of wine. The night was a glowing memory, warm and soft as the flicker of light on the dark water and the white flowers. It was such a clear image, right up to its suspiciously abrupt end, the moment when everything went still and black.

He could so easily imagine a dark mirror of that scene, like an inverted image in the pool's shadowed water.

Ziede must have felt his growing tension. She ran a hand through the long curls of his hair, working the tangles out. "What are you thinking, Kai?"

He was thinking that maybe he had been a gullible fool, that maybe he had made an enormous mistake. "There's a way to place a heart pearl, without asking for consent. I'm not sure it would work on a mortal, but on me . . . If the pearl was formed and then ground up in water—or wine. If I drank it. It would take a while to form, and it would depend on . . . a lot of things. But it's a possibility."

"And?" He could hear the worried frown in Ziede's voice.

"If someone did that. If he used it to put me under his will. And if then he drowned me." His throat had gone tight. "If that is what happened."

"Oh, Kai."

There was too much sympathy in Ziede's tone now and he forced himself to laugh. It came out more like a sardonic squawk. He said, "I'm starting to think that a mortal Prince-heir who wanted to consort with a demon in human form may not be a completely trustworthy person."

Ziede sighed again. "You think? The first one we met was."

Kai's smile was bitter. "He was an exception."

THE PAST: THE BEGINNING

I dream of the world as it was: Suneai-arik and a hundred car-
avans a day from the north, with silks and icewine and amber
and books, canal barges from the ports of the Arkai with the trea-
sures and curiosities of the archipelagoes. The people, familiar
and strange, merchants from Nibet, Enalin scholars and diplo-
mats, sailors of Erathi and Palm, even a solitary Grass King
from the far west. The food, the music, the laughter.

They say that Salasi the satirist saw what was coming and
flushed the birds from their cages in the forum garden. But they
all fell from the sky when the voice of the Hierarchs' Well rose.

—Letter found in the Benais-arik archives, attributed to
an unnamed survivor of Suneai-arik

Kai had only been in the late Enna's mortal body for two full
rounds of the seasons, when he woke his cousin Adeni by fling-
ing himself on top of him. Adeni groaned and used his pillow and
sharp elbows as a shield against Kai's flailing arms. "Stop! You're
going to break the beds!" Adeni hissed at him.

Kai braced himself against the heavy guide rope that steadied
the bunks against the canvas wall. It was just barely dawn; the
roof slope of the great tent of Kentdessa Saredi stretched high
above, still deep in shadow. The light, falling through the venti-
lation holes where the stabilizing cables ran through the canvas,
was still a deep gray. Kai kept his voice low to keep from waking

everyone else in the sleeping partition. "I'm not! Come on, get up, we're going to be late."

"All right, all right." Adeni sat up and swatted him with the pillow. Kai just laughed and swung over to the side of the scaffold to climb down past the sleeping forms of his mortal cousins.

It was darker down in this part of the partition, where the wall-curtains blocked the dawn light from the lower level of the tent. But even in Enna's mortal body, Kai could see the painted scenes covering every bit of hide and canvas, all from stories about the clan's ancestors, the rich colors shifting in the dim light. The evening candlelight would make them appear to move, something Kai found just as fascinating to watch as his cousins did. It felt a little like his old home, in the changeable landscape of the underearth.

Kai dropped to the tent floor. Up toward the top, Adeni was throwing his blankets around, but everyone else was quiet except for snoring.

Other parts of the tent were already awake. Pottery clattered somewhere a few partitions over, and Kai heard distant voices. He dug into his chest of belongings and changed out of his light sleeping shirt into a tunic and pants and embroidered tabard. The warmer season meant there was no need for a heavier outer coat; he didn't feel the cold like mortals did, but the clan captain had told him to try to emulate his cousins whenever possible, as a courtesy to Enna's remains. He found his boots buried under the lowest bunk in the stack, currently occupied by a snuffling Aunt Laniaa, and slipped through the opening between the curtains.

He followed the passageway between the sleeping rooms to their section's eating area. It was a wide circular space, with coal-filled braziers for pots of millet porridge, and smaller kettles of hot water for goat milk tea. Kai sat down on a mat and by the time he got his boots on, Adeni arrived and plopped down beside him.

Uncle Guardi filled the warming pots from a bigger kettle brought in from the outdoor kitchen. Passing Adeni a portion of porridge, he said, "Kai-Enna, do you want these?" He held out a bowl with treats left over from last night, mostly twists of dried goat meat flavored with sorghum syrup and hot spices.

"Yes, please, Uncle." Kai took the bowl happily. He could last a long time, half a season maybe, without food, but it was better not to and he liked the taste and texture.

With his mouth full, Adeni demanded, "Hey, why does Kai-Enna get treats and not me?"

Kai was pretty certain it was because he was currently the only demon in the Kentdessa clan and one of the youngest in the Saredi. There were about a hundred demons right now scattered throughout all the clan tents camped here, and more in the clans traveling to the south. Uncle Guardi said repressively, "Because Kai-Enna didn't wake half the herder night shift barely two hours after they crawled into bed last night."

"Respectfully, I think you're exaggerating, Uncle." Adeni's voice was muffled by porridge.

Kai added, "It was a third of them at most."

Uncle snapped a towel at them.

Kai finished his bowl while Adeni was still eating, then fixed his braids that had come loose while he was asleep, fixed Adeni's braids, and answered a dozen questions from people heading out to chores about where he and Adeni were going so early.

Finally Adeni finished and they started out, stopping by the stores partition to collect bows and quivers before following the passageway out to the tent's main entrance.

The day was bright, the breeze was cool and brisk, scented with sweet grasses, dung from the goat and horse herds, and woodsmoke. Kentdessa loomed over them like a small domed mountain of canvas and cable. It was part of a roughly circular cluster of enormous clan tents, standing on the plain above a wide shallow river that glittered in the morning sun. The endless stretch of grass spread out behind them, dotted with the occasional stand of tall spreading trees. Kai couldn't see it from this angle, but each tent roof was painted with the individual clan sigils and colors. The paint was fading now, worn down by sun and weather, but would be renewed at the big gathering that marked the end of the Cold Wind season. They passed the outdoor kitchen with its firepits and clay ovens, the cooks busy making breakfast and bread for the day, and Kai managed to drag Adeni past before he could stop to eat again.

It was a fair walk to the river, since the camp was set well back to be safe from seasonal flooding. If Adeni had been alone, he would have taken his horse. But the Saredi horses were distrustful of demon-scent and it wasn't worth the time it took Kai to calm one for this short a journey.

The clans had been situated here since the start of the Golden Light season and would stay until the end of Green Changes season. They were downstream of the wooden pipes and trenches that carried water to the gardens and drinking tanks, and upstream from the latrines and bathing pools. It was a sensible system, even though the clan's spirit-workers would regularly purify the water. They passed the outskirts of the last tent, Elinvassa, and started across the grassy floodplain, when Adeni said, "So who are you going to marry?"

Kai laughed. "Nobody. I'm only supposed to have babies." Grandmother had explained that on the first day Kai had awoken in late Enna's body. The clan hoped for at least one baby, would be pleased for more, but Kai was absolutely not to do anything that might cause a baby for three more full rounds of the seasons. It wasn't because they were waiting for Enna to change; her body would stay as it was at the moment of her death until Kai left it. But Grandmother said the delay was to make sure Kai understood mortal life. He had one more season to go, though he felt he understood it pretty well at this point.

Adeni pulled his quiver higher on his shoulder. "Right, but that doesn't mean you can't marry someone, too." He flicked a quick smile at Kai, somehow shyer than his usual broad grin. He was

half a season round older than Enna's body and had been the first
one to grab Kai's arm and drag him outside after the awakening
ceremony. They had run all the way around Kentdessa, under the
giant cable web of the outer supports.

"Marry who?" Kai demanded. Then he had a sudden suspicion.
"Marry you?"

"Well, me and Varra and Iludi." These were two other cousins.
Kai spent a lot of time with them but most of his adventures had
been with Adeni. Everything from exploring the caves where
the bear-people Liberni hibernated to scandalizing the elders by
climbing the outside of Kentdessa, though that one had almost
ended disastrously. But the four of them also just talked and told
stories, out all night with the herds, lying in the grass under the
stars. Adeni added, "Just think about it."

"Think about sleeping in a double bunk with your smelly feet?"
Kai said, mostly because he wasn't sure if Adeni was joking or not.

Adeni grinned and gave Kai's shoulder a shove. "If I'm willing
to put up with getting tossed out of bed before dawn every day,
you can put up with my feet."

They were almost to the river, with more mud and pebbles underfoot than grass now. It was nearly three hundred paces broad
at this point, with a wide band of shallows along the bend, though
the current changed and carved out different channels with every
rainstorm along its course. There must have been a storm in the
hills upstream sometime late last night; the broad banks were
littered with broken tree branches. A splintered trunk as wide as
Kai was tall had jammed in a sandbar that marked the edge of
the deeper water.

It had also destroyed the rope bridge the builders had strung
across the narrowest part of the river, that Kai and Adeni meant
to use to get to the hunting grounds on the far side. The ropes
and shattered planks were mixed in with the debris along the
sandy banks, the support poles wrenched half out of the ground.

Kai halted in disappointment. "Well, this is shitty. How long do you think it will take to fix it?" It wasn't going to be this morning, that was for sure. They would miss the perama migration completely.

Adeni watched him a moment, then smacked him on the back. "Come on, we can wade across."

"I can't." Exasperated, Kai waved at him and pointed to his eyes. "Remember?"

"Water doesn't hurt, does it?" Adeni poked Kai in the shoulder. "I've seen you take baths."

"No. It just feels strange, when it's between me and the ground." Like he was hollow and empty, like part of him was missing, but that was hard to explain to a mortal.

"It won't take us long to wade across. And our clothes will dry fast." Adeni nudged Kai again. "You've been looking forward to this, you don't want to miss it."

Kai didn't want to miss it, and he didn't want Adeni to miss it. They would have to wait a full season round for another chance at hunting perama. He looked around. They were the only ones out by the river, and a large stand of cedar blocked them from the view of the camp. "All right, but don't tell Grandmother or the captain."

"Sure, that's the first thing I'll do, go to our Revered Ancestor and the captain and say, 'Guess what I talked Kai into?' And then we can both shovel goat shit and dig latrines for the next season." Adeni tugged on his arm. "Come on, let's hurry before anybody sees us."

Kai followed Adeni down the gentle slope of the bank into the shallows. As soon as both his feet were in the water, he felt his connection to the underearth fade to a trickle of awareness. He took a sharp breath. It wasn't something he thought about all the time, but losing it felt like stepping off a cliff. He felt alone and oddly unmoored.

Adeni had stopped to watch him. "All right?"

Kai nodded. He supposed it was a good idea to get used to it;

he would be spending a long time on the upper earth and he was sure to need to cope with running water over and over again. "Let's hurry."

They picked their way forward. The fast-moving water carried a chill that Kai could just feel through the waxed leather of his boots. He was a little afraid Adeni might think it was funny to push him over, but Adeni showed no sign of that, instead forging ahead to find the shallowest water, leading them over the sand-bars and finding pathways between the branches and debris. Every time Kai stepped onto a sandbar or climbed atop a tree trunk, his connection to the underearth returned, a warm flicker under his skin. This wasn't as hard as he had expected and he was glad Adeni had talked him into it.

They were near the large broken trunk caught on the island when Kai stepped onto a sandbar and had a moment of . . . not warning, just a pulse from under his heart, where his connection to his real body in the underearth lived, a shiver through his skin that made his eyes water. But there was nothing in this river but fish and a few snakes. Adeni was ahead by ten or so paces, closer to the trunk, looking for a route that didn't involve Kai wading into deeper water. "Adeni, wait—"

Water exploded just past the trunk. A gray shape rose up to tower over them. It opened a round mouth with a rictus of fangs and slammed the shattered tree aside. As it barreled toward them, Adeni yelled for Kai to run and flung himself sideways. Kai didn't run, he bolted forward.

If it hadn't been for the water, Kai would have made it. But to reach Adeni he plunged into thigh-deep shallows. Even with his underearth-given strength, it was like moving in slow motion. The creature whipped around as Adeni struggled up the slope of the island. Adeni's knife was in his hand and he stabbed at the wide maw looming over him.

Kai reached the island and scrambled up the soft slope. His hands closed around the roll of fat at the creature's neck. He had never done this before on anything but plants, with the eldest demon in the clans standing by to make sure his control didn't falter. He felt his real body, held in suspension in the rock under the realm of the Fourth House with all the others who had taken the Saredi bargain to come to the upper world. He touched the life inside this river creature, the blood running through its veins like streaks of light, and pulled it out through his hands. The Saredi called this "eating life." It wasn't something demons could do in the underearth, only here in the mortal world.

The creature's life flowed into Kai, a stunning burst of energy like a too-close lightning strike, energy he had no idea what to do with. Then the creature flung its head to the side and Kai was in the air. He tumbled over its body and slammed down on the wet sand of the island.

Kai couldn't move, all that power running uselessly under his skin. The river creature staggered away, then slumped down into the water, half its body dried and collapsed like an empty air bladder. Then he saw Adeni.

He lay on his back just a few steps away on the other side of the little island, his legs trailing into the water. His blood soaked into the sand, but his chest was still moving. His head was turned toward Kai, eyes unfocussed.

Stolen life was still sparking off Kai's hands. He tried to push himself up. If he could reach Adeni, could he give him the life before it faded? No one had ever suggested this was possible but suddenly it seemed as if it might be, as if this was the natural thing to do with all this sparking light in Enna's veins.

Kai struggled so hard to drag himself forward his vision blurred and he suddenly saw his own body, Enna's body. Slumped on the ground, his eyes still open, hands stretched out, fingers digging into the sand. In the next heartbeat it was his body again, grit grinding under his fingernails, staring into Adeni's fixed, empty gaze.

⸺◦◦◦⸺

Kai was barely aware of frantic splashing through the water and someone carefully lifting him. He remembered being carried back into the shadow of the great tent in dreamlike fragments.

He came back to himself gradually, lying on soft blankets, the heavy scent of river cedar incense in the air. His throat felt raw, like he had breathed and swallowed water, or been crying in his sleep. He rubbed his face and Grandmother's voice said, "Ah, there he is."

He opened his eyes to see her right above him, and realized he was lying with his head in her lap. "Where's Adeni?" he tried to say, and it came out as a barely audible croak.

"He died, little one," she said, stroking his hair. "Did you try to step out of Enna's body into his? You shouldn't do that, Kai, you might not be able to get back in."

"I don't know," he said. Grandmother was the only mortal who could travel back and forth to the underearth; if she said he had tried to leave his mortal body, she should know, but Kai hadn't thought it was possible. "I didn't know I could."

"It's possible he did," another voice said. Kai turned his head a little and saw a dozen people sitting on cushions and mats in Grandmother's room. The clan captain, the sub-captain, family elders of Enna's line, and demons from other clans. The demon who had spoken was Doniqtian in the body of the late Kaened of clan Garoshon, the oldest demon in the camp. "He shouldn't have been able to drain that beast, and yet. And in water, too."

"It wasn't deep, and he would have been standing on the island," said Arn-Nefa, a demon from the tent of Kanavesi. She was in the body of an older mortal man, but she had only been in the upper earth for four rounds of the seasons longer than Kai. She and her mortal sisters had often gone hunting with Kai and Adeni. "Kai is very fast. If he couldn't kill the beast in time, it couldn't be done."

A mortal Raneldi elder asked, "But why was he placed in the body of a small youth?"

"Because he is a youth." Grandmother stroked his hair. "And Enna was dying, and the honor was due to her line." Enna's elders eyed the Raneldi without favor.

"He should not have gone in the river," someone else said. "It was careless, foolish."

"No one questions that," Grandmother said, in the tone that meant she was tired of hearing it. "Children are often careless. Is there any word where that animal came from?"

"We know it should live closer to the coast, somewhere downriver in Erathi, and it was under geas, driven here by foreign powers." That was Benati, captain of Kentdessa, her voice calm but with an undercurrent of worry.

"A scout," Grandmother said, a frown in her voice. "A spy? Have there been messages from our allies in Erathi recently?"

"Not since the last trade caravan, that was at the beginning of this season," Doni-Kaened said. The Saredi and parts of the borderlands got their metals from the Erathi, who traded for it from the other sea people.

Grandmother's brow furrowed. "Send riders, and ahead of them send crow-messengers. Those who can speak Witch, send to the eastern Border Hills sanctum. Ask them to See for us toward the coast." She stroked his hair again. "Kai, do you wish to visit Adeni's body?"

Kai's throat closed and he couldn't speak, but he nodded.

"If you can stand, I'll take you." Her strong hand gripped his shoulder. "But you mustn't try to look for him in his body, he's gone now. Swear to me you won't."

"I swear," Kai managed, tears making his vision swim.

Kai knew it had been the death of his mortal cousin, but he hadn't known it had been the beginning of the death of the Saredi. That Erathi had already fallen and the Hierarchs' forces were on their way.

THREE

Kai flailed back to consciousness to the gentle rocking of the shell-whale. Morning light fell down the entrance hatch. Ziede and Sanja were seated on the floor, sharing the contents of a clay pot. Ziede watched him with a lifted brow and Sanja's forehead was furrowed in alarm. He realized he had kicked two of the cushions out of the cubby and possibly had a fight with a quilt.

So far the voyage hadn't been as bad as Kai had feared. But waking up dead and entombed had invited some unpleasant memories into his dreams, mixed with fading nightmares still written into this new body's flesh. Like so many aspects of mortal life, sleep was overrated. He said, "Do you know where we are?"

Ziede wiped her hands on a rag. The meal was pickled cabbage and strips of something that might have been dried fish. "The compass says southeast. I checked outside at dawn and saw volcanic plumes."

"Good, that's good." Kai had thought they must be getting close. He rubbed his face, climbed out of the cubby, and retrieved the bedding. He found the whale compass on the shelf and went up the steps and outside into bright daylight.

The platform at the top swayed with the whale's motion and the fresh wind tore at his hair. The sky was a limitless vault of blue, the last remnants of the storm they had outrun a few days ago nothing but gray streaks of cloud. The islands in the distance were jagged dark shapes. He leaned against the inward curve of the nautilus and touched the bone in the center of the compass.

It was easier to ride the song of the whale's consciousness this time, maybe because it was more alert as it swam. It had a good sense of the arrangement of the Gad-dazara islands ahead, though Kai had trouble interpreting the images it sent him. It thought of the world as large objects that blocked currents, which was hard to translate into anything that could be expressed on a paper map. Fortunately Kai didn't need to find an active volcano, any seamount would do.

This one, he told it, picking out what looked like the nearest island with the easiest landing, *as close as you can safely go*.

He drifted with the whale's internal song until it signaled its agreement. Coming up out of its awareness into the bright day left him calm and pushed the nightmares away, at least for now. He propped his folded arms on the smooth pearl edge of the shell and watched the shapes on the horizon draw closer.

From below, Ziede was giving Sanja a history lesson, because she couldn't stand ignorance. "This was sixty-seven years ago by Rising World reckoning. Or sixty-eight, I suppose, however long we've been in that tomb." Before the Hierarchs came, Ziede had been a teacher in the Mountain Cloisters of the Khalin Islands, instructing the novices in the history of their craft. After the Hierarchs' defeat, there had been rumors that the cloisters were being rebuilt, but Ziede had never gone back. Everyone she knew there had been killed. "Before the Rising World alliance, the Hierarchs controlled most of the world, stopped only by the northernmost ice sea."

"And they really used demons to fight their wars?" Sanja was speaking with her mouth full.

"No, that was another lie. They enslaved demons and Witches as familiars, to give to their expositors, to help them focus their power," Ziede corrected. "They also used the Well of the Hierarchs to close off passage to and from the underearth, trapping demons in their mortal bodies so they couldn't escape. This also prevented the Witches who had gone there from returning. And for a time, no one in the mortal world could speak to the underearth."

Sanja took that in for a moment. Then she said, "The stories say the demons couldn't cross water. And we're . . . crossing water now."

"We've already established that sometimes the stories lie." There was a dry smile in Ziede's tone. "But it is true that demons couldn't use much of their power while crossing water."

"What about now? Can demons go to the underearth now?" From her tone, Sanja understood perfectly well that this was not just an idle question. "Since the Hierarchs are all dead?"

"It's still difficult. Even before the Hierarchs were defeated, cracks formed in the seal, that let wisps like imps and other small creatures slip back and forth. But it will never be like it was before. Even to talk to the underearth, you have to find a place with a deep conduit, something with power of its own, that will help you send your spirit there to speak."

"And that's what we're doing now, looking for a conduit?" Sanja asked. "What will he do when we get there?"

"He's going to try to talk to someone. They may know what happened to our people." Ziede's voice turned wry. Possibly at Sanja's disappointed expression. "No, it won't be exciting to watch."

There was a short silence. Then Sanja asked, "Are we going back to the Mouth of Flowers?"

"I don't know. It depends on what Kai finds out." Ziede was thoughtful. "Do you want to go back to the Mouth of Flowers?"

"No," Sanja said immediately. From the little she had told them, she had been a street feral, attached to a loose pack of other children. She was so small, Kai found it unlikely that she had ever been successful as a thief. She looked like she had spent enough time starving to stunt her growth. Sanja added, "Unless you're going to burn it to the ground."

Ziede laughed, her first real laugh since waking in the tomb. "You hate every person in the city so much?"

"Most of them," Sanja said. After a long moment of obviously reluctant consideration, she added, "Not all of them."

"Something to keep in mind, when hoping for mass destruction." Ziede added, seriously, "Believe me."

There was a pause. Kai swayed as the whale crested a wave. Then Sanja said, "Can you kill people like he does?"

"You can call him by his name."

There was a hesitation. "Can you kill people like Kaiisteron does?"

"Not exactly like. I have my own methods. But I can kill." Ziede's pause was more deliberate. "You're not afraid of us."

"I was. I am. I'm not stupid. But you're . . . you're not afraid of anything." Kai touched Ziede's mind for permission, then used her pearl to extend himself into her consciousness, just enough to see through her eyes. Sanja was looking down, flicking the tie of her boot wrap. Her jaw set and she looked up, lifting her chin. "I'm tired of being afraid."

"No living creature is immune to fear." Ziede's voice was serious now. "You saw what happened to us."

Sanja's throat moved as she swallowed, and her gaze dropped again. "That happened, because somebody powerful is afraid of you."

"You're not wrong." Ziede's tone turned brisk. "Now, do you want to hear more about the Fall of the Hierarchs and the rise of the Arike Prince-heirs, and the Rising World alliance?"

Sanja said, "Yes, please."

―――⌘―――

By the time the sun moved into afternoon, the whale reached Gaddazara. Ziede and Sanja came up from below and Kai moved to a perch on the edge of the shell to give them room on the platform.

Peaks rose from the sea, stretching away in either direction in a great curving archipelago. Some were weathered and worn down, others still breathed long furls of smoke into the air. The dark cone of the nearest volcano loomed over them, dominating the sky. Its last eruption had almost destroyed the land mass around it; the sea had crept in between shattered cliffs and ridges and spawned a hundred tiny satellite islands. Seabirds rose in white waves from rocky beaches, clusters of smaller fins fled the whale's approach.

The whale circled around the broken island and wove its way through what had once been the busy harbor of a fabled city; they passed small rocky remnants of land still supporting ruined columns or walls, even whole tumbled buildings. On the slopes above the broken shoreline, hardened lava and windblown vegetation had taken most of the city, but half-buried obelisks or broken walls were still visible. There had been ports all through this chain of mountain islands, right up until some disaster had broken the power that kept the fire beneath the earth under control.

The muscled stone legs of a giant statue towered over them as the whale drew near the harbor's ruined breakwater. The remnants of the jumbled stone dike had stretched to protect this side of the port.

The whale seemed content to rest and wait here. Kai made the jump to the dike and climbed to the top. Ziede summoned one of the many wind-devils at play in the air currents and had it fly her and Sanja up, meeting him on the platform near the statue's weathered big toe. "Will this do?" Ziede asked. She was hiding her impatience well, but Kai could sense it through her pearl. Hopefully he could get her some answers soon.

"It should." From what the whale had shown Kai, the statue was actually built on an old seamount that had been incorporated into the breakwater. He could already feel the restless stir of heat and power in the earth at its root, it was more than deep enough to let him open a passage. Kai brushed off the warm stone and sat down, folding his legs up under his skirt. "What are you going to do?"

Ziede wrinkled her nose and plucked at her cotton shirt. "We might look for a place where we can bathe."

"Watch out for pirates," Kai said, settling himself and closing his eyes. "And if you find any, save some for me."

"Stop showing off in front of the child," Ziede retorted, and led Sanja away down the breakwater. "And don't antagonize the Overlord!"

"I can't help it," Kai muttered to himself. His continued existence would be enough.

The faint sounds of their steps on the stone faded away. With nothing in his ears but the wind's bluster against the rock, the lapping of water, the slow breathing of the whale, Kai separated from his body and sunk through the stone.

The underearth was not actually in the ground somewhere, the way mortals thought, but it was the connection with the rock and the living heat far below the surface that made it reachable now. When Kai had first come to the mortal world, he could step between his borrowed mortal body and his original form in the underearth anywhere. Now the underearth body Kai had been born into was gone and he had to send his spirit down like a Witch. But after what the Hierarchs had done, he was lucky to be able to have even this poor pathway open to him.

Kai found his way through the conduit, a sensation not unlike merging with the whale's song, until he sensed the underearth form around him, a coalescence of sound and sensation like nothing in the mortal world. He had to pretend his body into existence here, imagine himself with flesh and limbs. If he let go of the illusion for even one instant, his spirit would disunite and drift, and he would have to put himself together again before he could make the trip back to the upper earth.

Kai would never again see the underearth as it was. He couldn't even take on a shadow version of his original body and was constrained to appear here in a semblance of his current mortal form.

He opened his eyes to see a great canyon in place of the sea, the bottom shaped into mountains and valleys. The sand was pearl white, with swaying fields of red grasses and delicate coral-like trees. Beautiful, but no more real than a mortal dream. These were only shadows of the physical location of his mortal body.

The ruined city loomed over him, but preserved as an echo in the rock of the island, just the way it must have looked the day before its destruction. Columned terraces marched up from the circle of the port to slopes covered with tiled houses and the colorful awnings of market stands, the whole capped by an array of palaces with brilliant blue stacked hip roofs. There was no echo of the original occupants; the flickers of movement on streets and stairways were not mortal or human.

Kai twisted around to see the statue was gone. In its place was a round pavilion with gauzy white fabric hanging from the eaves. The fact that she hadn't made him walk across half the sea was encouraging. Travel here could be more than difficult without the anchor of a physical form. Kai got to his feet and walked up the steps.

The floor was carpeted by a thick wooly hide, the skin of an animal that hadn't walked the upper earth in centuries, a vague echo of the ancient Saredi grasslands. Its fangs curved up on either side of the throne, a wide chair made of skulls. They were all relics of the Overlord's family, kept for sentimental reasons.

Kai bowed formally, an Arike court salute, to the figure curled on the seat. She had pale horns curving back from her head, a muscular scaled body ending in a long powerful tail that spilled off the throne, the tip a narrow spade-shape that flicked impatiently. Her pale wings, the texture of mortal skin, were half-furled. He said, "Overlord."

"Since you're still alive, you might call me Mother," she said, her voice dry. "Sit. Where have you been?"

He sat down on the carpet in an easy sprawl, since apparently this conversation was going to be friendly. Kai was considered a renegade by all the other demon lines and sometimes the Overlord of the Fourth House found it more politic to agree with them. "I've been trapped for a while, Mother. Underwater."

Now that it had become obvious there wasn't going to be a fight, others crept up to the pavilion, or dropped down from its eaves. They were smaller versions of Mother, with blue or black shading on their wings. Some had tails split into two or more segments, some even had human-like legs, but with heavy dark claws on their feet. Vaiisterite, one of Kai's siblings, landed beside Mother's throne and crouched at its foot. Mother tilted her head skeptically and said, "Surely this was not a surprise to find yourself in a trap, considering the mortals you associate with."

She wanted an argument, which Kai wasn't going to give her. "I wasn't surprised, just disappointed."

Her eyes narrowed, the same solid black, whiteless eyes that Kai wore in every mortal body he had taken. "I assume you're not coming here to discuss returning to take up your duties and be married. I have two acceptable prospects who may be enticed to accept you in mortal form without too much argument."

Kai didn't sigh. For some reason the prospect of marrying into whichever demon line would grudgingly accept him, producing half-mortal children, and then having to fight off his new relatives' attempts to trap him here had never sounded appealing. He knew the Overlord thought she was doing him a favor, and that made it even worse. "No, thank you, Mother."

"It was good enough for your grandmother."

"Grandmother wouldn't be here if her mortal body hadn't been murdered, Mother." Kai had to add, "The next time I'm trapped in a glass box at the bottom of the sea, I'll consider it."

Vai, crouched by the throne, did sigh.

Mother bared her fangs. "Stop being overdramatic."

Kai would have loved to, if dramatic things would stop happening to him. "With your permission, I came to pay my respects to Grandmother."

There was a flutter of hissing comment among the watching crowd. Mother studied him a moment more, but there were too many pacts written in demon hearts' blood protecting Grandmother's place and power here, and he had every right as a survivor of both the mortal and demon direct lines of her issue to speak to her. Mother said, "And do you intend to ask her for favors?"

"No," Kai said, not quite honestly. Grandmother, still Saredi to the bone, wouldn't consider it a favor. "I just want to listen to her reminisce."

Eyeing him suspiciously, Mother leaned back on her throne, tucking her tail in. "Your sister will take you there."

Kai rolled to his feet and bowed again. Vai rose up on her tails, and he followed her down the steps.

He walked beside her up the long colonnade that had taken the place of the breakwater, as the memory of the city shifted to a dream of some other place. Night was falling over the hipped-roof palaces, dissolving them with shadow.

"You're different," Vai said.

"I have a different mortal body," he told her. "You didn't notice? I got taller."

"They all look the same to me." Vai sniffed. "You smell strange, that's all."

The colonnade split off into a stone-paved street with walled houses to either side, their gates broken and flowering brush and lush vines flowing out as if their garden walls had burst like rotten fruit. Kai didn't recognize this place at all; it was a memory of somewhere he had never been. The darkness settled in like a fog but it sparkled with white flames: a cloud of imps, leading the way like tiny floating torches.

The street opened up into a round court, lush vegetation enclosing it in a flowering green wall. At the back rose a large wooden house built atop tall pillars, a style from the Erathi coast, meant to resist the storm waves common to the low-lying barrier islands. The Saredi clans had often sent traders there in the dry seasons, to exchange goods directly with the sea people ships that came to shore along it. When Kai had gone there, all the coastal towns had already been burned by the Hierarchs.

As Vai led the way across the court, Kai could hear the ocean now, waves crawling up a sandy beach, not the rocky coast of the volcanic island in the mortal world. It had been a statement, at one point, for Grandmother to choose the image of a house meant to survive the ocean storms, here in a place where deep water was the enemy. She had kept it for so long now that possibly she just liked it.

It was made of heavy logs, the roof thatched, and a long flight of steps led up to a wide porch with wooden sliding doors. Vai stopped at the stairs, coiling up to wait. Kai hesitated despite himself and asked, "You won't come in?"

Vai showed her fangs and said sourly, "You're her favorite."

Kai sighed in frustration and climbed the steps. "She can't make you a favorite when you don't talk to her."

Predictably, all that got him was a hiss.

He scratched at the door and a server opened it immediately. Dressed in a light cotton tunic and cropped pants, her dark hair coiled around her head, she was part mortal, as all Grandmother's servants were. She could have passed as a human woman except for the split pupils of her green eyes and the prominent fangs.

She nodded to Kai and led him down the white-plastered central hall, which was open all the way up to the peaked roof. It went through to the back of the house and a breeze drifted down it, salt-tinged by the invisible, illusory sea somewhere behind the wall of foliage.

The servant stopped and gestured him through the door into a large room, with wooden slatted windows allowing in the scents of the flowering trees outside. Grandmother sat on a low couch, wearing a gray-trimmed black silk coat. She still looked like an entirely human woman, with fine lines at the corners of her eyes, and white streaks in the coils of her dark braids. She said in Saredi, "There you are," as if she had known he was coming, as if she had been expecting him.

Her sight was of the underearth, so there was no question about her recognizing him even in the shadow of a different mortal body. He saluted her like a Saredi clan captain and she gestured for him to come and kiss her cheek, and then to sit with her on the couch. Kai curled up beside her on the cushions, feeling the tightness around his heart ease for the first time since he had woken in his glass coffin. "Are you well, Grandmother?"

"As can be expected." Grandmother lifted a hand and two more part-human servants carried in a covered tray. They set it down on a stand within reach of the couch, lifting the lid to reveal the tiny decorated sweets and savory morsels that had been customary for entertaining guests in the great tents of the Saredi. Long before the Hierarchs had conquered the plains, when Grandmother had been a young, fully human captain of scouts, before she had been wooed away from the mortal world. "You've lost your body again, I see," she said.

The servants settled on the floor to listen, two curling up on the floor cushions, one starting to prepare a kettle for the ginger almond drink that always accompanied the sweets.

"This is the first time I've lost a body in years and years," Kai protested. From Grandmother's expression, she wasn't impressed. "They tried to get Ziede, too. I came to ask if you could see Avagantrum for me. We've been gone from there at least a full round of seasons and we're worried about the family."

"Ah, they always did like to do away with the whole line, once they turned against you." Grandmother picked up a tiny cake, her expression grimly reminiscent. "But that was the Hierarchs, and they're gone now. They blur together, after you're conquered." She gestured to the watching servants. "Lika, go and bring a seeing bowl, we'll summon some wraithlings."

Lika stood and left the room. Grandmother pushed the plate

toward Kai and he took a savory roll. Here in her own domain, she commanded the underearth to such an extent that the shadow even tasted like Kai's memory of the real thing. "We were taken from Benais-arik but Tahren Stargard wasn't with us, and Ziede can't find her through her heart pearl. Can you think of anywhere that mortals could possibly imprison an Immortal Marshall that would keep her from hearing a pearl's call?"

She frowned, and pushed the plate toward the servants, who shifted forward to take some of the delicacies. "I never understood why a Witch like Ziede wanted to lie with a Hierarchs' dog."

Kai was patient. He knew trying to rush her wouldn't help. "Tahren betrayed the Hierarchs, that's why they call her 'the Fallen.'"

"Hmm." Grandmother selected another cake. "How is Ziede?"

"Angry, but alive." Kai added, "She would be better if she knew where her wife was, and if her family is all right."

Grandmother couldn't argue with that. "Let me think. She's Fallen, so the places of the Blessed"—she turned her head to spit on the floor—"curse their shadows, would not admit her. They might put her in one of the old Witch cells."

Another servant took out a cloth and wiped the spit off the floorboards, frowning repressively at Grandmother, who waved a dismissive hand.

"Witch cells?" Kai asked, before Grandmother could get distracted. "Are they like the Cageling Demon Court?"

"No, not much like." Grandmother settled back against the pillows. "Water doesn't do anything to Witches except make them wet. And the Cageling Demon Court was also a show of power, they used to walk every visitor past it. You probably couldn't see that from where you were inside."

"No, I remember that. A little." It had been hard to see anything outside the court, the colonnades around it screened by the perpetual rain. Sometimes he had seen figures moving by, the glint of light off jewels and rich fabrics. It was the feel of the place that was etched into his memory: the cold, the stench of rotting bodies, the helplessness.

Grandmother's sharp gaze shifted away as she searched her own memory. "Witch cells were meant to hide their occupants from everything, including demon eyes." She flicked her fingers in the same way that Mother did, though neither of them would have admitted to sharing anything except their blood. "And for a true Immortal Marshall, whoever wanted to hold her prisoner would have needed strong binding cantrips, which are written into the cell walls."

Kai believed Grandmother that these cells had existed, but all the Hierarchs' places in this part of the world had been destroyed or taken over by the Rising World, or one of its allies. He had a hard time believing that if a Witch cell still existed, he hadn't heard about it. Or that someone hadn't tried to put him in one. "But this sounds like something that would have been in the old Summer Halls."

"I'm not dim, you little snake, I know that place was destroyed." Grandmother took another cake. She paused while a servant stood to hand them both cups of the ginger milk. Kai accepted his and the scent was like a breath of childhood. Meeting Grandmother here for the first time, when she had visited in mortal form, in a place dreamed to look like her rooms in the tent of Kentdessa Saredi. She told him and his siblings about their mortal relatives and their demon ancestor, and how she had made her bargain with him in the upper world, and what had come of it. And Mother yelling at her to stop filling their heads with nonsense. Before Kai had been called to the mortal world to his first human body.

Once the servants settled back on the floor to share the rest of the drink among themselves, Grandmother continued, "Witch cells are old, far older than the Hierarchs. But they were no good for holding expositors; no one in the borderlands knew what an expositor was, when the cells were built." She snorted in derision. "So Hierarchs found them in the borderlands and took the marked walls apart and carried them away. If they did it, so could the Rising World."

When she put it that way, it was a stronger possibility. But if the cells had been looted from some Hierarch storehouse, they could be anywhere now. "Do you know where they might have taken them?"

Grandmother shook her head. "All the places I remember are rubble or ash. You would have to ask a Hierarchs' dog."

Another Immortal Marshall, she meant. One not Fallen like Tahren. That was a terrible idea.

Kai thought he might very well have to try it, if there was no other way.

The servant Lika returned, carrying a clay bowl of water. The others hastened to move the plate and cups from the stand, so Lika could set the bowl down. All the servants gathered around and Kai sat up to see better. Floating just above the surface of the bowl was a wraithling. Lika said, "This wraithling lives above the mass grave along the ruins of the old western trade road in Saleos, up from what used to be the port of Lossnos."

It looked like wisps of gauzy cloud, wrapped around a narrow body with a lot of spiny legs and arms, its head a diamond shape with tiny green spots for its eyes. The little creatures had an attraction for altars, sanctuaries, tombs, and graves. They were generally harmless unless abused.

Lika had summoned it so she would have to do the questioning. Grandmother motioned for Kai to speak, and he said, "Ask it if it can see Avagantrum." Now that they were close to answers, his heart was starting to pound from nerves, and he swallowed the tension down. Allowing his agitation to show wouldn't help Lika concentrate.

Lika's fangs dug into her lower lip with the effort. Then she said, "It sees the outer walls and gates."

"Nothing like an attack? No sign of fires, explosions?" Kai tried to think of anything that would indicate a battle to something as disinterested in mortal life as a wraithling. He didn't want to ask if it saw any recent ghosts; he was too afraid to hear the answer. "Any sense of an expositor's intentions?"

Lika shook her head slowly, her eyes hooded as she kept her connection with the wraithling. "No, Fourth Prince. It remembers nothing like that. Not recently. If there had been death, it would sense it. It feels life there. Mortal lives, Witch lives."

The tension in Kai's chest eased. If the place had been attacked in their absence, there might be mortals there, but there wouldn't be Witches. "An Immortal Marshall's life?" he asked, just in case. Even if something had happened to Tahren's pearl, he didn't think she would just be sitting there, waiting. She would be off somewhere searching for them.

Lika's brow furrowed as she concentrated, then she shook her head. "If it can see that, it won't show me."

Kai needed to see inside. "Can you get it to go any closer, maybe let us communicate with someone?"

"I'll try, Fourth Prince. But it's not much interested in speaking to the living. The only thing it likes is old death." Lika settled herself again, her gaze turning inward.

Kai considered the problem. Avagantrum was an old Nossian step-fort. It had a heavy outer wall, an interior court, and then an inner wall that turned into a series of interlocking squares, each one carved deeper into the earth. Its water source and living chambers were in the center, underground, and now carefully warded by the Witches who lived there; the wraithling couldn't get in even if Lika could convince it to want to. But the former inhabitants had died out at some point before the Hierarchs' arrival, which was why the place had never been attacked. Their graves were still there. "In the outer court, near the gardens, there are old tombs buried in the earth. Can you get it to go there?"

Lika nodded once. "That may work." She was silent for a long moment, her face set in a frown of effort. Grandmother took a little olive cake, watching with interest. Lika said, slowly, "It sees someone. A mortal person working among the plants in the garden." Before Kai could ask, she said, "The wraithling sees differently than we do, especially colors, so it's hard to describe. But this person wears Arike woman's clothing, their appearance is older than mine, their skin is darker than mine, their hair is dark, with tight curls, tied back." Lika made a gesture behind her head. "It makes a halo."

"It sounds like Tanis, Ziede's oldest daughter." Kai wanted to jump up and pace but he knew Grandmother would hate that. Relief was heady; he had been more worried than he had allowed himself to realize. "Can we speak to her?"

"She has seen the wraithling. But it can't make words like we do." Lika frowned in thought. "I don't know how—"

"It can move the grave dirt," Grandmother said, selecting another cake. She had the detached interest of someone watching other people play a forty square game.

"Ah." Lika's expression cleared. "In Saredi characters?"

"Old Imperial," Kai said, trying not to bounce with excitement. "Tell her, 'Tanis, this is Kai. Is everyone all right?'"

Lika's hands moved to shape the characters in the air as Kai waited tensely. Then she said, "The person Tanis speaks: 'Uncle Kai, yes, we're all well here! But where are you? Is Mother with you? Grand-aunty sent a messenger to the Benais-arik, but they said you left months and months ago! You're not dead, are you?'"

"Not dead. Ziede is with me." Kai kept it short, watching Lika form the characters, knowing the wraithling would only stay still so long. But he wanted to make sure he understood Tanis. "Do you know where Tahren or Dahin are?"

Lika translated, "The person speaks: 'No word, none at all, but Uncle, we thought Tahren was with you. We haven't heard from her since you left. And nothing from Uncle Dahin since that last message when you were here. Uncle, are you all right?'"

"Tell her we're fine," Kai said, even if it wasn't true, and would be even less true once Ziede heard that Tahren wasn't safe at home.

Though that had always been a far-fetched hope. "We'll come back when we can."

Lika wove the message, and added, "I should let the wraithling go, Fourth Prince, before it grows tired. If I press it, it might start showing me things it remembers from the war, and that will confuse us."

Kai sat back on the couch, accepting that reluctantly. "Can you find another wraithling near the Benais-arik Palace?"

Lika waved the first one away, and after a moment of concentration, called up another little creature, this one with a glittering red carapace. "This one is from the tombs outside the palace walls. It sees the mortals on the roads and the canals, the wagons and palanquins that go in and out of the gates, and nothing seems strange."

If Benais-arik had been a smoking heap of rubble, Kai would have bigger problems to worry about, but at least the attack on him and Ziede would seem less personal. He let out his breath slowly. "I think that's all, Lika. Thank you for your help." As Lika dismissed the wraithling, he added, "Grandmother, one more question. Do you remember the cantrips that seal the Witch cells? And how to get past them?"

She tapped her temple. "That knowledge I have engraved on my eyelids, little snake."

Time was as mutable as the rest of the underearth and night had flowed back into dawn by the time Kai left the house. Vai was curled up on the steps. She rose and stretched when he stopped beside her. He said, "You should have come in, she had the ginger drink you like."

Vai huffed in exasperation, flowing to her feet, and only said, "You're going back up there, aren't you."

Kai couldn't live down here, not as the demon prince he no longer was, and not with Grandmother as a part-human, insulated in the perpetual past of a world that he had seen violently destroyed. And Vai had never lived in the upper world, would never understand what having a mortal family was like.

"I left my body there," Kai said only, starting the walk back through the silent city.

———⚬⚬⚬———

Kai came back to himself in the smoke-tinged wind and warm sun of the Gad-dazara, under the broken statue. The city was a ruin frozen in black rock and overgrown weeds again. He took a deep breath and pushed to his feet, stretching.

In the water below, the shell-whale lifted its massive blue head and blew a plume of spray through its breathing hole. Something about it seemed uneasy. Kai climbed down the rocks to where he could jump back down to the shell's top platform.

The compass was where he had left it, tucked into a curve of nacre. As soon as he touched it, he felt the whale's sense of another moving body in the water.

There were a lot of things in the sea big enough and dangerous enough to catch the whale's attention, but none would come this close to the surface. And this wasn't something the whale knew as a predator; it was unnatural, like the shell on its back. It had sensed it sometime earlier at a distance, but not close enough to concern it. Now it was too close. *Show me,* Kai whispered.

The shape was long, with fins and a fish tail and an oddly shaped head, but there was no perspective for Kai to be able to tell its size. Something dangled off it, four narrow shapes that might be tentacles. Kai's knowledge of most of what lived in the water was limited to things that ended up hung for display in market stalls, but this didn't look unnatural—then one of the tentacles bent and the end opened into a hand. A human hand.

Kai recoiled, breaking the contact. *Shithead expositors,* he thought. He had known there would be an alarm set on their tomb prison to alert their captors. He hadn't been expecting something that would follow them. If it had come near enough for the whale to get this good a look at it, pursuers were likely close by.

Kai turned and leapt back to the rocks. He climbed to the top of the breakwater, feet sliding on the slippery stones, and headed toward Ziede and Sanja.

Close to where the breakwater met the port's sea wall stood a circle of broken columns with an old basin in the center. High waves had filled it recently and Ziede and Sanja must have used it to bathe. Ziede sat on one of the broad steps tying her sandals back on and Sanja was knee-deep in the water, her tunic and pants dripping. Ziede hadn't been incautious; the air above the basin flickered with the presence of wind-devils.

Ziede stood as Kai approached, her brow furrowed at his haste and his expression. Kai said, "There's an expositor's amalgam in the water."

Ziede grimaced in annoyance. "I was hoping our enemies were stupidly overconfident." She lifted her hands. The wind-devils swirled above her, then scattered in all directions. "They could be close."

"We'll know soon." Kai was glad they had come here first, that they hadn't made straight for Avagantrum or tried to meet with any possible allies. It would be just him and Ziede against whoever pursued them, no interference, no potential hostages to fate. Except one, and he didn't intend to risk her.

Sanja hurriedly climbed up out of the basin. She was breathing hard, eyes wide. She said, "Are they going to get us?"

Kai brushed a spiral of hair out of her face. "No." Prediction, not bravado.

Sanja stared up at him, and her throat moved as she swallowed. Then her expression hardened, and she nodded. "No, they won't."

Still looking up after the wind-devils, Ziede asked, "Well? Was your grandmother able to help?"

"I spoke to Tanis. Everyone at Avagantrum is fine, there's been no attack," he told her, giving the good news first. "But Tahren's not there and they haven't heard from her or Dahin since we left. There was no sign of a disturbance or attack at Benais-arik, either." It was hard not to feel like he had less information now than before he had gone to see Grandmother. The trip had given him some ideas, but that was all he had to work with.

Ziede looked out to sea, her face set in tense lines. She would have been hoping against hope that Tahren was home, even if Tahren was there because she was holding off an attack on their household. Then at least they would have known exactly where to go and what to do. "At least the children are all right." She let out her breath. "Tahren wanted to look for Dahin, she'd had word he might be traveling the Arike states, visiting archives in the other cities. Wherever they are, they may be together."

Kai thought that was wishful thinking. Dahin was more than capable of avoiding his sister when he wanted to. And it would have been hard enough for their enemy to take Tahren unawares; if she had been with Dahin, Kai didn't think it would have been possible at all.

It could be an attempt to interfere with the Rising World coalition renewal. As the first Immortal Marshall who had rebelled against the Hierarchs, Tahren was part of the treaty agreements with the Blessed Lands. And she had significant influence on the Rising World council. There were members who would put her word well above Bashat's. If she was the target, it was an important piece of the puzzle. "If they wanted Tahren out of the way before the renewal—"

"They would have had to remove us first," Ziede agreed grimly. "But our underwater tomb wouldn't have held her."

Kai wasn't sure of that, but there was just too much they didn't know yet. "Grandmother had an idea about how someone might keep an Immortal Marshall prisoner." He told Ziede about the Witch cells, how likely it was that they would still exist somewhere. "If they did take Tahren, they wouldn't want to move her very far, whatever they did to her." If anything, taking on an angry Immortal Marshall, even a Fallen one, was a riskier proposition than attacking a demon. Kai's mortal body could be killed more easily than Tahren's. It would take an Immortal Blessed blade to kill her. But she could be hurt, made insensible long enough to move her somewhere.

"We need a way to track her—" A lone wind-devil slipped down through the gusting wind back to Ziede. Kai followed its movement by the odd hardening of the air and the shifting light, as if the sun was reflecting off something that wasn't there. Ziede listened to the faint high-pitched whisper with a frown. She said, "There's something to the west. Damn it."

Kai looked around for a good vantage point. At the end of the breakwater stood the blocky remnants of a four-story tower. "We can see from there."

Ziede led the way and Kai followed, holding on to Sanja's hand to help her over the bigger cracks in the breakwater. They had to jump across a large gap to get to the slab where the tower's foundation stood. A set of broad stairs, broken and half scraped away by the lava, led to the cracked platform on top.

In the distance, past the ruined city and the hardened lava flows that marked the edge of the island, a ship cut through the blue water. It was long and low, a galley with the prow ornamented with a massive scowling face that looked like it was angry at the sea beneath it. The three big masts held sails, still furled, and the oars were shipped. If Kai needed any other clues, the hull gleamed a dull copper and was embossed with sun signs. "Immortal Blessed." He was bitterly amused. It was somehow the least surprising thing that they were involved in this plot. "They make a religion out of not minding their own business."

Ziede spared him a glare. "Not Tahren."

"Of course not Tahren." Kai snorted. He didn't think of Tahren as an Immortal Blessed anymore, anyway. "Do I have to say it every time?"

Ziede gave him a shove to the shoulder. "Yes."

Piqued, he shoved her back. Before she could retaliate, Sanja said, "Stop fighting!"

"We're not fighting." Ziede shaded her eyes again. "I don't think those are Immortal Blessed."

Kai still wanted to argue. "How can they not be when the ship is clearly—Oh wait, you're right." The figures on the upper deck were dressed in dark rich colors, not the whites and light yellows of the Blessed. But there had to be at least one Immortal Marshall onboard or the ship would have to use its sails or oars. "I need to get over there."

"They'll be expecting us to come from the air. And before you ask, no, I can't conjure a storm, the conditions aren't right." Ziede dropped to a crouch and began to brush away the broken bits of stone paving on the platform. Quick-witted Sanja hurried to help her, and Ziede sat back on her knees to open her bag and shake out a collection of charcoal sticks and powdered chalks she had gathered from among Menlas' belongings on the shell-whale. "But I can use all this smoke and ash in the air." She nodded toward the volcano on the island across the strait, with its steady plume that stretched up to join the low gray clouds.

As Ziede sketched the diagram for her cantrip, Kai tried to see a way he could reach the ship without taking to the water. Whoever was aboard would be looking for a landing, probably heading to the breakwater and the old docks, where the whale was. Kai didn't want to fight a running battle all over the island. He grimaced to himself; he would have to go through the water. "I'll need the whale. Anything you left aboard the shell that you want?"

Ziede shook her head absently, lips pursed in thought as she added a carefully curved line to her cantrip. Air spirits were already starting to gather, little drifts that stirred the dust. Sanja looked up and said worriedly, "Will the whale be hurt?"

He shook his head. "No, it'll be free, sooner than we originally planned."

Sanja was relieved but dubious. "Then how will we get off the island?"

Kai nodded toward the Immortal Blessed craft. "On our new ship."

THE PAST:
THE FALL

The mountain and hill lands that surround the Grass Plains are said to be the first birthplace of the Witch. They are born of the union of mortals and demonkind in mortal form, who came forth during the great war between the legions of the underearth and the Grass Kings. From there they spread, or fled, through the east and south.

—*Night-Tales of the West,* transcribed by various hands

Kai was with the other demon scouts, lying on his stomach and propped up on his elbows in the dirt. They were under the cover of a small tent-shelter, to prevent any wind damage to the map and to hide it, if it was true that the Hierarchs could use birds and spirits as spies, like the Witches said. "I told Treris he was too far west," Dae-Fera from Raneldi Saredi said for the third time.

Kai, making his additions to the dirt map, threw a pebble at her. "We know! At least think of something else to complain about." He ignored the groans of agreement and the chorus of protests. It had taken several long days and nights to assemble this new information and they wouldn't be able to rest until the plotting was done.

Someone kicked his foot. Before he could kick back, Arn-Nefa of Kanavesi Saredi said, "Kai-Enna, Captain Kentdessa wants you."

Kai wriggled backward away from the map to keep from disturbing the edges. The mortal chroniclers were waiting outside to memorize the finished version and transfer it to cloth maps to be shared with their borderlander allies. "Up on the ridge?" Kai asked Arn-Nefa. The ridge was where the commanders were meeting. "Am I in trouble?" He had been pushing his luck, leading his scouts close to the Hierarch camp. Closer than the captains had told them to go.

She snorted and pulled one of his braids. "You probably should be. But that's not what they said. They want to talk to you and Dae-Fera."

As Arn-Nefa continued on her way, Kai caught Dae-Fera's eye and signed *come with me* in Witchspeak.

Dae-Fera wriggled away from the map and they ducked out of the tent. It was surrounded by scraggly trees, tucked down among the rocky slopes of the hills; a large part of the allied force was camped through here, with new groups from the borderlands arriving all the time.

Kai followed the path that wound up slope in the shadow of stunted trees and brush, pebbles skittering under their boots. It was warm but the morning sun was weak, hidden behind clouds. At the top of the hill the view opened up to the plain, and the Hierarchs' camp toward the eastern side.

Most of the enemy activity was hidden behind trenches and a tall earthwork made out of sandy dirt, though the sheer size of the encampment and the smoke of hundreds of cooking fires made it obvious how numerous their troops were. Past the rough wall, Kai could make out the sea of peaked red tent tops, the furry backs of the wallwalkers stabled among them, and some ornate wooden structures that the borderlanders said were probably siege engines. Which didn't make a lot of sense, because the nearest borderlander walls were to the west, up in the mountains; all the people of these lands were nomadic, like the Saredi.

The assembled warriors of the grassplains alliance had been fighting skirmishes for days, driving the Hierarch forces away from the central plains back toward the Erathi coastlands. The older demons had been leading war parties, while the younger ones acted as scouts. Kai had been scouting and organizing scouts from Kentdessa and the other clans, and had been shot with a lot of arrows. He had been drawing heavily on his body in the underearth to repair the damage, and had had about an hour of real sleep in the past day. Dae-Fera, younger and with a less responsible position, bounced with energy.

Kai had never relied this heavily on his connection to the underearth before and he knew his reserves weren't limitless. It was something he should talk to Grandmother about, but there was just no time.

He and Dae-Fera followed the flattened grass of the path down a short slope and around to a flat rocky space sheltered by the cliffs of the higher hills. Erina had said she had heard it was the remains of an old fort, and that the circular hill blocking it from the view of the plain was actually a buried tower. Whether that was true or not, a path ran up the side to a vantage point on top.

On the rocky flat, a meeting was underway. There were a dozen or so commanders from the borderlanders, from the different territories along the edges of the grassplains. Some wore metal armor over silk robes, some bright-colored headscarves and tough leather clothing, others in hooded garments with wooden face masks. Joining them now were Erathi leaders in the loose cotton pants and tunics and jackets of sailors' gear. Their ships had landed at the cove to the west a couple of days ago and their fighters had joined the growing coalition last night. The Erathi coast had been hard hit by the Hierarchs, many of the towns and ports utterly destroyed. Kai had never seen or heard of anything like it, and the shock lingered.

Witches were scattered through the group, dressed in dark draped fabrics and veils, their feet bare on the rough ground. Grandmother, who knew a lot of Witches, said the story was that they wore the veils and the concealing drapery so that they could take them off and walk among mortals without anyone knowing.

But since that would work for just about any kind of distinctive clothing, she doubted it was true.

Everyone was in groups talking or listening, with translators whispering or signing Witchspeak to those who couldn't understand. Dae hesitated, but Kai tugged her coat sleeve to follow him and wove his way through the fringe of the group. He found the Saredi and stopped behind Captain Kentdessa, who was a different Captain Kentdessa from the one that Kai had known since being given Enna's body. When the Saredi had decided to create the alliance against the Hierarchs, a new captain, someone thought better suited for leading fighters, had been selected by vote. This captain was older, her braids more iron gray than black. She was part demon herself, descended from one of the first demons to take Grandmother's bargain and come to the mortal world in a Saredi body. The borderlander commanders probably didn't realize it; her demon blood was visible only in the darkness of her eyes. She wore her Kentdessa antelope sigils wrapped around the buckle of the belt cinching her leather coat.

She listened to a Witch, a stocky person only a few inches taller than Kai, their veil draped over a black broad-brimmed hat. The Witch broke off as Kai and Dae appeared, and said, "Children."

Kai ducked his head in a salute. "Kindred." Dae, having only been in the mortal world less than a season and still shy, hurriedly copied him.

In a light voice, the Witch said, "Kaiisteron, Prince of the Fourth House, Daevavopta, Knight-Guardian of the Seventh House."

Captain Kentdessa said, "Kai-Enna leads our clan scouts. He assembled the map of this area and came closest to the camp's walls. Dae-Fera was with him."

The Witch turned to face Kai and their almost undivided attention felt like a warm fire. "When you were near the walls, did you feel anything?"

He knew the Witch meant anything from the underearth, or

other powers. "I could tell there were expositors." By now, Kai and most of the Saredi fighters had seen enough dead bodies to become experts in the effects of expositors' intentions, but they hadn't known what expositors were until the first attack on the Erathi. That was when refugees arriving in the grassplains had described the way the invaders seemed to draw power from the death of mortals.

It had sounded like a story at first, something heroic Saredi ancestors encountered in their adventures. Grandmother had to travel to the underearth to find demons who had encountered expositors before and could describe their abilities. The way they drew power from death, the more death the better, and shaped this power into intentions and designs that were entirely different from the Witches' spirit workings. Grandmother was still there now, negotiating with Kai's mother and the principals of the other Houses to get passage for demons in mortal bodies to use the underearth to get behind Hierarch lines. Once they were able to do that, the mortal forces would push forward and the Hierarchs would be trapped between them. The Witch seemed to expect more, and Kai added, "They've set their intentions all along the walls, to keep us from getting through, but they weren't pushing past that, as far as we could tell."

The Witch said, "Not the expositors. Something else."

"You've had omens?" Captain Kentdessa said, her brow furrowed.

"Not enough." The Witch made a gesture of displeasure. "We need more information."

Captain Kentdessa turned to Kai. "The Witches want you to speak to Grandmother."

Kai glanced around. There were a lot of mortals who were not-Saredi standing around, watching the conversation. The borderlanders had been allies with the Witches for a long time, as long as they had been living in the fringes of the grassplains. But the Saredi didn't get many visitors to their tents, and most borderlanders would never have seen demons before the war. Kai had encountered some in the field who were afraid, and it had made him feel uncomfortable and awkward in Enna's body. "Here?"

"Here," Captain Kentdessa said. Then she smiled a little, deepening the wrinkles at the corners of her mouth. "It's not a secret."

Kai sat down on the packed earth and pebbles, folded his legs, and breathed out to relax. Dae sank down into a crouch beside him.

He closed his eyes and rode his connection to the underearth down to his real body.

He was curled up in a bubble of water deep in the protective rock, the darkness warm and comforting on his scales. He uncoiled his tails and focused on finding Grandmother. He shifted the underearth around him, followed the spark of her presence. As he drew closer he could tell she was with others of the Fourth House, their shadows in the underearth long and defined. It meant he wouldn't be able to talk to her in private, which was disappointing. He slid into the space they all occupied and opened his eyes to a large chamber.

He knew the Overlord was here too so he dropped to his knees on the floor, which was softened with heavy furred skins. Tusks and massive bones lined the walls, arched inward as if they supported the weight of the curving roof. Openings between the bones looked out onto a landscape of forested hills, not unlike the area around the Saredi-borderlander camp, but these trees were much taller, with long waving fronds of black and red.

Mother and Grandmother sat nearby, having tea out of the skulls of favored ancestors. A few dozen of Kai's siblings sat back along the walls. His brother Veditiron hissed, "Honored Mother! Kaiisteron is here!" in the sort of tone normally used to announce an intruder.

"I can see that, Veditiron," Mother snapped, her horns flaring in impatience. "Kaiisteron, you're interrupting. I hope you have a good reason."

He said, "Captain Kentdessa wants to speak to Grandmother."

Grandmother's spirit was here in a body that had been made for her, part of the long-ago treaty she had forged with the underearth. It was as malleable as everything else here, so she looked the same as the last time Kai had seen her, before Kentdessa's fighters had left to join the southern clans at the meeting point. Her white hair was braided back, silver-bright against her dark brown skin, and she wore the elaborate embroidered coat of a Saredi ancestor, the antelope sigils of Kentdessa repeated on the cuffs and across the back. She motioned for him to come to her. "Come here, Kai. What does the captain want?"

Kai scooted over, his tails making it a much more elegant motion than it would have been in his human body. "The Witches have questions."

Disgruntled, Mother gestured. "We all have questions." She added impatiently, "We still haven't been able to see these creatures closely. They have protections against us. That hasn't changed from the last time the mortals asked."

Kai knew all the Houses under treaty with the Saredi had been searching for clues to the origin of the Hierarchs. Grandmother and the captains thought it might be possible to attack their homeland or supply chain through the underearth, the way the demons had attacked the grassplains in Grandmother's youth. But searching the upper earth from the underearth was about as easy as searching the sky or the ocean. Grandmother's expression was dry as she said, "If you were as all-knowing as you think you are, this would be over by now." She told Kai, "Tell them to ask what they will, little one."

Kai's perception of the mortal world was dim and fuzzy now, narrowed to nothing but the darkness behind his eyelids. He made Enna's body say, "She's here. Ask."

Captain Kentdessa's voice came to him as if he was at the

bottom of a canyon. Kai repeated, "The wooden towers inside the Hierarch camp. The Witches say they may be structures for a kind of long-distance weapon."

Grandmother frowned. "I thought the borderlanders said they were siege engines."

Kai had Enna's body repeat her words, the lips of his original body moving silently as he spoke aloud for Captain Kentdessa and the Witch. Kai translated their answer, "The remains found in the destroyed Erathi cities did look like siege engines, but the Hierarchs have also built them in this camp, where the only walls are their own." He heard wind in the distance, rising over the plain. Enna's body didn't smell rain, so it probably wouldn't affect the attack plan.

Mother looked bored. The structures of the underearth were constantly moving and malleable; she probably didn't understand what they were asking. "What does it—"

Grandmother held up a hand, her brow furrowed in consternation. "But there were patterns of destruction that looked as if they radiated out from those towers. I was told they were supports for battering rams."

"That was wrong," Kai repeated. "They think now . . ." The voices cut off and he shook his head a little. "I'm sorry, Grandmother. They stopped talking." The wind had risen to a howl. Maybe it would be a storm. "The wind came up—"

Kai slammed back into the mortal world so hard it turned his vision black and Enna's body fell into the dirt. He shoved himself up, got his eyes open, and saw something terrible.

The howl wasn't the wind, he wasn't hearing it with his ears. It was a pressure, something that staggered every mortal in the fort. Bodies sprawled in the grass. The Witch had turned away, their hands lifted, an invisible force ripping at their veils. Beside Kai, Dae rocked back and forth, hands clapped to her ears. That pressure was inside Kai, pressing the air from his lungs, tearing the strength from his limbs, filling his body like water, like it would burst him like an overfull barrel.

Captain Kentdessa grabbed his collar and dragged him to the path, dirt and grass catching in his clothes. She shoved him away and tossed Dae-Fera on top of him, and then death rolled over the hills.

Kai came back to himself choking on blood. He shoved himself up to his hands and knees, and spat out a red mouthful. He was on the path below the hilltop fort, in the shelter of the stunted trees. Dimly, as if there was something wrong with his ears, he heard screams, moans. Dae huddled in the roots of a tree next to him. He grabbed her shoulder and she fell, her small limp body uncoiling. "Dae! Dae." He shook her and her head lolled back and he saw her eyes. Brown, mortal eyes. Dae was gone, Fera's body was empty. Reflexively he tried to touch the underearth to find her, to make sure she had gone back to her original body. There was nothing.

It was like groping for something with a phantom limb. An empty hollow, like when he stood in running water. There was no connection to the underearth. Just a dead cold nothingness.

The mortal world had never felt this unreal and this raw. The air was heavier, Kai's skin too sensitive. He staggered to his feet and struggled back upward, toward the hilltop. The others would be hurt; he had to help them, he had to find the captain and tell her Dae-Fera was gone, that something was terribly wrong. But when he climbed the path there was no sound of groaning or outcries.

He reached the top and saw nothing but tumbled bodies. No movement, no gasp of breath. The Saredi, the borderlanders, the Witches in their tangled veils, all lay as limp as discarded heaps of clothing. The faces he could see were stained with blood. Their eyes had bled, their ears, noses, mouths. Like something had gotten inside their veins and forced the blood out.

He realized his boot was against something solid and looked down. It was Captain Kentdessa.

She sprawled at the top of the path, facedown in the dry grass and pebbles. She must have turned back after pushing Kai and Dae down the hill, gone back to try to get someone else. He dropped down beside her and rolled her over. Her eyes were as blank as Dae's, her nose and mouth filled with blood.

Kai didn't know how long he sat there, looking at her. Then footsteps pounded up the path. He managed to lift his head and saw Tahsia, a Kentdessa sub-captain. She said, "Kai-Enna, get down to the camp," and climbed past him up the slope.

Sick and cold, Kai pushed to his feet. He stumbled down the path. When he reached the bottom, familiar bodies sprawled in the dirt outside the tent where they had constructed the map. He crouched to feel for breath on the mortals, to look at the demons' eyes. They were all gone.

He found his way through the trees from one clearing to the next, where the Kentdessa had pitched their round tent-shelters and lean-tos. There were bodies everywhere, mortals huddled in unmoving heaps. Horses in the pickets had fallen where they stood, birds had dropped dead from the sky. He spotted other moving people, running frantically. He tried to look for his cousins, for his aunts and uncles, but there was nothing but death. He could still hear yelling, screaming, but when he followed it, everyone was dead.

He reached the clearing where Captain Kentdessa's tent stood. It was on fire; someone must have knocked over a brazier when they fell. The smell of smoke and sudden death choked him.

He sank to the ground near the burning tent. His connection to the underearth was still silent, cold, severed.

He sat there until Tahsia and two fighters with Raneldi sigils came from the direction of the hill fort. Arn-Nefa staggered after them, blood dripping from her ears. It should have been a relief to see that not everyone he knew was dead, but he couldn't feel anything right now. Kai watched Tahsia and the others stride by, but Arn-Nefa grabbed his arm. She dragged him to his feet and shook him like a rattle. "Kai-Enna, are you still here?"

Being touched made his skin crawl. He jerked his arm free, snarling, "Get off me."

"Kai-Enna!" she snapped. "Find a horse and ride to the landing. Tell the Erathi boats to flee. The mortals they sent to stand with us are dead, the rest will be slaughtered if they wait. Here." A Raneldi demon he didn't know ran toward them and stumbled to a halt, holding out the black and green Erathi totem. Arn-Nefa snatched it and shoved it at Kai. "Give them this."

He took it automatically. Arn-Nefa said, "Now go! Then follow us to the last meeting point."

Kai stumbled away from her. He searched until he found a horse either too stunned to dislike his scent or just so grateful to be led away from all the death that it didn't resist him, and rode away from the ruin of the camp.

He reached the cove in time to warn the Erathi ships. On the way he ran into a lost band of Hierarch legionaries, and proved to himself that even without the underearth, he could still drain the life from mortals. But when he got to the meeting point, only a few demons were there among the mortal fighters, and Arn-Nefa and the Raneldi demon who had been with her never appeared. Tahsia was the highest in rank and so, with her leading, they rode on through the plains back to the main camp.

When they arrived, the Saredi clan tents were already burning.

FOUR

Leaving Sanja with Ziede, Kai climbed down from the platform to make his way back to where the whale drifted beside the breakwater. He suspected it might like this plan a lot better than he did.

The smoke-laced wind was already gusting, driving waves and spray further up the tumbled rocks. The shell swayed under Kai's feet as he leapt back to it, but the motion subsided as he found the whale's mind again and sunk into its consciousness. *I need to change our bargain,* he told it. *I need you to take me somewhere, not far, just to the strait on the other side of this island. Then we'll be finished with each other. But first I'll remove the shell.*

The whale's sharpened interest washed the murk from its thoughts, leaving the stream fresh and clear. Kai concentrated on turning his plan into a series of images it could understand.

When the whale agreed, Kai took off his skirt, leaving him in the expositor's long tunic and leggings. He wadded it up and pitched it over onto the breakwater. He didn't know if he would be able to retrieve it later but it was nice to have the option. Then he swung over the side of the shell's platform and climbed down to place his bare feet carefully on the whale's slick hide.

It was smooth and cool, with a very slight give. Kai let his breath out in an uneasy hiss. He didn't trust easily, something he felt was validated every time some supposed ally murdered him and stuck him in an underwater vault. And it was ridiculous to expect the captive, abused whale to trust him. But its consciousness had never felt vengeful and he was hoping being set free would buy him enough gratitude for it to fulfill its part of their agreement.

He crouched to put both hands on the curved ribbed surface of the shell, sinking into the web of intentions that held it in place. It was fitted onto a chain harness that stretched around the whale's body, but it was the expositor's design that really anchored it. Undoing the structure took hardly any pain at all, and Kai picked apart and broke the strands of power until something under the shell cracked.

He edged back, closer to the whale's blowhole, and stamped his foot twice in their prearranged signal.

The whale's body rocked as its fins propelled it away from the breakwater. Kai leaned down to keep his balance, bracing his hands on the whale's cool skin. The sky was growing darker, telling him he needed to hurry.

Unmoored, the shell shifted with the motion, then rocked sideways. The nacre underside was slimy, pocked with seawater parasites that had wormed their way under it. The whale's deep blue skin was mottled with bruises and scars and raw wounds. The harness below the shell was a raised ridge of netting, made of knotted cables woven from braided scaled hide and secured with chains. Kai hadn't been sure how it was constructed and it was a relief to see it would work for his purpose.

He crept back toward the harness, wary in case the shell toppled in his direction. They needed to leave soon; a haze rolled over the water as Ziede's air spirits drove the smoke down to the sea's surface.

The whale half rolled again and the shell toppled into the water with a tremendous splash. Barely keeping his balance as the spray rained down, Kai stretched forward and grabbed the edge of the harness. The whale could easily throw him off, could roll and dive fast enough for him to lose his grip, but it didn't. It waited until he climbed around to face forward, finding handholds and footholds in the old gaps and tears in the netting. He signaled he was ready with a slap on its hide. *Now for the awful part,* he thought. It had been a long time since he was a young demon in a mortal body, easily made helpless by water and expositors' intentions. But the sea would still inhibit his power and water was an impossible element for witchwork. Not that he would have time to create a cantrip if he was drowning. This whole plan was objectively a very bad idea for a being of the underearth or a Witch. Not that that had ever stopped him before. He huddled down and squeezed his eyes shut.

Kai felt the whale tilt down. He tightened his hold as cold saltwater slammed into him. A ball of terror formed in his throat and the urge to scream was almost overpowering. He forced it down, thinking of Ziede and Sanja on the island. If this didn't work, they could be trapped or recaptured. The harness ground into his hands and feet. He could last without breathing for the time it would take to reach the ship but water leaked into his throat and lungs despite his clenched jaw. He told himself how much worse this would be if the whale was actually trying to dislodge him.

The dive evened out, the force of the water lessened. Kai steeled himself and opened his eyes.

The water was clearer than he expected. The whale was still fairly close to the surface, moving slowly. He couldn't make out much except startled fish and rocks as the whale curved away from the shadow of the breakwater, but it was so strange under here that it almost made him forget how terrified he was.

The expositor's amalgam was still out here somewhere. A perfect choice of opponent for a demon; since its life was created only by an expositor's design, Kai couldn't drain it. But it should follow him specifically, ignoring Ziede's presence on the island. And it would have been designed to track his position but not try to stop him.

Out of the dark water a long, lethal shape arrowed toward him. *Or maybe it* was *meant to stop me,* he thought, frustrated. He took one hand off the net to draw Tarrow's knife. The drag of the whale's motion made him sway back and he huddled closer to its body. *It would be nice if just one thing was easy.*

The amalgam swooped down, sharp fins cutting through the water, close enough for Kai to see the oddly shaped skull was actually a jumble of human and bulbous squid heads. Multiple eyes tracked the whale as the tentacles stretched out, their obscenely human hands reached for him. Kai ducked and stabbed at the nearest hand, but the water slowed every motion. He had to keep it back. If it hurt the whale enough, his ally might scrape him off against the nearest rock.

As Kai tried to think of something clever, the amalgam circled toward him again. Then the whole world went sideways.

Kai dropped the knife to grip the harness, helplessly dizzy, realizing the whale had rolled. Then suddenly he was right side up again. The rocks and the shadow of the island were gone; this must be the more open water of the strait. Whatever the whale had done, the amalgam was nowhere in sight.

Then the whale pushed upward hard enough to flatten Kai against its body. In the next instant they broke the surface as foaming waves rushed down its slick hide.

Kai clung to the harness, hair dripping in his eyes, trying to quietly hack up a lungful of water. When he had spat out enough to get a breath of smoky air, he tossed his hair back and looked up. The sky was invisible past the now dense smoke but the embossed coppery curve looming beside them was the hull of the Immortal Blessed ship. It sat dead in the water, angry muffled voices sounding from the upper deck.

The smoke hung in such a thick cloud now that everything above the hull seemed shrouded in gray veils. He had hoped the smoke would force the crew to halt the ship or at worst slow down; even an Immortal Blessed craft had to be careful of ramming into rock. Kai wasn't sure exactly where they were; the smoke blocked any view of the island that should be on his left. A pale hand floated by, still attached to the torn remains of an arm: all that was left of the amalgam

Kai patted the whale. *Good job, friend.* He used a little effort to draw out what little life remained in the braided hemp cables of the net, just enough to shrivel the fibers to brittleness and unravel the knots. He felt the cables sag under him until they were loose enough to come apart during the whale's next dive. Kai pushed to his feet and padded carefully across the whale's skin to the side of the ship.

The copper hull was figured with flowing wave and wind designs embracing and surrounding the sun imagery of the Immortal Blessed. Kai crouched and jumped, caught the bottom ridge of a raised band. He looked down to watch the whale sink almost silently below the surface, its dark shape disappearing under the hull. *At least one of us got out of this whole mess better off,* Kai thought.

He scrambled up, finding footholds in the other sacred symbols. He couldn't hear any voices or movement. He peered through the oar port expecting an empty rowing bench. Shadowy figures loomed and he jerked backward so violently he almost fell off the hull.

Kai hung from the port, cursing under his breath, waiting for someone to raise the alarm. But nothing happened. *How is it so quiet,* he wondered. No jostling movement, no coughing. No breathing? Mortals were never that quiet. Demons were never that quiet.

Kai pulled himself up again. The figures on the bench hadn't moved. They were shoved together, maybe six human shapes crammed into a space meant for only two Immortal Blessed. He risked his head to lean further in and get a view down the length of the rowing deck.

The whole space was filled with silent bodies. All mortals, they were locked in absolute stillness. The air was tainted with fresh blood and rot and unwashed skin.

It was obvious now that expositors' intentions hung heavy throughout the deck. From a distance Kai had mistaken it for the Immortal Blessed's Well of Thosaren, which could be used to sail the ship without any human effort. The Blessed only rowed their ships on ceremonial occasions, or during the war, when the Hierarchs would punish them by restricting their Well. They would certainly never let mortals corrupt their property by touching even one sacred oar. Someone else had control of this ship now.

Kai pulled himself up and wriggled through the port, glad this new body was agile enough to manage it. Inside he balanced on the oar, blinking as his eyes adjusted and he made out more detail.

Rank after rank of frozen mortals filled the benches. Their clothes were ragged, the wood beneath their hands was stained with blood and pus. They stared straight ahead, their breath shallow, eyes unblinking. Kai grimaced, sickened. And confused.

Someone had created a life-well here, had enchained these people with intents and designs to drain their lives, as a way to power the ship in place of the Well of Thosaren.

Maybe these mortals had been brought aboard, told they would be rowers, and once they were seated at the benches the expositor had sunk them into this half-life, draining them to build the intention that let him keep the ship in motion. An expositor could be executed under Rising World law for something like this. Kai had caught and executed lots of them for similar crimes, if not on this scale.

Kai stepped along the oar, carefully avoiding the rower's hands. Their eyes gleamed in the dim light, and he had the suspicion they were just aware enough to know someone was here. There had to be at least one expositor aboard to keep this tanglement of obscenity working. Kai hopped down to the catwalk and ran silently toward the narrow spiral stair at the stern.

Just as he reached it, the wood creaked and the rope handrail twitched. Someone above had put their weight on the top step. Kai slid sideways into shadow. Booted feet came into view, then a mortal in a long sleeveless coat with a cursebreaker slung over his shoulder climbed down. As he reached the bottom and turned toward the rowers' benches, Kai slipped up behind him and clapped a hand over his mouth.

Apprentice expositor, Kai identified, as he drained the man's life. He could always tell. He stored the vitality and power like another heart in his chest, burning a little with its fresh intensity. He was sure he would need it soon. When the convulsions ended, Kai dropped the desiccated body to the deck. The last bench was unoccupied so he picked up the cursebreaker carefully by the handle and eased it out the oar port. The splash was fairly quiet. Kai took the long curved boat knife off the man's belt, tucked it into his own, and started up the steps.

He climbed upward, past the landing for a service deck. From the way these ships were usually designed, it should be closed off from the rest of the lower compartments. He paused only long enough to make sure it was silent and empty.

At the hatch at the top of the stairs, he took a cautious peek first. This was a large stern cabin, the space lavish, with a central hall lined with cushioned benches built against the walls. Above them were gold-embossed panels depicting soaring mountains and deep valleys. Curtained arches led to smaller sleeping cabins. At the stern, below the two eye-shaped ports, was a platform with a petal-carved throne for the Immortal Marshall who would use their power to sail the ship. It was currently empty.

The Immortal Blessed would go shit-raving over the idea of an expositor controlling this craft. But then they would go shit-raving just the same over Kaiisteron or any other Witch putting their dirty feet on one of their sacred decks.

Gradually he had the sense of a live body in the room, someone breathing. He spotted a figure curled up on a couch, apparently asleep, just a shape buried under a silk blanket. The one bare leg hanging out was pale white. Not the light but weathered skin of Menlas' unfortunate archipelago crew, but the white of a light-skinned person who was never let outside.

Kai climbed up onto the polished wood floor. His clothes

were still dripping seawater, his wet hair stuck to his chest and shoulders. He stepped toward the figure, and lightly nudged the leg with a knee. The person sat up abruptly and stared at him. They were young and small, probably female, with a gossamer mane of light-colored hair, barely dressed in a silk wrap. A jeweled collar with a bone binding token was clamped around her neck, put there by the expositor who had enslaved her. She frowned up at Kai, confused, as if expecting him to be someone she knew. Then her eyes widened and her breath hitched. She had seen his eyes.

Kai raised his brows and held up two fingers for silence, tapping them against his lips in case she didn't recognize the gesture. She nodded and briefly pressed her hand to her own mouth, then her throat, which was Witchspeak for *compelled under an intention*. So not just an enslaved mortal, then. A Witch, turned into a familiar. Kai signed back that he understood.

Kai eased closer, trying not to alarm her, and took the bone-carved token between thumb and forefinger. The expositor's intention buzzed under his skin like a trapped bee. He drew it out, released it into the air to fade, and pressed down on the suddenly weak material. It turned to powder between his fingers.

The familiar pressed a hand to her chest and drew in a shuddering breath.

Kai stepped away and paced toward the open hatchway at the far end of the cabin. He stopped when he was close enough to see outside. The open deck was shrouded in smoke; he could barely make out the first mast and the bow might as well have been lost in another world. Ziede would be out there somewhere, waiting for his signal.

Just outside the hatch was the upper deck, ringed with more of the low couches stuffed with white cushions. In the center stood the metal pillar housing the ship's steering mechanism and the sacred relic that was supposed to connect the hull to the Immortal Blessed's Well of Thosaren. An expositor stood next to it, dressed in a ruby and purple coat and skirts, fine enough for the court of an Arike city-state. Two other mortals stood with him, in similar dress but far less rich. One was probably another apprentice, and the other wore the chain and leather armored tunic of a soldier or bodyguard over the finery. Expensive armor, with snake heads on the pauldrons. Silk rustled as the freed familiar crept up to stand beside Kai.

The expositor spoke to someone on the lower deck: "—defenses arrayed above us. The demon can't get past the water."

Kai didn't snort.

A voice below, muffled by the heavy air, replied, ". . . whole ship. You don't know that."

"Insolent," the apprentice commented.

"If we didn't need her, I'd throw her over the side," the expositor agreed, his voice dry.

"Surely that would be a waste." The apprentice seemed worried. "She could be useful, if we need a death for another set of intentions."

"We have plenty of fodder. I might still throw her over the side, and the spy with her." The expositor was unconcerned, confident, secure in his power. "We're close now and I have no intention of losing our quarry."

The odor of perfume hung on the damp smoky air of the deck, overpowering the light incense that clung to the fabrics in the cabin. Kai grimaced. It reminded him of the Benais-arik palaces, of why he was so fucking angry right now.

Creating an intention would take too long, and the expositor might notice. Kai crouched and sketched a quick diagram on the wood where the damp had settled on it. A set of witchwork cantrips, nothing much by themselves but enough to mesh with the power of Ziede's air spirits and weave the smoke veil into something more opaque and closer to the texture of a cloth net. The familiar crouched beside him to watch attentively.

Kai knew she saw the cantrip completely differently than he did. For a real Witch, a cantrip was using words to paint reality into a different shape, shifting a tiny piece of the world into a new configuration. Witches didn't see the world the way mortals, or demons, or anything else did. They said they saw spirits, but it was more accurate to say they saw the animating forces, what expositors might call energies, of everything. But the secret was that it was all they saw.

As Kai drew, the argument outside continued, with the expositor insisting there was no way a demon could get aboard and whoever was below equally insistent that they should risk hulling the ship on the rocks to leave the strait. Kai added the signs to exclude Ziede and Sanja, and the familiar. When Kai finished, he blew gently on the sigils to send the cantrips ghosting across the deck.

Kai pushed to his feet and leaned against the side of the hatch to watch. The familiar lounged on the deck, smiling faintly. The cantrips drifted over the polished wood of the hatch lip and across the upper deck, until they curled like mist around the feet of the mortals by the helm. Then they spilled down the steps to the lower deck, still invisible in the smoky fog.

Muffled again, the other voice spoke irately from the lower deck, "What do you expect me to do about it?"

Evidently as out of patience as he was ideas, the expositor snapped, "Come up here, Ashem."

The sound of footsteps barely penetrated the thickening air, but a figure rose into view as it climbed the steps to the upper deck.

It was a mortal wearing the dress of an Arike Rising World soldier, a light armored tunic over wide pants, with a sash identifying her as a garrison officer. Other coalition soldiers had adopted Arike dress, but she looked like an Arike, short and sturdy with brown skin and tight dark curls cut close to her head. She wasn't wearing a helm or hood and there were no weapons at her heavy leather belt. She walked like she was frustrated by everything and especially weary of the expositor. Another figure followed behind her, obscured by the smoke.

At the top of the steps she said, "If you're going to shout at me, call me Cohort Leader. And I—" Then she glanced up and met Kai's gaze. She froze, dark eyes widening in shock.

He had never met Cohort Leader Ashem before, and even if he had, she couldn't possibly recognize Kai in this new form. But she knew a demon when she saw one. Instead of shouting the alarm, her expression turned grimly amused. She said, "Well, you were certainly correct, Aclines, he's very nearby."

Aclines, the expositor, demanded, "What are you saying? How do you know?"

Ashem nodded toward Kai. Aclines and the other two turned. Or tried to. The cantrips had woven the smoky mist into a tight net and tied their legs in place. The apprentice jerked a cursebreaker out of his belt and lunged forward. His feet failed to move and he fell flat on his face. The cantrip web wove a cocoon of gray mist to pin him down. He would probably smother in the thick smoke but it wasn't as if Kai hadn't been planning to kill him anyway.

Aclines didn't waste time on exclamations; he drew power from the life-well of mortal misery on the rowing deck and flung it toward Kai.

Kai was already moving. The bodyguard was behind and to one side of Aclines so Kai ducked out of his reach, stepped on the prone apprentice, and drove the boat knife in under Aclines' chin. The half-formed intention scattered as Aclines clawed at the knife.

Someone yelled, "Behind!" in Arike. Kai spun away from the expositor just as something slashed past him. The bodyguard had snapped out a telescoping staff to nearly six paces in length. The end glinted in the smoky light, studded with razored slivers.

The bodyguard cursed, and shouted, "Ramad, you traitor!"

Aclines, knife still lodged in his throat, wavered as his knees buckled. He fell into the mist, crumpling in a heap of fine silk. The cantrip threads seized and held him, even as his body shuddered and blood soaked his clothes.

The figure behind Ashem had called the warning. From this vantage point, Kai recognized him. It was Ramad, one of Bashat's vanguarders, an inspector of his spies and scouts. Kai had seen him at Bashat's side a few times at the Rising World court.

He was a young man, tall for a southern Arike. His curling dark hair was long and braided back, and he wore the working version of traditional Arike men's dress, a cotton coat belted over a tunic and split skirt. The colors were faded grays and blues, washed out and dim against his amber brown skin.

It was interesting that Ramad was here, and that was putting it mildly. But between him and Cohort Leader Ashem, they should be able to get some answers.

The familiar stepped up beside Kai. She held up a hand, asking for permission. Kai jerked his chin in assent.

The familiar eased forward, almost within reach of the desperate bodyguard's staff. Aclines' death was a power well of its own, and until he finished dying she was still connected to him. Kai could just sense the movement of energy as she drew back the life he had been stealing from her to fuel his intentions. She lifted her hands.

The bodyguard froze, his throat worked as something constricted his breath. He dropped the weapon and clawed at his face. Flowers erupted from his mouth, his nose, ears. White asters, plum blossoms, the rich blue-purple blooms of something Kai didn't recognize. Yellow petals squeezed out of the tear ducts in the man's eyes. Kai was impressed. "That's a good one," he told her. She must have an affinity for ground and plant spirits, the way Ziede did for the air.

The bodyguard jerked, stiffened, and collapsed backward.

Ashem tried to lunge for the bodyguard's staff. She jerked and nearly fell; her feet were tied to the deck by the net of smoke and mist. Ramad reached to steady her and then had to grab the stair rail to keep from falling himself. The muffled shouts of alarm and cursing told Kai that everyone else on the lower deck was now caught in the net.

Kai paced toward Ashem and Ramad and stopped out of arm's reach. He found himself more curious than angry, which was new at least. He asked, "Now what are Rising World officers doing working for an expositor aboard an Immortal Blessed ship?"

Ashem eyed him grimly. "We're here against our will."

Ramad's brow furrowed with something that might be consternation, but certainly wasn't fear. "That is you, isn't it. Kaiisteron?"

Kai knew he was smiling and that it wasn't a pleasant expression. "I'm flattered you remember me."

Ashem's hard gaze was wary. She was clearly just as suspicious of him as he was of her. "Aclines said he was looking for a demon, I didn't realize it was you."

Ramad added, "There was one other apprentice, he had a cursebreaker. I don't know where—"

"He went below. I ate him already," Kai said.

Ashem's expression tightened at the reminder of what Kai was. "There are no other expositors on board." She gestured down at the smoke. "You could release us from whatever this is."

"Why would I do that?" Kai glanced at the familiar for confirmation that the only expositors were dead. She moved her hand in the Witchspeak sign for *truth*.

He signed back, *Were these two prisoners?*

She answered, *They seemed to be, with the rest of the crew.*

Aclines had set defensive intentions in the ship's furled sails and around the deck, ready if anyone attacked; Kai felt the structures collapsing with the expositor's death, not strong enough to last without Aclines' connection to the life-well in the rowing deck. Sparks of captured life force drifted down, dissolving in the air, and it made Kai's exposed skin tingle. He stretched out to tug gently on Ziede's heart pearl. *I've taken the ship.*

He felt Ziede's sigh of relief. *It took you long enough. I thought you were fighting a ship full of Immortal Blessed.*

Ashem demanded, "Why won't you release us? You know we're Imperial officers."

Kai told Ziede, *I found a ship full all right but it's not of Immortal Blessed.* He said aloud, "Aren't you here to help Aclines hunt us down?"

Ashem's wary expression turned mortally offended, as if Kai had insulted her family back to her first ancestor. "What?" she snapped. "Are you accusing me of treason?"

"It's as Cohort Leader Ashem says, we were taken prisoner." Ramad's expression was thoughtful, almost more interested in picking meaning from Kai's questions than getting free. "The rumor was that you left Benais-arik abruptly. Did Aclines have something to do with that?"

Kai didn't know much about Ramad but rumor said he was an excellent vanguarder and in Bashat's confidence. "Where did Aclines get this ship?"

"That I don't know." Ramad jerked his head toward Aclines' cooling body. "When he came to the outpost at Scarif, he already had it."

Ashem flicked a repressive look at Ramad. "Don't answer his questions until he releases us."

Ramad gave her a wry glance. "He has a Rising World rank too, Cohort Leader, and higher than yours."

Ignoring them, Kai looked at the familiar. She signed *truth* again.

He signed, *Do you know where Aclines got this ship?*

She touched her forehead. *He took my thoughts at Scarif. If I was with him before then, I don't remember it.*

Appalled but not surprised, Kai signed, *He took all your past? Your home, family?*

Her face twisted in despair, before iron control shuttered her expression again. *Everything.*

One way expositors protected their secrets was to destroy their familiars' memories of their captivity. Kai swallowed down anger like a thorn in his throat and reminded himself Aclines was already dead. It would make it nearly impossible to find out where the familiar had come from, to return her to her family line.

"What is she saying?" Ramad asked, politely.

During the war, some of the Arike vanguarders had known Witchspeak. That was years before Ramad's time but the knowledge might have been passed down. Kai said, "She knows what you know. So it sounds like I don't need you."

Ashem folded her arms and gave Ramad a frustrated look, as if this was his fault for answering questions. Ramad seemed to take the statement as a bargaining point rather than a threat. He said, "There are only two aboard who are Aclines' followers. I'll point them out for you and she can verify my claim. The rest on deck are captives, Cohort Leader Ashem's cadre. Release them and I'll help you."

That was an interesting assumption on Ramad's part. "Help me do what?" Kai noted that Ashem's jaw had tightened.

"Whatever you left Benais-arik to do." Ramad was matter-of-fact. If he thought this was like trying to negotiate with a feral animal, he was too good a diplomat to show it. "Your absence in the year before the Imperial renewal of the Rising World was noticed. I assume the Witch King doesn't disappear without a good reason."

Ashem was too impatient for Ramad's careful haggling. She grated out the words, "Aclines captured my cadre and a cohort of soldiers from the outpost at Scarif, so he could control this ship. They may be dying. If you ever had any loyalty to Bashat, release us, and my cadre can help them."

Any loyalty to Bashat. Kai had endless loyalty to Bashat's family line and he wanted, oh how he had wanted, to believe Bashat personally deserved it.

The smoke in the upper air thinned as a breeze moved across the deck. Ziede was gently, slowly releasing her air spirits and their control over the atmosphere in the strait. It wouldn't be long before she arrived, and she was going to want answers. Just because Aclines had been planning to kill Ashem and Ramad as power for his intentions or throw them overboard because they were annoying didn't mean they hadn't originally been in the plot together. Expositors turned on each other all the time. "Why would I release anyone? Maybe I want to drain their lives and eat their bone marrow."

Ramad pressed his lips together, betraying some exasperation. "Of course you'll release them. You're not an expositor. You've been an ally of the Rising World longer than we've all been alive."

If only Kai was sure that was still true. He turned away to drop down onto one of the couches intended for the Immortal Blessed to survey their ship. "What were you doing when Aclines captured you, Ramad?"

Ramad coughed at a stray drift of smoke and rubbed his eyes. "I was traveling, and had stopped at the cohort outpost to stay the night." Ashem's gaze slid sideways, skeptical. She didn't think he had been there by chance.

Kai didn't think so either. "And why were you in Scarif?"

Ramad said, "I'm happy to answer your questions if you'll answer mine." Kai's expression went flat and Ramad added, "I mean no insult. I'm a historian. You knew the Great Bashasa. I have many questions."

Ashem grimaced in so much irritation that Kai said, "Ask one."

Ramad didn't hesitate. "There's a rumor that you were an immortal servant of the Hierarchs and Bashasa released you from the Summer Halls. Is it true?"

Kai had the feeling that this at least was not a trick, that whatever else Ramad was here for, he was serious about seizing this opportunity. "There were immortal servants of the Hierarchs. I met some. I wasn't one of them."

Ashem looked up at the mast as if asking it to bear witness to her pain. "Why do we have to do this right now?"

Ramad ignored her. "What were—"

Kai stopped him. "You don't want to owe me a debt, Ramad, even if that debt is only a truthful answer."

Ramad looked briefly thwarted, before he smoothed his expression again. He said, "I was looking for Aclines."

Ashem turned sharply to glare at him. "You were?"

Kai had to say, "And here you thought you'd be bored by this conversation, Cohort Leader."

Ashem pressed her lips together. Ramad told her, "I didn't know he intended to attack your outpost, or I would have warned you. I had word, mostly rumors, of an expositor who was heading toward Scarif. I came to investigate. I was obviously far too late."

The smoke had thinned enough for Kai to see the lower deck, to make out the scatter of figures trapped in the cantrip web. Ashem's cadre, all focused on the drama playing out on the upper deck, and among them the two who Ramad had said were Aclines' surviving followers.

The familiar had checked the bodies and collected the cursebreaker from the apprentice who lay face-first in the cantrip web. She nudged him with her foot, and signed to Kai, *This one is dead now, too.* She lifted the cursebreaker inquiringly.

"Throw it over the side," he told her. He signed, *Were they cruel to you?* and nodded toward Ramad and Ashem. *Or any of her cadre?*

No, she replied. *They didn't seem to know what I was.* She pitched the cursebreaker over the rail. *Though I think the vanguarder suspected I wasn't an ordinary mortal servant.*

Will you travel with us for now? I can't promise safety, Kai signed, and pointed at the telescoping staff. "We'll keep that."

She picked it up, collapsed it back into a rod. She tossed it to him and signed, *I know who you are, the demon the mortals call King of the Witches. Do you promise revenge?*

Kai tapped his heart three times, the Witchspeak sign the Saredi had used for *I swear.*

She smiled. *My name is sister Tenes,* she signed, and padded back into the stern cabin.

Ramad watched her, brow furrowed. "She can hear but not speak?"

And Ramad called himself a historian. Witchspeak had been a language as long as Witches existed, but it had become even more important in the Hierarchs war. But they never taught any of this anymore. There was no reason for most mortals to know it, but the Arike of the Prince-heirs' courts, especially Benais-arik, should remember. In a strange way, it hurt that they didn't, and Kai was a fool for letting it. He said, "Expositors take away the speech of their familiars, among other things, so they can't reveal any secrets. It goes back to the Hierarchs."

Cohort Leader Ashem frowned. "But there's no point to that. She talks in sign."

Ashem was too naive for this world if she thought people were only cruel when there was a point to it. "The Hierarchs' expositors used to cut their hands off, too." Kai scratched his head with the tip of the rod. The salt drying in his hair was making his scalp itch. "Where's Tahren Stargard, called the Fallen?"

Ashem's suspicious frown deepened. She said, "Why would she be here? She has to be in Benais-arik for the Immortal Blessed's part in the Imperial renewal. If she isn't there to give her assent on their behalf, it could be disastrous. You must know that as well as we do."

Kai ignored her, watching the way the tiny lines at the corners of Ramad's eyes tightened. Ramad met his gaze with what looked like honesty and said, "Then she isn't with you."

Kai said, "Why are you really here, Ramad?"

Ramad breathed out, and admitted, "I was looking for Aclines.

Because Tahren Stargard did not arrive at Benais-arik when expected, and Bashat fears that something has happened to her."

Kai kept his expression neutral, though he thought he was finally getting to the truth. "And what brought you to Aclines?"

"Rumors, whispers, at first." He inclined his head back toward the lower deck. "Then I followed his two coconspirators to Scarif. Unfortunately, Aclines was more astute than they were."

Kai leaned back against the soft cushions. Trying to get the mortals in the rowing deck to the nearest port alive was going to be hard without help. It would be easier with Ashem and Ramad and the cadre, though Kai couldn't possibly trust them. But he couldn't think of another solution. "That is not going to be good enough for Ziede Daiyahah, called Scourge of the Temple Halls." People always thought Kai was the one to be afraid of.

Someone on the lower deck called out in alarm. Mortals stared up in fear as Ziede drifted down out of the dissipating smoke, holding Sanja against her side. The wind-devil, visible only as a shape outlined by fading mist, opened to let them take the last step down to the upper deck. Sanja ran to throw herself down on the couch next to Kai. "This is much better than the whale," she whispered.

Ziede crossed the deck with slow deliberate steps and stood where the trapped crew could see her. She planted her hands on her hips and focused on Ashem and Ramad. She said, "Let's start the way we mean to go on. Whose skin am I going to peel off until someone tells me where my wife is?"

THE PAST:
THE MEETING

The Arike are by nature hospitable but seem to divide their people into only two genders, signaled by clothing style. This is similar to some ways of the scattered sea peoples of the southern islands but they are not so strict about it, as I understand. It must be a confusion, to be Arike. What they think of us, I have been too polite to ask.

—*Book of Travels,* by Talon-re, an Enalin chronicler
and poet

The rain in the Cageling Demon Court never stopped, falling on the chained demons scattered across the painted paving stones. Today the trickle of water was the only sound.

When Kai had first been brought here, he had snarled and fought and tried to break the chains. Looped around his wrists, ankles, and throat, the tiny braided links looked delicate but the diamond dust embedded in the metal worked with the expositors' designs to trap him. The water prevented him from eating their lives and stopped his body from healing itself. After three days in the Court, he had sobbed and called out for his grandmother until his throat was raw.

Now he was as silent as the others imprisoned here, his skin deadened by the rain soaking his clothes and hair, his body aching as he fought to stay upright. The demons who collapsed were rotting where they fell; the Hierarchs' Great Working had sealed away the passage to the underearth and they couldn't escape to their original forms. Not even the destruction of their mortal bodies would release them.

The rain was a stifling blanket over Kai's senses and a dull burn in his brain. He had never felt as much like a spirit in a dead husk; it was hard to remember that he had ever felt warmth in Enna's body.

Sometimes shadows moved in the lighted colonnades, Hierarch nobles coming by to stare and gloat over the prisoners. But the only mortals Kai saw in the court itself were the expositors who moved among the captives. They came to find the demons fallen into a death-like state as their mortal bodies failed. Some they took away, others they left to lie and rot in the water. Kai had no idea how they decided who to leave or take. He had screamed at them, growled, talked, but they acted as if he was already an inert lump of flesh like the others.

When a figure stopped beside Kai now, he just leaned away from it, expecting a prod from a cursebreaker. But someone knelt next to him.

He turned his head just enough to see through the mist. It was a mortal man, dressed in a gold and blue brocaded coat over a white skirt. He crouched beside Kai, his jeweled leather sandals already soaked. He whispered, "Can you hear me? Can you speak?"

Kai flinched and turned his face away. No mortal had spoken to him directly since he had been captured. This had to be a trick, a new sick torture.

"Ah, you're alive. I'm Bashasa of Arike and currently a Hierarchs' dog."

Kai slid him a sideways look. The mortal Bashasa was sitting on his heels, broad-shouldered under his finery, with dark curly hair and warm brown skin. He had an open face, and was smiling, which was infuriating. And Kai suddenly wasn't too dead to care. He lunged for Bashasa's throat.

The chains caught him with inches to spare. Bashasa jerked

backward and sat down hard on the wet paving. The effort took what little was left of Kai's strength. He collapsed, catching himself on his elbows in the pooling water. His vision swam, blurred.

"Do you want to try another one?" a voice whispered behind Kai.

"No. No, this one." The cold burn of a cursebreaker touched the back of his neck and Kai toppled into darkness.

Kai woke slowly, in a dimly lit space, his whole body a bone-deep ache and his skin stinging like it was riddled with hot needles. He realized gradually that he was lying on something soft, under a gray-blue canopy. Not a tent; there was no odor of horses or goats, no noisy chatter. He had been dreaming about Kentdessa Saredi, running with Adeni and Varra under the heavy ropes of the outer structure.

He squinted and the shadows solidified into a stone wall and the frame of a curtained bed. Frantic, he twisted sideways to see more, but he was alone in the bed, alone in the room.

With a hiss of pain, Kai shoved himself up a little. The space was warmed by a small fire in a stepped center hearth cut down into the stone floor. Cloudy gray daylight spilled from a wide doorway opening onto a court. There were plain blue hangings on the walls, woven rugs on the floors, wide wooden seats stuffed with cushions, a set of cups and a carafe in a rich blue glaze sitting next to the hearth. Outside he could see the corner of a dry fountain choked with overgrown weeds.

This was strange and new and terrifying. Kai had never seen any part of the Summer Halls except the Cageling Demon Court; he had been dragged there in a hemp bag, already wrapped in the chains and expositor's designs that suppressed his power.

But at least those chains were gone. He was away from the Cageling Court, away from the rain; he tried not to feel pathetically grateful for that. His hair was still damp but his skin and clothes, the ragged remains of the pants and long tunic he had been wearing when captured, were almost dry.

A voice said, "Ah, you're awake." The mortal, Bashasa the Hierarchs' dog, stepped through the door from the open court.

Kai slid to the cool stone floor to lean back against the bed. He hoped it looked like he meant to do it. He was too weak to stand yet but he didn't want this mortal to know that.

Bashasa strolled forward to the hearth. "Let me assure you, no one here will harm you. Do you want food or water, or wine? I was told your kind do not need to eat, but I found it hard to believe."

Kai just watched him. His head was fuzzy and the world was distant, like he was still stuffed in that bag. Free of the continuous rain, he should be able to drain life again, but he was so weak. He would have to wait and endure whatever Bashasa meant to do to him until Enna's body recovered.

Bashasa lifted his brows. "I know little of your people, but perhaps more than some. The Hierarchs say that the Grass Kings traded their dead for demon slaves, that they sacrifice children for power. A blasphemous practice that the Hierarchs used to rouse their loyal followers to take the grasslands." He sat down on the carpet, so he was eye level with Kai.

Bashasa seemed very confident about his ignorance. "Grass Kings" was what the mortals past the borderlands called the Saredi clans. Bashasa had to have some other protection in the room. And there was a cursebreaker around somewhere; Bashasa's companion had used it to get Kai out of the Court.

Bashasa said, "But when I was a boy I traveled in Erathi, along the grassland coast, and heard a different story. That Grass King clans trade the death of a clan member for a young demon, for the chance to hear the last thoughts of the dead. That the young demon takes up the dead one's place, and works, fights, even bears or sires children." Bashasa stopped to pour a cup from the carafe. Whatever it was steamed, and smelled like hot rancid berries. "It sounds more to me that it's not the Grass Kings sacrificing children to demons, but demons sacrificing children to the Grass Kings. But it's also said there is no sacrifice at all, that only a natural death will do."

It wasn't always natural. Kai's third sister Dranegepte had come to the upper world in the body of a murdered man, and been asked to name his killer. But maybe to a Hierarchs' dog, murder was natural. Enna had died of a wasting disease and Kai hadn't been able to share her last thoughts with her family until he had finished coughing the congestion out of her lungs. It had not been the best awakening, but he would have been happy to stay with the Kentdessa forever. Should have stayed with them forever.

Oblivious, Bashasa continued, "I also heard the Grass Kings send their people to the lower realms, in fair trade, to marry demons. Perhaps that's where the rumors of sacrifice come from."

Kai's eyes narrowed. Grandmother's mortal body had been burned by the Hierarchs, trapping her forever in the underearth. He didn't think Bashasa understood what the word *sacrifice* meant.

"You can understand me?" Bashasa asked suddenly, doubt creasing his expression.

Kai said, "Why wouldn't I?" His voice came out in an unused croak. Bashasa was speaking Imperial, the language that the clan captains had ordered all the advanced scouts to learn. It didn't have any other name, as far as Kai knew, and the Erathi said that was because the Hierarchs meant it to be the only language spoken in the world.

"Ah, good enough." Bashasa sipped from the cup, recovering his confident pose. "Am I right, about what I've said?"

Kai was going to kill every mortal he could catch even if the expositors destroyed Enna's body and left him trapped in whatever was left of her flesh. If they didn't, if they took him back to the Cageling Court and the chains and the rain . . . "Does it matter?"

"Perhaps it doesn't, to the Hierarchs. They certainly knew their tales of rampaging demons and children sacrificed in pyres were lies when they spoke them. I wanted to demonstrate that I knew the truth. Because I have a proposition for you." Bashasa leaned forward. "Help me destroy the Hierarchs." He sat back and waited expectantly.

Most of Kai's mind was still stuck in the sick terror of the thought of returning to the Cageling Court. He didn't have the resources to react to whatever this was.

"So, obviously you don't believe me," Bashasa concluded after a long moment of silence. "What can I say to convince you?"

The question was apparently sincere. Maybe this wasn't torture. Maybe Bashasa was just that stupid. "The Hierarchs let you take me from the Cageling Court." Something occurred to Kai, though maybe it was too devious. There was nothing subtle about the Hierarchs' cruelty. "Isn't it more likely that they want me to kill you?"

"No, no, there's been a misunderstanding! My fault, I should have explained." Bashasa gestured with the hand holding his cup and some liquid slopped out. Possibly he was a little drunk. "They don't know you're here. I replaced you with a dead body, about the same size." For the first time, he seemed uncertain. "I know it seems . . . That's how I chose you, you were the right size. I apologize. But my plan is to liberate all of the demons in the Court. So you would have been free regardless, even if I hadn't picked you today."

"Uh." Kai wondered if he was hallucinating. If Bashasa was hallucinating. That seemed more likely. "Demons don't die like . . . A mortal body won't look the same."

"That's been taken care of." He made a gesture, looking away. "And her eyes are closed." He seemed to shake some thought away and continued determinedly, "They won't notice immediately! No alarm has been raised. We will have a few days at least. That's all I need." Bashasa added urgently, "Will you help? I have a good plan, but releasing the demons in the Cageling Court is the core of it. We can't proceed without you."

If Bashasa was mad enough to be telling the truth, if he really meant to release the other demons, Kai couldn't pass up this chance, no matter how stupid it was. And whatever happened, he still needed to recover before he could kill anyone, so it was best to play along. But when Kai said, "I'll help you," he felt a tiny stir of hope in Enna's broken heart.

The other mortals here, Bashasa's servants and guards, were afraid to get near Kai, so Bashasa kept telling them to do things and then getting exasperated with the fearful delay and having to do them himself. So it was Bashasa who led Kai to a bathing room off this court and left him there, while the servants who had prepared it ran away immediately.

Like the firepit, the bath was carved out of the stone floor, filled by taps in the shape of fish heads. The sight of the water made Kai flinch and breathe hard. But the skin on his arms and chest was still stained with ground-in dried blood from the battle when he had been captured. It was Tahsia's blood, who had become Captain Kentdessa when everyone else had been killed. His hair was full of blood and grit from the Cageling Demon Court's paving. And the water was warm, drawn from a steaming and clanking boiler somewhere nearby, and the soap smelled a little like a red-spice tree, though there couldn't be one anywhere near this place. He compromised by sitting next to the bath and using a wet towel to scrub off with, and hanging his head down in it to rinse out his hair.

They had left a tray of food: a small bowl of some kind of fish with tiny green onions, nuts, and pieces of root vegetables he didn't recognize. It was another reminder of how far away home was. He ate the fried sweet cakes and drank the water flavored with sour fruit and wished desperately for any kind of milk.

They had already brought him clothes, though Bashasa had sent the first set back, saying, "No, not servants' clothes, those are inappropriate."

Kai couldn't quite hear the whispered objection. Bashasa made an annoyed noise in response. "Get something out of my sister's trunk, then."

This time they brought clothes as fine as what Bashasa wore, wide pants and a long tunic, with a coat to belt over it. The coat was different than the Saredi version, made of fabric instead of leather, wider sleeves, longer but with splits in the sides for easy movement. It was dark blue with white geometric patterns along the hems and very fine, and there were sandals made of a soft leather. The worn and stained leather band with Kai's Kentdessa clan sigil, two tiny wooden antelope curled into sleeping positions, had still been braided into his tangled hair. He tied his wet hair back with it again and wondered if anyone else from Kentdessa had survived. If any part of his mortal family existed anywhere except for Grandmother, trapped in the underearth now.

When he walked out to the court again, Bashasa was there, bouncing with nervous impatience. "Do you feel better?" he asked.

"No," Kai said, startled into honesty. "Not . . . no."

"Ah." Bashasa clearly had no idea what to do with that answer either and turned to lead him out to a wide stone corridor.

The Hierarch palace was different from any mortal habitation that Kai had ever seen before. High, heavy stone corridors and colonnades bordered small courts open to the sky, at least on this level. Kai could tell they were some distance above the ground.

Bashasa's guards wore unfamiliar armor, mostly leather with reinforcing metal chain. Though they wore bright cotton coats and sashes over it, their clothes were a little battered, with signs of careful or clumsy repairs. Some seemed a little young to be trained warriors, some too old. Many were scarred, one was limping, one had a missing hand.

Bashasa said, "This is a section of the Hierarchs' Summer Halls set aside for the use of hostages from the lands they have conquered. We are here for the amusement of the Hierarchs' servant-nobles, who come from the far south, like their conscripts. In the neighboring courts around us are other Arike Prince-heirs and their families or dependents, from what used to be the free city-states of Arike before our Hierarch rulers turned their greedy eye on it. I was brought here as a hostage for the good behavior of my family and my people, the state of Benais-arik."

"They didn't slaughter all of you, then," Kai said.

"Not yet." Bashasa shrugged. "They persuaded a cousin to assassinate my aunt, who was the Speaker of our city assembly, and then he took power in a bloody coup. Then the Hierarchs said he was mad, and they kindly assassinated him for us, and installed another of my cousins as regent, with one of their own servants as his helpful advisor. Now we are what they call a client state, which means they take what they want from us and we pretend to like it or die."

And you're living in a palace and all my mortals are dead, Kai thought, but said nothing.

They came to a doorway with a guard, but a different kind of guard than the others. She was tall, a full head taller than Bashasa or any of the other Arike, with short light golden hair that stood up in spikes, as if something drastic had been done to it recently. The skin of her face and hands was unnaturally pale, like she had never been out in the sun. She wore a plain metal breastplate under a plain, long leather coat. Her light-colored shirt and pants looked more like indoor wear but her knee-high boot wraps were battered and stained. Bashasa said, "Ah, Tahren. Has she asked for anything?"

"No. She understandably prefers not to communicate with me." Tahren frowned down at Kai. "This is the demon from the Cageling Court."

"I'm aware." Bashasa's smile was strained. "You knew my plans."

Kai looked up at Tahren and bared his teeth. The pointed ones were a sign of the underearth, a change to Enna's body like his whiteless eyes. Tahren wasn't a mortal; she had power from a source Kai couldn't see, running through her body like a rushing torrent. Then he recognized it. "You're an Immortal Marshall."

Tahren's expression went even more still. In a voice without inflection, she said, "I was."

Kai felt something hot move up his spine. He had thought he was numb, but no, he was still capable of feeling bitter seething anger. The Saredi hadn't known much of the Immortal Blessed before the Hierarchs attacked the Erathi coast. Just wild stories about powerful beings who flew through the air on golden wagons. But then they had encountered the Immortal Marshalls, fighting alongside the Hierarchs, and the borderlanders passed on rumors of how the Immortal Blessed had become the willing allies of the invaders, trading their warriors and power to the Hierarchs for the safety of their lands. "How many Saredi did you kill?"

Tahren's smooth brow knit, just enough to be noticeable. "None that I know of." After a moment, she added, "I was not sent to that region."

Bashasa put his hand on Kai's arm and said gently, "Come, we are all prisoners of the Hierarchs here, one way or another. Fighting with each other is the last thing we should do."

Kai looked down at the hand on his arm, and wondered if Bashasa was not being manipulative and clever but that he was ill, in his mind, in a way that made him not fully aware of his actions. He looked up to meet Tahren's gaze and realized they were both thinking the same thing.

No mortals other than the Saredi ever voluntarily touched a demon; Kai hadn't been touched by any mortal not Saredi since waking on the upper earth. Not counting the Hierarch legionaries he had killed with his bare hands.

Apparently unaware of any undercurrent, Bashasa continued, "Could you open the door? It will be easier if we speak about this together, I think."

Tahren's expression indicated that she didn't think anything would be easy, but she tapped her knuckles on the door and then opened it.

The room was octagon shaped, with narrow window slits high in the walls. There was another curtained bed, a sunken hearth, rugs, but what captured Kai's attention first was the woman floating almost four paces off the floor.

She was in a sitting position, her legs folded under her. Her skin was a darker brown than Bashasa's and the other Arike, and she had a gold sunburst painted on her high forehead, gold lining her eyes and lips, and her hair was woven into dozens of braids and wound around her head. She wore a red-brown patterned long-sleeved tunic and wide pants tied at her ankles, under a tabard cinched at her waist. Her eyes were closed in a repose Kai didn't believe; the tension in her body was coiled and alert. And for the first time since he had been chained in the Cageling Demon Court, Kai didn't feel more than halfway to dead.

He knew a Witch when he saw one. She wasn't anything like the borderlander Witches, but a Witch nonetheless.

Bashasa coughed. "I've brought someone to meet you, sister."

"Don't call me that." The Witch opened her eyes. Her dark gaze went to Kai first. She knew what he was, the way he had recognized her. "You chose a demon in the body of a child?"

"You haven't told me what to call you." Bashasa's voice was tight. "And it's a young woman."

Watching the Witch, Kai corrected, "It's a Prince of the Fourth House of the underearth, late Enna of the tent of Kentdessa Saredi."

Bashasa turned to stare at him, startled. "Prince?"

"You didn't ask," Kai said, his gaze not leaving the Witch.

"You're an idiot," the Witch told Bashasa. Her gaze turned to

Kai again, and she unfolded her legs and stepped down to the floor. She was tall, not as tall as Tahren, but close. If all her people were like that, it explained why she thought Enna's body was a child. Enna had been a little short even for a Saredi, but her body had finished growing before she left it. The Witch said, "I am Ziede Daiyahah. What are you called on this level of the world, Fourth Prince?"

He said, "Kaiisteron. Kai."

Bashasa looked from Kai to Ziede and back. "I apologize for my misunderstanding."

Ziede said, "When a demon is called to the dead of the Grass Kings, they don't bother to match age or gender. They do match rank." Speaking Saredi, she asked Kai, "Was the late Enna from a descended line?"

Her accent gave the words an odd ring, but Kai could still understand her. He replied in the same language. "Through our mortal ancestor, who wed an Overlord of the Fourth House's heir to seal the grassplains treaty with the underearth." He didn't mean to, but the words came out anyway. "She's trapped in the underearth now, they burned her mortal body. Were you a prisoner here too?"

"No. I was a teacher in the Mountain Cloisters of the Khalin Islands. That's the oldest convocation of Witches in the southern shelf. Or it was, I should say. Everyone there was killed, of course, when the Khalin Electors surrendered. I had been sent away as a scout and a spy, and when I heard the news I came to this city, hoping to find a way to . . . hurt it. Somehow." Her gaze went to Bashasa, and she switched back to Imperial. "I got word that a man from the palace was sniffing around looking for Witches. I sought him out meaning to kill him, but I listened to him first, and here I am."

"And lucky we are to have you with us," Bashasa said, apparently serious.

Ziede crooked her finger and Kai went to her. She took his

hand, and her skin was warm, and he felt the underearth in her veins. Not the same as it was in his, but it was the first familiar thing he had felt in ages, in forever. He wanted to wrap himself around her and cry on her chest. She said, "The other demon prisoners here will listen to you?"

Kai could lie, but there was no point. He had been as good as dead since the great tent of Kentdessa collapsed in flames, since the passage to his body in the underearth had closed, and everything now was borrowed time. "I don't know. They'll listen to me more than they would a mortal."

Ziede nodded. She told Bashasa, "Then this may actually work."

"Well, then." Bashasa cleared his throat and turned to Tahren. "This is Tahren Stargard, called the Fallen, who has agreed to help us."

Ziede regarded Tahren with a disdain that had razor-sharp edges. "To help us? And not to give in to her natural inclination to murder us?"

"That inclination is not natural," Tahren said, managing to look both bored and acutely uncomfortable.

A faint line appeared between Ziede's brows. She said, "Was that supposed to intimidate me?"

Tahren stared at the far wall. "No."

Kai said, "I have one condition." He instantly had their attention. "You have a cursebreaker here. Maybe more than one?" The more Tahren spoke, the more he was certain that she had been the second person with Bashasa in the Cageling Demon Court, that she had used the cursebreaker to knock him unconscious. "Destroy them." He knew they wouldn't do it. A cursebreaker was the most effective way to stop a demon in hand-to-hand combat; it would be their only way to keep Kai under control.

There was a long silent moment. Bashasa and Ziede both watched Tahren, waiting. Then Tahren lifted her brows briefly, in a way that seemed to be her version of a shrug. She took a long black wooden cane out of an inside pocket of her coat, and snapped it. The released power made a faint pop of displaced air, a tug Kai could feel in his bones. Tahren said, "Just the one."

Ziede let her breath out and folded her arms.

Bashasa smiled. "Now that we're all getting along, I'll tell you the plan."

FIVE

Kai said, "Ziede, murder later. We need to get moving." The smoky air had cleared as much as it ever did in the strait of Gad-dazara. The peaks of the islands were visible again, outlined against the ash-tinged sky, the dark billows of volcanic rock lapped by the waves. Kai felt too exposed; with their luck, one of the volcanoes would go off at any moment.

Ziede's jaw set as she eyed Ashem and Ramad. "Was it them?" she asked without looking away. "Were they the ones who did this to us?"

Wide-eyed, Sanja looked from her to Kai and back. Kai sank further into the cushions and pretended it was a casual conversation. "I don't know. Cohort Leader Ashem says they're here against their will. Vanguarder Ramad says Bashat sent him to look for Tahren when she failed to reach Benais-arik, and he followed two suspicious characters to Aclines."

He had pitched his voice to carry. From the lower deck, someone snarled, "Ramad, you traitor." The words were in the lowland Arik dialect, as if Kai and Ziede wouldn't know that language.

It's the forgetting, Kai thought again. That was what hurt. *We were there. They have to know that. Don't they?*

Ashem's response was a grimace of eloquent dislike. She called back, "You idiot, now they know who you are. We wanted to use you as a bargaining point."

Ramad ignored the interruption. He said reasonably, "Even if you don't trust our word, you must see the people in the rowing deck are innocent captives."

Ziede hissed out a slow breath as she controlled her temper. She said, "The rowers?"

"Alive, turned into a power well," Kai told her. He needed to decide what to do about that. "Aclines had a familiar aboard, too."

Tenes had been listening. She stepped out of the main cabin, trembling. She had taken off the jeweled collar and put on real clothing instead of the wisps the expositor had made her wear: a long tunic and a man's split skirt that probably came from Aclines' wardrobe. She went to Ziede and dropped to the deck at her feet.

Ziede bared her teeth in annoyance. "Get up. What's your name?"

"She's sister Tenes," Kai supplied, as she scrambled to her feet. "He took her voice and her memory up to the point he brought her aboard."

The waves of rage emanating from Ziede's body should have been physically visible. "Go over there, Tenes," she ordered through gritted teeth.

Tenes hurried to sit next to Sanja, curling her feet up on the cushions. Kai leaned his head back and groaned, a theatrical gesture only partly faked. He was going to have to partially dismantle the power well in the rowing deck. If he just let it go all at once, many of the mortals might die instantly. And the survivors would need food and water and medicine, and Kai doubted there were large enough stores onboard. Some might attack their rescuers out of panic, or fear of whatever stories of Witches, or of Kai himself, had been drummed into their brains. Many could die before the ship reached a port. If he could gradually ease the drain on them, put them into a suspended sleep, it would be far safer all around. "Ziede." Through her heart pearl, he added, *We need to go. If another ship shows up with a power well full of captured mortals, I'll lose my mind. I don't know what I'm going to do with the ones I have now.*

She cursed under her breath and lifted her hands. "Make them drop the sails."

Kai took that for the agreement it was. He said, "Cohort Leader Ashem, I'll release the mortals in the rowing deck as best I can, if you cooperate and don't attempt to attack us."

Ashem hesitated, eyeing him. Ramad told her, "I believe we can trust Kaiisteron's word." He added dryly, "And it's our only choice."

She spared Ramad a glare, but said, "Let the others on deck out of this—" She gestured at the smoke-net tangling her legs. "Whatever it is, and my cadre will sail the ship for you."

Ramad added, "Except for those two." He twisted, awkward without being able to move his feet, and pointed out two men: the one who had cursed Ramad in lowland Arik and another standing near him. Kai would have probably been able to pick them out anyway. They were older than the others on deck, their traveling clothes finer. The noisy one glowered impotently at Ramad, the other looked away.

Ziede's jaw was going to crack if she couldn't keep her temper. "Just tell them to drop the sails." She moved her hands, shaping precise angles as she gathered the trailing threads of Kai's cantrips. The net on the lower deck puffed out and dissipated. Released, the mortals there stumbled or stretched their legs in relief. Except for the two expositor's men. And Ramad and Ashem on the upper deck, still wreathed in smoke from the knees down.

Ramad didn't seem surprised. Ashem grimaced but didn't protest, just twisted to address her cadre and instruct them in lowland Arik. She told them to do what Ziede ordered, and added that they should not be afraid and not resist.

Ziede stood like a statue while the cadre climbed into the rigging. Most looked Arike or Enalin with a few islanders, which was common now for a Rising World cadre from the vicinity of Benais-arik. All the Arike were women, which was still traditional for Arike soldiers, and they wore conventional long tunics and loose pants under light leather chest and back armor. The others wore a mix of styles, plus a few wore Enalin robes, the sides split for ease of movement. Enalin clothing didn't differentiate gender, unlike Arike traditional clothing. In the years since the war it had been adopted by some Arike for that reason. All the cadre members were clearly working soldiers, the colors they wore soft and weathered, the leather well-worn.

Most had also obviously been on a large ship before and got the sails lowered with a minimum of shouted instructions at each other and no one falling off the rigging. The big sheets of canvas were dyed red and painted with giant gold sun signs. Kai snorted; they were making their escape in the most obvious craft on the sea.

Sanja had been watching Tenes with wary curiosity. "Who is she?" she asked Kai.

"She's a Witch, but the dead expositor on the deck there captured her and made her his familiar. She's free now." Tenes looked young, but age wasn't always easy to tell with borderlander Witches. But she could also be from one of the witchlines that had followed Bashasa to the Arik.

Sanja looked at the expositor with distaste. "Like that Menlas was going to do to you?"

"Just like that."

Tenes leaned forward to sign to Kai to ask what Sanja's name was. Kai told her and Sanja tried to imitate Tenes' signing, asking, "Is this like talking? How does it work? We had hand signals in the gang but it didn't make words." They passed the time teaching Sanja a few basics of Witchspeak.

When the ship was ready to sail, Ashem said, "If you release me, I can steer for you." Ramad, who seemed to know more of Kai and Ziede than they knew of him, said nothing.

Ziede didn't even bother with a glance of contempt. Years ago she had sailed small boats all around the Khalin Islands, and commanded larger craft. She held out her hands and called the wind-devils again. *Avagantrum?* she asked Kai silently.

Since they didn't know where Tahren was yet, it was the only choice. Even though they might be heading in the opposite direction from where she was being held. *Yes. For now.*

The sails snapped and filled with air, and Kai pushed to his feet. His clothes were almost dry and he needed to get to work.

First he searched the cooling bodies of Aclines, his apprentice, and the bodyguard. He set a few things aside to look at later, and tossed several potentially dangerous intentioned items over the side. Then he started a search of the rooms off the upper deck cabin while Tenes found the ship's chart box and took it out to Ziede. Sanja helped him search, and he showed her what to look for and what to be wary of.

Only five of the curtained rooms off the cabin had been occupied, so the work went quickly. Aclines had left no convenient diaries explaining his plans, no letters to his masters, no documents naming Ashem and Ramad as coconspirators. But maybe that sort of thing was only done by the villains in romantic Arike novels or Enalin poetic epics.

Kai checked the lavish bathing room on the service deck just below. It had basins that could be filled with water pumped up from the ship's cistern, and Kai took the opportunity to stick his head under a tap and quickly rinse the saltwater out of his hair. The galley was small, meant only to serve the Immortal Blessed occupying the stern cabin, but it was stocked with dry staples like lentils, chickpeas, and millet, with fresh stores of dates and figs. Provisions for Arike and the other south- and eastlanders, not the kind of food the Immortal Blessed preferred.

Aclines hadn't looked Arike, but now, after more than two generations of refugees resettling and trade and travel, that didn't mean he hadn't been born in the region. And Arike food, clothes, and customs had always been popular in the southeast even before the Hierarchs, but had now spread throughout the Rising World alliance.

Finished with that part of the search, Kai sent Sanja to stay with Ziede, to give her an extra set of eyes to watch her back and to bring her anything she needed. In the stern cabin with Tenes, out of sight of Ramad and Ashem on the upper deck, he signed, *Did Aclines ever speak of me or Ziede?*

Tenes answered, *That he wanted to find you before anyone else did. At Scarif, when we came aboard this ship, he had me help him make the intention to follow the hunter-beast.* She meant the amalgam that the shell-whale had destroyed.

He didn't brag to anyone about being the one to capture us? Kai asked. She made a negative gesture. That didn't mean much, there were obviously secrets Aclines had meant to keep from his familiar, or he wouldn't have taken her older memories. *Did you ever hear mention of an expositor called Menlas?*

She gestured *no* again and touched her head to remind him of her missing past. Kai chewed his lip and tried to think of better questions. *Did it seem as if Aclines had this ship for some time, or if it was first brought to him at Scarif?*

I first saw it near there at anchor, before we went to the Arike outpost where he stole all those mortals. She hesitated, frowning around at the cabin. *But I must have been on it before then. I knew where to find things in the cooking place when he told me to make food.*

"Huh," Kai said aloud. To sail to Scarif, the ship had needed either an Immortal Blessed or a mortal crew. Or, Kai guessed, another power well of mortals in the rowing deck who Aclines had already driven to death and then dumped overboard, before taking the Rising World cohort as replacements. The most obvious answer was that an Immortal Blessed had brought the ship to Aclines at Scarif and then left. But just because it was obvious didn't mean it was right. Giving it up for the moment, he gestured to Tenes to follow him. *Come help me search the rest of the ship.*

They needed to look through the secondary cabins in the deck below this one. On a normal voyage, it was where any Lesser Blessed who were traveling aboard would stay. Aclines had quartered Ashem's cadre there, which made sense if she was telling the truth and they had been unwilling conscripts. Or Aclines was just a snob who didn't want to share the luxurious stern cabin with common soldiers.

There was no direct connection between the service deck below the stern cabin and the secondary under the bow; Kai could have gone back down to the rowing deck and up from there, but he didn't want to expose Tenes to that energy at any closer range than she already was. So the two of them walked down the steps and across the lower deck, past the captured cadre.

Ashem and Ramad were still trapped in the cantrip web and Ziede had contributed her own additions to the bonds on Aclines' two surviving men: their arms were bound in front of them with more solidified air. After setting the sails, the soldiers had climbed down from the rigging and now stood at the rail or sat on the deck. None moved or spoke as Kai and Tenes went by, most averting their eyes or trying to stare surreptitiously. Ashem ignored them. Ramad was the only one who turned to watch.

The secondary cabins were accessed via a sheltered hatch. A narrow stairwell continued down to the rowing and supply decks. Kai sealed that passage with a minor cantrip, so no one could use it to come up on the stern cabin from below. The area already stank with the rotting-flesh odor of a dead expositor's failing intents and designs. Leaning close to sniff the polished wood of the doorframe, Kai detected a tangle of intentions, something meant to monitor the crew when they were out of sight. The apprentice's work, probably. Aclines was far more powerful, some of his more complicated workings surviving his death to take on spirit-lives of their own.

Tenes watched closely as Kai drew the wards and warnings, and frowned a little as he cut his arm for the spark of pain to power the seal, not understanding his technique. She didn't ask for an explanation and he didn't offer one.

The cabins in the secondary deck were smaller and windowless, meant to be shared, but not much less comfortable. The Immortal Blessed considered themselves superior to their Lesser Blessed cousins, but they also considered the Lesser Blessed far above common mortals, who wouldn't have been allowed on the ship in the first place.

The beds were narrow but stuffed with soft linens and silk quilts, with gauze drapes for privacy. The rooms were cooled by a system of tiny round vents that funneled in air from the wind and the movement of the ship. There was a bathing room, smaller and not as well-appointed as the one below the stern cabin, and a larger galley with more food stores. There were signs the cadre were using a brazier to cook; Aclines must not have bothered to expend the power to make the Blessed stove, a block of stone set with metal plates, work like it was supposed to.

It was more support for Ashem and Ramad's version of events, at least the part about how abruptly the crew had been conscripted. There was almost nothing down here that wouldn't have already been on the ship: no extra clothing, no combs or hair oil, no makeup or remedies for ailments, no paper or writing implements, no books or counters for games, nothing that soldiers going traveling might choose to carry with them. There were also no hidden cursebreakers, no poisons or intentioned devices that might send or receive messages or leave traces to be followed. There were no weapons of any kind.

The search of the stern had already told Kai that Aclines and his minions had known to bring supplies for a long trip. And Aclines had brought a chest full of writing material and ingredients for complex designs; he had meant to stay aboard for some time.

With the search finished, Kai and Tenes went back up on deck. The breeze was cool and the sky was still overcast, though clear blue was visible to the north. The ship was out of the strait now, their course bending away from the smoke and haze of Gaddazara, the dark islands off the starboard side growing smaller already. The Immortal Blessed ship was much faster than the poor burdened shell-whale.

They crossed the deck again in silence under the eyes of the cadre, the wind pulling at Kai's still-damp hair. On the steps he paused to tell Ashem, "Order the ones Ziede doesn't need to go below." Tenes had already reached the upper deck and stood with Ziede. To see if Ashem or Ramad would attack him, Kai plucked the web of cantrips around their feet and let it drop. "You too."

Ashem stepped back, slowly, careful to make no sudden moves. She turned and went down the steps to the lower deck and spoke to her cadre, posting a watch and telling the others to go below.

Ramad turned to Kai and said, "I'll stay up here, if you permit." Without waiting for an answer, he sat down on the top step.

Ramad was a vanguarder, he wanted to glean information. Kai climbed to the upper deck where Ziede eyed him critically. Sanja stood on the couch, gripping a line to steady herself and looking back toward the islands shrinking in the distance. The natural wind had risen a little but Ziede still had full control of the ship through her wind-devils. She probably had some controlling the ship's direction and others napping in the sails to keep them filled. Ziede said, "Can you at least put some clothes on?"

"At what point did I have time for that?" Kai protested. His damp tunic and leggings still clung to him. He lowered his voice. "I'm going to try to stop the power well and put the rowers to sleep."

She took a sharp breath, but didn't argue. "Just be careful."

Kai went past her into the stern cabin. Tenes followed and he signed to her to make sure no one came in. She signaled understanding and settled on the deck near the hatchway.

He picked a room that hadn't been occupied and sat down on the knotted silk rug. There was only one bed, larger than in the secondary cabins, filmy drapes protecting the linens from the salt wind flowing through the open port. There were cabinets on the wall, forming part of the sun sign–carved decorative panels, and a fragrant sagewood chest. Kai had checked all the storage spaces in these rooms, to make sure no one had been clever enough to conceal a trap, or had left anything interesting behind.

How did an expositor get his filthy hands on this ship? Kai thought. He had the feeling the answer would explain a large chunk of what had happened.

If the Immortal Blessed had made a deal with Aclines, surely one of them would come along as part of it, to guard and sail the ship. There was no sign of the battle that would have ripped through all this finely crafted wood and metal if Aclines had fought an Immortal Blessed caretaker, injuring them so badly they returned to the Well of Thosaren.

Aclines had time to stock the ship with supplies meant for mortals; there were even soaps and oils in the stern bathing room below this deck. He had expected to have the use of it for a long time. *And he didn't expect to be hunted for kidnapping a Rising World cohort.* Because he had been given permission to take them? Or because he thought no one would trace their disappearance to him? Maybe the ship had been payment for Aclines' part in whatever was going on here.

Which took them right back to where they had started; betrayed by someone high in the Rising World, someone with Immortal Blessed allies who could obtain this ship with no repercussions.

If they were lucky, Aclines' surviving followers knew.

Kai couldn't pierce his skin with this new body's blunt bitten fingernails, so he had to use his knife to draw enough blood to write the Saredi word *reveal* on the wooden deck. It would help him navigate the expositor's intention and set an anchor for him to return. Then he took a deep breath, let it out, and sank his consciousness into the lower air to look for the complex web of designs and intents that controlled the power well.

Expositors didn't draw power from pain in their own body, like Kai did, or by forming relationships with the spirits inherent in the different levels of the world, both living and otherwise, like Witches. Expositors drew their power from life: new life, stolen life, life on the point of death. It was why they were so dangerous, why greed was their driving force. It was why their power was so susceptible to a true demon's ability to steal life from anything living or once living. But that was something the Saredi hadn't realized until it was too late.

But that affinity for stolen life let Kai's consciousness follow the chains of Aclines' work down to the rowing deck, and examine the delicate intention that bound all the mortals together. That held them in suspension so Aclines could feed off them like a wasp off a trapped caterpillar.

He had to follow each thread separately before he could understand the shape of the whole structure. Once he found the design that drained the victims and fed the power to its maker, he picked it apart. He left the bonds that held the mortals in suspension without need of food or water, but funneled more power to an unused branch that would reduce their awareness of their circumstances. That would make the experience less like a waking nightmare and more like a genuine sleep.

When he was certain it was done, he drew himself up and back to earth. Kai opened his eyes to a darkened room. The deck swayed in time with higher waves, and the sky visible through the single port was fading to purple. His head swam; it had been delicate, difficult work and that one apprentice he had eaten was a long time ago now. He let himself slump down and curl up on the rug, sinking into sleep.

SIX

Kai woke to firelight on his eyelids and grimaced. The sway of the ship told him where he was even if his brain felt slow and waterlogged. He managed to make out Sanja standing over him with a small clay lamp. She called to someone, "Yes, he's alive."

Kai sat up, shoving his hair out of his face. He was still on the floor of the cabin but someone had put a cushion under his head and a quilt over him. "What?" he demanded.

"Now he's awake," Sanja reported over her shoulder.

"Did you eat? Does Ziede need a rest?" Kai scrubbed his eyes. He called a swarm of imps and they flitted around the room and out into the main part of the cabin, shedding a soft white glow on the polished wood and gold.

"Ziede's fine. The sailors made lentil dal and they didn't try to poison us or anything." Sanja pinched the lamp wick out with her fingers. She wore a new tunic with the sleeves rolled to fit her, and her hair had been fixed into a neat cap of finger coils. "Ziede says the wind finally picked up in the right direction so she can let the air monsters steer for a while. She wants you to find out from those people, the cohort leader and the spy, and the other two, what they know."

"Right." Kai pulled himself to his feet. "Give me a moment and then tell Ziede to make them come in here."

Sanja padded out. Someone had left clothes draped over the chest by the wall. Kai changed into the dark blue long-sleeved tunic and split skirt, and kept his battered water-stained belt and bare feet. It wasn't cool enough for the coat inside the cabin, despite the strong breeze coming in through the ports. These clothes had probably belonged to Aclines; the woven grass silk was soft and fine, the dark blue iridescent on the folds. Kai's hair had dried into a curly, frizzy mane. He shook it out and didn't bother tying it back.

He pushed the drapes aside and walked out to the main cabin to take a seat on the Immortal Blessed throne. Sanja was already back and had settled on the couch along the starboard wall. Her legs were tucked up and folded but one knee bounced impatiently.

Kai called the imps to gather overhead and leaned back. Through the large forward hatch he had a view of the upper and lower decks, where a few oil lamps had been lit along the railings. Aclines must have brought those aboard for the crew; the Immortal Blessed made their own light and wouldn't need anything so primitive.

Aclines' two surviving followers entered first, the wisps of solidified air still binding their limbs, loosened only enough to let them walk. Ashem and Ramad came after, and then Ziede, outwardly calm but Kai could read all the suppressed tension in her shoulders and jaw. Ziede had changed out her tunic for a finer one, but had kept her cotton pants since there weren't any spare women's clothes aboard except what the Arike soldiers were already wearing. Tenes remained outside on watch, though Kai spotted sinuous movement in the dark, an indication that Ziede had called more wind-devils to guard the deck.

Ashem watched Kai steadily, glancing aside only when Ziede paced deliberately past her. Controlling her impatience with visible effort, Ashem said, "What about the cohort?"

Her concern seemed real. Kai said, "I've altered Aclines' power well. They'll sleep until we get to a place where they can leave the ship."

There was a flicker of relief in Ramad's expression. But Ashem was still clearly suspicious and deeply dissatisfied with this solution. Her jaw tightened and she said pointedly, "You refuse to release them?"

Before Kai could make a flippant yet vaguely threatening response, Ramad told her, "What Aclines did isn't easy on the body or the mind. It's better this way. If he just lets them go, they could panic, injure themselves. And we don't have enough supplies to keep them fed."

Ashem hesitated, reluctant, but she was obviously finding Ramad's point persuasive. Finally, she grudgingly nodded. "I see."

Kai said, "I'm glad you approve, Cohort Leader." It was unsurprising, but still a sour bite that a random vanguarder's word was better than his. He jerked his chin toward the two expositor's men. "Introduce your friends."

"Safreses and Kinlat, lords in the court of Nient-arik." Ashem added with a grimace, "Not my friends."

Nient-arik had been one of the first Arike city-states to fall to the Hierarchs, who had assassinated the presiding Prince-heir and replaced her with a distant relative willing to submit to them. Which was interesting but not proof of anything. Something similar had happened in Benais-arik, though not until most of Bashasa's family had already been murdered.

"You're a traitor, Ashem," Safreses said, furious and afraid. "You and the vanguarder will burn along with the Witches for this."

"You kidnapped me, and my cadre, and an entire cohort," Ashem retorted, exasperated. It was the first unguarded reaction she had shown yet. "You're the traitors. The Witches have Imperial favor—"

"It's lies, lies—" Kinlat burst out, as if he couldn't hold it in a moment more, even to save his life. "There was never an alliance, it was never—Imperial Arike destroyed the Hierarchs with no help from these abominations!"

"The Arik wasn't an empire back then and technically it isn't even one now," Kai corrected. He had heard all this before, which didn't make it any easier, but at least it wasn't new. He could tell these two had been subjugated to an expositor's will, whether they understood that aspect of their relationship with Aclines or not. It made them vulnerable in a way that Ashem and Ramad and the other mortals on the ship wouldn't be. Kai used a little of his stored power to set his voice in a tone that would resonate with that vulnerability and compel answers. He said, "Who ordered us captured and trapped?"

"Aclines," Safreses said immediately. "It was his doing."

The response had been too quick. Safreses was apparently clever enough to pretend to be under Kai's influence. Aclines had been taking orders from someone. This ship was proof enough of that.

"It wasn't Aclines alone, it couldn't be," Ramad contributed. His arms were folded, his expression cool and thoughtful under Safreses' enraged glare. Ramad continued, "It has to be someone closer to the Rising World court."

Kai did not appreciate the interruption. "I know that. I don't need your help."

"Shut up, Ramad, or I'll rip your tongue out." Ziede was clearly at the end of her small store of patience. "Kai, get on with it."

Kai focused on Safreses. Unfortunately for him, pretending to be under the influence of Kai's will just made him more easily affected. Safreses lifted his chin defiantly, apparently less frightened than Kinlat. It was usually the ones who wouldn't allow themselves to express their fear that broke first. Kai took a more oblique tack and said, "Who told you it was Aclines?"

"He did . . . No." Safreses shook his head, pretending to be uncertain. "You can't make me—"

Kai leaned forward. A drop of sweat trickled down his forehead. This was almost pure will, and it wasn't easy, even on two mortals whose minds had been subjugated already, even on overconfident Safreses. "Why did you think it was Aclines?"

Safreses fought to keep his lips closed but Kinlat blurted, "He had the strictures and intentions for the working. The signal that told him when something went wrong. He knew the tower had opened. He knew how to find you." Kinlat struggled to move his arms, as if he wanted to stop up his own mouth. "He knew the traces to follow the hunter."

That jibed with what little Tenes had been allowed to remember, and suggested Aclines had been the one to create the tomb. Safreses was still resisting, so Kai tried, "Do you know an expositor named Menlas? He was strong enough to command a shell-whale."

"He left to . . ." Kinlat looked confused. "No, no." Safreses' mouth twitched, an involuntary spasm.

"Who is Menlas?" Kai persisted, adding emphasis through their tenuous connection. "It can do no harm to your plans to tell me."

"He was Aclines' apprentice." Kinlat's confusion deepened, as if he heard the words but didn't understand that they were coming out of his own mouth. "Then he wasn't. He left. Aclines was angry . . ."

Aclines must have realized that Menlas had gone to the tomb, and been on the move even before Kai and Ziede had woken.

"Kai," Ziede said quietly. Through her pearl she whispered, *Tahren.*

He didn't think it was the best moment to ask, but he knew how much pain and uncertainty Ziede felt. Kai said, "Where is Tahren Stargard?"

The abrupt change in subject slipped under Safreses' defenses. He blurted, "I don't know."

Kinlat's expression twisted into pure malice. "Dead! The Fallen should be obliterated, the ashes scattered!"

Ziede stepped forward, the faint tremor in her voice a danger sign. "If you're so anxious to see someone burned—"

They weren't done yet. Kai said sharply, "Ziede. He doesn't know." She halted, her hands clenching and unclenching. Kai focused on Safreses. "Where is Dahin Stargard of the Lesser Blessed?"

Safreses clamped his jaw shut again but Kinlat gasped, "At Nient-arik, in the court, I saw him—" He shook his head, sinking his teeth into his lips.

Ziede tensed, and Kai's heart leapt. He said, "Saw him do what?"

Kinlat choked out, "He was going to meet with someone in Bashat's circle."

Ziede flashed a startled look at Kai. He had no idea what this meant. But Dahin was pursuing his own work, and it might be related to that. "Who did he meet with?"

That answer came easier. "I don't know!" Kinlat snapped. "You can't make me say what I don't—"

"Did you see him leave?"

Kinlat gasped and said, "Yes! I saw him board a canal barge."

Perhaps he was never a target, Ziede said through her pearl, *or he was never caught. He might be looking for Tahren. Or us.*

He might have no idea any of us are missing. You know he hardly ever sends letters, Kai pointed out. Dahin liked to go his own way. This whole conspiracy might have missed him because he was off reading in some forgotten archive, and no one thought he was important enough to track down.

Ziede frowned in acknowledgment and said aloud, "Why were you watching Dahin?"

"Because he is Fallen like his sister and all the Fallen should die," Kinlat said with great satisfaction.

Even Ashem let out an exasperated breath.

Kai knew he could only keep this up so long. He needed to move on to other questions. "Where are the Witch cells that the Hierarchs took from the borderlands?"

Safreses stayed silent though his face was so red he might have a stroke at any moment. Honest confusion flicked over Kinlat's features. He said again, "I don't know. I don't know what that means."

Ramad had been following the conversation with almost as much concentration as Kai. "If they were Hierarchs' loot, they might be at one of the old storehouses in Benais-arik."

Ashem threw a glare at Ramad. She said, "Are you giving away a state secret?"

It was Ramad's turn to look exasperated. "Cohort Leader, please remember, they were there when the Hierarchs fell." He gestured to Kai and Ziede. Before Kai could press the question, Ramad added, "And it's no secret. My maternal great-aunt was one of Prince-heir Bashasa's wardens. She told us about removing the Hierarchs' relics from what was left of their strongholds. She never mentioned Witch cells, but if they were powerful artifacts, they would have been taken to Benais-arik with everything else."

"I don't remember that." Kai wasn't sure he believed Ramad or not. Whether he wanted to believe that Ramad was so willing to help them.

"It's not well known, outside the Benais-arik bureaucracy." Ramad made a helpless gesture. "It was a confusing time, and you must have been occupied with other matters. The location of the Hierarchs' treasures probably was concealed at first. Years later, it just became something else for the Rising World's accountants to keep track of."

Ziede was still skeptical. "And you know this because as a young boy, you hung on your aging aunt's every word?"

"As a young man, I did," Ramad told her with some asperity. "I was a court historian before I became a vanguarder."

Kai had been in no condition to pay attention to what was happening at the end of the war. He knew the Rising World had made efforts to return looted treasures to their original owners, if any of them still lived; he had seen the things that had been sent back to the Erathi and the sea people's ships, and the few Saredi who had taken refuge there.

Safreses trembled with exhaustion from resisting and Kinlat's shoulders sagged; they had both relaxed, thinking the interrogation was over. Kai tilted his head at Safreses, focused his will again, and asked, "Where did Aclines get this ship?"

"I don't know," Safreses said, then looked appalled at his lapse.

Kai pressed, "Where did you first see it?"

"When we met him in Scarif." Safreses ground the words out through gritted teeth, just as Kinlat said, "He was given it, for the holy purpose."

Kai kept his gaze on Safreses. "Why did you go to Scarif?"

"We were ordered—" Safreses' mouth worked, his jaw tightened, horror dawned in his eyes, but the words forced themselves out. "To meet him."

Kai pushed harder. "Ordered by who?"

Safreses gasped, "Brehama, the . . . the Prince-Speaker. It was—He—" Blood sprayed from his lips as he bit his tongue.

Ashem was frankly startled, as if until now she had still suspected all this was some kind of trick on Kai and Ziede's part. Ramad's expression was intent, intrigued but not surprised. "Brehama is the Prince-Speaker of Nient-arik." He nodded to Kai. "You just made my job much easier."

Kai's heart pounded with the effort and a spike of pain lanced through his temple, there and gone like the stab of a long needle. Ziede said, "That's enough." Through her pearl, she added, *You're pushing yourself too hard.*

Blood on his lips and chin, Safreses' face flushed dark and his gaze burned with hate. Kinlat's eyes had gone vague, a sign that Kai's will was starting to turn his brain. And Kai had a weird floating sensation that had nothing to do with the motion of the ship. He released his will.

A tightness in his chest gave way and he took a full breath, startled. He hadn't been aware of the slow-building pressure until now. He let himself fall back against the throne.

Ziede lifted her hand and picked up the reins of the cantrips. She tightened her grip until both men choked, stumbled, and then collapsed to the floor. With both unconscious, she opened her hand and let them breathe again. She said, "I was tired of listening to them anyway."

Ramad watched Kai with sharp attention. "Now the question is, is Brehama the only one involved, which I doubt. Nient-arik has long wanted to take Benais-arik's place as the ruling capital of the Rising World. They claim their Prince-heirs have blood-line ties to one of the Great Bashasa's cousins, which is true, but irrelevant to the Rising World's charter. But the Imperial renewal is their best chance to sway the coalition and supplant Bashat bar Calis."

Ashem's frown turned confused. "Didn't the Imperial renewal already happen?"

"No, but soon, it's the last day of this quarter-month." Ramad added, "With Kaiisteron Witch King and Ziede Daiyahah missing from Bashat's court during the time of the renewal, it makes it look like Benais-arik has lost your support, and the support of the Witchlands. With Tahren Stargard missing, it's worse. It puts the treaties with the Immortal Blessed at risk. It could disrupt the whole empire."

"It's a coalition, not an empire," Kai said, pressing his hands to his temples. The spikes of pain faded but his head still felt like one of the Gad-dazara volcanoes, all pressure and heat.

With deliberate emphasis, Ashem said, "Kinlat's holy purpose is killing you, if you didn't get that."

"Yes, Cohort Leader, we know that." Ziede's voice was dry. "The only reason we're not still locked in coffins is that another expositor opened the tomb. He meant to make Kai his familiar."

Ashem's brow furrowed in apparent surprise. Ramad's quick startled glance seemed genuine. He said, "A tomb?"

Ziede tilted her head, examining him. "At the bottom of the sea. Just deep enough to hold Kai forever."

Ashem glanced narrowly at Ramad, whose frown deepened. Kai wasn't in the mood to parse whether Ramad's disconcerted expression was real or an act. "What?" Kai asked. "Did you think we disappeared because we were off somewhere having a good time?"

Ramad shook his head slightly. "The expositor that found you . . . That was the Menlas you asked about?"

There was something in his tone that was genuine, concern or consternation or just surprise, it was hard to tell. "You've heard of him," Kai said, not making it a question.

"I'd tell you if I had." Ramad was preoccupied. "Expositors steal each other's secrets, especially ambitious apprentices. He might have thought to gain so much power through you that he wouldn't need to fear retribution."

"I am tired of being told things I already know," Ziede said contemplatively, apparently to the air. Sanja had gotten up and circled around the two unconscious men. She nudged one with a foot. Ziede added, "Sanja, get away from that."

"What will you do with them?" Ramad asked, his expression opaque again, whatever had disturbed him carefully tucked away.

Ashem eyed both men with disgust. "I would like them alive. They committed crimes against the Rising World by attacking and taking prisoner the cohort and my cadre. I assure you, they won't go unpunished." She glanced at Ramad. "And if they're part of a Nient-arik dissident faction, trying to undermine Benais-arik or the renewal, then they must be questioned by the Rising World council."

Ziede glanced at Kai and said silently, *She's right. They're valuable as witnesses, if nothing else.*

Much as I'd like to drop them over the side, Kai replied. Whoever had given Aclines the ship would probably prefer them dead and not speaking to Ashem's Rising World superiors.

Ziede said aloud, "Put them down in the hold with the cohort. They'll be drawn into the well and sleep." She made an elegant gesture. "Cohort Leader Ashem, if your cadre could make themselves useful . . ."

Kai watched from the throne while Ashem called a couple of

her people in from the lower deck. Ziede gestured for them to follow her, and Ashem and the two soldiers hauled the unconscious Safreses and Kinlat down the narrow stairs to the rowing deck.

Sanja padded over to Kai and sat down on the dais. Frowning, she asked, "Why didn't you kill them?"

"Someone in the Rising World might know better questions to ask them." Wearily, Kai propped his head on his hand. This throne was uncomfortable but he needed to wait until his head stopped swimming so he didn't stagger across the deck like a drunken mortal. "They're not expositors. They're just tools."

"Are you going to eat them?" Sanja asked.

Kai lifted his brows at her. She shrugged. "I'm just trying to learn how everything works."

Ramad took a step toward them and without looking up, Kai said, "Careful, you wouldn't want to startle me."

Ramad glanced at Sanja. "A word in private."

That was interesting. Kai told her, "See if Tenes is all right."

Eyeing Ramad with suspicion, Sanja pushed off the dais and went outside. Ramad lowered his voice and said, "I can confirm one thing, Kinlat was speaking the truth about Dahin Stargard. He was at Nient-arik and he did meet with a Benais-arik official before he left, but I don't know who it was."

Kai leaned back in the throne, wary of betraying too much of his reaction to Ramad. It was odd, since Dahin had long ago made it clear he wanted nothing to do with the Rising World politics. "How do you know this?"

Ramad made an open-handed gesture, as if the answer was obvious. "Immortals visiting such courts as Nient-arik are always interesting to the Rising World." Because Nient-arik had surrendered to the Hierarchs, making possible the fall of the city-states around it, and none of the Arike had ever gotten over it, even all these years later.

Ramad continued, "If the Nient-arik meant to disrupt the coalition renewal, perhaps they should have recruited you. I've read accounts that say you thought the Rising World should have released the coalition members from their agreements after the last Hierarch was killed."

"So did a lot of others, at the time." Kai couldn't tell if Ramad was setting conversational traps for information or thinking aloud. Better to shift the subject, and there was one thing he was genuinely curious about. "Why are you so helpful to us?"

"I'm just as interested in discovering who is behind all this as you are. And finding Tahren Stargard is my mission." Ramad hesitated, as if contemplating his own shift in subject. "And I think our arrangement was a question in exchange for an answer."

"Maybe not just as interested." Kai eyed him narrowly. "Ask, then."

There was a trace of the banked fire of scholarly interest in Ramad's gaze, so familiar from Dahin, from Ziede, from the sisters who studied at Avagantrum. "The other rumor I'd like to dispel is that you were a Witch, a renegade of their kind, who met Bashasa after the escape from the Summer Halls. And that you traded a Hierarch's life for your demonic power from the underearth."

"I was born a demon." Kai snorted derisively. "And Witches don't have renegades."

Ramad took that in. "I admit, I'm partial to the history that says you and Bashasa were always allies. That you fought your way out of the Summer Halls together, that you were there when he killed the first Hierarchs."

Kai regarded him and said nothing. There were parts of the story he had no intention of sharing with anyone.

Footsteps on the stairs signaled the return of the others. Ashem looked grave and the two cadre members seemed stricken. This must have been the first time they had seen with their own eyes what Aclines had done to the cohort. Ziede followed a moment later and said, "I think that's all the excitement for tonight." She pointed toward the hatch.

Still subdued, Ashem gestured for her cadre members to go and followed them out. Ramad hesitated, but went when Ziede's expression made it clear she meant him, too.

Kai heaved himself out of the throne and crossed the cabin to lean in the hatchway. Out in the cool night wind, Tenes perched on the railing, Sanja sitting on the bench at her feet. Clouds framed the moon, and the wind had that aftermath-of-a-lightning-strike quality that meant there was a storm somewhere behind them. That, or it was a lingering trace of the charged air of Gad-dazara.

Ashem sent her people down the stairs to the lower deck, but paused and said, "What are you going to do?"

Ramad paused, too, standing at the top of the stairs. Ashem was looking at Kai, so he answered, "Get revenge." That was what they were for, after all.

Ashem jerked her chin toward Sanja. "And this child? You'll take her with you on your quest for revenge?"

Sanja glared at her in outrage. Kai suppressed a surge of irritation. Ashem was too young to remember the Arike under Bashasa, where the cohorts had scooped up survivors and fled in front of the oncoming legions, leaving them in the first place of safety and going back for more. That wasn't what Ashem was objecting to, anyway. She thought their influence would corrupt an innocent girl.

In the Mouth of Flowers, Sanja had no one to protect her and nothing to believe in. If anyone, even a greedy shit like Menlas, had shown her the slightest bit of attention and offered even a sliver of safety, she would have attached herself and fought to the death for them. It was far better for Sanja and her murderous potential to be under Ziede's care. Kai just said, "What do you want us to do, abandon her alone in an unallied port city like the one she came from? Why so cruel, when we could have left her on an active volcano?"

Ashem wasn't deterred. "Where did she come from?"

Sanja stood, her jaw set. "The Mouth of Flowers. Menlas bought me from the child-catcher as a sacrifice to bring them back, so Kaiisteron could be in my body and Menlas could make him a slave." She added decisively, "So fuck you."

Ziede said, "Sanja, if you're going to swear, don't do it in Old Imperial. If you use their curses, you'll take on their beliefs."

Sanja blinked, distracted by that thought. "That's the only language I know," she pointed out.

Kai told her the Saredi word that meant "go into the wetland and eat shit-mud."

Sanja repeated it twice, trying to get the vowels right. Ziede said, "Go back in the cabin and sleep, Sanja. Cohort Leader Ashem, why don't you go belowdecks and lecture your loyal cadre on morality. You can chide us from your pedestal of Rising World superiority later. Ramad, go with her, or leap off the boat, whichever you prefer."

Ashem pressed her lips together and stomped down the stairs to the lower deck. Ramad, with an ironic twist to his expression, gave them a court salute, touching his hands to his forehead and bowing, then followed. Sanja obediently wandered back into the stern cabin.

Kai watched Ramad cross the lower deck, saw Ashem pause to speak to the cadre members on watch. Then they both disappeared down the forward stairs.

Shaking his head, Kai went to sit on the cushioned bench. Ziede sat beside him, and through her heart pearl, he silently told her what Ramad had said about Dahin.

Ziede let her breath out in a long, aggrieved sigh. "He might be lying."

Kai leaned against her shoulder, warm under her silk sleeve. The moon threw a broad reflection on the water, like it was pacing the boat, flying along beside them. "I don't think he's lying. Not about that."

Ziede snorted under her breath. "Be careful, Kai."

"Of what?" There was so much to choose from right now.

"You know what I mean."

He sat back and stared at her. "I don't."

Silently, she said, *Ramad reminds you of Bashasa.*

"He does not," Kai said aloud, offended. "Ziede!"

Ignoring him, she continued, *He's kind, in his way. Or pretending to be. And he has the same nose. He's probably distantly related, you know how many relatives that family had, despite all the ones who were murdered.*

Kai didn't know whether to go with anger or try to laugh it away. Since it was Ziede, he tried the truth, and said, *Don't poke me in places that hurt.*

She sighed and leaned against him again. "Sorry. I just . . . sorry."

They watched the moon in silence together, while Kai struggled to find his composure. As if it was a lost object he had left somewhere. Probably back in Benais-arik, sixty years ago. Finally he said, "You should get some rest while you can. Tenes, you too. I can wake you if the wind changes."

Across the deck, Tenes looked up at her name and hopped off the rail. She signed, *Call if you need me,* and went inside.

"I don't need rest, I'm fueled by spite." But there was a thoughtful frown in Ziede's voice. "So do we believe this whole plot was the doing of Aclines and the Prince-Speaker of Nient-arik?"

"Nient-arik has a motive, to make themselves the capital of the Rising World." If they had some support among the other coalition members, and managed to join with the dissident Immortal Blessed who wanted to end their Patriarchs' treaty with the Rising World, they might have a good chance to pull it off.

There had always been Immortal Blessed who wanted to return to the position they had held before the Hierarchs, extracting tribute and taxes from the small polities in the north and doing whatever they wanted to whoever they wanted. The Rising World prevented all that; under its treaties, all coalition members were equal under Benais-arik's leadership, and the Immortal

Blessed's power was strictly contained within the Blessed Lands. It had been a small price to pay, for a former ally of the Hierarchs. If not for Tahren, the coalition might have demanded that the Blessed be utterly destroyed. Kai added silently, *But they aren't the only ones with a motive to remove us.*

Bashat had to be behind this, Ziede answered. *No one else could arrange for us to be secretly taken from Benais-arik. Aclines must have had two masters.*

Whether the Nient-arik knew it or not, Kai agreed. Maybe it had been Bashat's idea of mercy, to forbid Aclines from attempting to take Kai as a familiar.

If Aclines had attempted it, this whole thing might have been over much sooner.

Ziede followed the tenor of his thoughts. She said wryly, "Menlas thought he was powerful enough to keep you."

"A lot of famously dead expositors have thought that." Kai leaned back and rubbed his face. This topic was too much after a long day. "Do you think Ashem is right about Sanja? This isn't going to get any less dangerous."

"No." Ziede looked off into the dark, the light from the imps reflecting off her eyes. "If we ever reach a safer place, I won't send her away. But I will give her every opportunity to run, just like the others."

"She won't," Kai said. Sanja had been studying Ziede like a treatise. "You should start teaching her." He took a deep breath and added, "I have an idea."

Ziede turned to regard him. "Is it a terrible idea?"

"Probably." It had occurred to him while he was talking to Grandmother, but there had been no way to attempt it until now. "We can use this ship, the connection to the Well of Thosaren, to call an Immortal Marshall."

"Ah." This was the last thing Ziede should want to do, but he could see she was considering it. "There are too many places

Tahren might be, Benais-arik, Nient-arik, others we haven't thought of yet." She took a sharp breath. "The bottom of the sea. A Marshall might know how to find her."

They were sitting on an Immortal Blessed ship that someone had given to Aclines as payment for whatever deal he had struck with the Nient-arik faction. Kai admitted, "We might have to fight. Anyone we call could be involved in the plot against us."

Ziede's voice was wry. "Kai, I will do anything to find Tahren. Even invoke my kin-right."

He hated to ask her to do that. But it was better than just summoning a random Immortal Marshall. "In the morning, then."

Ziede's gaze turned inward. "How did it come to this, Kai? I remember how we started. Now you're all razor barbs and I'm an angry shrew."

"No," he said, stung by that description of herself. "You're righteously furious. You've always had the high ground, Ziede. Don't let them say you don't." She was still looking away into the dark. "You're right about me and the razors, though." Most of the time Kai felt like he was made of razors, bleeding from the inside.

She reached over and squeezed his hand. "I've always liked your razors, Kai. They've cut us out of a number of tangles. But it would be good if one day you could stop bleeding." She stood and walked back into the light of the cabin.

Kai let the imps on the upper deck flutter away, so he could sit in the dark and watch the racing moon.

THE PAST:
THE PLAN

The Well of Thosaren was said to be the first source of potency that could be taken from raw spirit form and shaped to usefulness by living beings. The Immortal Blessed use it for prosaic tasks that mortals are able to perform for themselves, yet claim to have created it via the sheer power of their collective faculty—but that is an unlikely bit of posturing. Wells of potential are created by great deaths, like the Well of the Hierarchs, or the natural forces of the earth, from which the Witches coax strands of power at will, or other means unknown; not because those of privilege will it.

—The History of the Hierarch War: Volume Three:
An Introduction to the Civilizations of the North and East
by An Interested Yet Unbiased Party

Bashasa and his reluctant guards led Kai, Ziede, and Tahren to another room off the court, with a sunken hearth and rugs and seating cushions.

The Saredi clan tents had been divided up into spaces for sleeping, and eating and talking. This was the same, except divided by stone walls rather than curtains. If this was the way the whole place was arranged and not just the hostage quarters, it seemed awkward; there was no obvious way to repartition the space when another family married into the clan or if you had a large number of visitors. But then Kai had no idea how the Hierarchs actually lived. Maybe they ate their families, who knew.

They took seats on the cushions near the hearth and one of

the obviously terrified servants brought Bashasa more of the rancid red drink. Ziede accepted a cup, too. Tahren refused with a quietly appalled expression. Bashasa said, "Now that we are all here—Ah, Dahin, come in, sit with us."

Someone had stepped into the doorway from the court. A young person, pale like Tahren except for a dusting of freckles across their cheeks, with short straw-colored hair. They were dressed like Tahren, too, in a long light-colored tunic, wide pants, and tabard. Bashasa said, "This is Marshall Tahren's brother, Dahin."

Dahin came inside, hesitated, then dropped onto a cushion next to Kai. Tahren said, "Dahin. That's a demon."

"Oh." Dahin looked at Kai blankly. "So is it all right if I sit here?"

Kai said, "Yes." Dahin's resemblance to Tahren ended at his clothes, hair, thin lips, and sharp features. There was no sense of power from him, no strange current of connection to something on an unearthly plane. He wasn't entirely mortal, though, Kai could tell. "What are you?"

Dahin's expression said no one had ever asked him that question before. He looked at Tahren for help.

Her mouth was stiff, as if this were the worst question in the world. She said, "We are Blessed. *Were* Blessed. We have left their ranks."

Kai knew Immortal Marshalls were part of the Immortal Blessed, that had been obvious even to the Saredi, who before the war had thought them only stories. But he couldn't stop being a demon, so he didn't understand how an Immortal Blessed could just stop being an Immortal Blessed. He said, "What do you mean, 'left their ranks.'"

Ziede had been grimly sipping her drink, wincing between each taste. "It means she fought for the Hierarchs until it became personally inconvenient."

Tahren's expression was somehow both stony and profoundly uncomfortable. She said, "Our Patriarchs made the decision to grant the Hierarchs' petition for Marshalls to aid their forces. I did fight for them. I did break my sworn allegiance and turn against them for personal reasons."

Dahin held up his hand. "Me. I'm the personal reason. Part of the agreement was that some of the Lesser Blessed be turned over to the Hierarchs to become priests in their temples. I was supposed to be one of them." He sounded mildly embarrassed about it. He must have seen that Kai found the explanation wanting, so he added, "Lesser Blessed can't draw from the Well of Thosaren like the Higher Blessed can. We live a long time, compared to mortals, and we can use most of the things made from the power of the Well, and . . ." His brow furrowed. "I suppose that makes us expendable."

Her expression solidifying into cold granite, Tahren said, "If you are understandably unfamiliar with this, becoming a temple priest requires the candidate to give up every part of their soul and power to the Well of the Hierarchs. It is unlike a connection to the Immortal Blessed's Well of Thosaren in every way. The Hierarchs' Well hollows out those connected to it like wooden dolls and they become . . . lost to their former lives. So you are correct that it was a personal reason, a very personal reason."

Ziede lifted a brow. "I didn't say I disagreed with your reason." She offered Tahren her cup of the drink.

Tahren winced away from it. "No, thank you."

Betraying exasperation for the first time, Bashasa said, "Is that done now? Are we done with this?" He set his cup down. "Because we have only so long before the Hierarchs realize what I have done and come in to kill everyone here."

Dahin said, "I have a question. Tahren, why shouldn't I sit next to a demon?" He turned to Kai. "Will I die if I touch you?"

"No," Kai said, eyeing him. He seemed utterly sincere. "But don't touch me."

"Oh." Blinking uncertainly, Dahin folded his hands in his lap.

Ziede said to Tahren, "That one was your fault."

Outrage flickered across Tahren's still expression. "If you would like to continue this discussion—"

Bashasa's jaw went tight and this time Kai was on his side. Kai said, "Tahren, Ziede, fight afterward."

Ziede saluted Kai with her cup and a dry smile. Tahren stared grimly at a wall, clearly embarrassed.

Bashasa let out his breath. "Thank you, Prince of the Fourth House." He regained his easy demeanor so quickly it was a little disturbing. "Two days from now, four of the High Hierarchs will be in this palace, at a ceremony to be held in the Imperial Halls, an investiture for the new regent they will be installing in Stios. This is obviously an opportunity that cannot be missed."

For the first time Kai felt the stir of anticipation. Bashasa had everyone's attention now, even Ziede, who already seemed to know something of the plan. It was an opportunity, an incredible one. The Hierarchs never made themselves vulnerable on the battlefield, at least as far as the Saredi and borderlanders had been able to discover before their defeat. There had never been an opportunity to strike at them directly.

Bashasa knew he had his audience now. The tension had gone out of his shoulders. "Our plan is simple. Tahren has discovered the source of the magics that create the perpetual rain in the Cageling Demon Court. Ziede believes it can be suspended or even destroyed. If we can do so, we can free the demons there and, hopefully, persuade enough of them to attack the Imperial Halls to provide confusion and disruption. While we target the four Hierarchs."

"We?" Kai repeated. It couldn't be as mad as it sounded. "Just us?"

"Us, and my personal guard." Bashasa either didn't pick up on the sarcasm in his tone or ignored it. "As I explained, there are Arike hostages from other city-states here, living in separate households in other courts. But I trust none enough to include them, at least at this stage. When we make our attempt, I will invite them to join us."

Tahren still wasn't looking at anyone, but her expression had turned thoughtful. "This would not be a survivable situation, particularly for mortals. Are your people here so willing to die for vengeance?"

"Not so much for vengeance, as to buy a chance for the others who will come after us." Bashasa was deeply serious. "You will know that except for the local conscripts, the legionaries all seem to come from the upper regions of the south. Before the invasion, we of the Arik had no contact with them, and the archipelagoes had little more. The Hierarchs must have been preparing this for at least a generation, raising and training these people to conquer the rest of the world." Kai had known some of this, that the light-skinned legionaries who looked like the sea people of the archipelagoes actually came from further south, from lands even the Erathi traders had rarely visited. Bashasa continued, "They think themselves superior in all ways and are filled with wild stories about us. I was asked if I had children with my sister, and how we picked which ones we would eat."

Without thinking, Kai said, "Like the story that the Saredi sacrificed children to demons."

"Exactly like that." Bashasa nodded to him. "They think of us all as barely better than animals, you know. They mean to slaughter us, all of us, from the eastern sea to the western, to the far north. They have already slaughtered so many of us." He focused on Tahren. "I cannot imagine that they intend to keep their agreement with the Immortal Blessed once they are no longer needed."

Tahren's gaze went to Dahin. "Their agreement is already too . . . unsupportable."

Bashasa made an open-handed gesture. "I will only bring the members of my guard who volunteer. The others, and those too injured to fight, will wait with my dependents and hope for a chance to escape the palace in the confusion. If they succeed, they will spread the word of what we've done and inspire others to resistance and rebellion. At least, I hope so." He reached back to pick up a round wooden thing that when opened turned out to be a case for papers. Bashasa unrolled a scroll and flattened it out using the cups, ignoring the drops of red liquid that stained it. "This is a map of the area around the Imperial Halls—a partial map. I've only been called there a few times, it's all from memory."

Everyone leaned in to look, even Tahren.

After the talking finished and Bashasa was called away by one of his guards, Kai walked out to the court to sit by the dry weed-choked fountain. It was late in the afternoon, the sky growing dimmer somewhere above the heavy gray clouds. He propped his chin in his hand and watched ants walk along the basin. His part of the plan was simple: persuade a bunch of pain-maddened demons he had never exchanged a word with before to go and attack the expositors and legionaries and Hierarchs in the Imperial Halls instead of taking the opportunity to escape.

Other than that, it sounded simple, it sounded as if it would work. Despite the fact that the map looked like Bashasa had drawn it with his feet.

Two servants came into the court, saw him, and bumped into each other trying to get out of his eyeshot. Kai was tired of being treated like something corrupted that might infect anyone who got too near. Could Bashasa really trust these people not to betray his plans to their captors? It seemed a really obvious course of action to Kai, and he wasn't even a mortal who had been made to be a servant and dragged off to be a hostage in a foreign palace through no fault of his own.

And even if they could rely completely on Bashasa's people, Kai had no idea if he could rouse the other demons and convince them to help.

So many Saredi clans had been destroyed, the demons in the court might have no mortal families to go back to, even if their borrowed bodies weren't worn down by torture and deprivation. When they were released, they had no reason to stay and fight. They might run, kill as many mortals as they could. Or find a place to hide and wait, hoping that the passage to the underearth might someday be restored and they could return to their original bodies.

If Kai had any sense, he would do that, too, as soon as he could get out of this place. At least he had Grandmother and his demon family living in the underearth. But some part of him didn't want to let go of Enna. She was all he had left of Kentdessa. Every other member of her family, their family, was dead.

Dahin crossed the court and sat down next to Kai, staring at him expectantly. He said, "I've never seen a demon before."

Kai lifted a brow. "There's a whole bunch of us chained up in a court not too far from here."

"I know, but sister wouldn't let me go look." Dahin shuffled a little closer. "I'm in hiding, too. Sister came here to petition the Hierarchs not to take me, and they refused to hear it, and Bashasa said he'd hide me for her as long as he could. She told everyone she sent me back to the Blessed Lands. Only our family knows where I really am. So if you're worried we'll tell about you, we won't. If we did, somebody would punish us, either the Hierarchs or the Immortal Blessed Patriarchs or both." He reached to nudge a pebble out of the path of the ants.

"Punish?" Kai echoed. It didn't sound as bad as painful death, which was what everyone else here was facing.

"They would encase Tahren in ice rock," Dahin said, his voice completely sober for once. "And execute the rest of us. But if we don't kill the Hierarchs, they're going to figure it out, sooner or later. Probably sooner."

All right, so it was just as bad for the Blessed as it was for the rest of them. It made Kai more inclined to listen to Dahin.

Though the thought of Immortal Blessed running and hiding from the Hierarchs just like everyone else wasn't exactly a sad one. They should have fought when they had the chance, before the Hierarchs killed the world. Kai asked, "Why don't you run away? Hide somewhere else."

"When they realize I'm not in the Blessed Lands, they'll ask the Hierarchs' expositors to find me." Dahin stared at Kai. His eyes were a blue so light, it looked unnatural. "Why is everyone so afraid of demons?"

Kai snorted, though it wasn't funny. Where he came from, no one was afraid of demons. "We don't die."

Dahin looked as if he was unsuccessfully hiding skepticism. "That sounds like a superstition, stories mortals tell each other. How do you know—"

That was too much. Kai plucked the knife out of Dahin's belt and sliced deep into his own wrist. Dahin's jaw dropped as the gash closed even as blood welled up. Kai's flesh flowed back together like water. The cut was just a red smear. "Oh," Dahin finished. Kai handed the knife back hilt first and Dahin took it, tucking it back in its sheath. "How does it work?"

Kai was even more annoyed. "It's not a trick."

"No, I meant . . ." Dahin gestured at himself. "The Immortal Blessed come from the Well of Thosaren, we're consecrated in it when we're born and that gives us long lives. The Marshalls and the other Higher Blessed can draw power from it. Everything else is just hard work and training."

Kai added, "And an inflated sense of superiority."

"Well, yes, that," Dahin admitted with a smile, which made it hard to stay angry and hostile. "But where does your . . . come from?"

Kai sighed. But there was no reason not to explain, it wasn't a secret. "This isn't the body I was born in. My body is in the underearth. When demons come here, into offered mortal bodies, it give us abilities that we didn't have there. We're . . . malleable, in the underearth. Here that means we can heal so fast, it's hard to hurt us. Even now, when the Hierarchs have sealed the underearth passages so I can't return there, and no one who lives there can come here."

Dahin nodded slowly. "I guess the other part is true, too. Being able to destroy things with a touch?"

"Not the way mortals think." Kai plucked a leaf from one of the vines currently prying at the fountain's rim, and held it up. As he drained the tiny spark of life from the leaf, it browned and dried and crumpled between his fingers.

"I see." Dahin sounded like he did see. "It—the life force, the energy—goes into you?"

"Sort of." Kai didn't understand entirely where it went. When he killed legionaries this way, it just seemed to buzz around in his chest uselessly.

"And you can do that to a whole living thing? An animal, a person?" Dahin seemed too far gone in curiosity to know what he was asking. He met Kai's gaze, and looked a little abashed. "If it or whoever was attacking you, I mean."

"Yes." Kai flicked the leaf away. "It's not easy."

Dahin nodded. "It takes a lot of effort, then?"

"No. It's not easy to watch."

"Oh." Dahin seemed a little taken aback, but not so much as to end the conversation, which Kai had been hoping for. "I think I see now why demons are associated with all kinds of moral corruption in our lore, not just physical corruption. It seems to be a misunderstanding of your essential nature. Can you reverse the process?"

Kai frowned. "Reverse it?"

"Put the energy back in the leaf?" Dahin shifted excitedly, leaning over and plucking the dead leaf out of the dry fountain basin. "Try and see what happens."

Kai had never drained anything or anyone he hadn't wanted to kill; he didn't make a practice of destroying foliage or anything else that was useful or innocuous. But Dahin had sparked a memory: lying in the wet sand watching Adeni die, and believing it might be possible to give him the life of the creature who had killed him. Frowning, he took the dried leaf back and concentrated, feeling for the thread between it and that buzz of life in his body. It was still there, though fast fading. He tugged on it gently.

The leaf unfurled, green threading through its veins. "Huh," Kai said aloud.

Dahin nodded slowly. "Interesting." He turned to scrape through the leaf litter. "Now instead of sending the energy back to the same leaf, could you send it to another leaf? I think that's an obvious next question."

It was . . . strange. Kai hadn't learned that demons were terrifying to so many until the war had started and mortals from other lands had joined the Saredi and the borderlanders in battle. He had spent two full changes of the seasons walking or riding through camps where allies watched him with fear and loathing, to the point where he expected it, was used to it. Now Dahin was reducing the horrifying power of demons down to what was interesting and obvious.

Dahin picked out a likely, at least to him, selection of leaves and set them out on the cracked stone of the fountain rim. But then a servant ran out of a doorway across the court and darted past, not even bothering to skirt around Kai in his fear. Two Arike soldiers strode into the court. Kai tensed, but then Bashasa came out of the room behind him and made an abrupt gesture. The soldiers wheeled to hurry through another doorway.

Bashasa stopped beside Kai and Dahin and said, "Go to Ziede. She'll hide you with her—"

Another servant stepped into the court and pressed herself back against the wall. Her wide-eyed, frightened gaze seemed to send an urgent message to Bashasa. He hissed out a breath and said, "No time. Stay where you are, drop your eyes, pretend to be—"

An expositor walked into the court.

Kai had no idea what he and Dahin were supposed to pretend to be but they were both small and sitting on the ground playing with dead leaves like children, so he went with that. He ducked his head and kept his gaze on the moss-covered paving. Next to him Dahin stiffened and his breath hitched in dismay. Kai wrapped an arm around him and pulled him close, and Dahin tucked his head into Kai's shoulder. Maybe it would help; surely no one in the Hierarchs' palace would think a mortal would voluntarily touch a demon. But then Dahin wasn't truly mortal. If the expositor could sense that . . .

Sounding a shade too hearty, Bashasa said, "Ah, Cantenios. What an honor to have you visit us. What brings you here?"

Bootsteps moved toward them, more than one set. The expositor had brought a retinue, probably palace legionaries. "Prince Bashasa," a voice said. Before Kai had lowered his gaze, he had a bare glimpse of an older man with pale skin and a neatly trimmed beard, dressed in a gold coat over a black and gold tunic and skirt. A dangling gold and enamel ornament hung from the collar of his tunic, and a gold veil was folded back over his dark hair, pulled just low enough to shade his eyes. A dark cane cursebreaker hung off his belt. "I heard of your recent bereavement and wanted to deliver my condolences in person." He spoke Imperial with an accent that Kai couldn't identify. "Hierarch's Voice Raihankana also sends his . . . regrets."

There was a pause. Then Bashasa said, "I thank you, and I thank the Hierarch's Voice for his condescension." Now he sounded rough and a little unsteady, and Kai wished he thought it was an act. "I also thank the Hierarch's Voice for allowing me to return her body to our home for rites."

Whose body? Kai wondered.

"Yes, that has been allowed, hasn't it." Cantenios paced closer, close enough that Kai could see the gold beading at the bottom of his skirt and on the toes of his black boots. "I assume you will send someone to accompany the coffin box?"

"One of my family dependents, her nurse. As is our custom." Bashasa sounded harried, distracted. "Do you think I'm taking the opportunity to . . . remove someone from this palace? The Hierarch's Voice flatters me with his attention. But I have no one else to remove."

"Not even your new guests." It wasn't a question.

"You mean the Immortal Marshall?" Annoyance crept into Bashasa's voice. "Yes, she has graced my household with her presence. Ah, here she is."

Tahren's steps were soundless but Kai sensed her approach through the thread of power in her blood. The fabric of her tabard whispered as she stopped, the third point of a triangle formed by Bashasa and Cantenios. She said, "Expositor."

"Immortal Marshall. It's always so invigorating to see a member of the Blessed."

"Is it." Tahren was laconic.

Kai bit the inside of his cheek. Bashasa was all over the place, careening from one emotion to another, and now Tahren was going to get them killed, not by betraying them but because she was a stubbornly proud ass.

The expositor said, "But I wasn't speaking of the Immortal Marshall. I was speaking of these guests."

Kai's skin prickled and he knew the expositor was looking down at him and Dahin. Cantenios continued, "Surely you can stand and greet me, Dahin of the Blessed. Excuse me, the Lesser Blessed."

Kai felt Dahin's chest rise and fall with a sharp breath.

Cantenios continued, "There was some fear that young Dahin might be lost in the palace or the city, so the Hierarch's Voice Raihankana lent me this." He lifted one of the ornaments chained to his belt, a flat gold plate set with an obsidian disk. Kai suppressed a twitch, then wasn't sure why. The disk affected the air around it in a way just beyond his senses, like an itch inside his brain. Cantenios added, "A finding stone. It senses the locations of Immortal and Lesser Blessed."

Dahin slipped out from under Kai's arm and pushed to his feet. Voice a little thick, he said, "I apologize, expositor. I've been . . . upset."

"Overcome with the honor of joining the Well of the Hierarchs?" The expositor sounded as if it was funny, as if he understood Dahin's fear, as if he had seen it so many times before and it had never stopped entertaining him.

Tahren's voice was icy calm. "It is an honor not required of all expositors, I understand."

"No, it is not. Many of us are valued for our independence." Cantenios added, "And when is the happy day for young Dahin?"

Tahren answered, "It has not been set, that I know of."

"I will inquire for you," Cantenios promised. "And who is this?"

Spikes of hot fear crept up Kai's spine. Fear and disappointment. They weren't even going to have a chance to try Bashasa's doomed, desperate plan.

Bashasa managed to sound offhand, as if it didn't matter. "One of my dependents, only. Keeping Dahin company."

Cantenios was calm and amused. "She isn't dressed like a servant."

Kai bit his lip to keep his expression blank. That was Bashasa's fault, at least, giving him clothes that suited whatever the Arike thought Kai's station was.

Then the expositor reached down and put two calloused fingers under Kai's chin.

Something in Kai's brain went white and still, like a light filling him up. It should have felt like rage, but it was too big for that, too big to name, too much to feel all at once.

He is going to see my eyes and know what I am, and kill everyone here, from Bashasa and Ziede to the soldiers and the people who bring food and clean the rooms, Kai thought. *He is going to see my eyes and die.* Both outcomes were equally possible, but Kai had already made his decision.

This wasn't the plan. He was doing it anyway. As the expositor lifted Kai's chin to reveal the dark wells of his gaze, Kai smiled up at him. And grasped his wrist.

He had never managed to get a hand on an expositor before. In his mind he saw Cantenios' power, the way it ran through his body in the same veins as his blood. He heard the remnants of the mortal sacrifices that had caught that power and held it there for Cantenios' use, as if their last cries and sobs still rang out.

Behind him, Bashasa said, "Shit."

Frozen in place, Cantenios resisted, formed intentions to make his power a wall against Kai. Kai had never faced anyone or anything who could fight back like this before. It was an intoxicating challenge. The legionaries seemed to move in slow motion as they realized what Kai was, what was happening. Bashasa moved much faster, a knife suddenly in his hand as he stepped forward and drove it into the nearest legionary's throat.

Kai pushed forward with everything he had, knowing if he didn't conquer Cantenios now, the expositor would have a chance to use his own power, drawn from the Well of the Hierarchs. He would attack with an intention or pull the cursebreaker off his belt and Kai would collapse helpless on the paving. Tahren flashed past in the corner of Kai's eye, her straight sword slashing down onto another legionary. Bashasa's soldiers stormed into the court, bodies slammed into bodies and weapons clashed at the edges of Kai's vision.

Kai pushed forward with everything, felt Enna's body go numb, felt his head swim. Then Cantenios' power gave way with a sensation very like biting into a ripe pomegranate. Kai pierced through it, found the heart-life hiding in the man's chest, and drew it out.

Cantenios' desiccated body tumbled limply backward into the

dry fountain and Kai pushed to his feet. He looked down at Dahin, who huddled on the paving, staring up at Kai with his jaw dropped. Kai's mind was empty of everything except the conversation they had been having. He said, "That's what it looks like."

Tahren, Bashasa, and a scatter of Arike soldiers stood among the sprawled bodies of the legionaries. Bashasa had a smear of blood on his forehead. Ziede stood across the court, eyes wide with shock. Frightened or avid servants peered out of doorways. Bashasa dropped the legionary sickle sword he held and stepped toward Kai. Kai was riding too high on the unexpected deluge of power from the expositor to be properly wary, but he still didn't know what to expect when Bashasa grasped his shoulders. "You did it," Bashasa said, his dark eyes a little glassy. "You killed that monster."

Even with the heady rush, it was dawning on Kai that he had ruined all of Bashasa's careful plotting. Kai said, "But the plan."

Bashasa gently shook him. "The plan," he repeated, as if he had no idea what Kai meant. Then he went still and his eyes widened. "The plan."

Tahren said, "What are we going to do?"

It should have been gratifying to see an Immortal Marshall at a loss, to hear an urgent note in her voice, but Kai just felt growing dismay as cold reality sunk in. He had ruined their chance to show that Hierarchs could be killed.

Ziede stepped over the bleeding body of a legionary, her brow knit in consternation. "I can weave a chimera . . . But someone will come looking for them . . ."

Bashasa turned to face her, one hand still on Kai's shoulder. He said, "No. We move. Now."

"The investiture," Tahren pointed out. "The other two Hierarchs aren't here yet."

"Fuck the investiture," Bashasa said with conviction. "We have a chance to take two Hierarchs, that's better than anyone else has ever managed." He turned to Kai again and squeezed his shoulder. "Yes?"

Kai couldn't believe Bashasa was touching him after what he had just seen, with Cantenios' body a desiccated heap at their feet. But there was nothing in Bashasa's face except grim purpose. Something in it made Kai believe anything was possible. Kai said, "Yes."

Bashasa nodded. He released Kai and turned to his people. "It's almost time for the Hierarchs to speak their daily prayers in the Temple Halls. This will be our new goal. Those who will fight, assemble here. Those who will take the news of our vengeance home, make ready to leave."

Tahren stepped toward Ziede, betraying a little uncertainty. "I can show you the intention for the Cageling Demon Court."

Ziede nodded sharply. "Yes, whatever we do, if we can at least accomplish that—Bashasa, we're going!"

Bashasa waved an acknowledgment as he strode out of the court.

Tahren seemed to settle into her skin, calm determination making her expression opaque again. "Good. Kaiisteron, you're with us. Dahin, stay with the group who are leaving. I'll find you later."

Dahin stood, his face anxious. "Sister—" She threw a quelling look at him and he swallowed any objections. "Just be careful."

Tahren and Ziede started for the archway. Kai stepped over Cantenios' body and ran after them.

They were in the corridor when a voice called out, "Fourth Prince!"

Kai turned. A young Arike soldier with a scar across one eye hurried after them. She stopped a few paces away and held out something, a tool with leather-wrapped handles. Kai took it automatically, confused. It had bladed pincers at one end and looked like a farming implement. "For chains," the soldier explained in halting Imperial, and made scissor-cutting motions with her fingers.

"Right, yes!" Kai said, understanding. "Thank you!"

She nodded and ducked back down the corridor. Kai ran to catch up with Ziede and Tahren. Taking long strides, Tahren glanced down at the tool in Kai's hand. "That's for making Blessed armor. The blades are well-born steel. It's what we used to get you out."

Trying to tuck it inside his tunic without stabbing himself in the breast, Kai felt a little thread of hope. Bashasa, at least, thought they still had a chance to make this work.

SEVEN

As the sky brightened with dawn, Kai stood out on deck with a cup of hot ginger water while the others were still inside eating. In the bow cabins, the cadre had made a millet porridge, and Ramad had sent some to the upper deck. Despite the fact that they seemed to have a truce arrangement, Tenes and Ziede had both tested the food for poison.

Now the low rise of the Arkai coastline lay in the distance, where they meant to find a safe landing to leave the unconscious cohort. If Tahren was being held somewhere in the Arike city-states, it might be best to leave the ship and head overland. If she had been taken to an outer Rising World territory, this ship would be the fastest way to get there and he and Ziede would need to keep control of it. Not knowing was like being poised on a knife's edge; if they didn't get answers from the Immortal Blessed, Kai had no idea what to do next.

Go back to Benais-arik and ask Bashat, face-to-face, Kai thought. Yes, returning to the Rising World court would go well, if he wanted to chance ending up at the bottom of the sea again. Especially after Bashat found out what Kai had done.

Kai rubbed his eyes. This was probably a bad time to try to plan anything. He had spent most of the night out on deck, keeping watch while Ziede slept, waking her whenever it was time to placate the wind-devils again. He had slept a little before dawn, when Tenes had come out to take his place.

Ashem and Ramad were down on the lower deck conferring. Kai watched while they seemed to come to a decision, then both came up the stairs. Ashem shook out a fabric map and said without preamble, "There's a place nearby where the cohort could be released." She opened a folded writing stand from the end of the curved bench and spread the map on it. "This is Orintukk. It's an empty city."

Sanja, still chewing, wandered out of the hatch. Frowning, Kai turned the map to the angle he was used to visualizing it from, and said, "I've heard of it. It was hit early." He had never been there. Avagantrum was further inland, and Kai had always traveled there overland; there had never been a reason to approach it from this direction or go to Orintukk. Like Ashem said, it was an empty city, a decaying monument to its murdered inhabitants.

"Yes, the Hierarchs landed their legions there when they first came to the Arkai." Ramad leaned in to trace one finger down the coast, following the route the Hierarch ships might have taken. Kai eased back a step. Ziede's comment about Ramad was making him a self-conscious idiot. Oblivious, Ramad said, "They kept it for a while as a staging area. It never recovered, but there are probably some surviving farms in the area around it."

Ashem said, "I was there once. From what I remember, the piers and breakwaters are still standing." She tapped a point above the drawing that marked the city. "There's a Rising World outpost here, upriver. I can send messengers there to get help for the cohort."

Sanja leaned around Kai's elbow to see. "Why is the city empty?" She stabbed one nail-bitten finger on the image for Orintukk, a little line drawing of onion domes and walls with water flowers and fish woven around them. "Is it all ruined, like the city on the fire mountain?"

"It wasn't destroyed. The Hierarchs just didn't leave anyone alive when they were done with it," Kai told her. "Mortals might live near it, or on the outskirts, but there weren't enough left to live in the city again."

"No people means no shipping, no caravans, no markets," Ramad contributed.

"But what about all the people who live through here." Sanja spread her fingers on the map, along the river and the valleys spreading out from Orintukk, the lines where the old roads and canals ran. Her brow was tightly furrowed. "They don't want to live in the city?"

"There aren't many people there. Most of them died." Kai looked down at her, watched her tremble on the edge of a terrible understanding. "The world used to be a much bigger place, with so many more people in it."

Ashem was turning impatient, but Ramad asked Sanja, "You said you were from the Mouth of Flowers?"

Her gaze turned a little mistrustful, but she said, "Yes."

He nodded. "Did you ever cross the bridges to the landward side, and see the walls and canals?"

She nodded, still frowning. "I saw it from the seawall. There's nothing over there. It's just a big garden, no one lives there."

"They used to, when it was part of Nehush. Most of the city used to live there, in houses along the canals, and they would sail little boats across the bay into the port. Hundreds, thousands of people." He looked at Kai, who stared back at him and said nothing. Did Ramad somehow know Kai had first come to the mortal world as a Saredi? It meant his "historical" questions yesterday had been an elaborate pretense of ignorance. But if they were, it didn't make sense to reveal that now.

There were no empty cities on the grassplains. The scars where the great tents had burned had been scoured away by the wind and blossomed back into grasses. If you traced the courses of the rivers, followed the herds of now wild goats and horses, you might find the remnants of irrigation channels that had been dug during the Golden Light and Green Changes seasons for garden plots, you might uncover rusted tools and arrowheads, if you looked very hard.

Sanja had either taken in the idea or set it aside for later consideration. She said, "Is Orintukk filled with ghosts?"

"Is that a problem for you?" Kai asked her.

"Ghosts steal your face," Sanja said. Then she squinted up at Kai and amended, "Not your face."

"Not my face," Kai agreed. Ashem watched them with a frown. He wondered if she thought it was now too late for Sanja, already corrupted by Witches and demons. He said, "We'll stop at Orintukk and you can take the cohort off the ship. But first, Ziede is going to use the steering column's connection to the Well of Thosaren to call an Immortal Blessed, probably an Immortal Marshall, to answer a few questions. She'll invoke her kin-right, but depending on which Blessed comes, they may still try to kill us."

Ashem's frown deepened. "Wait, what? An Immortal Marshall may try to kill you?"

Kai leaned on the rail and shrugged. "You'll know when we do."

Ramad, who seemed committed to his role as the Reasonable One, said instead, "Orintukk is close. Can we dock there and take the cohort off first?"

"No, because I may need them as hostages." That was a lie, but it was the lie that Ashem and Ramad would believe.

If the Immortal Marshall who answered their call wasn't involved with the plot, but decided to ignore Ziede's kin-right in order to kill them for old time's sake, then the cadre and the enspelled cohort should be safe. The Immortal Blessed had never had clean hands where the Hierarchs were concerned, but they did have a justified reputation for not harming non-combatants and bystanders unless it was expedient. If the Marshall who arrived was involved in the plot, anyone who had been on the ship with Aclines would likely be dead, even if they had already landed the mortals at Orintukk.

Kai added, "If the Marshall kills us and Tenes, I'd appreciate it if you'd say Sanja is with your cadre."

"Hey!" Sanja objected, disturbed at the idea. "I don't want to be with their cadre!"

Ashem was not pleased with anything she was hearing. "This is exactly what I was taking about last night," she said with heat. "This is why you—This is why people fear Witches."

That was so completely unfair Kai couldn't let it go. "It should be why they fear the Immortal Blessed."

Ramad's expression of disbelief was turning to consternation. Apparently he had thought Kai was exaggerating. "Will it really come to that?"

"Your guess is as good as mine." Kai folded his arms and looked out to sea.

Ziede stepped out of the main cabin, dusting crumbs off her fingers. Her mouth a grim line, she said, "Let's get this over with." She crossed to the steering column, pushed the metal plate up, and put her hand on the white stone mounted below. Kai felt the change in the air, the sudden tingle of heat across his skin. The Well of Thosaren wasn't like the Well of the Hierarchs, but it was still alien, still inimical to what he was.

Ziede said, "I am Ziede Daiyahah, wife to Tahren Stargard, and I invoke my rights to formal hearing as kin to the Blessed."

<hr>

"Was this really the best plan?" Ramad studied the blue cloud-streaked sky, his expression only slightly desperate. The sun was a little higher, but Kai knew it shouldn't take much longer.

"Ramad, I don't care what you think," Ziede said, patiently for her. "I've made it as plain as I can and I don't know how else to explain it to you."

Ashem, her arms tightly folded and her expression somewhere between furious and disgruntled, said, "It will serve you all right if the Blessed kill you. I just wish you weren't planning to take the rest of us with you."

"Cohort Leader, I don't actually want to take you anywhere," Kai told her.

"Believe me, the sentiment is mutual," she said.

The more powerful Immortal Blessed could use the Well of Thosaren to transmute their bodies from one location to the other, but only if there was a Well-source on each end. Sending a summons through it with kin-right should mean the Immortal Blessed who responded would be one of Tahren's relatives, honor-bound not to hurt Ziede. But it might also draw the attention of Aclines' Immortal Blessed coconspirators.

Kai explained all that to Sanja, when she asked why they were looking up instead of scanning the horizon for ships. He finished, "If they could send themselves anywhere they wanted, we would never have got them out of the war. They would have been every-where, like fleas."

Ramad's expression was set in grim lines. "You're going to—What if the Immortal Marshall—" but he stopped there.

What was he going to say? Kai wondered. *You're going to die. What if the Immortal Marshall kills you?* Ramad had to be worried about the fate of the cohort and cadre. Then Kai spotted the spark of light high in the bright morning air, too high and defined to be a trick of the sun or a reflection from the ship. "Run inside the cabin," he told Sanja. "Cohort Leader, get your cadre off the deck."

Sanja hesitated for a heartbeat, staring up, then bolted for the hatch. Ashem turned and shouted a command. Her cadre scrambled for the forward stairs. Tenes paced deliberately out of the main cabin and came to stand beside Kai and Ziede. Kai told her, "You don't have to."

Her gaze on the sky, she signed back, *I want to.*

The bright figure grew in size and detail as its meteor-like fall slowed. It was an Immortal Marshall, not just a Blessed. They wore a gold breastplate and forearm guards over a light-yellow tunic with tabard, and full pants tucked into high gilded leather boots. Their hair was cut all the way back to the scalp until it was just a light dusting of silver on tawny skin. They carried a lance tipped with the white flag of the Blessed.

"Ostentatious, condescending . . ." Ziede's inaudible mutter became audible. "Oh, it's Saadrin. Well, if we have to kill her, at least it'll be no loss."

From past interactions, Saadrin felt the same way about Ziede. Saadrin was related to Tahren distantly, but Immortal Blessed family lines were longer and more branching than even demon houses or Saredi clans, and Kai had no idea how.

During the war, Saadrin had been one of the Immortal Marshalls who fought for the Hierarchs. She had also been a negotiator for the treaty between the Immortal Blessed and the newly born Rising World, but then that didn't mean much. After the fall of the Hierarchs, negotiation with the coalition had been the Immortal Blessed's only option.

"It could have been someone worse," Kai said. Tahren had relatives who were much more hostile.

Saadrin landed lightly on the deck in front of the steering column. Her glare passed over Kai and Tenes, skipped Ashem and Ramad entirely, and went straight to Ziede. "How did you get this ship?" she demanded, gray eyes furious. She spoke Old Imperial. It was the language the Immortal Blessed had decided to use to speak to lesser beings, and nothing had changed their minds about that, even with the Hierarchs dead and gone.

Kai said, "What, you aren't going to greet your marriage-sister by name?"

Saadrin's perfect jaw hardened but she said, "Ziede Daiyahah. What are you—and that demon—doing with this ship?" Saadrin couldn't possibly recognize Kai in this new body, but she knew from his eyes that he was a demon. And there was only one demon Ziede Daiyahah traveled with.

Kai could tell from the set of her shoulders that Ziede was tense, but he didn't think it would be obvious to anyone else. Especially Saadrin, who probably didn't notice much of anything about the people she considered lesser beings. Ziede's brow knit thoughtfully, and she said, "Since you ask so politely, we took it from the expositor Aclines."

"An expositor." Saadrin's voice dripped with disgust and disbelief. "Bring him to me."

"Impossible, sadly. He's being nibbled by crabs at the bottom of the sea." Ziede tilted her head inquiringly. "So you weren't the one who gave him this ship?"

"Why do you say such a thing?" Saadrin's eyes narrowed. "What are you doing here?" Her gaze flicked to Ashem and Ramad, as if noticing them for the first time. "How does this concern the Rising World?"

Tight and controlled, Ashem answered, "The expositor took my cadre and an Imperial cohort prisoner, and forcibly brought us aboard. That's how it concerns us."

Saadrin's expression darkened. "Why?" she demanded.

Whatever reaction Ashem had been expecting, that wasn't it. She made a strangled noise of incredulous rage. Ramad, who must have dealt with a lot of Immortal Blessed, said dryly, "He didn't discuss his motives with us."

They could have said we captured them, Kai thought, *if they really wanted us dead.* But perhaps they thought it was better to take the chance that Kai and Ziede would keep their promise to release the cohort at Orintukk.

"So many questions." Ziede lifted her brows. "Like an innocent asking for instruction."

"You might answer one of my questions." The skepticism and suspicion in Saadrin's gaze was growing. "Who is this Aclines? How did he get this ship?" She frowned at the embellishment above the stern cabin hatch. Kai suspected it told her the ship's name and other information, but she didn't enlighten them.

Ziede spread her hands. "I've told you all we know. I look to you for answers, Immortal Blessed."

Saadrin's expression turned more thunderous but she managed

to ignore the sarcasm. "A mortal—even an expositor—could not steal this ship."

Ziede didn't argue that point. "We don't think he did. That's why I asked if you had given it to him."

Saadrin seemed genuinely furious. "Why would I do that?"

With a patience designed to annoy, Ziede said, "That would have been my next question, had I ever been given an answer to my first."

Saadrin grated out, "I did not give anyone a sacred ship of the Well of Thosaren, let alone an expositor." She looked at the deck, her lips thinning in disgust. "This ship's aura has been tainted. Did that abomination Kaiisteron do something to it?"

Ashem, having wrestled her own fury under enough control to regain the power of speech, said, "I told you, Aclines captured an Imperial cohort. He used them for his foul purposes aboard this ship. If any Immortal Blessed had a hand in it, the Rising World will not be pleased! The treaty is already at risk with—" Ramad touched her arm and Ashem stopped, her jaw tight. She had been about to reveal that Tahren was missing, but fortunately Saadrin was clearly not listening to her.

Ziede smiled indulgently. "As she says, Aclines created a power well with captured Rising World mortals. Possibly that's what you sense."

Saadrin's face twisted in disgust. "Where is the Fallen? Is she here? Is she a party to this?"

Kai had a bad feeling Saadrin was just as baffled as she seemed.

"More questions," Ziede said, folding her arms. Through her pearl, she admitted to Kai, *She's not that good a liar.*

She isn't, Kai agreed silently. *She doesn't know where Tahren is.* It was unlikely Saadrin was the one who had given Aclines the ship. If she had, she would have been trying to kill them already, not arguing in circles. It meant they might be able to trust Saadrin's answers, if they could get her to give them any.

"Answer me! Is she here?" Saadrin demanded.

Ziede kept the sinking disappointment out of her expression but Kai could hear it in her inner voice. "Are you telling us you don't know where she is?"

Saadrin ground out the words, "I wouldn't have asked if I knew where she was!"

Ziede eyed her, then made her decision. She said, "Tahren has been taken by an enemy, possibly along with my marriage-brother Dahin. I called on right of kin to the Blessed to ask if you have a way to find them."

Saadrin's expression turned deeply annoyed. She demanded, "Is this true? Even the Fallen would not shirk her duty at this time."

At least Saadrin wasn't pretending to be unaware of the upcoming coalition renewal and Tahren's place in it.

Ziede was derisive. "Why would I lie about such a thing?"

"I have no idea, but I'm sure there might be a reason," Saadrin assured her grimly.

Ziede didn't take the bait. "I know the rules of kin-right. You cannot deprive Tahren's dependents of her if you know where she is."

"I don't know where she is. Believe what you want." Saadrin tried to stare Ziede down, but Kai could have told her that was impossible. "I have no knowledge of Dahin's whereabouts, either. But even you must understand the Lesser Blessed's connection to the Well of Thosaren is not the same."

"I understand." Ziede paused, to let Saadrin think for a heartbeat that she might give up. Then she said, "But you must know of a way to find her. I've seen you do it before."

From the tightness around her mouth, Saadrin clearly didn't want to talk about that stain on the Immortal Blessed's history. But she admitted, "Our ways of searching for errant Blessed are not as comprehensive as they were under the Hierarchs. The Fallen has not been considered a criminal for some time." She didn't sound as if this was a development she agreed with.

Ziede nodded, and prompted, "But you can find her."

"I cannot." Saadrin was obviously more than reluctant; the kin-right to a Witch must drag at her like an anchor stone. "But the Conventiculum of the Immortals at Stios has the finding stones."

Finding stones? Ziede asked Kai silently. *She means the finding stones that the Hierarchs used to keep track of their pet Immortal Blessed?*

Probably. The Rising World would have handed them over during the treaty negotiations, Kai replied.

The Conventiculum was on an island in the harbor of Stios, the city that had been the principal port of supply and travel for the Hierarchs' Summer Halls. It had been a sea people city-state before the Hierarchs took it, and many of the inhabitants had been killed. It had fared better than Orintukk, since the Hierarchs had moved in a new population to be the dockworkers and shipwrights and sailors. It was a trading city now in the Rising World, though not as populous as either of its past two incarnations. The wrecked hulks of the Hierarchs' ships still cluttered the water and made navigation into its port tricky.

The Conventiculum still belonged to the Immortal Blessed; treaty agreements had allowed them continued ownership of some of the places the Hierarchs had given them. The Rising World coalition had wanted them out of the war more than they wanted the territory returned. The people who had lived there before the Hierarchs were all mostly dead, anyway, or scattered to the winds.

Through her pearl, Ziede's mind felt bright and hard with suspicion and disbelief, though she let none of it show on her face. *The Hierarchs used those stones to keep the Immortal Marshalls on a leash, and she's just told us—us!—where to find them?*

Convenient, isn't it? Kai told her, *But it's given me an idea.*

Ziede said aloud, "If we go there and ask, we can find her?"

"If they will admit a Witch or a demon." Saadrin bared her perfect teeth in an expression that was not a smile. She obviously knew something about the Conventiculum that they didn't, but if it was just the unlikelihood of the caretakers admitting them, it was hard to tell. Saadrin continued, "Now tell me how you will return this stolen ship."

She obviously expected Ziede to argue, but Kai said, "Tell us which Immortal Blessed it belongs to and where to bring it to dock, and we'll take it there."

Saadrin's brows knit as she searched for a way to argue with that. She didn't want to claim responsibility for the ship herself. If it had been handed over to an expositor without the knowledge of the Immortal Patriarchs, in violation of the Rising World treaty and Blessed law, someone was going to be in deadly trouble. "I told you, I don't know."

Ziede, taking up the threads of Kai's thought, said, "When you find out, send me a message. I don't wish to abandon this ship where any pirate or thief could take it."

Saadrin's mouth thinned in irritation. "You cannot expect me to leave it in your care."

Ziede was unmoved. "I have not renounced my kin-right. I need this ship to go to Stios to the Conventiculum and find my liege-sworn wife."

Saadrin folded her arms. "Then I will remain with it."

Ziede let out a breath and looked at Kai. Silently she said, *Can we fight to the death instead?*

The river that met the sea at Orintukk was mated to the old canal network that joined the Arkai to the Arik and beyond. *Only if you really want to,* Kai replied silently, *but I think I know a better way.*

———

Skeptical, Ramad said, "Will she really help you?"

They had withdrawn into the stern cabin. Kai sat on the cushioned bench, leaning back against the wall. Ziede had taken a seat on the throne, where she could lounge with her chin propped on one arm, locking stares with Saadrin, who still stood out on the deck next to the steering column. Kai said, "Help us by fighting, if we're attacked? No."

Ashem frowned. Despite all her distrust, justified and otherwise, she was a practical person. She said, "Surely she won't just stand there."

"That's exactly what she'll do," Ziede said, not moving, not blinking. "Stand there and watch."

Ramad shook his head slightly, as if he understood none of this. "And she's your kin?"

"It certainly wasn't by choice on her part." Ziede's voice was dry. She added, "One of us will have to stay with the ship until we're done with it, or she'll make off with it." Her brow furrowed a little. "And she knows the Conventiculum won't admit us. They'll certainly know a demon when they see one."

"There are ways around that." Kai looked out toward Saadrin's stubborn silhouette. Off the bow, the land was growing larger on the horizon, enough to see heavy green jungle above low cliffs, the hills rising behind it. "While you're taking the cohort off the ship at Orintukk, I'll have a look around."

Ziede sighed, audible even from here. Through her pearl, she said, *If the Conventiculum is obviously a trap, you don't need to do that disgusting thing.*

It might come in handy, he replied.

Sanja poked her head out of a cabin. "Can I come out? She's not going to kill us?"

Tenes patted the cushion between her and Kai, and Sanja came to plop down on it.

Frowning in Saadrin's direction, Ashem asked, "What is the Conventiculum? A temple of the Immortal Blessed? I've seen it from the Stios harbor, but I didn't realize it was in use."

Ziede said, "The Hierarchs gave it to the Immortal Marshalls for a command post during the war. The story was that the Hierarchs made sure they had some kind of power over the building. The Blessed still keep it, but I don't think they do much with it."

Ramad clearly found all this increasingly dubious. "Are you certain you want to trust her? The stones might not be there at all. And the place is surrounded by Witch-flags so she obviously knows you can't get in. This kin-right doesn't seem to restrict her from lying to you."

They needed to stop talking about this before Ramad figured out they had another plan. Kai said, "The Immortal Blessed are such wonderful people that they need all these rules telling them not to murder their own relatives." He asked Ziede silently, *So, we're decided?*

Yes, we're decided, she answered. Aloud, she said, "Cohort Leader Ashem, get your people ready. You'll be taking the cohort off at Orintukk as soon as we dock there."

Ashem pushed to her feet in relief, clearly ready to be done with Witches and their problems. Ramad stood to follow her, but his expression said that he knew there was something he wasn't being told.

EIGHT

From a distance the white walls of Orintukk gleamed under the bright sunlight, standing just above the waves washing against the rocky shore. As the ship drew closer, it was easier to see the untended cracks and weathering, the places where the white outer covering had worn away to show the rough blocks underneath. There were occasional signs that a road had once run between the wall and where the ground dropped off toward the water, though it was badly overgrown. There were still tumbled piles of stone visible, and a few statues or pillars that might have been distance markers.

Kai leaned on the rail, concentrating on being enigmatic and not looking as if he was frantically trying to come up with alternate plans if Orintukk didn't have what he needed. They couldn't make too many preparations in advance without alerting Saadrin or the others to their intentions.

Ziede sailed the ship around a small peninsula where dull red rooftops and tall willow trees were visible above the walls. As the ship rounded it to enter the great harbor, they saw the full sweep of the city.

Sanja whistled in startled admiration. "It's so big. I thought nothing was bigger than the Mouth of Flowers!"

The city curved nearly the whole way around the circle of the natural harbor. It was broken only by the mouth of the river, which was bridged by a structure more than four stories tall, each level terraced with round columns. The buildings along the harbor basin and on the gentle slopes behind it looked mostly intact, especially from a distance. But as they neared the docks that lined the inward curve, Kai spotted a few fallen walls, and leafy foliage standing high above the remains of collapsed roofs.

Frowning, Sanja added slowly, "It is all empty."

His voice wry, Ramad asked her, "Did you think we weren't telling you the truth?"

"No. No, but . . ." Sanja shrugged as though it didn't matter, but she was still frowning. "I just . . . couldn't really picture it in my head." She turned to Kai. "They killed everyone?"

"Everyone." Kai leaned on the railing and tried not to think about Kentdessa. "It's a big, beautiful grave marker."

"It was much written about, in its day." Ramad's expression was regretful. "They said no one ever went hungry here. Food was so plentiful, everyone got a share of millet and teff whenever they needed, just like getting water from the well. The methods for it were adopted by the Great Bashasa to feed the refugees and partisans, and are still used across the Arik and other Rising World territories today."

That was true, it was a little living piece of Orintukk preserved. Just like the way the Saredi system of tent assemblies formed the basis for the Rising World's council. But Kai said, "I heard it was honey wine and almonds," just to get on Ramad's nerves.

Annoyingly, Ramad refused to be baited. "I don't think they made much wine here. It's more gourd country."

The long stone docks were mostly empty, except for a few small fishing boats clustered at one end, almost hidden by the tall pilings. The fishers were living in the port itself; a large stone market pavilion was strung with nets, and smoke from campfires stained the white walls.

But as the Immortal Blessed ship angled to draw up to a dock, the new vantage point let Kai see past the mouth of the river. There was a smaller set of docks there for travel inland, the broken remnants of old barges half-sunk between the rotting wooden pilings.

That'll do, Kai thought in relief. It wouldn't be easy, but it would work. Easy would have been finding an intact craft they could use, but this would be enough.

Saadrin was still out on the upper deck, standing at the opposite rail, arms folded, keeping her face expressionless, though she couldn't seem to control the air of disgruntlement hanging over her like a cloud. Kai suspected she had been looking forward to watching Ashem's cadre fumble while trying to dock the large ship, but Ziede's air-devils had no trouble guiding and nudging it into place at the long merchant pier.

From this vantage point, the fishers were visible, gathered on a patch of sand and rocks down where the port's retaining wall had collapsed. They had been washing clothes and crockery in the small pool formed by the fallen blocks. Now they watched the Immortal Blessed ship's arrival with open astonishment and curiosity.

On the lower deck, Ashem directed her cadre to climb down the side to secure the mooring. Kai turned to Ziede, who stood a short distance away sketching a finding circle in the palm of her hand with a mix of spit and blood. Tenes was at her elbow, watching with interest. Kai didn't move any closer so he wouldn't block the air currents Ziede was calling.

Ziede drew in the airborne spirits from the forest to tell her what predators hunted through the distant scatters of habitation outside the city. The empty countryside would be tempting to people who had nowhere else to go, with ruins that could be rebuilt and the wild remnants of the dead city's crops and livestock. These people would be isolated and vulnerable, the prey of creatures that lived on the margins of the mortal world, drawn here by the Hierarchs' passage or the power well created by so many mortal deaths.

As the spirits moved the blood mixture on Ziede's hand, telling her about the entities they brushed past in the surrounding forests, she muttered, "Some soul-stealer ghosts, bone-eating vines, not really anything too terrible."

"There has to be at least one," Kai said. They clung to the fringes of death wells like cockroaches to middens.

"Hush," Ziede told him. "Wait, here we are." She drew more lines on her palm, turning it into a rough map. "That's the old road, that's the river, and here it is."

Kai stepped closer to see. It was a very rough map, but it told him which direction to start out in. Once he got closer, he would be able to track the predator. "I'll be back as fast as I can." He signed to Tenes, *Try to get the supplies together without Saadrin noticing. Sanja can help.*

With a flicker of a smile, Tenes signed assent. Kai didn't think she would be sad to see the last of this ship.

Ziede looked up and grimaced. The ship was tied off, and the cadre was now working on opening the door in the railing so the gangway could be attached to the side. Ramad and Ashem had already gone down the dock toward the port buildings, probably to look for a place to shelter the cohort while they waited for help. "Getting those people ashore is going to take a while."

The cadre members leaned over the side, trying to get the gangway positioned. Kai thought they should have attached the hooks to the rungs on the deck first, but it was a little late to offer that advice now. Saadrin just watched with an unhelpful sneer. Sanja had gone closer to see, but was too innately cautious to get within arm's reach of any of them. He told Ziede, "Just stay alert." She would have to go down to the rowing deck to help Ashem. They would need to detach each unconscious mortal from the now static power well.

Ziede pressed her lips together, studying the group at the railing. She had probably noticed they were doing it backward, too. But she said, "We're giving them what they want." The words *they have no reason to attack us* were unspoken.

Kai didn't snort in derision, because he didn't want to annoy her any more than Saadrin already had. "When has that ever made a difference?"

She sighed. "Just take care. If you're killed in a ridiculous way by a mere ghoul, it will be embarrassing for all of us."

Kai squeezed her hand, and vaulted the railing to drop down to the dock.

Ramad and Ashem had reached the retaining wall and climbed down to speak to the fishers. Some had the darker brown skin of local Arkai, with a few lighter archipelago natives scattered among them. All had their clothing and hair tied up for wading in the rocks. They seemed naturally wary, but also a little excited, as if nothing interesting had happened here for a long time. They were all as barefoot as Kai; he needed to feel the currents of the land and it was easier with direct skin contact.

His route to the big avenue took him past the market pavilion. Inside were a few elders and children, and bags, baskets, drying laundry, a hearth built from salvaged stone, the other debris of a long-term camp. The children stopped playing to watch him, and he heard someone whisper the old sea people word for Witch. The open arches were hung with protective charms, little constructions of shells, twigs, broken glass, and polished pebbles strung together with string.

Once out of the sea port, the central road was wide and unobstructed, though weeds grew in every drift of dirt. Kai walked past the dusty sun-bleached walls of empty houses, arcaded pavilions, round mausoleums, cracked plazas. It was quiet, except for birdcalls, the buzz and click of insects, and the occasional voice echoing from the port. Under the calm of a deserted place, there was power here, rising up from the ground in waves like heat on hard-packed earth. The Hierarchs had turned Orintukk into a major power well but never completely drained it. Kai had wondered if that would be the case; he could have done this working without it, but an exterior power source would make it easier.

Kai made his way around toward the river, emerging from the avenue to see the wide stretch of muddy water, bordered by terraces and buildings covered with intricate carvings of people, sea creatures, ships, unfamiliar symbols. He followed a walkway down past a couple of bridges, until he found the docks, just behind the four-story colonnaded structure built across the river's mouth. A broad pavement led to stone stairs down to what had obviously once been a bustling river port, but now was a decaying mass of wood along the weedy bank.

The docks had mostly rotted away under the constant force of the river, and rushes grew along the banks and between the wrecked remnants of barges. Kai picked his way through the silt, searching for the right one. It wasn't the state of decay he was interested in, but the remaining resonance. A barge that had been used longer, preferably by the same set of mortals, would have the most willingness to return to its former state.

He found one half-sunken, not much left of it but the long, curved prow and the ribs. Ankle-deep in mud, Kai squelched closer until he could put his hand on the sun-dried wood. *Yes, this one.*

He climbed back up to the bank and spent some time clearing a spot on the broken pavement, wishing he had thought to borrow a broom. Did the Immortal Blessed even use brooms? Kai didn't think he had seen anything like one on the ship.

Once that was done, he drew his knife and made a mixture of his blood, spit, and the mud the barge had been decomposing in to draw a cantrip roughly the size of the original craft, leaving one small section open. This was a combination of an expositor's intention and a Witch's working. The cantrip let him speak to what was left of the barge's inhabiting spirit, to draw it out and let it shape itself inside his design, where he could feed it power like an intention, drawn from the well of death that had formed inside Orintukk.

Once the spirit had fully entered the cantrip, Kai closed it off with the last of the blood mixture. With everything in place, there wasn't much more to do than wait. But he had one more errand, one that would explain his absence.

He left the river port and found the avenue that led toward the city's outskirts. It was warmer and wetter here, and he was glad he hadn't bothered with a coat. At the city's edge, the buildings had all turned into collapsed piles of stone and tile, and lush growth invaded the pavement. Ramad hadn't been joking about the gourds, Kai found himself tripping over their vines every other step.

The brush and tall grass gave way to larger trees, with smooth reddish bark and heavy branches twisting down to rest on the ground. The thick canopies blocked out the sunlight, leaving the path winding through a dim green cavern, noisy with the roar of singing cicadas. He wondered if the people who had lived here had harvested them to eat the way they did in Erathi. As the path grew darker, Kai called a chorus of imps, not so much to light his way but to let anything that might trouble him know that it was better not to.

Well-traveled pathways often created a sense of disturbance that he could feel cutting through the flow of energy in the earth. But these pathways weren't well traveled anymore. The maze of small roads and walkways for surrounding villages and farms was overgrown. The big stone-paved road that had once led toward the next major Arkai city was still there, unused and slowly being overtaken by grass. In that state it was far less disruptive to the land's flow of power and so harder to sense. But the roar of life that was the jungle and grassland was divided by a dead zone that he knew was the river, its waters opaque to him.

He slipped through the brush to step onto a nearly invisible pathway marked by broken chunks of paving, and made his way toward the predator Ziede had located. Ferns and colorful vines took advantage of breaks in the tree canopy and it was even warmer here than in the city, sheltered from the wind off the sea. He passed a scatter of ramshackle huts with gardens bounded by stick fences, and heard mortal voices somewhere past the trees. No one tried to approach the lone figure accompanied by the darting lights of underearth imps.

Kai knew he was close to the spot marked on Ziede's map when he felt a sense of malicious intent. He banished the imps and cut through a thick band of trees, the undergrowth tugging at his skirts. The woven stick wall of the dwelling blended so well with the brush he almost walked into it.

There was no sound from inside, and he felt his way around until he found a door. It was curtained by a leather drape that smelled of rotted human skin. *This must be the place*, Kai thought dryly. He brushed it aside and stepped in.

Mold grew across the thatched rafters, illuminating the interior as Kai's vision adjusted. The wooden walls were covered with bamboo racks holding the body-stealing ghoul's hoard. Arms, legs, hands, and feet were the most obvious, from a very dark brown through to the pale of almond milk, all the colors of the mortals who lived around Orintukk or passed through here on their way somewhere else. There were also organs—hearts and livers mostly, some others that Kai had never learned to recognize—plus tongues, entire heads, and finally, eyes. There was no buzz of flies or crawling maggots; the ghoul's inherent intent kept its bounty from spoiling.

The Hierarchs' legionaries had always talked of how horrific the underearth was, when their own homegrown monsters were so much worse.

Thrashing in the trees told him the ghoul was nearby, aware that an intruder had entered its hut. A few heartbeats later, it shoved through the doorway.

It looked like an ordinary male mortal, maybe a little more well-fed and prosperous than was normal for this empty land, his long cotton tunic and wrapped skirt less ragged. His graying hair was tied back and his face was weathered. If he hadn't been carrying a dead mortal body, there would have been nothing unusual about him.

"Ah, a customer!" he said in Old Imperial. He dumped the corpse on the packed dirt floor. "Incautious of you to simply walk into my home. I might be short of wares." He leered, showing sharp bloodstained teeth. "What are you willing to offer me, I wonder, to make you worth more as a buyer than as"—he gestured to the racks of glistening limbs and organs—"a lovely addition to my stock?"

Kai was suddenly sick of these grabby mortal predators, huddled in their filth, greedy for pain. He called the scattered imps to him. As their little bodies filled the hut with light, he said, "So you get many customers out here? I thought this was more a hobby than a vocation."

The ghoul made a gargling noise and whipped around to flee. Kai reached to find the tendrils of design and intent around the creature and pulled. The ghoul froze in place.

Kai stepped close, circled to face his prey, and wrapped his hand around the ghoul's throat. "Do mortals just walk into your charnel house all the time? Am I one? Am I stupid?"

The ghoul choked out, "I didn't know you were a . . ."

"Say it." Kai smiled.

". . . a demon."

"You idiot." Kai leaned closer to whisper, "I'm *the* demon."

THE PAST:
THE BATTLE

The Immortal Marshalls' part in the Hierarchs' war was always in dispute . . . The Immortal Blessed have always valued isolation and claimed superiority, setting themselves above the rest of the world. They would never want to admit to being as helpless before the force of the Hierarchs' invasion as the mortal lands. It was an unprecedented concession when the Immortal Marshalls eventually revealed that they initially resisted the Hierarchs but were ordered to capitulate when they found themselves unable to protect the Blessed Lands from attack. There was no shame, the whole of the known world was helpless then. But the Immortal Marshalls were seen to serve the Hierarchs so the Immortal Blessed will always be viewed as willing allies to their conquerors. That Tahren Stargard rebelled when she did is their sole saving grace.

—Writings of Weranan, historian of Seidel-arik

They left the Benais-arik Hostage Courts through an open door that led into a much bigger, better-tended court. Large trees grew in planting beds, their canopies like a tent roof overhead, a scatter of red leaves like blood spatter across the paving. There were only two legionaries, not particularly alert. Tahren walked briskly up to them as if she meant to speak, then whipped her sword around and took off both their heads at one stroke.

As Tahren reached the archway at the far end of the court,

Ziede said, "Wait!" There was no gate, but Kai sensed something across the opening, something that tasted of an expositor's power.

Tahren stopped, glancing at Ziede with lifted brows.

Keeping her voice low, Ziede explained, "There's an intention across the opening. If the Hierarchs decide to kill everyone here, they don't want to waste time breaking down doors and gates. But they want to know whenever anyone enters or leaves."

Tahren made a gesture for her to go ahead. The still air shifted as a tiny wisp of power slipped from Ziede's hand and into the archway. Kai couldn't tell what its source was, except that it was soft and insubstantial, something like the air right before a sun rain. Kai said, "Is this how you got in without the Hierarchs knowing?"

She nodded, preoccupied. "Yes, Bashasa got me to this point rolled up in a rug, then I suspended the barrier long enough to slip through." She moved her hands in slow fluid gestures, weaving something out of air.

"It's why they kill Witches," Tahren said.

Kai turned to face her and Ziede slid a languid look over her shoulder.

Tahren looked from Kai to Ziede, and appeared to realize she needed to clarify. "Your abilities are different from the expositors'. You slip through the cracks no matter how powerful they are. It frightens them."

"It should," Ziede said. She turned her attention back to the barrier. "I suspect it was Cantenios who this was meant to warn, but there may be others." She added, "There. This will stay open long enough for Bashasa's people to get through without setting off any alarms."

Tahren nodded toward Kai. "Speaking of alarms."

"I know, I know." Ziede started untying the sash at her waist.

"What?" Kai didn't understand. Oh, his eyes. "Wait, are people going to be able to see us? Aren't we . . . going a back way or—"

Tahren's eyebrows quirked. "There is no back way."

Ziede shook out her sash, a filmy diaphanous gold. She draped it over Kai's head where it rested like a cobweb, low enough to screen his face. "Now let's go."

The archway led them through a short tunnel, the end opening into a wider corridor. Tahren paused and said to Kai, "There are people from all over the conquered territories in this palace. No one should notice us, if we behave as if we have nothing to hide."

"I get the idea," Kai said, annoyed. He knew he must look nervous. His shoulders were as stiff as if he had rigor mortis. These wide, high-ceilinged stone corridors were like walking through a cave where something might leap out at you at any moment. The veil made it hard to see and the material kept sticking to his face. He kept his gaze on the floor, the worn paving stones and the moss or occasional scrawny flower growing between them.

Ziede took Kai's hand. "We're visitors, escorted by an Immortal Marshall."

Tahren gave her a nod and they walked out into the corridor. It was wider, taller, more brightly lit, with silk banners and painted emblems mounted on the upper levels. Bashasa would be coming out soon with the Arike soldiers. The investiture would have meant more people moving through here, more confusion that they could have taken advantage of. "I'm sorry," Kai whispered, his breath stirring the veil. "I shouldn't have . . . done that."

Ziede squeezed his hand. "I don't see how we would have gotten out alive if you hadn't."

Tahren added, "The Temple Halls and the Imperial Halls are both equally . . . impossible situations, so it hardly matters."

Kai grimaced. That really didn't help.

Ziede snorted quietly. "Thank you for that reassurance."

Tahren glanced back, her expression dry.

They passed a quartet of legionaries going the other way, following two figures so wrapped up in veils that Kai could tell nothing about them. After they passed and were out of earshot, Ziede winced. "We need to look more natural."

Tahren said, "An admirable goal."

In a low but conversational tone, Ziede said, "Kai, did Bashasa tell you how he and the Immortal Marshall got you out of the Cageling Court without anyone knowing?"

Kai hadn't retained a lot of what Bashasa had said right after he had woken, but he remembered that. "He said he left a dead body in my place."

"Yes. It was his sister's body."

Startled, Kai looked up at her, not that he could see any subtleties of expression through the veil. Cantenios had said something to Bashasa—taunted Bashasa, actually—with condolences for a death. And Bashasa had told the servants to bring clothes from his sister's trunk. He had just assumed the sister was around somewhere.

Ziede glanced down at Kai. "His younger sister. She was weapon training with a few of her soldiers, in a practice court they were given access to. Some servant-nobles from the Hierarchs' court appeared and challenged them, supposedly to a friendly sparring bout. The girl was struck in the stomach and the back with the end of a short spear." Tahren was listening, too, her head cocked slightly. "She seemed well at first, then became badly ill and died a day later. Bashasa has no doctor of his own, and the one provided by the palace was useless."

Another group of nobles and legionaries passed, these in a kind of dress Kai didn't recognize, long gauzy robes in rich greens and pale yellows, their heads shaved, gold circlets standing out against dark skin. Listening to Ziede, Kai barely took them in, and knew he and Tahren must look much more like people who belonged here, having a conversation as they walked through the corridors.

Ziede continued, "This was before I came here, so I only saw the girl after she died. The nobles claimed they weren't responsible for the death because there was no open wound, only bruises. For all I know, they believe it." She dropped her voice again, cautious of any listeners. They had turned into a higher open hall, one wall all archways looking down into a larger court filled with trees and ornamental ponds and streams. "The servant-nobles who came here from the south are appallingly ignorant about medical matters, anything to do with their own bodies, which are considered profane by their own dogma. Bashasa had paid one of the lesser expositors to suspend the corpse's natural corruption, to preserve it, supposedly so it could be transported back to Benais-arik to the family mausoleum. I think that's when Bashasa had the idea to free the demons in the Cageling Court." She tightened her grip on Kai's hand. "He said he had seen the demons and thought it was cruel, and typical of the Hierarchs, and a great pity they couldn't be let out to ravage the Hierarchs' elite who took so much interest in staring at them. And he felt that way before they killed his sister."

Tahren glanced back and said, "So, he's a grief-stricken madman."

At first, Kai had thought Bashasa was angry about being a hostage, angry in an abstract way about losing control over his city-state, losing his political power. But his anger was more visceral than that. He said, "He's just like us."

Ziede's smile was wry. Tahren ducked her head for a heartbeat, as if concealing an involuntary expression.

They took a turn down another corridor, and Kai heard the patter of rain. Enna's heart thumped in his chest and he almost stopped, but managed to keep his legs moving. There was a short flight of upward stairs, and then he got a lungful of damp air laced with the coppery odor of blood.

Kai didn't falter, he thought he was controlling his expression, but he was grateful for the concealing veil. Ziede tugged him closer. At the top of the stairs they crossed into the roofed gallery, placed here specifically for the entertainment of the court, so they could look down on the captured demons and admire the Hierarchs' power without getting wet. The open balustrade allowed a view down onto the court where light rain and mist fell in continuous waves. Kai kept his eyes on Tahren's tense back and his gaze averted from the huddled chained figures on the pavement.

There were several servant-nobles here now, leaning against the balustrade and deep in conversation, as if the view wasn't any different from the garden court with the ornamental streams. A half dozen legionaries, probably tasked as the nobles' bodyguards, were stationed at each end of the gallery. Tahren passed them without a glance. Their gazes followed her watchfully but they didn't speak.

Tahren led Kai and Ziede to the exit at the far end of the gallery and down a short flight of steps, the stone damp with mist. They turned into a smaller corridor, out of sight of the viewing gallery. A single legionary stood there, near a metal door set deep into the stone wall.

The face under the close-fitting metal helm was young, open, guileless; this wasn't an important post. One of the first things the Saredi and their allies had learned about the Hierarchs was that many of the common legionaries were conscripts from conquered peoples.

Tahren said, "A word, please," and then slammed the legionary's head back against the stone. His helmet banged off the wall and she drove her fist into his face. Bone cracked. She caught the limp body as it slid down the wall.

Ziede let go of Kai to move closer to the door. She hissed, "They heard that."

Kai stepped back into view of the gallery entrance and said in Imperial, "Sorry! I dropped it." He leaned over as if scooping something up from the floor.

Ziede raised her voice to add, "Careful, child."

Kai flicked a glance toward the nobles and legionaries and saw them turn to continue their conversation. He stepped back out of sight and whispered, "Be more shitting quiet." If they were caught now, Ziede and Tahren might seem plausible long enough to bluff it out, but Kai was a demon under a flimsy veil with a Blessed cutting tool stuffed in his tunic. Even for the dullest legionary, those connections were going to be obvious.

He expected Tahren to ignore him or be angry, but she just mouthed, "Sorry," as Ziede wove air through the intentioned lock on the door handle. She pushed it open to reveal a narrow well. A spiral stair led upward to a source of wan daylight. Tahren hauled the limp legionary inside and Ziede and Kai slipped in after her. Kai tugged the heavy door shut. There was no way to bar it.

Ziede said, "I'll create a seal—"

Tahren held up a hand to stop her. "A seal can be undone, as you've just demonstrated." She took a sheathed dagger out of her tunic and slipped it through the metal loop on the door to hold it shut.

"I'm impressed," Ziede said dryly.

Tahren flicked an unreadable look after her. Kai just wanted to get on with it and raced up the stairs.

At the top, lit by daylight falling down from a shaft in the low ceiling, was a large square stone basin, maybe twenty paces long and wide. It was waist-high to Kai, the water swirling gently.

There was no power in it that he could sense, not in the damp air above, not in the water when Kai tentatively flicked his fingers in it. He leaned over the stone lip to look down, but it was empty all the way to the bottom, the water a little clouded but not enough to hide anything. He turned, looked around the room desperately. He must have missed something.

In the far wall, the one facing into the court, was a row of windows. Kai ran to the first and had to stand on tiptoes to see out. The wall was thick, more than the length of his forearms. He couldn't get more than a glimpse of the decorative scrolling on the roof of the opposite gallery, just above the heavy layer of mist.

Kai turned back to the basin. Whatever controlled the court had to be in there. The rest of the room was empty, just a bare chamber. He circled around, baffled, and finally noticed there were holes drilled under the inside edges of the basin, just above the waterline. Some drained water away, some filled it with steady streams.

Tahren and Ziede still searched the room, looking for hidden panels in the walls and floor, apparently as confused as Kai. He said, "It has to be this basin. There's nothing else here. How do we break it?" The stone was thick, twice as wide as the span of Kai's hands. He couldn't drain the life from stone.

Ziede looked pointedly at Tahren. Tahren said, "I was told it was delicate."

"Told by who?" Ziede demanded.

"Expositors brag while in their cups," Tahren said pointedly. "I explained this before."

"I don't care what you were told," Kai said. He knew he was being unreasonable but they were so close. "This is not delicate. This is stone and water. There's no life in it, no power."

Ziede grimaced in frustration. "The intention that drives it must be hidden somewhere. This is just the water it uses."

Kai snarled. He slammed a hand into the water, splashing Tahren's light tunic. If he tried to go into the court with the rain still falling, he wouldn't be able to fight, he could be caught by any legionary with a cursebreaker. "We have to go back down, you have to try to stop it from inside. I can't—"

"Block the holes," Tahren said.

Ziede blinked. "Ah." She grimaced again, but the irritation seemed directed at herself now. "We could do that. Of course."

Kai stared at Tahren, the breath harsh in his lungs, as the simple solution sunk in. He said, "I'm sorry I splashed you."

Tahren made a slight movement indicative of a shrug.

Ziede braced her hands on the lip of the pool and a breath of damp air brushed past Kai's face. A breeze flowed in through the windows. The water shivered, wavelets chased each other in odd

crossed patterns. Ripples grew at the waterline. Ziede's brow furrowed and she muttered, "This is harder than it looks."

"It looks hard." Tahren's gaze was on Ziede, a faint line of worry
between her brows.

The breeze grew harsher, plastered Kai's veil to his face so he
pulled it off. He flinched away as the water rocked and slopped
out of the basin. But the waves settled and troughs formed at the
rim, created by the air Ziede manipulated. The troughs forced
the water away from the sides and the drain holes. Kai's fingers
curled into claws as tense moments stretched. Then the streaming water abruptly slowed to a trickle.

Kai dashed to the first window again, reached through to hook
his hands around the outer sill and pull himself up to see. In the
court the mist was clearing, the patter of rainfall slowing to a drip.
He dropped back to the floor, heart pounding. "It's working!"

A hollow metal bang spun him toward the stairs. It came
from the room below, from the door. Tahren winced. Ziede, jaw
tight with effort, all her concentration and attention on the basin, didn't move. Someone must have noticed the change, come
to investigate, and sounded an alarm when they found the guard
missing.

It didn't matter. Kai had known there was no way out of this.
He turned and jumped up to grip the wide sill of the window
again. "I'm going down there."

Tahren said, "I'll hold them as long as I can." She vaulted the
stair railing and dropped into the room below.

Kai dug his sandals into the rough stone wall, heaved himself
up and through. Before he could think too much about it, he
rolled out of the narrow window into the sick misty air of the
Cageling Demon Court. He turned the fall into a flip and landed
feet first on the edge of the gallery roof. The slate was slick with
water and he crouched to keep his balance.

The mist had almost dissipated. With it gone, Kai saw the

arched ceiling overhead for the first time, the carved designs of clouds. The whole space was taller than he had realized and there were open balconies above the viewing gallery that he had never noticed. The light rain was now barely a dampness in the air, though the eaves still dripped. He felt his feet slide, turned it into a controlled fall and landed on the wet paving below.

He had never been able to stand up in the court and it looked different from this angle, like an unknown if equally horrible place. The floor was dotted with what looked like heaps of ragged soaked clothes, attached to clumps of dark tangled hair, brown limbs. The demons who were sitting up were curled in on themselves, their heads drooping. There were around fifty captives, but that was counting those who looked as if their borrowed bodies were abandoned. And Bashasa's poor dead sister.

Kai had no idea what happened to a demon who tried to leave their body when a return to the underearth was impossible. The idea that it might be less painful than the court was unlikely.

Kai's heart pounded and every instinct in Enna's body screamed at him to run, to jump for the gallery and fight his way out. Instead he pulled his coat open and dug out the cutting tool. He threw himself down beside the nearest slumped figure.

The stench of rotting waterlogged skin, the feel of the wet pavement made his hands shake. He fumbled for the demon's chains. It felt like an endless stretch of time but it was really only a few heartbeats before he figured out the trick of cutting at the joins. He snapped the three connections, to free ankles, wrists, and neck, of the unmoving demon. Then he remembered he should be talking to them. He shoved to his feet and went to the next. "I'm a Prince of the Fourth House, late Enna of the line of Kentdessa Saredi." Kai raised his voice to carry, speaking Saredi so the legionaries on the gallery wouldn't understand. "Two Hierarchs are in the Temple Halls. We're going to kill them, and ask you to fight with us!"

Alarmed voices shouted from the gallery. Kai ignored them,

frantically cutting chains, moving from one huddled demon to the next. Some faces turned to him, crusted eyes opened, but he was too frantic to do anything but cut their chains and move on. Bashasa had expected him to know how to convince them to fight but he had no idea what else to say.

As Kai stood to reach the next demon, something slammed into his back. The shock of it knocked him forward. His forearms hit the slick paving and the tool jolted out of his hand and clanged on the stone.

Kai snarled, tried to shove upright and found his right shoulder stiff and unmoving. Pain grew in it like a hot poker under his skin. With a wince, he reached back and groped for the source. His hand found metal and he pulled; it hurt even more coming out. Hissing in fury, he found himself holding a metal crossbow bolt, fired from somewhere on the gallery.

He tossed it aside and crawled forward, grabbed up the tool again, and cut two more chains. Another bolt clanged off the paving somewhere to his left, then a second thumped into his lower back. From the new tearing agony, it had just missed his spine. Enna's body was held in a kind of stasis while Kai was in it, and any hurts would heal almost instantly, once he could get the bolts out. But Enna's body could be torn apart, or peppered with so many metal blades that it collapsed and left Kai trapped.

He got the last chain on the current demon, who tried to crawl away. Kai reached back and managed to pull the new bolt out. Two more thudded into his hip and lower back. *I don't have time for this!* Kai half lifted himself and shoved with his feet to reach the next demon. At least there was movement in the court now, freed demons scrambling or dragging themselves toward the walls, others struggling to their feet. Something thumped his left leg and he threw a look over his shoulder to see another metal bolt. Kai growled and yanked it out.

A shout, then a choked-off cry sounded from above. The next

bolt went wild, clanging off a pillar across the court. The limp body of a legionary flew out of the gallery to slam into the paving. An instant later Tahren vaulted the gallery rail and landed in the court. She ran to Kai, sword raised, then twisted away at the last instant and leapt up to slash at something in the air. Her sword rang like a bell and another bolt clattered to the floor. She said, "He's up in a balcony, I can't get to him." She glanced down at Kai, one brow lifting. He must look like a pincushion. "Is there anything I can do?"

"Pull them out!" he told her, crawling for the next set of chains.

Tahren spun to deflect another shot, then dipped down. She plucked bolts out of Kai like a child picking flowers.

It was like being torn open, but that was the only way to let Enna's body repair itself. With the bolts gone, Kai shoved forward on his hands and knees to the next cluster of demons. "Is Ziede—" A freed demon reached for Tahren's leg and Kai lunged toward them. He grabbed the demon by the scruff of the neck and shook them. "No! Don't hurt her, she's helping us! Any of you touch her, I'll tear you apart!"

He tossed the demon away and they scrambled toward the wall of the court. Still-chained demons edged away from Kai and Tahren, staring. That had got their attention in a way his appeal for help hadn't. Kai stumbled to the next demon, limping on his injured leg, his back aching as his flesh stretched to close the open wounds. As he reached the huddled shape, they lifted their head, shaking back a mane of tangled hair. "Kai-Enna?"

He stared down. The demon was in the body of an older man. His clothes were rags but pinned to the tattered coat was a small plainswolf carving, the sigil of Kanavesi Saredi. And then he recognized the face. "Arn-Nefa?" Kai flung himself down and hugged her. He almost hadn't known her. Arn-Nefa's cheeks were sunken, the skin around her eyes deeply bruised, she looked like a different person. Under the rot, she smelled like the grassplains, like the underearth in her veins.

She put her hand on his face. "I thought I heard you—I tried to call back to you, but . . ." Her voice was thick and raw.

Kai had no time for relief, no time to tell her how glad he was to see her, that she lived. "We're going to fight. There's a mortal, an Arike prince attacking the Hierarchs in the Temple Halls." He pulled back and hurriedly cut her chains.

He helped her get upright and she stumbled toward the gallery, stopping to grab another free demon's arm and haul them with her.

Encouraged, Kai raised his voice to carry. "If you want to kill Hierarchs and legionaries, follow us to the Temple Halls. Or you can lie here and rot like useless piles of shit!"

Kai cut more chains. More bolts peppered the court, striking the trapped demons. But some demons pulled the bolts out, helped others, staggered or crawled toward the walls. They were finally waking from the daze of their long painful captivity. Tahren followed Kai, her back to him as she covered him. She was trusting him to protect her, the way she was protecting him, he realized. As if his question hadn't been interrupted, she said, "Ziede sealed the stairwell. She told me to help you."

Ziede surely couldn't maintain that difficult air manipulation for much longer. They had to work faster. "Can you cut the chains with your sword?"

Tahren didn't answer and Kai spared a look up at her. Her expression was faintly troubled and he thought she was afraid of the other demons, afraid of a touch that could drain some of her immortal life away. He didn't think that would happen, that the demons now understood she was helping them. Even if it did, it was a chance he was willing to risk to get the rest of them out. But she said, "You'll be unprotected." She punctuated this by twisting and batting aside another bolt.

"I'll be fine, go! Please." His desperation must have come through because Tahren gave a short nod and whirled away across the court.

She was faster than Kai, far faster when not having to watch out for him. Her sword struck chains with a sound too high and pure to be called a clang, she moved too fast for even a confused demon to try to catch her. Kai turned back to cut the next set of chains and immediately got struck in the back by another bolt.

But recovering demons climbed the wall to the gallery and as they swarmed up mortals started to scream. The legionaries on the upper balcony aimed their crossbows at the carnage there, which allowed Kai to move faster. He cut the last set of chains in this part of the court, saw Tahren would finish the other side faster without him. He turned to help the more mobile demons drag the others toward the walls. "We have to get them to the gallery," he told the nearest, still using Saredi. "A Witch is holding the water back but she can't do it for long."

"What tent?" someone asked him.

"Kentdessa. Kill the Hierarchs in the Temple Halls, not the Arike, they're helping us. Tell the others." He repeated this over and over, hoping they were listening.

Someone else pulled the bolts out of his back. Then the demons on the gallery wrested a crossbow from some dying mortal and the legionary archers on the upper balconies tumbled down to the paving stones.

Kai turned back for another demon to drag to shelter and found himself looking at an empty court. A muted thump shook the walls and water abruptly gushed down from above. Kai staggered, his limbs suddenly weak, all the strength knocked out of him in one hammer blow. He fell to one knee, gasping for air.

It wasn't the deluge, a brief exposure shouldn't do this. It was the memory of helplessness, of being trapped here . . . It left him stunned, froze his blood. He flailed, tried to struggle upright. Then Tahren was suddenly beside him.

She grabbed him around the waist and the world swung as she lifted him and slung him over her shoulder. He couldn't see anything but the back of her tunic but he felt her take a long step. Then with a jolt they were in the shelter of the gallery.

She lifted him down and set him on his feet. Freed demons crowded near as the rain poured down into the court. Tahren plucked a last bolt out of Kai's arm, then took his shoulders and shook him gently.

"What are you doing?" Kai managed. He was rattling around inside Enna's body, like he might drift out of it any instant.

"Trying to revive you," Tahren said. Her expression was grave and calm, not at all as if they had done the impossible.

"Stop, stop," Kai said, pushing her hands away. "Please, thank you." Water dripped from his clothes and hair onto the gallery floor. Demons watched him, battered, sick, angry. Mortal bodies lay underfoot, desiccated or bloody. Kai drew in a breath and made himself focus. "The Temple Halls. Which way?"

Tahren pointed. "Out that side, then the leftward hall."

"Go!" Kai yelled. "Kill the Hierarchs in the Temple Halls! Leave the Arike, they're allies!" He was a little shocked when the demons actually turned to stream down the gallery.

"There." Tahren breathed the word in relief. Kai hadn't heard her express that much emotion about anything and glanced at her in confusion. Then he saw Ziede floating down to the floor of the Cageling Court.

She must have crawled out through the narrow window like Kai had. Her clothes were soaked from the rain and disheveled, her gold eye-paint smeared.

Tahren stared at her as if stricken.

Huh, Kai thought. That was a surprise. But everything today was a surprise, like finding Arn-Nefa, like the fact that they were still alive for the moment.

Ziede drifted almost to the gallery railing and said, "What are you waiting for? Have you lost your minds? Get to the motherless Temple Halls! If I did this for nothing I will end both of you myself!"

Tahren seized Kai's arm and pulled him along, until his brain caught up with his body and he pushed forward through the demons. Ziede's appearance invigorated them, especially those who had been held captive longer, were more ragged and battered, their borrowed bodies worn down and closer to collapse. "A Witch," voices murmured, in the dialects of the far western grasslands clans, of the borders of Erathi. "Witches are here, Witches are with us."

By the time Kai and Tahren got out of the gallery and reached the leftward corridor, they were in the front of the pack. Tahren let go of Kai and strode forward to lead the way and he jogged to keep up with her.

Alarms must be spreading through the Summer Halls. Legionaries charged from a cross corridor and with barely any chance to scream went down under a pile of demons. Kai remembered Bashasa describing his plan, saying that the legionaries in the palace were not experienced soldiers, they were jailers and torturers. All they would know about demons was how to hurt them, when they arrived bound and helpless to be carted into the Cageling Court. *Right again,* Kai thought. For a grief-stricken madman, Bashasa had been right about a lot of things so far.

Tahren led them past a junction of smaller corridors, then took the next turn down a wider, taller processional avenue. The upper walls were lined with the banners of conquered places, the mounted heads and bones of defeated leaders, stolen treasures of gold headdresses, jewels, weapons, wooden masks, ivory icons, everything imaginable. Somebody angry had passed along this way before them. Trophies had been pulled down, a decorated shield discarded on the floor, scraps of fabric left spiked into the wall from where banners had been torn away. Then shouting and screams and the clash of weapons echoed from the end of the avenue. Kai ran faster.

He reached the archways a step behind Tahren.

They were at the top of a broad set of stairs, the vast Temple

Halls spread out before them. It was a canyon with multiple levels of galleries lining its walls, the pitched glass roof letting in shafts of sunlight. Against the far side below the Hierarch banners was a set of raised platforms; they were empty now, all the fighting concentrated in the center of the chamber.

Kai expected a confused melee but Bashasa and his soldiers and a random assortment of other mortals had been corralled into the center of the room, and were completely surrounded. Kai couldn't see any Hierarchs or expositors, just a few officers' tails among the legionaries. Someone in Bashasa's group waved a blue and purple banner, probably an Arike trophy taken from the processional hall. This was hardly the grand gesture of resistance to fuel rebellion that Bashasa had hoped for.

Kai felt his mouth shape a grin. *Let's see what we can do about that.*

He plunged down the steps and sprinted across the marble floor. He didn't care if the other demons followed or not. The only goal was to cause as much carnage as possible, to do to this place of honor for the Hierarchs what they had done to the grasslands.

Kai hit the first legionary from behind, caught hold of armored shoulders and pulled himself up, slapped a hand over the mortal's face to rip his life away. As the man collapsed under him Kai launched himself forward. He landed on another legionary who fell under his weight; Kai took him through the gap between helmet and collar. Someone drove a knife into his chest and he gripped their hand, draining their life before they could pull away. Screaming, panicked shouting, the heady taste of enemy life filled Kai's brain and there was nothing else.

Kai didn't come back to himself until he stood in an open circle, dead legionaries scattered around him. His clothes were bloody, he had cuts and slashes he didn't remember. The astonishing part was that the other demons were here, too. The fighting was everywhere now, decayed bodies scattered across the hall. He spotted Arn-Nefa, leading a dozen other demons, driving panicked legionaries across the floor like frightened ducks. The demons had broken the siege on Bashasa's people, rolling over the Halls like an avalanche.

More legionaries burst in through an entrance in the side wall, but scattered groups of armed mortals poured in from the processional avenue. Some must be the other Arike from the Hostage Courts, but there were so many others of all different descriptions and dress.

Maybe Bashasa actually had ignited a rebellion, at least among the other hostages inside the palace.

The nearest demons looked at Kai and he realized they were waiting for orders. *Uh-oh*, he thought. Kai had never been a captain. He needed to find Bashasa or Tahren, somebody who knew how to organize the chaos.

Across the width of the chamber three legionaries suddenly flew up into the air, then slammed into a wall. That had to be Ziede. Kai spotted Bashasa and Tahren on the platform at the far end of the chamber, flanked by Arike soldiers. Bashasa fought with a short legionary spear, a torn remnant of the recaptured Arike banner wrapped around his chest. But Tahren fought like an Immortal Marshall, moving almost so fast all Kai could see was the flash of her sword. He started toward them.

He didn't realize the nearest demons moved with him until three legionaries charged him and went down under the swarm. That explained why so many of his potential opponents seemed to be scrambling to get out of his path.

Kai reached the platform and climbed the stairs, draining and tossing aside the legionaries in his way. Other demons raced up the steps on either side and crashed over and through the resistance. Suddenly the way was clear.

On the platform Arike soldiers spread out into defensive positions around Bashasa. Others took advantage of the respite to retrieve their wounded. As Kai reached the top, Tahren lowered her sword. The only signs of how hard she had fought were the bodies piled on the surrounding platforms, the few beads of sweat on her brow, and the flecks of blood on her tabard. A bubble of quiet seemed to form around them as Kai stood beside Bashasa. He turned to the demons waiting on the steps below and said, "This is Bashasa, he's your captain now." He used the Saredi word that there was no real Imperial equivalent for, the one that meant more "leader in traveling to danger."

The demons murmured assent as Arn-Nefa and her followers reached the bottom of the steps.

Bashasa stared as if he had never seen Kai before. Kai knew his clothes were covered with slashes and blood, that his braids were unraveled because someone very foolish and now dead had grabbed his hair from behind and tried to cut his throat.

Bashasa was just as disheveled, his brocade coat sleeves slashed bloody, his knuckles scraped raw. He said, "You have a knife in your chest."

Oh, right, he did. That was what was wrong with his right arm. Kai reached to remove it but the angle was awkward.

Bashasa's brow furrowed. "You're just going to pull it out?"

"Sure." Kai didn't have the words right now to explain how Enna's body worked.

"Wait, let me." Bashasa gripped the hilt and jerked the knife free.

Kai let out a huff of breath. That did feel better. He looked out over the cavern-like space and saw the pockets of fighting growing smaller, that the new arrivals focused on the platform, watching them. Maybe they were something to watch, standing at the nave of the Temple Halls where the Hierarchs were meant to be worshipped, surrounded by dead legionaries. He asked, "Who are all these people?"

"Arike, Enalin, Ilveri from Nibet, the Grale, others I don't recognize. Hostages, emissaries of conquered client states, enslaved captives who have freed themselves," Bashasa said. He nodded toward the knots of unfamiliar Arike soldiers taking up guard positions around the Halls' entrances. "Prince-heirs Asara and Stamash have broken free of their courts and joined us." He turned to the tall gold doors behind the platform. "We think the Hierarchs are there."

Air whipped around, tossing Kai's hair and making the Arike banner flutter. Ziede dropped to the floor beside them. She said, "What are we waiting for?"

"For you," Bashasa said, no hesitation. He stepped back from Kai and dropped the legionary spear. He held a hand out and one of his Arike soldiers put her own sword hilt into it. He faced the door. His soldiers and all the others on the platform gathered behind and beside him.

Kai watched Ziede brace herself, her clothes drifting in the breeze as she drew her remaining power to her. From her guard position on Bashasa's other side, Tahren glanced at Ziede as if hoping for a look in return, but Ziede didn't notice. Kai made himself focus on the door; he knew this was the end.

A breath of air that smelled of blood and recent death tugged at Kai's clothes, ruffled Tahren's short hair. It grew rapidly stronger until Kai had to plant his feet to keep from leaning into Bashasa. Smaller mortals stumbled sideways or set their spear butts on the platform to stay in position. It didn't touch Ziede, standing like a statue in the eye of her growing whirlwind.

She made a sharp gesture and the wind slammed into the doors. The crash reverberated through Kai's bones. One heavy door buckled, the other flew off its top hinges and spun inward with a sharp crack of gilded hardwood.

Bashasa shouted and lunged for the opening. Kai surged forward with the soldiers. Then the mortals started to scream.

A heartbeat later, an invisible force closed around Kai's body. It squeezed his lungs, sapped his strength. Bashasa and the other mortals staggered, fell, lurched away. Ziede's face knotted with furious effort as she held her ground, struggling against the crushing force. Tahren kept her feet but she strained to move, barely inching forward. Kai managed a look over his shoulder and what he saw made his heart contract in despair.

The effect spread off the platform, rolled like a fog across the room, pushed even the other demons back. The unsuspecting mortals who still fought staggered or dropped to the floor, legionaries and rebels alike.

Kai had felt this for the first time on that terrible day in the hills, when it had killed Saredi and borderlanders and Witches in droves. He had never been this close to the source. Now he knew it was the Hierarchs' Great Working, preparing the power of their Well to rain death on everyone in range.

Kai stepped toward the doorway and felt a shove against his chest, like a hand planted there pushed him steadily away. It froze his heart, made his legs shake. It was draining his life, but Kai had been draining mortals all across the Halls; all that life now flooding Enna's body gave him the strength to force his way forward.

He reached the broken door and clambered across it into a chamber that was clearly some kind of retreat. Lamplight flickered against walls of figured marble and an ivory floor. Mortals were scattered around, legionaries with officer tails, richly dressed servant-nobles, all helplessly sinking under the indiscriminate effect of the conjuration. But Kai only focused on the Hierarch who stood in the center of the room and the expositor shielding him.

Kai had never seen a Hierarch this close but the stink of the Well, of pain and stolen lives, came off him in waves. He looked like a small man, dressed in a white and gold gown, with pale white hands, a pink unlined face with shaved brows and a trim white beard and long white hair. His expression was mild, as if this was only an inconvenience. And maybe it was; so far it was only his legionaries and servants who had been killed.

The expositor in front of him stood with hands outstretched, a slim figure all in black with features concealed by a veil. Frozen in place like a statue, the expositor used the Hierarchs' Well to flood the room with the numbing power that would kill everyone in range, then feed their lives back into itself.

Kai didn't want to die, didn't want Ziede and Tahren and Bashasa and all the others to die just to cause a moment of inconvenience to a Hierarch. He flung himself forward.

It was like swimming through cold mud that sapped the blood from his veins, the strength from his muscles. A flicker of movement in the corner of his eye warned him just in time to catch the arm holding the cursebreaker before it touched him.

But the wielder was just as hampered by the power of the Well as everyone else. Kai yanked them sideways and drained their life. Shoving the corpse down, he stumbled over its legs and pushed forward the last two steps toward the expositor. This close the vortex of power had the weight of a mountain and he collapsed under it.

This was what it felt like to have your life eaten away. The Hierarchs' Well pressed Kai down into the cool ivory floor as his bones creaked and bent and snapped. Neck muscles straining, he forced his head up just enough to see the expositor's gilded sandals under his skirt. Kai dragged his arm up to stretch out and grab a bare ankle.

The Well ran through the expositor's body and it should have overwhelmed Kai instantly, but it was all flowing outward to kill the mortals in the Halls. Something about that connection must have kept the expositor from fighting like Cantenios had; Kai felt the expositor's life leaching into his veins and was so shocked he almost let go. He had never expected this to work; he had just wanted the Hierarch to feel fear, to see how close one demon Saredi could come.

The crushing force of the Well ceased, rage-filled voices screamed, a heavy boot stepped on Kai's leg, then pain stabbed down into his spine. Some kind of cursebreaker, a short spear with a demon-killing intention on it, he wasn't sure. But if he was going to be forced out of Enna he was killing this expositor first. He clutched at the expositor's life with everything he had left.

Then the world went dark.

Kai came back to feel the soft scrape of ivory tile under his hands and he rolled over. He remembered crushing weight and splintering bones but nothing hurt now. Except his swimming head and the sick knot in his stomach. He saw white skirts and looked up, expecting to see the Hierarch standing over him. But it was Bashasa.

Bashasa flung out his arm. "Stop, stop!" He stared down at Kai in horror. "Sister Witch!"

Kai blinked up at him, then down to where the Hierarch sprawled in blood-soaked robes, just past Bashasa's boots. The Hierarch was dead. "Bashasa. You did it," he croaked.

Kai should have been happier about that, but he just felt exhausted. Oh, right, because he had broken all Enna's bones and a powerful cursebreaker had done something terrible to him. This was what being knocked adrift from your body was like. Except not, because Bashasa was clearly staring at him and a mortal wouldn't be able to see an adrift demon.

Ziede's voice said, "Kai?"

Bashasa said, "Here. He's here."

Ziede lunged into view, throwing herself down beside Kai. Her brow knit in an incredulous frown, which at least was better than horror-struck disbelief. She said, "Kai?"

He said, "Ziede?" His voice still sounded strange inside his own head. "Bashasa killed the Hierarch. Didn't he?"

Ziede's gold makeup was a smeared mess. He tried to reach up to wipe it away. "Kai." She took his hand. Her hands were warm and he realized how cold he was. "Did you . . . mean to do this?"

This? "To kill the expositor," Kai managed. His ankle hurt, his back ached. He was freezing cold. Worse than lying outside in an ice storm without a coat. Why did his voice sound so strange?

She squeezed his hand. "Yes, Kai, but did you mean to do this?" She took his shoulders and turned his body toward where Bashasa still stood like a statue. No, past Bashasa toward the crumpled form that lay near the dead Hierarch.

Kai was looking at himself. He was looking at Enna's body. Her eyes were open, but they were mortal eyes. Kai had never seen Enna's eyes; when he had woken in her body the first time and been shown her face in the polished metal mirror, her eyes were already the flat black wells that marked a demon habitation. Now they were brown flecked with green, dull and still with death. "Uh," he said, and his voice came out in a different tone. "That's me." Then the sick pain in his stomach welled up and his vision went black.

NINE

On the way back, Kai stopped at the edge of the forest and made a cantrip to call a messenger. He had wanted to do this earlier, but Enalin was landlocked and their cantrip didn't work on seabirds. After a time, a long-legged river bird walked out of the trees, and stood in Kai's cantrip. The message he had written there dissolved into the dust, and the bird took wing.

When Kai reached the outskirts of the sea port again the sun was shading toward afternoon and the smell of roasting fish was in the air. He went to the river docks to check the working for the barge and found it nearly complete.

On his way to the Immortal Blessed ship, he followed the dregs of Aclines' dismantled power well to a stand of tall overhanging trees. They sheltered a long low stone building with thick walls that might once have been a storehouse for perishable food. Ashem had probably chosen it because it was cool and protected from the sun, and not far from an intact well house, a little round building topped by a sculpture of leaping fish.

Kai paused in a drift of dead leaves to glance inside the storehouse. The dusty interior was now full of the semi-conscious, raggedly clad bodies of the cohort, sprawled on the hastily cleared floor or leaning back against the mossy walls. The cadre moved among them, washing faces and tending to the abraded skin on their hands, trying to make them comfortable. It was quiet except for murmuring voices and the occasional cough, though the cool air held the smell of unwashed bodies and mortal sickness.

Ziede would have released what remained of the web of intentions gradually inside the ship, and the cadre had to walk or carry them all up here, so it was a testament to Ashem's organization and the cadre's hard work that it was already done. Blankets, water jugs, baskets holding food stores had been brought from the ship to help, and Kai wondered if Saadrin had been petty about it, or had decided it was beneath her notice.

He went back up the walkway and down the broader road past the fishers' market pavilion, spotting Ramad standing with Ashem at the top of their dock. Some fishers were working on their boats, others sitting outside their pavilion repairing nets. Kai didn't see Ziede out on the upper deck and touched her heart pearl to ask, *Everything all right?*

Her reply was reassuringly immediate: *It was tedious rather than dramatic. Ashem sent two runners to the Rising World outpost right after you left. It will take them at least a day to get there, but I suspect the faster we leave, the better. Were you successful?*

On both counts. We should be able to leave soon.

Always a relief. We've packed up some supplies and we're ready when you are.

Good. I'll be aboard in a moment. Kai went down the steps and detoured toward the fisher dock. They paused their work when they saw him coming, alert and watchful but not afraid. When he dropped the ghoul's head on the salt-crusted pavement, several leapt to their feet. There was a splash and thrashing as someone fell off the boat.

Without waiting for further reactions, Kai turned to go along the retaining wall toward Ramad and Ashem. He had their complete attention already. Ramad's gaze flicked between Kai and the fishers, who had cautiously approached the ghoul's head, one leaning down to examine it with a long stick. Ashem looked aghast. Before either could get a word in, Kai said, "If there's anything else you need from the ship, get it now."

Ramad started to speak, then stared at Kai, eyes widening. Ashem took a full step back with a muffled curse. "How?" she demanded. "Is that a chimera?"

It wasn't really any of her business, but Kai asked, "Does it look like a chimera?" He brushed at the dried blood on his cheekbones. It felt strange and made his vision watery on the edges. Saadrin's attention had been drawn by the noise and she glared down at him with a thunderous face.

"No. It looks real," Ramad assured him, clearly trying to conceal mild horror. He glanced back at the fishers still poking at the ghoul's head. One made a loud exclamation of relief and another started an old sea people prayer-chant. "Who was that?"

"And did you kill him for—those?" With a grimace, Ashem jerked her head in the general direction of Kai's face.

Kai hissed out a breath. He didn't owe either of them an answer, but he was tired of being misunderstood at every turn. "It was a body-stealing ghoul. If you think it was pleasant for these mortals to live here with it nearby, you're wrong."

Ashem admitted, grudgingly, "I've heard of those. We had one sniffing around a waystation when I was first posted to the south coast."

"Body-stealing," Ramad repeated, brow furrowed as the implications set in. "And you got . . . those . . . from it?"

Kai resisted the urge to scratch or poke at his borrowed eyes. The only mirror he had been able to find was a still pool off the path in the jungle. He knew they looked natural enough to fool anyone but another Witch, which he doubted would be a problem. "The Immortal Blessed don't let Witches and demons wander around holy sites looking for old artifacts they used to use to harass and punish each other. Now do you need anything else from the ship?"

Ashem let out an annoyed breath but said with surface courtesy, "No, thank you. You're taking it to Stios now?"

Saadrin withdrew from the rail with an expression of distaste, but Kai was certain she was still listening. He told Ashem, "We're going to Stios overland. Once Ziede leaves the ship, Saadrin will take it away immediately."

Ashem's eyes narrowed, as she glanced up at the rail where Saadrin probably still lurked. She said, "The Rising World council will have questions about all this."

Ramad began, "I think it would be best if—"

Kai lost the rest as Ziede's urgent voice said, *Kai, we're out of time, the stone under the steering column is glowing.*

That meant more Immortal Blessed were coming, using the ship's Well-source as a focus. Kai held up a hand for Ramad to stop talking. *Did Saadrin call them?*

Ziede's inner voice was breathless. *She said she didn't and if that's true, they've tracked us some other way—*

Ziede—He heard a scramble on the upper deck and Tenes ran past the rail. He didn't know what his expression was doing but Ramad looked concerned and Ashem's brow knit. Kai said, "Cohort Leader, tell your cadre to hide, stay quiet. Immortal Blessed are coming, maybe the ones who gave Aclines the ship." Kai bolted back down the retaining wall.

He skidded to a halt near where the fishers gathered around the ghoul's head. They turned to face him, wide-eyed and curious. He remembered the shell and pebble charms surrounding their camp and made the old Witchspeak sign for *danger from the sky*. If they understood, it would eliminate the need for a lot of wordy explanation.

A heartbeat of appalled realization, then the fishers burst into motion. Some turned to leap back down toward their docked boats. Others scrambled up to the market pavilion, calling warnings. People scattered out of the camp, small children under their arms, running deeper into the city.

Relieved, Kai turned away. Maybe the warning to the fishers had convinced the Arike. Ramad sprinted toward the storehouse. The cadre members up on the retaining wall grabbed their supplies and retreated up the road toward the shelter of the port buildings and trees. Ashem followed, walking backward, waving for the stragglers to catch up.

When Kai reached the bottom of the ship's gangway, Sanja and a couple of leather travel bags flew off the deck in one of Ziede's wind-devils. Kai caught Sanja as the wind-devil dropped her and let the bags fall to the dock.

"They're coming, someone's coming," Sanja said, anxious and frightened. He set her on her feet and leaned down to grab the bags. She had a new tunic pulled on over her other clothes and had been hastily bundled into one of Aclines' less ostentatious coats. "Ugh, what happened to your eyes?"

"I know, and it's a disguise." He slung both bags over his shoulder and took Sanja's hand to start back up the dock. This was far too close to Kai's worst prediction, that one or more Immortal Blessed were involved and would come to kill them and all the mortal witnesses. They could stay and fight but it would increase the risk that the cohort would be found and killed. These might just be Immortal Blessed looking for the stolen ship, but they couldn't take the chance.

Sanja trotted to keep up with his longer strides. "Are they coming? The people who want to kill you? What's going to happen?"

"Someone's coming and we're not sure who." Kai pulled her up the steps to the top of the retaining wall. "We're going up the river." He started to look back but a whoosh of air blew his hair into his face as Ziede's wind-devil dropped her and Tenes to the paving. Ziede was grim and Tenes worried. Both carried bags of supplies.

Kai headed for the big avenue. Ziede said, "If Saadrin tells them we're going to the Conventiculum—"

"Will she?" Kai didn't think Saadrin was involved. She hated expositors almost as much as she hated Witches and demons; he couldn't see her entering into any conspiracy that included them. And she wasn't imaginative enough to give such a convincing performance of ignorance when Ziede had questioned her. If she resisted these newcomers, she might end up in the same prison as Tahren. Which would serve her right. Though with kin-right invoked, they would just have to rescue her, too.

"I warned her they could be the Blessed who gave the ship to Aclines." Ziede shook her head, her mouth a thin line. "That's all I could do."

"If she's smart, she'll leave through the Well," Kai said. He didn't think Saadrin would be smart.

"Hah," Ziede commented.

They passed a warren of empty two-story houses, the white walls weathered and stained with moss, overgrown gardens dripping off balconies and rooftops. Kai turned right, led them under a big tree whose roots had pulled up the paving and out onto the terrace above the river. The Immortal Blessed should be focused on the ship, at least at first, but being in the open made the back of Kai's neck itch.

Down on the flat beside the rotting docks, their new barge had rebuilt itself inside the cantrip, floating a pace or so above the muddy ground. It was semi-transparent, woven out of the memories of its former self and Orintukk's death well. It was a long boat with a narrow, curved prow and a broad stern. Mostly open, the sides were low to make it easier to lift cargo in, and a faded blue and white striped canopy sheltered the mid portion. Baffled, Sanja said, "What the shit is that? A ghost?"

"It's the memory of a barge. Here, hold these." Kai dumped the bags in her arms and jumped down to the flat.

As he crouched to check the cantrip, Sanja said pointedly, "But it's not a real boat."

"It'll work, Sanja," Ziede said. She hopped down to the muddy flat and held up her arms for Tenes to hand her the bags. "It doesn't know it's not a real boat."

"Confidence is very important in these kinds of workings," Kai pointed out, pricking his wrist for more blood to close the cantrip. He held his breath as he made the seal of completion, then opened the boundary. It was touch and go for a long heartbeat as the barge's image shivered. But it didn't fall to pieces and Kai tried not to show how relieved he was.

He shoved to his feet and gave the prow a push toward the river's edge to make sure it would hold together in motion. It was just as ungainly as a real barge, and because it was floating in the air didn't make it any easier to maneuver. As translucent as parts of it were, it remembered the weight of its former existence. He was going to have to walk it to the water; it wouldn't know what to do with itself until he could get the river current under it. He turned back to help Ziede and Tenes toss the bags aboard, then gave Sanja a boost over the side as the others climbed in.

Once they were aboard, Kai braced his feet in the mud and leaned his weight against the barge's side. As the translucent bulk shifted reluctantly toward the rushes, Tenes crouched on the deck, sketching the outline of a cantrip. Ziede summoned her wind-devils and said, "We're going to need you for the chimera, Kai."

"Coming." Another shove got the barge off the mud flat into the shallows. With water under it, the translucent hull darkened into solid wood, or at least the appearance of it. But then it decided it was heavier. Kai gritted his teeth and braced his shoulder against the side.

At the thud of running bootsteps, Kai whipped around. But it was Ramad. He jumped down from the terrace into the packed mud. As he sloshed into the rushes, Kai demanded, "What happened?"

Ramad put his shoulder to the hull. "There are bright lights in the sky to the southeast, coming this way. Saadrin is taking the ship out of the harbor."

Kai had more questions but right now getting the barge into the current was more important. With a shove from both of them, the barge shifted further out and Kai splashed into thigh-deep water. The rushes bent under the hull, snakes and water spiders skittered away. Saadrin moving the Immortal Blessed ship might distract their pursuers. Kai was sure any help Saadrin gave them was unintentional and due to her own impatience to leave and her stubborn disregard of anything else going on around her. And Kai appreciated the report but he had no idea why Ramad was here. "You need to hide with the cohort," he said, leaning into the barge's side.

Ramad shook his head, timing his next shove with Kai's. "I'm going with you to Stios."

Distracted, kicking away a large river gar, Kai almost lost his footing in the mud. "What? Why?"

"Dammit, Ramad." Ziede leaned over the side. "Is this on Ashem's orders?"

"I am not under Cohort Leader Ashem's command. We'd better get—" Ramad looked down and noticed the barge was not actually touching the surface of the water. "—aboard whatever this is. What is this?"

"No, answer my question." Kai hooked his elbows over the lip of the low rail as the barge found the current, or at least where the current had been when it was new, before the silt and overgrowth had changed the shape of the river. "Why do you want to come with us?"

Ramad held on to the rail, determination in the set of his jaw, as the barge towed them along. "My mission is to find Tahren Stargard. I want to hear what she has to say. I want to know who's behind this."

"It's none of your concern," Kai told him, trying to glare. With his stupid new eyes, and the barge dragging him through mud and spiky rushes, he knew it wasn't nearly as effective. At least it wasn't having any impact on Ramad.

"There's no time!" Ziede slapped the rail impatiently. "Get up here, both of you! We need to go."

Hissing in frustration, Kai swung a leg up to hook over the side and heave himself aboard. Ramad boosted himself up on the rail and rolled in, neatly except for the amount of water and mud that came with his trailing skirts and coat.

Sanja sat under the awning next to the bags, her expression pinched with worry. Kai dragged himself and his sopping wet clothes up to the bow where Tenes crouched next to the sketched cantrip. He added his intention to it, drawing from Orintukk's death well for more power. Tenes leaned over to close the cantrip.

The intention flowed out from the circle of intent, a cool dampness like a winter mist. It rolled over the barge as it drifted further into the river, then wound up the poles to the ghost of the striped awning. Kai chewed his lower lip, and glanced back at Ziede. If the current caught them and carried them out into the harbor, they would be in trouble. Her expression was abstracted and he knew she was guiding a wind-devil overhead, seeing through its senses. Finally her tense shoulders relaxed and she opened her eyes. "We're good."

Kai slumped back against the rail, relieved. "Let's get out of here."

Ziede called the wind-devil down to settle behind them, and a heartbeat later the barge jerked into motion. It pointed itself up-river and plowed through the muddy water. They gained speed as they passed rotted wooden docks, empty pilings, the hulks of half-sunken boats. Ziede would need to let her wind-devils switch out frequently to maintain this pace. The river port fell behind and they moved past stone walls covered with faded paint and carvings, arches, stepped terraces with still-flowing waterfalls, overgrown flowering vines and brush. Sanja's head swiveled back and forth, eyes wide as she tried to take it all in. Tenes sat up on her knees beside her, tugging on her sleeve to point things out. "Did you do the wake?" Kai asked, just to make certain.

"Yes, the wake and the bow wave." Ziede was intent, her gaze on the water ahead as she made sure they didn't hit any floating debris. "This isn't my first time, Kai."

Ramad watched them, brow furrowed, but Ziede's calm seemed

to convince him they knew what they were doing. He wrung out the skirts of his dripping coat. "What was that fog?"

"That was a chimera." Kai settled against a bench. He told himself it was all right to rest, that they had a long trip ahead where he could do nothing but wait. It was hard to make his racing heart believe that. "To make the barge match the rest of the river water." It would have been easier to make it look like a drift of branches, but then a drift of branches wouldn't be powering its way against the current as fast as a ship under full sail. "You should have stayed with the cadre."

"It's Ashem's cadre—" Ramad began.

"Ramad. What do you think you're doing?" Ziede cut him off. "We're not your friends, no matter how much you would like us to believe we are."

"We both want to find Tahren Stargard. And I meant what I said, I want to know who's behind this." Ramad dashed mud off his face with his equally muddy sleeve, but his voice was passionate. "I'm a Rising World Imperial officer. And I'm an Arike. I know what you did for us."

Kai slumped into the bow. They were in the heart of the city now, the oldest part. The stone buildings were three or four stories tall, with broad balconies, the paint that had decorated their eaves faded to pastel shadows. The mouth of what had been a processional avenue went by, the trees lining it so overgrown that it was a green tunnel. "You don't know what you're getting into."

"I can help you at the Conventiculum." Ramad was determined. "All I want is to speak to Tahren Stargard and hear what happened to her. Who she saw, who she believes is involved."

Ziede shook her head wearily. "I can't decide whether you're a bad spy pretending to be an innocent or a good spy pretending to be a bad one to lull us into complacency."

Ramad sighed. "Ziede Daiyahah, I have been an envoy to the Talai-alaou in the western archipelago and I assure you, you cannot have a lesser appreciation of my intelligence than they did.

But if you are trying to annoy me with insults, you have succeeded."

"Good." Ziede was unmoved.

Ramad's jaw set but he was too practiced a diplomat to lose his temper. "Saadrin knows you're going to the Conventiculum. She'll tell them, whoever those Immortal Blessed were who came for the ship. She thought we were lying about a conspiracy."

"If she doesn't believe they're working with expositors, yes, she'll tell them," Kai agreed. If they didn't kill her first. He was very much hoping she would tell them. "Especially if they imply she was helping us."

Ziede snorted. "She wouldn't lie for us even if the possibility occurred to her."

Ramad was so far gone as to let himself appear openly exasperated. "Then what are you going to do when you get to Stios? Surely you have a plan?"

Kai hesitated, and through her heart pearl Ziede said warningly, *Kai, if you tell him, we have to keep him with us. It would be safer to make him sleep and dump him on a bank somewhere. If we do it soon, he won't even have that long a walk back to Ashem and the cadre.*

She was right. And Kai didn't trust Ramad even if he was grudgingly starting to like him. He told Ziede, *I know. But I think we can use his help.*

He thought she would be annoyed, but her mental voice was resigned, and wry, *You really want to drag someone else into this?*

No, Kai told her. But he also believed in letting people make their own choices. Aloud, he said, "We're not going to the Conventiculum or Stios. That's a trap. Either the finding stones were never there, or they were only sent there to be destroyed. Saadrin would never have let us get near them. Whatever's waiting there, it's nothing that can help us."

Ramad's frown deepened, and he looked from Kai to Ziede and back. "What about the kin-right?"

"It won't let her attack us directly." Ziede brushed drying mud off her pants. "But she's quite capable of lying to us and telling herself it's for our own good."

"She did seem like that sort of person." Ramad seemed relieved to know Saadrin wouldn't be figuring into their plans anymore, if they could avoid her. "So where are we going?"

"To the Summer Halls," Kai said. "Or what's left of them."

THE PAST:
THE CHANGING

. . . demons could steal mortal bodies, it was that they would not, or had been forbidden it . . .

. . . that was how they fought the Saredi in the great war between the grassplains and the underearth, before the treaty that ceded the Witchlands to their issue . . .

. . . such buried knowledge not even the Saredi know much of it, only that the war happened and Witches came from it . . .

—Fragments of documents recovered from a western mountain Hillfort, burned during the Hierarchs' invasion of the grasslands, from the Rising World Archive at Benais-arik

Someone patted his face with a warm hand. Ziede's voice said, "—this happen?"

Kai got his eyes open and saw he was somehow lying half in Bashasa's lap, his head pillowed on Bashasa's thigh. Bashasa no longer looked horrified at least. He was frowning but his face wasn't made for that, so he just looked distressed. This close Kai could see new flecks of blood on his cheeks, on the rich blue brocade of his coat and the tunic under it. *Hierarch's blood*, Kai thought. Had anyone ever drawn Hierarch's blood before? Bashasa smiled down at him and said, "Ah, there you are again. Do you want to sit up?"

Kai didn't know what he wanted but he nodded. Bashasa took his shoulders and helped him sit up. His hands were warm and reassuring. Arike soldiers and other mortals moved in and out of the room. The broken doors had been pushed to the side. The Hierarch's body was gone. Enna had been wrapped in a dark mantle, her face covered. The expositor's body wasn't there either. Then Kai remembered. *Oh, right,* he thought. He drew a shaky breath. His lungs and chest felt different. Longer, bigger?

Ziede stood a few steps away, speaking to Arn-Nefa and another demon in the body of an older Saredi woman. Her ragged coat still bore the crow design of Raneldi. Arn-Nefa said, "He is the demon called Kaiisteron. That's all I can tell you."

The Raneldi demon added, "It doesn't happen often, or at all, if that's what you're asking. When we leave our gifted bodies, we return to the underearth, but with the passage sealed—" She made a helpless gesture.

"I'm asking if he'll be all right," Ziede said, her voice harsh. "He won't lose his hold on it, this body?"

An edge in her tone, Arn-Nefa said, "We don't know." She turned away. Kai wanted to call to her to stay, but she walked out. The Raneldi grimaced in frustration and followed.

Ziede snarled under her breath and turned back to them. "Bashasa, get off Kai and go lead the mortals."

Kai didn't want Bashasa to go, though it felt weak to admit it even to himself. Bashasa might not know what he was doing any more than Kai did, but at least he was able to confidently fake it. But Ziede was right. Kai pulled away from Bashasa and said reluctantly, "You need to go." The different sound of his own voice made his teeth ache, like another person was in his head.

"You're right, you're right." Bashasa squeezed his arms and said, "Just take care. You've had a shock." He stood, looking down at Kai, concern in his gaze. Then he pulled off his coat and draped it over Kai's shoulders.

As Bashasa walked out, Ziede crouched down to Kai's level and said, "Do you understand what happened?"

"Uh, yes. I took this body." He lifted his hand to push his

hair back and startled at the texture. Straight, like Enna's hair, but thicker, dressed with oil that smelled like unfamiliar flowers. "I . . ." *It almost happened before, when Adeni died.* Grandmother had warned him. "I knew it could happen, sort of. But I didn't mean to do it."

Ziede glanced at the shrouded form. "The other demons said you couldn't go back to her."

"No." Enna was gone now, just decaying flesh, nothing inside her to reach out to.

Ziede sat back on the ivory floor and dug in the pouch at her belt. She handed Kai a small hand mirror with a carved wooden back. Kai took it and stared at himself in the silver surface. His skin was a more golden brown now and his hair a darker black. Everything was different. His face was longer, less round, had high sharp cheekbones, dark brows, full lips. His teeth were different, with no points on his incisors. He didn't look Saredi anymore, and that made something in his chest hurt. The only thing that was recognizably his was the flat black wells of his whiteless eyes.

He wore a black silk tunic belted over a skirt, the black veil he remembered lying across his lap. A small ornament, a web of thin silver plates connected by tiny delicate chains, was pinned to his collar. He started to rip it off, but something made him hesitate. Cantenios had worn something similar. The plates were enameled with characters in unfamiliar writing, the blue and black standing out against the silver.

He poked at his hair again. It hung past his shoulders, partly secured with emerald-tipped pins. He had never even seen an emerald before. *Wait, what?* He squinted at the polished green stones in the mirror. *How do I know these are emeralds?*

Ziede said wryly, "At least you're pretty."

Kai stared at her and she winced, and said, "Sorry. I suppose it's too soon for humor."

Kai rubbed his forehead. The disorientation and nausea were fading but that didn't make it any easier to think. "The Hierarch.

There was only one Hierarch. Wasn't there supposed to be two?" The body was gone, but from the wide swath of blood leading across the ivory tiles and out the doorway, Kai could guess where it was. They had dragged it out on the platform to display their success to the other mortals.

Ziede's expression went tight with worry again. "There were two, at least. We're sure of that. But the other one must have been late to the ceremony."

When Kai had first woken in Enna's body and shared her last thoughts with her grieving family, her memories had faded quickly into dreamlike images, barely to be grasped. He had retained a few things, like being able to speak Saredi. The faces of her family had been familiar, though he didn't know their names. He had recognized her horse, been able to find her bed in the Kentdessa tent. But that was all. He and Adeni and Varra and Iludi had made a game of it, trying to see what Kai could guess or remember.

Kai knew a lot more than that about this expositor. "His name is—was Talamines. He was from Irekan." Kai didn't know where that was. Somewhere to the far south, in the path of the Hierarchs' progress across the world; even Talamines wasn't certain exactly. "He was taken from there as a child, he barely remembered anything about it. I know what his rooms here in the palace look like. I know how to get there. I know . . . so much I can't . . ." He shook his head. He knew too much, it was all a confusing jumble.

Ziede looked increasingly worried. "I thought demons didn't retain the memories of their hosts."

"Saredi call us to take the bodies of their recent dead. This Talamines was alive. It's all still here." Kai handed Ziede back her mirror, and turned his hand palm up. There was so much knowledge it was overwhelming, but some things were more vivid than others. Like the first use of power Talamines had been taught.

Kai knew better than to touch the Hierarchs' Well. Even still shaking with shock and wearing a stolen body, he knew that would be a terrible idea and would probably tell the missing Hierarch and every expositor within range where he was, right before the Well flooded his body and possessed him. But Talamines had known a lot about how to source power.

Pain was the most readily available; pain of other mortals, their life force, their deaths. The obvious solution was to use the legionaries but it wasn't the solution Kai wanted. Grandmother's body had been burned, trapping her in the underearth never to walk the mortal world again, and Captain Kentdessa and all the others were dead, killed by the Hierarchs' Great Working or cut down in battle afterward, but Kai could picture their expressions if they knew he was even contemplating it.

But Bashasa and Ziede could have left him to recover or not on his own, or be killed as an expositor by someone who didn't understand what he had done, or be killed as a demon by someone who understood it all too well. He had to figure out a way to help them.

The horrific emotional consequences of the worst mistake of his life aside, Kai had an idea. *I could use my own pain,* he thought. The power structures his new brain remembered didn't seem to care what the source was, as long as it existed. *There's no reason why not.* And Talamines had parted with his body in a lot of pain, it was all still there, stored in a hot mass under Kai's stolen breastbone. And there was Kai's pain. He looked at Enna again, shrouded under the black mantle, and wanted to climb under there with her. She was his last connection to Kentdessa and all that it had been, all that was gone now. The ache of that thought sparked power and he used it to form an intention on Talamines'—his—palm.

A flame, yellow and wavering, heatless but bright, appeared above his hand.

Ziede's brows lifted in astonishment. "Kai—What the—You're not drawing from the Hierarchs' Well, are you?"

"No, Ziede, I'm not an idiot." Kai's exasperation extinguished the flame. With another effort, he brought it back. Concentrating to keep the shape of the design, he told her, "I'm using my own pain."

Ziede's eyes narrowed. "It's not nearly as likely to destroy your consciousness and enslave you to the Hierarchs' Well, but it's hardly an inexhaustible source."

Kai huffed a laugh, though it wasn't funny. "Isn't it?"

Ziede bit her lip and he could see she knew he was right. "You're taking all the fun out of killing a Hierarch's High Expositor and stealing his power, Kai."

It wasn't much fun at all, as more of this body's memories drifted to the surface. "Did you know some of them were enslaved? Cantenios wasn't, but this one was."

"I'd heard rumors," Ziede admitted. "It may be only the High Expositors who are controlled that way." She made a gesture and a breath of air brushed across his palm. He kept the flame stable, managed to make it a little bigger. She added, "So you're an expositor, now. I might be able to teach you witchwork, too."

Witches were supposed to be born of the mix of demon and mortal blood during the long-ago war with the underearth, at least in the borderlands. But maybe there were other kinds of Witches. Were expositors just Witches who had been twisted out of shape? Not all of them, not Cantenios, but Kai thought Talamines might have been. But he had a more urgent question to answer first. Was he even still a demon?

Kai wet his lips, still maintaining the flame, and drew the fingers of his free hand through the patch of wet blood staining the ivory tile. He brushed his thumb through the blood, and drew the life out of it. In the next breath it was black dust, flaking away like ash.

Ziede's surprise was turning into something very like awe. And calculation. "If we survive this day, this could be very, very helpful." Her brows lifted as another idea occurred to her. "Did this expositor know anything immediately useful? Like where our missing Hierarch might hide?"

"I'm not sure." This body's memories were too much and not enough at the same time. Grimacing in frustration, Kai closed his hand to halt the intention and dispel the flame. "The demons— Did they go with Bashasa?"

Ziede looked like she was coming to a decision. Abruptly she pushed to her feet, reaching out to grab his arm and tug him upright with her. He almost fell down again. He was taller now, only a little shorter than Ziede, and for a heartbeat it felt like he was balancing on unsteady stilts. Determined, Ziede said, "Let's see."

Kai struggled into Bashasa's coat and tucked the veil into his belt, then hesitated. He crossed the room and crouched to gently tug the shroud away from Enna's face. Her body was already starting to decay, her cheeks and the skin around her eyes sinking. He had been happy when he was Enna, before the war. That part of his life had been gone since the Hierarchs' first decision to invade the grasslands; this was just the final separation, the chasm that would never be crossed.

But he turned her head and gently unthreaded the leather band with the Kentdessa antelope sigil from her hair. Then he pulled the shroud back over her and stood.

Wrapping the band around his wrist and tucking it under the tight tunic sleeve, he followed Ziede out onto the platform in the Temple Halls. The Hierarch's body lay on the gray-white marble, its white robes drenched with blood. The severed head had been placed on the chest.

The Temple Hall was scattered with fallen bodies, mostly legionaries. But there were bright heaps of blood-stained fabric that marked other mortals, though there was nothing now to show what side they had fought for. A haze drifted in the shafts of light from the glass roof, mingled incense and smoke from a smoldering fire somewhere. The wounded had been brought to one side of the hall, where mortals, some in court dress and some in plainer servants' clothes, moved among them, bringing water or bandaging injuries.

In contrast to that useful activity, the demons sat on the steps of the platform, staring at Kai. Their gazes were dull or angry or just bored. Some had been in the Cageling Court too long; he recognized those expressions of disinterest, of a demon barely attached to their own body anymore. It was a wonder so many had reached the Temple Halls at all; he was certain some must have dropped away from the group in the corridors along the way. Arn-Nefa and the Raneldi demon stood with them, just watching him.

This inaction was maddening. Kai hissed out a breath. "What are you doing? There's still a Hierarch in this place, why aren't you helping look for him?"

Arn-Nefa's opaque expression didn't change. Another demon said, "Why did you violate every covenant by taking a living mortal body?" She had a wooden heron sigil on her torn coat, from the tent of Soliasar.

Sick shame hardened like a rock in Kai's stomach. The unfairness of it was grating but he knew saying *I didn't mean to do it, it was an accident*, wasn't going to help. He said, "This was an enemy. How many expositors have you killed?"

A few stirred, and their black depthless gazes watched him with more interest. But then Arn-Nefa said, "You broke your oath to the Saredi."

It stung, worse than if she had slapped him. He fumbled for a heartbeat, unable to answer that. He deserved that contempt. He had done something that the Saredi would have thought obscene, a rejection of every covenant between grasslands and underearth. But if he hadn't none of them would be standing here now. "The Saredi fell. We're all that's left. Are you giving up?"

"These mortals aren't fighting for us," the Raneldi demon said.

Kai was incredulous. "Why should they? You're going back to

the underearth as soon as the passage opens again. Do you want revenge first or not?"

"The passage won't open again," the Soliasar demon said. "No one will defeat the Hierarchs. We're trapped here."

Kai looked helplessly at Arn-Nefa. She just stared at him, her expression now edged with contempt. "You fought the legionaries in this room! What changed?"

The Soliasar demon's mouth moved in a not-smile. "You changed."

He wasn't their leader, he was just the one picked to free them from the Cageling Court. He didn't want them to fight for him, he wanted them to fight for themselves. "Then pick someone else to lead!" He knew he sounded desperate. He was desperate. "Arn-Nefa, you do it!"

"No." She pressed her lips together and shook her head regretfully. For a moment, her expression almost looked sympathetic. "We did what we could. These mortals are dead, even if they don't know that yet. There's no point."

"They know that." Kai lifted his hands, exasperated. He wished that Bashasa was here; he had convinced Kai, he could surely convince the other demons. He pointed to the Hierarch's corpse, stinking in its pool of blood on the sacred platform. "Bashasa— these mortals—killed a Hierarch. No one's ever done that before!"

"Isn't that enough?" The Raneldi demon sounded weary, as if she wanted nothing more than to lie down and die. "We can't kill them all."

Would they fight, if more legionaries poured into this room? Probably, until the surviving Hierarch arrived to overpower them with the Great Working and drag whatever survived back to the Cageling Court. Kai had to convince them. Maybe he could get them to go to Bashasa, to listen to him. He stepped closer to Arn-Nefa, lowering his voice. "Arn-Nefa, please, come with me and speak to—"

She grabbed his throat. Kai froze, too startled to react. And she was an older demon, in an older Saredi body, two things that gave her authority over him.

Then he felt a weird pull at his heart, at the store of stolen life under it. He didn't understand. Her expression was grim, determined. Suddenly he knew. She was trying to kill him, to decay his body like he was a mortal.

Kai grabbed her hand and bent it backward. Arn-Nefa jerked free and stepped back, a snarl on her lips.

Kai didn't feel anything except a deep chill in his bones. He said, "Not friends anymore, then."

Arn-Nefa tensed for an attack. Uncertainty crept into her expression when Kai just stood there.

He turned away and crossed the platform, past the dead Hierarch, to where Ziede waited.

The scatter of Arike soldiers around her, wounded and not, looked away hurriedly. Kai and the demons had been speaking Saredi so no one had likely understood the argument, or known what they were watching. Except for Ziede, whose brow was furrowed in dismay. Her voice low, she said, "Are you all right?"

Kai folded his arms, glad for Bashasa's coat. The cold still clung to him and he wanted to shiver. He said, "We're on our own. They won't help."

An Arike soldier, her face vaguely familiar from Bashasa's court, approached. She gave them both an Arike bow, touching her forehead. In accented Imperial, she said, "Excuse the interruption, Sister Witch. But can you make this person speak?" She pointed back to where a small group of Arike stood on the lower floor below the platforms. They surrounded a kneeling prisoner, a legionary with an officer's tail. It hung from his head down past his shoulder, a hank of hair braided with jeweled chains and bright-colored threads.

"I can try," Ziede said grimly. Witches manipulated elements and spirits, not mortal minds; Kai thought that if the Arike hadn't been able to force the officer to answer their questions, then Ziede couldn't either. Then Ziede glanced at Kai. "You might be able to."

The Arike focused on him, wary but managing not to look disgusted or terrified. "Will you try, ah . . ."

"Kaiisteron," Ziede supplied. "Call him Fourth Prince."

It was another sharp jab to Kai's heart. He wasn't Kai-Enna anymore. And he had never used his underearth title with the Saredi, it would have been laughable. "Just call me—" Kai started, but Ziede kicked him in the foot. "Ziede, don't," he grumbled, hopping out of range. The ankle he had used to transfer into Talamines was still sore.

"Will you try, Fourth Prince?" the Arike asked.

Kai rubbed his face, trying to shake off the numbing cold. At least the Arike thought he might be useful. "Sure. What are you called?"

She touched her shoulder where her sash was tied. "Salatel, Second Shield Bearer to Prince-heir Bashasa. Please come."

As they followed Salatel, Ziede demanded, "Where is Bashasa?" in a tone that suggested she had considered saying *where is that idiot Bashasa*. Kai didn't expect an answer.

But Salatel stopped, as if the question had come from her captain, and pulled a folded cloth map out of her coat. She motioned a subordinate over and spread the map out on the woman's back. Kai recognized Bashasa's handiwork in the awkward drawing and almost smiled. "He's here." Salatel indicated a spot with her finger. "This court. To hold it, to keep the legionary auxiliaries back. They think the Hierarch is somewhere in this area, but they aren't sure where."

Kai stepped closer to see, and Salatel only shifted a little nervously. Talamines' memory was turning patchy; Kai could visualize the interiors of rooms and halls Talamines had known well but couldn't tell where they were on the map. He spotted what might be the Cageling Court and pointed to the large open space near it. "And we're here?" To save Salatel's nerves, he didn't touch the map on the soldier's back, though she had to know he couldn't drain someone's life through cloth and leather. Or maybe she didn't know. "And the auxiliaries are coming through here?"

"Yes, Fourth Prince."

Kai stared at her. "That's not good." They could be overrun at any moment. The Hierarch was probably waiting for the legionaries to break through and corner the majority of the rebels in this part of the Halls before drawing on the Well. They were still all going to die, even though they had won themselves some extra time.

"No, Fourth Prince, not good," Salatel acknowledged grimly.

She folded the map again and they followed her to the lower floor below the platform, where several Arike soldiers waited, looking down at the legionary officer on his knees. He had been stripped of his weapons, helmet, and plate-armored tunic, but his expression was sardonic and amused. The memory of Kai's new body told him that the braided tail meant the officer's rank was high, that he was a Right Hand of Wrath.

Salatel motioned to the Arike soldiers and they eased out of the way. She said, "His name is Vilgies, a high officer of the legion, part of a Hierarch's own guard."

As Kai stepped in front of him, Vilgies frowned, his gaze moving up to Kai's face. His jaw dropped a little. Vilgies breathed, "What . . . what is this? It's impossible."

Kai had been poking Talamines' reluctant memories for some detail about the man, or better yet some way expositors had of reading minds, but nothing was coming to him. But Vilgies recognized Talamines so he decided to wing it.

Kai dropped to a crouch so they were eye level. He let his movements be sinuous, borrowing from his lost body in the underearth. He banished the stray thought: *Even if the passage reopens, how will you ever see Grandmother again.* He said, "Are you telling us a Right Hand of Wrath has never faced demons before?"

"Demons are nothing but spear-fodder for the barbarians,"

Vilgies said. His jaw set, all contempt and disdain. "They can't follow orders."

Couldn't they? Kai had been very obedient, for all the good it had done. He knew the Hierarchs' legions didn't understand how the Saredi were organized, but the Saredi had still been destroyed, so maybe it didn't matter. "I'm following orders now." He reached out and brushed his fingers across Vilgies' face.

The man jerked backward, his breath coming hard, but he said, "I won't tell you—"

"Oh, I know, I know," Kai assured him. "You won't tell me where the Hierarch might be hiding, and besides, we both know there's no point. Everyone here's going to die. You just won't live to see it."

Vilgies schooled his face to contempt again. "I'm not afraid of death."

That's not a lie, Kai thought. Vilgies would die without telling them anything, or at least anything true, no matter how slow and painful Kai made it. The Hierarchs' dogs were loyal, though Kai didn't understand it. After the first attacks on Erathi and the borderlands, the Saredi and their allies had thought the legionaries were intentioned to obedience somehow, their minds entrapped. Why else would they die for no reason except for the greed and aggrandizement of the Hierarchs? But when the Witches had tried to find the intention on legionary prisoners, there had been nothing, no trace of any kind of compulsion.

And Kai would rather not waste time on this when they should be going to find Bashasa. He didn't even know yet if Dahin and the rest of Bashasa's household had managed to leave. They might be able to buy time for more hostages and prisoners to flee.

Kai sat back and looked up at Ziede. In Saredi, he said, "I'm just going to kill him, unless you have any ideas." At least there would be one less Hierarch's Right Hand in the next battle against whoever survived to resist.

"Wait," Ziede said in the same language. She tapped her chin thoughtfully. "I think we're going about this the wrong way. Have you ever seen an expositor do a hunt-follow intention?"

"I've never seen it, but we were warned about it." Expositors could trace scouts back to their camps if they were spotted while too close. Kai had always found that if scouts were spotted while too close then they were going to be too dead to worry about it.

"We could use it," Ziede said. Not understanding their speech, the Right Hand pretended not to watch them. "That alabaster emblem he's wearing on his belt, with the gold embossed cup. That shows he's in direct contact with a Hierarch, one of their guard-servants. If he's been to the place the Hierarch is hiding within the past few hours—or it may be since dawn, we were never quite sure how the intention worked—tracing his movements would tell us how to start."

"Do you know how to make it work?" Kai asked.

"No, Kai, but you should," she said, not patiently.

"You're an optimist, Ziede." There was no certainty in Talamines' jumbled brain. Kai sat back on his heels and concentrated, but there was nothing he could remember about the hunt-follow intention. Something told him Talamines had not known many designs and intentions, he hadn't been that kind of expositor. *He helped the Hierarch focus power through the Well*, he thought, and wondered what that meant.

Did the Hierarchs need an expositor like Talamines to use the power of the Well on a large number of mortals? If they did, it would explain why the other Hierarch hadn't acted yet. But that was speculation so pure it might as well have been one of the Saredi fire-stories about people who lived in the sky.

But Talamines had ways of finding hidden information. Kai was pretty certain he wasn't imagining that. But it wasn't by reading minds. It was by reading . . . objects. "Does stone and wood and metal have a memory?" he asked Ziede.

"What?" Ziede was thrown for a moment, then apparently decided he was serious and said, "In a way, but those memories are hard to tap. Usually only"—she used a word in a language Kai didn't know—"can stay still and silent long enough to see them." She hesitated, biting her lip in thought. "But you aren't talking about a boulder in a field, you mean made things. Those can borrow memory through close contact with a person. But it has to be close, intimate contact. Like a piece of jewelry worn all the time."

Kai reached and pulled Vilgies' alabaster emblem off his belt. "Like this." Like the emblem that gave a Right Hand of Wrath leave to serve a Hierarch.

Vilgies snarled profanity and struggled until Kai shut him up by grabbing his jaw and draining enough of his life so he slumped over on the floor. Kai needed to concentrate.

Just holding the emblem and trying to think of where the Hierarch might be did nothing. But Talamines would have focused the power of the Well on it. Kai tried using a little of the life just taken from Vilgies, and suddenly saw a string of images. Most were a confusing mess, like a fading dream, but one was clearer than the rest. Figures in a large room, voices, water, lots of glass looking down onto a court. "The walls are gold, with an ivory and enamel design. It's two levels above the floor of a court. There are fountains and pools."

"Salatel, the map, please," Ziede said in Imperial as Kai squeezed his eyes shut and concentrated on the image, holding it in his mind. "Have you seen a room with gold walls and ivory and enamel decoration? No? Ask the others."

Shouts echoed through the court, soldiers spreading the question around the hall in Imperial and Arike. Then Ziede said, "Kai, describe it again, anything you can."

"The pools are long and shallow. One is big, curved and deeper, like you could swim in it." There was something off in the way the shadows fell, the way the sun came through the windows into the gold-walled room. "Oh, the court outside isn't open to the air. There's glass in the roof, but not all of it, like this one."

"I think we've got it," Ziede said, her voice taut.

Kai opened his eyes to see more mortals had joined the Arike soldiers. Most were in fine brocades and silks, bloody and disheveled from the battle. A person in a voluminous coat and a headwrap sat on the floor with Salatel's map as Ziede crouched beside them. The person was filling in detail on the map with a lead stylus.

Kai pushed to his feet and went to look. People stepped away to give him room but no one actually fled. Salatel reported, "This is an attendant of the middle servant-nobles, who saw a court like this once."

The person sketched in a section of the Halls that was not on Salatel's original map, though it wasn't far from the spot where Bashasa had gone to try to hold back the legionaries. "Bashasa never saw this area?"

"No, Fourth Prince." Salatel made an open-handed motion. "They pretend hostages are part of their court, but they don't allow us to see much of the Halls, just the most public areas."

The attendant finished and sat back. "If it's not right," they asked, in Imperial, "will you come back and kill me?" They didn't sound that upset about the prospect.

"No." Kai leaned over to commit the new section to memory. "Because if it's not right, I'll be too dead to think about you."

"*We'll* be too dead," Ziede said. Kai looked up and met her gaze. She didn't look like someone who expected to be dead. She looked like someone who had a plan. She added, "Let's go kill another Hierarch."

TEN

Ziede drew from a small host of wind-devils to keep them moving at speed upriver without exhausting any one of the wild spirits. The bulk of Orintukk was left behind for lush green country where gardens and crops and orchards had once grown, interspersed with thick forests and the occasional rotting docks or stone pilings for long-vanished towns.

When they were still in Orintukk, Ramad, calmly enough, had asked, "Why are we going to the Summer Halls, the most reviled and forbidden place in all the Rising World?"

"We need a finding stone to locate Tahren," Kai had explained. "There's one in the Summer Halls."

Ramad's grim expression had turned startled and thoughtful, as if that was a far more rational explanation than he could possibly have expected. "I see. In a location that isn't a trap, that no one will know we're going to. And a finding stone no one else knows about?"

"The Immortal Blessed know there were finding stones in the Summer Halls." Ziede studied Ramad critically. She had taken a seat up toward the bow near Kai. Tenes and Sanja were still in the stern, excitedly watching the city flow past. "But it's certainly not going to be the first spot that leaps to mind."

"And I know exactly where this one is," Kai said, and thought, *as long as it didn't float away.*

Ramad had nodded slowly. "So it's worth the risk."

They hadn't spoken of it since then. Kai thought Ramad was holding back his questions, trying not to push, trying to appear trustworthy. Or possibly actually being trustworthy. Kai still didn't know, and the whole thing made him want to groan.

The only way to know was to trust Ramad and then wait for the knife in the back.

Tenes had brought some of the Immortal Blessed ship's silk blankets, and they used them to fashion a tent in the stern under the awning. The weather was hot now during the day so it was worth it for the extra shade and the occasional need for privacy. Everyone had taken off their coats, and Kai and Ramad had tied their skirts up to keep them out of the water.

The country turned hilly, with the sharp walls of low bluffs on either side of the river. After they had taken their first turn into a canal, they passed a place where a cliff loomed above a pool so round it clearly wasn't natural, even with the trees and brush that grew all around its banks. The skeleton of a building stood against the striated rock, taller than the cliff itself, with stone pillars still supporting heavy wooden beams. It was overgrown with vines, but it formed an odd shape, like a giant wagon wheel.

Leaning out of the boat, Sanja asked, "What is that big round house?"

Kai was about to say it was probably an old fort, but Ramad pointed to the top of the cliff and said, "This is Lu-draya. There used to be a waterway that led from a lake somewhere across the plateau to a stone basin on this cliff. The structure was like a waterwheel for barges, lowering them down so they could reach this canal."

Of all the things Ramad might be lying about, being a historian was not one of them.

Not long after, Tenes spotted a few plumes of woodsmoke rising over the trees in the distance. As they drew closer, they found a small harbor had been dug into the canal bank and a set of well-kept docks held a scatter of sailboats, canoes, and an aging river barge. Trees had been cleared back from the bank to make room for a couple of blocky cargo storage houses. A wide path led through the forest toward the distant sound of voices, someone chopping wood, and a thread of music. Ziede scanned the sky for any signs of pursuit, then said, "We can stop here for supplies."

The chimera only worked from above, so they docked against the other river barge. It had taller sides and a small cabin, so their barge would be mostly concealed from the bank. That way if anyone came down the path from town they wouldn't immediately see something that shouldn't be floating, much less existing, and feel compelled to ask questions. When Sanja's back was turned, Kai tilted his head toward her and asked Ziede silently, *Send her alone, give her a chance to leave?*

Ziede hesitated, then shook her head. *Too close, I think,* she replied through her pearl. *If they search for us, they might find her.*

She was right, so Kai waited in the boat with Ramad as Ziede, Tenes, and Sanja climbed across the other docked barge and went down the path to the town.

Kai settled into the bow so he could keep watch up and down the canal. Ramad had stood to help boost Sanja up to the taller barge's deck, and Kai felt his attention as he took a seat again on the midship bench. Ramad said, "Something you said earlier . . . Why don't Witches have renegades? Because none want to rebel?"

"Because there's nothing to rebel against." Kai watched long-legged birds stride along under the trees of the opposite bank. It was clouding over, there might be rain later and they would have to figure out what that might do to the chimera.

"Witches have no hierarchy?" Ramad asked, frowning. "No organization? But they act in concert. Or they did during the war."

Kai shrugged. He wasn't the only one with these answers. "You want to use up all your questions on this?"

Ramad lifted a brow, and Kai watched him shift from something more genuine back into a professional mask. "How many questions do I have?"

Kai kept his expression completely serious. "That's one."

Ramad let out a breath, and a genuine smile flickered. He had been around Kai long enough to know that was a joke, and that was . . . somehow disturbing and warming at the same time.

Ziede was right, Kai needed to be careful.

Ramad reconsidered his question, his expression turning appropriately serious again. "The Great Bashasa spoke his last words to you."

That was disappointing. "Oh, not that." Kai pretended mild annoyance, rather than revealing his depth of exhaustion with people who wanted to know things they had never been entitled to. "Everyone asks that."

Ramad acknowledged this with a tilt of his head. "Then I won't ask what they were. I'll ask . . . why did he speak them to you?"

The approach was different enough to be intriguing. "Why do you think?"

Ramad shifted forward, bracing his elbows on his knees. He was clearly debating what to say, and there was something reluctant in it. "The rumor is that you were his lover. That you seduced him for power in the new Rising World."

Yes, they did say that. Kai just flicked his fingers in the water, like brushing away an annoying insect.

Without letting his gaze sharpen, Ramad added, "Others say the Great Bashasa would never have debased himself like that."

Yes, they said that, too. "Very provocative, Ramad. It's not exactly a new tactic." And he thought, *It'll be the next question, the one he really wants the answer to.* Ramad might be intrigued with Kai for more than one reason, but he couldn't help being a vanguarder any more than he could help being a historian.

Ramad lifted one shoulder in a deprecating half shrug, but Kai had the impression he wasn't enjoying this. "I've always wondered if it was the other way around. How he might have seduced—or persuaded—you to his service."

The answer was *Yes, but not like you think.* Not that anyone would believe that. Kai wasn't certain if he was falling for an obvious trick, or if it was something else that made him want to answer truthfully. He said, "What if I told you it wasn't like that at all? Would you believe me? Would you even listen?"

Ramad's eyes widened in unfeigned surprise. "Yes. I mean, I would certainly listen. And believe."

Kai was certain that Ramad had had absolutely no confidence that his tactic would work. Now he had the look of a hunter who had just realized they were tackling bigger prey than they could handle. "Have you ever heard of the Saredi? The people the Arike and Enalin called the Grass Kings?"

Ramad's brow furrowed as he obviously racked his memory. "Weren't they nomad herders, somewhere in the Witchlands? I remember a story about rather dark religious practices."

Yes, I was one of those practices, Kai could have said. "Dark compared to killing off entire cities because they're in your way?"

Ramad conceded that with a wry nod. "Not that dark, no. But I thought they were almost entirely destroyed by the Hierarchs. Did they lend support to Bashasa's alliance?"

"They formed their own alliance to fight the Hierarchs' advance, with the sea people and traders of Erathi, and the borderlanders, from the places the Arike called the Witchlands. But they didn't know how much of the world the Hierarchs had already conquered. They didn't know about the power of the Well."

Ramad frowned in concentration, taking this in as if he was memorizing every word. "Were you with them, before Bashasa?"

"I was with them." Kai abruptly felt he had said too much and not enough. Time to move on. "Now tell me how learning any of this will benefit the Rising World?"

Ramad sat back, shaking his head a little. "I'm not asking for the Rising World. I'm asking for myself. I'm still a historian by inclination. I've always been curious, since I first saw you in the court of Benais-arik."

Kai agreed, "I've always been a curiosity."

Ramad winced, and that looked unfeigned, too. "That's not . . . That's not why I wanted—You were there, when it all happened—"

Footsteps sounded on the dock and they both flinched.

Ziede and the others were back with bags full of supplies. Ramad seemed torn between reluctance to drop the subject and relief.

Ziede had traded some of the rich fabrics from the Immortal Blessed ship for lighter cotton clothing in sun-faded blues, yellows, and grays. Aclines' finery was already stained and torn from the mud and wrangling the ghost boat, and Kai found it a relief to get out of it and into a wrap tunic and a split skirt that was easier to tie up around his knees. Ramad kept his practical traveling clothes but Ziede opted for a short Enalin caftan belted over pants. Sanja imitated Ziede, though on her the same size caftan reached her ankles. Both wrapped their hair up in scarves to protect it from the dust in the wind off the hills and fields. Tenes wore a light patterned Arike long tunic over leggings. If they had to abandon the boat and walk or enter another town, at least they would look like ordinary wanderers. Kai used the pocket sewn under the tunic's lapel for the telescoping rod, their best weapon unless Ramad had something hidden on him, which he probably did.

They got underway again, and Sanja said suddenly, "Vanguarder, can you tell the story about the people who thought you were stupid?"

Kai, caught drinking from a bamboo water flask, almost choked. By the time Tenes leaned over to slap him on the back, he realized Sanja was being deliberately provocative, testing Ramad to see if he was going to lose his temper, if he was safe to travel with in this confined space. Probably testing all of them. He wiped his mouth and looked at Ziede, who sat there with her brows lifted quizzically.

Ramad turned to eye Sanja, but it was with the good humor of someone being hazed as the newest member of a group. He said, "Sanja, I'm afraid you're going to have to narrow that down."

Now Kai snorted, but discreetly, looking away at the huge cypress lining the far bank.

Sanja clarified, "The people on the island, the Tala-something."

"Oh, the Talai-alaou." Ramad sat back on the bench and wiped the sweat off his forehead. "They're interesting people but they have a whole code of strict rules of behavior. A little like the Grale, but without the courtesy and hospitality."

Ziede commented, "The Grale are the most reasonable people on the eastern continent, but also the most tiresome."

"They are as nothing compared to the tiresomeness of the Talai-alaou," Ramad assured her.

Tenes crossed the boat to settle next to Sanja to listen. Ramad was a good storyteller, self-deprecating about his effort to make friends on the Rising World's behalf with the stuffiest inhabitants of the whole western archipelago. Kai felt the muscles in the back of his neck unclenching and realized he needed the laughter. He was more tense about their destination than he had thought he would be.

As they traveled, the hills gradually fell away, leaving open fields and scattered copses of trees. The days were long and hot but the nights were cool, with sweet breezes and flickers of light in the brush from glowing insects or stray ghosts. They stopped only briefly, to clean the latrine bucket, or to scrounge supplies from the overgrown fields of long-abandoned farms. Sometimes they had to struggle to keep the boat from hulling itself on long-vanished sandbars. The barge's state made it hard to keep any clothing clean, and Ramad's erratic shaving and his beard stubble made him look even more like an itinerant river trader.

And they talked. Ziede spoke to Tenes in more depth, to try to help her remember anything she could about her past before Aclines had taken her memories at Scarif. There was depressingly little that Tenes could describe, and while Ziede could tell she came from a witchline that worked with ground spirits, that didn't narrow it down. Ramad told more stories about his travels, trips to distant allies, the occasional hunts for violent expositors. Kai wouldn't talk about the war, or Bashasa, but he talked about their travels over the years, or the trips he had made alone.

By the time the canal crossed the old border of the Sana-sarcofa, foraging proved inadequate, and they had to stop under some overhanging willow trees near the docks of another river trading village.

With a pocketful of Ramad's Rising World coins, they sent Sanja alone down the trail to find the town market. After she left, Ziede sent Tenes to follow her at a distance to make sure of her safety, but not to interfere if Sanja chose not to return.

"You're giving her a chance to run away," Ramad said, watching them.

Kai had settled down into the bow again, head propped on the soft wood. The sun didn't hurt his skin, so up here he had room to lie down and leave the awning and the tent for the others. He said, "Isn't that what you wanted, to get her away from us?"

Ramad's shrug was wry. "That was Cohort Leader Ashem. I believe in letting people choose their own path."

If only I believed you mean that, Kai thought.

Barely half an hour later, Tenes reappeared, smiling, to climb back in the boat. Then Sanja came down the path, a bag stuffed with food over her shoulder and carrying three wide-brimmed straw hats that she had purchased for herself, Ziede, and Tenes.

"Why didn't you get one for me?" Kai teased her, standing and giving her a hand.

"You wouldn't wear it," Sanja retorted, as she stepped carefully over the side. "You don't like things on your hair. If you need one for a disguise, you can borrow mine."

"Speaking of that." Ramad got up to help Kai push the boat away from the shallow water under the trees. They had poles for that now, acquired along the way. "What happens after you retrieve the finding stone and free Tahren Stargard? What is your plan?"

Pushing off the big tree roots and then the little island clumps of mud and weed got them back out toward the center of the river. The current tried to push them downstream, but Ziede woke a wind-devil to get them back on course. Kai let Ramad help him stow the wet poles along the side before he said, "You've been with us the whole time. Have you heard us talk about a plan?"

Ramad looked around for something to wipe the mud off his hands, then gave up. "I know you and Ziede Daiyahah have the means to speak without anyone else hearing you."

Ziede lifted a waterskin to him in a salute. "Very clever."

Ramad sighed. "I know I've said this before, but I can help you, if you let me."

"Why?" Kai settled into a forward seat so he had the excuse to watch where they were going when he needed to avoid Ramad's gaze. "Why are you so eager to help us?"

Ramad lifted his hands in exasperation. "I told you. There have to be more traitors at court working with the Nient-arik faction. They have ties to renegade Immortal Blessed, they employ expositors. This was all a deliberate attempt to disrupt the Imperial coalition renewal."

Kai flicked a look at Ziede, who was helping Tenes adjust the chin strap of her new straw hat. Kai said, "You know the Rising World was never meant to be an empire."

Ziede said silently, *Careful.*

"I know it was a temporary alliance that grew into something more." Ramad watched Kai intently, as if trying to read his thoughts. "You helped it grow into something more."

Grow like a tumor, Kai thought, but he didn't say it aloud. He knew he wanted to trust Ramad, that a mortal lifetime ago, Ramad would have fit into the cadres and scouts that Kai had fought and schemed with as they pried the known world out of the Hierarchs' clutches. *He reminds you of Bashasa,* Ziede had said, but it wasn't true. "We don't have a plan right now. We won't, until we get Tahren back."

———— ✖ ————

Kai woke before dawn on the day they would reach the Summer Halls. He was lying in the bow, his favorite spot on the boat, and at first he thought he had woken from nerves, from the thought of facing this place again.

The sky was still mostly dark, the trees along the edge of the canal sparser, tall canopies still in the predawn air. Then he realized something else had woken him.

He sat up. Everyone was asleep except for Tenes, sitting back under the canopy, taking her turn at watch. Kai nodded to her, and then glanced down in the water.

A shape glided under the surface, sinuous, nearly half the length of the boat. It glowed gently in the dark, impossibly brilliant white and purple and blotchy indigo. Frills like gold lace ornamented its fins. Kai rolled up his sleeve and trailed his hand in the water.

A scaly whiskered mouth brushed his palm, and he felt a little warmth. He pulled his hand up and read the message now written there. The characters faded from view and he took a deep breath in relief. He looked up to see Tenes watching him quizzically, and signed to her, *Tell you later.*

She nodded, and they both watched the messenger whip around through the water and flit away down the canal.

ELEVEN

The dawn had just broken in a cloudy sky when the last of the forest fell away to plain, and they finally came in sight of the Summer Halls. Kai stood on the rail of the boat, holding on to the canopy's support, to watch it grow more distinct in the gray light.

It wasn't much like he remembered. The towering earthworks still stood like a small flat-topped mountain, but the low growth of grass and flowers that had kept the dirt in place had grown into a heavy covering of brush and small trees. The broad sweep of canals that ringed it were heavily overgrown with rushes, at least on this side. Even from this distance the small city to the west of the structure looked overgrown, empty, and silent. The dark skeletal shapes strewn along its docks were the hulks of wrecked and abandoned boats and barges.

The others were still asleep, and there was no reason to wake them now. He did nudge Ziede through her heart pearl until she sat up, blinking and frowning at their surroundings. She groaned under her breath and said silently, *I hate this place. I forgot how much I hated it.*

It's the same weather as the day we escaped, Kai replied. He was suddenly uncertain. *Isn't it? I'm not imagining that.*

"No, it's the same," she whispered aloud. She made a complicated gesture and the boat slowed and wandered a little sideways as some of her wind-devils broke away to scout.

They were silent as the sun advanced somewhere above the clouds and the boat drew closer and closer to the man-made mountain of the Summer Halls. The bridge had been destroyed long ago, so there was no way to approach it by land now. Nothing was visible of the top, at least not from this angle. Kai could just barely pick out the fold on the slope where a set of stairs climbed it, now completely shielded by foliage. "Can you see anything of the inside?" he asked Ziede.

"No, not really." Ziede was distracted, biting her lip as she saw through the senses of her wind-devils. They were searching for human shapes and movement, and what passed for their eyes didn't always see the mortal world as it was. The image Kai could see in Ziede's pearl was only the shape of the open top of the earthwork. It was a perfect oval; Kai had never known that, never seen it from this angle. The wind-devils' perception could make out nothing inside, just a moving void of shadow. Ziede said, "There's too much . . . I suppose you could describe it as residue, of the Hierarchs' Well and the old intentions and designs of all the expositors who built this place." She shook her head slightly. "The wind-devils aren't seeing any sign of life on the mound, at least."

"No Immortal Blessed, no expositors, no Rising World cohort lying in the bushes in wait for us," Kai said. He meant it to sound like a joke, but it didn't come out that way.

"Not so far." Ziede's voice was dry.

Behind them, Ramad coughed. Kai glanced back at where he lay on a bench, a blanket bunched under his head for a pillow. He was bleary-eyed as he sat up and squinted at the earthwork ahead. "So we're almost there," he said in a rasp. He cleared his throat, and started to retie his hair. "I realized last night I'd lost count of the days. Yesterday was the Imperial Rising World renewal."

Kai locked gazes with Ziede. "Well, good to have it over with," he said, as if it didn't matter.

Tenes slipped out of the tent with a supply bag, Sanja behind her. They passed out food: some stale millet bread left over from their stop at the last market, as well as melon, pickled eggplant, and dried waterweed.

The earthwork's nearest brush-covered slope loomed larger,

close enough to clearly see the thorns on the spiky trees and the flowers in the scattered grasses. Alert now, Ramad said, "What are the chances of someone stationed here to guard this place?"

"As a Rising World vanguarder, you don't know?" Kai was honestly curious.

"I don't know every move the empire makes, no." Ramad actually sounded a little testy. This was the first time Kai had seen him betray any nerves. But for a historian, a child of the Arike generation who had fought and died under the Hierarchs, coming here had to feel like a tangible weight. "There must still be things of value, if no one's been in there since the Hierarchs fell."

"Others have returned here, or tried to," Ziede said absently. "I heard they made it up to the top, but realized there was no point in continuing."

"They did," Kai admitted. "That was when they destroyed the bridge."

"So the interior really is flooded, the way the stories say?" Ramad asked. He was looking back the way they came, studying the low trees and brush, as if watching for signs of pursuit.

"Oh, it's flooded all right," Ziede assured him. "Kai did it."

"It was an accident." Kai looked around to see Tenes was curious and Sanja judgmental. His first time in a new body, terrified and expecting at any moment to find out what dying meant for a demon in the mortal world.

Ramad was staring at him now, he had no idea why.

By the time Ziede guided the boat out of the main canal and into the innermost of the three moats that circled the earthwork, they had finished eating and put away the supply bags.

The rushes along the bank covered the foot of the huge slope. The further they got from the faster current of the canal, the more sluggish and dark the moat water became. The scent rising off it was foul, and the cool breeze had died away, leaving the air clammy and dank. Despite the thick foliage and lush flowers, there was no buzz of insects, no clouds of gnats or skitter of water beetles, no sign of fish, no waterbirds, no lizards basking on the banks. Kai knew why; this close he could practically smell the power well. "Can you feel it?"

Ramad's brow was creased. "Feel what?"

Tenes signed, *Cold death*, and took Sanja's hand. Sanja kept her gaze on the slope, worried and wary.

"It's become a power well," Kai said. They should have known this would happen. All that death, the bodies left to rot, the water. "A small one, no range at all. But I wonder if anyone's ever used it." He felt prickles of ill ease chase up and down the skin of his back.

Ramad was startled. "Like what Aclines did aboard the Immortal Blessed ship? Or Orintukk?"

"No, this is natural. Like . . ." Kai couldn't come up with an example that would make sense to Ramad. "The Well of Thosaren probably started as a natural power well. If someone worked long enough on this one, they could turn it into a well for expositors to draw from."

"It's had years to stew in its juices." Ziede sounded thoughtful. "We're going to need some protection from that water."

"The canal water?" Sanja asked uneasily. She drew her hand back from the side of the boat. "It smells bad. That means it's poison?"

"It's a good indication that it might be." Ziede said, "Kai, we're going into the harbor, correct?"

"Unless you can think of a better idea," he told her. If there was something or someone here guarding this place, the land harbor was the mostly likely spot for them to camp. Anyone staying in the city would have to put out in a boat to reach the Summer Halls, which would be impractical for trying to confront intruders.

If there was anyone here, they would be in the harbor, and it was better to meet them and get the confrontation and death over with.

It was Sanja who asked, "How did an accident make it flood?"

She had been unusually subdued, letting Tenes hold on to her hand.

"It's a long story. I'll tell you after we find what we're looking for." That was probably far more optimistic than their situation warranted, but Kai didn't want to talk about it now, not in the shadow of this place. And they were coming up on a sharp angle of gray stone standing out from the overgrown slope: the edge of the watergate into the harbor. Past it broken stone blocks rose above the surface, making navigation difficult. The blocks were the most visible part of the demolished bridge and there would be a lot more under the water. Technically the barge's hull was only partly existent in reality and therefore couldn't be torn open if it hit a rock. But Kai didn't want to end up arguing with a barge determined that it had been hulled and needed to sink; the canal was too deep for that.

Sanja grumbled something and Tenes poked her in the ribs.

Kai and Ramad used the poles to keep the boat off the stone debris just under the surface. Ziede guided her wind-devils to gently maneuver them past the pillars of the giant watergate. One rusted iron door had fallen off into the water, the other stood partly open.

Tucked into the side of the massive earthwork, the harbor should have been familiar, but Kai had only seen it briefly and never from this direction. The moat flowed into a big semi-circular pool, and at its far end was a tall arch, now closed off by heavy metal-bound doors, that led to a large cavern of docks and barge slips.

The years of abandonment showed in the plaza on the far side of the pool, where clumps of flowers and mosses had sprouted in every crack and gap. Stone stairs curled up the slope from the plaza, heavily overshadowed with brush but still mostly intact, as far as Kai could see. In the retaining wall between the stairs and the harbor pool, there was another archway, also closed off by heavy doors. It was easily tall enough for loaded wallwalkers to pass through, and would open into the cavern that had held the stables and storage for wheeled vehicles. In the high outer wall, the massive gate that led out to the now-demolished bridge was shut, and its locking mechanism of multiple bars and gears and chains looked rusted in place. The barred portcullis just inside it had also been dropped.

Kai thought the harbor doors would be locked; obviously the only reason the watergate was open was that it had fallen apart. But when their boat edged up to it, Ramad leaned forward to give one door an experimental push and almost fell in when it swung open.

With nudges from Ziede's wind-devils and shoves from the poles, they got the boat through the archway and into the cover of the shadowy cavern. There was no sound or sense of anything alive; Ziede's wind-devils found no trace of living intruders, not even any nesting birds or river rats. The place was as quiet as a room deep underground, the drip of water from the stone vaults overhead oddly loud in the dark. Kai called a scatter of imps and they flitted around, casting light on empty docks. There were only a few boats left, mostly small, rickety craft rejected by the refugees who had escaped here so many years ago. One large hulking half-sunken ornamental barge had also been left behind, its gilded wood glinting as the imps briefly swarmed it.

After a struggle, they got their barge close enough to a stone slip for Tenes and Sanja to jump off and help guide it in with the ropes. Kai said, "We'd better take our supplies off in case it falls apart." He wasn't sure how much longer the intention would last; unmoving, sitting here with the other wrecks, the barge was far more likely to forget its brief new life and sink again.

Tenes signed, *I keep forgetting it's not a real boat*, and turned to help Ziede with the supply bags. Kai helped them pull the tent apart, then stepped away to take a closer look at their surroundings. Sanja, with an armload of bags, said, "What is that?"

She was looking at the gilded barge. It was a good forty paces long, with two levels of colonnades draped with rotting silk curtains. The prow was shaped into a giant bearded face, set in a beatific expression. "It's a Hierarch's barge. For traveling along the canals," Kai told her.

"No, I figured that, I mean—" She pointed at the face. "Is that a Hierarch? Is that what they looked like?"

"Sort of," Kai admitted. He didn't recognize it as an individual. Maybe it was like a composite mishmash of all the Hierarchs. That was just the baffling sort of thing they might do. "They didn't all have beards, though."

"There was a face on the front of the big Immortal Blessed ship, too." Sanja was still frowning. "Did the Hierarchs copy them?"

"Huh." It was an interesting question. The Immortal Blessed were unlikely to copy anyone, especially the Hierarchs. "Maybe."

Then Ramad said, "Kai."

The tension in his voice made Kai and Sanja turn in unison. Ramad stood a few slips over, beside a low river boat about the same length as their barge. At first glance, Kai had taken it for another wreck.

But it sat higher in the water, in much better condition than the moldering barge and the other rotting boats that had been here since the escape. Then Kai's imps, drawn by Ramad's urgency, swarmed it and in their light the hull gleamed gold.

Kai reached it in one breathless heartbeat. He couldn't believe they had almost missed it, but in the gloom, the Blessed metal hull had faded into the darkness. The bright colors had been allowed to dim and mottle, but the sun signs etched along the sides were still visible. He didn't need to hear Ramad whisper, "This is an Immortal Blessed craft."

It was a practical boat, meant for canal journeys. Near the stern were storage compartments, built-in benches, and a rolled-up shade canopy stowed under the side rail. Ziede arrived so silently Kai almost jumped when she said, "There's no column for the Well of Thosaren."

Kai spotted the low plinth near the bow. "No, there was, but it's been removed."

Ramad looked worried. "Another stolen Immortal Blessed boat is surely an indication of . . . something."

"And it hasn't been here long," Ziede added. Kai agreed. The boat was clean, well cared for, there was no layer of grime or wind-blown dirt on the benches and cushions. The green water had only had time to leave a faint line of moss along the hull.

Sanja rotated like a spinning toy, trying to see every part of the dim cavern at once. "If they followed us, and got here first, why haven't they jumped out at us yet?"

"Because they didn't follow us, they came here for something else." Kai turned to Tenes, who was keeping a wary eye on their surroundings. He caught her attention and signed, *Keep watch here?*

Tenes signaled assent. Kai said, "Sanja, stay here with Tenes."

Uneasy, Sanja hugged herself and nodded. "You're going to find these people?"

"Only if we can't avoid it," Kai said. "We're going to find what we came for and get out."

<hr>

Kai, Ziede, and Ramad took a quick walk through the stables attached to the docks, just to make sure there were no more surprises. Ziede's wind-devils found no sense of mortal life in the dark echoing halls. Even the long-rotted bins of fodder left behind had drawn no rats or lizards or other scavengers, and no one had ever come for the tools and equipment.

Back out in the plaza, Ramad said, "Is it possible to climb to the top without taking the stairs? They might be watching that route."

Kai could have warned him but decided not to.

Ziede said, "We're not climbing." Ramad startled when she grabbed his arm but didn't pull away. Kai was used to that moment when the wind-devil closed around him and his feet left the ground, but Ramad drew in a sharp startled breath. Kai felt Ziede wait for a heartbeat, to see if Ramad would panic and fight. He didn't, and the devils lifted them upward.

Kai stopped worrying about Ramad as they cleared the high stable arches and moved up the slope toward the crest of the earthwork. He braced for what he was going to see. Ziede kept them so low the taller treetops brushed his shins. In moments they were at the top.

The paved rim that circled the earthwork had discolored from white to dingy gray, but wasn't as eaten away by grass as the plaza below. Part of Kai had expected the water to be clear, the courts and glass-roofed halls as visible as if it had all happened yesterday. But the water was a dark sour color, thick with rafts of rotting dead leaves.

Only rooftops, or the tops of the tallest towers or courts, were visible above the surface. The stone was pitted and worn, streaked with something like rust. The glass so mottled and discolored that it was as impenetrable as the water.

Kai realized his heart was pounding, though it was with relief instead of anything else. He wasn't sure what he had expected, but these signs of age and neglect and mortal rot were . . . reassuring. "You'd think there would be float-moss," he said. They were always having to clean it out of the still pools at Avagantrum. "That the whole place would be green."

"That only grows in healthy water." Ziede's suspicious gaze was on the Immortal Blessed supplication tower, nearly halfway across the width of the Halls. It was tall and narrow, meant only to give access to the landing balconies, and only a few levels still stood above the water. "They—whoever they are—must have carried a small boat up here."

If they were diving for relics, a structure with a mostly intact upper portion would make a good platform to work from. Kai spotted a much larger glass roof to the left, so huge only its peak was visible, the rest buried under leaves and some weedy growth. That must be the Temple Halls, and if it was, then he recognized that colonnade some distance past it. The whole top floor was above the surface. "Over there, that tall court. That was where we found the second Hierarch."

Ziede's frown deepened. "Hmm."

There had to be riches under the water, jewels and metals, but more importantly, intentions, devices, and other workings of the Hierarchs that might still be usable for expositors. Kai spoke silently to Ziede, *How many people still alive know how to find that court?*

At least one too many, apparently, Ziede replied. *If it's not just a coincidence.*

Kai doubted that anything that had happened so far was a coincidence.

Ramad studied the scene avidly. As an Arike growing up close to the Rising World court, he would have heard stories of this place all his life. "They came in an Immortal Blessed craft. They can't be ordinary thieves." Before Kai or Ziede could reply, he added, "No, I'm not being naive. I mean they must be either a Blessed, or an expositor like Aclines, someone who was given or stole a consecrated boat. And that seems coincidental for there to be two different groups of conspirators."

It was interesting that Ramad was thinking along the same lines as Kai and Ziede. Or at least, interesting that he was willing to admit it. Kai said, "Aclines' friends should be expecting us at Stios." Unless they hadn't fooled their pursuit at all, and someone had guessed their destination. Unless Ramad was their agent and had some means of communicating with them. The thought was sour; Kai was so tired of being suspicious.

Seemingly oblivious to any undercurrents, Ramad nodded. "Unless there's something here they want. Besides you."

Ziede said grimly, "Let's get a look at them." She took hold of

Kai's arm and the shoulder of Ramad's coat and stepped into the air again.

The wind-devil caught the breeze and floated out over the dark water, where it spun like a leaf. Unnerved, Ramad grabbed Ziede's hand where it rested on his shoulder. Kai thought the devil might be reacting to the power well now sitting like a bloated carrion toad over the ruin of the Summer Halls.

As they reached the top of the Hierarchs' court, Kai tapped Ziede's hand. She let go and he dropped onto the roof of the colonnade. He landed in a crouch, his feet slipping a little on the grimy slate. Then he slid forward to the edge of the roof and hung head down.

There was nothing on the colonnade but rotting leaves. The windows in the back wall opened into what had once been a grand, high-ceilinged space. He didn't need to call imps: toward the far right corner was the cool white glow of an Immortal Blessed lamp. It was at the wrong angle for Kai to see much. He had the sense of a shadowy human shape, and some lumps that might be packs.

I found the boat, tucked up under a window on the far side from you, Ziede told him through her pearl. *Small, not room for more than three people at one time.*

Someone's here, Kai replied. *I'm going to get closer.* He rolled forward and hung from the edge to drop silently onto the crusty stone floor of the colonnade.

All those years ago, when Kai had come to this court in search of a Hierarch, he hadn't seen this floor; the audience hall should be at least one or two levels below. It was too dark in the further corners of the room to see any doors or stair landings. He slipped silently across the colonnade and climbed in through the window.

The floor was just as crusty but also slimy and slippery. Kai stepped carefully, moving silently toward the lamp and the outline of a human shape sitting cross-legged near it. Water dripped constantly and he could hear breathing, the rustle of paper. Closer, and he made out the tarp spread on the grimy floor. There was a roll of bedding, some bags, and a wooden water container. A scatter of papers, book rolls, a stone ink bottle, and a few carved pens. Not just a camp, but a scholar's camp. Maybe this wasn't thieves or conspirators, but some historian like Ramad, with more curiosity than sense.

The preoccupied shape beside the lamp was a small person, hair tied back in a short queue, head bent over a stack of papers. Probably male, since he wore the tunic and skirt of traditional Arike dress, in dull cotton for work or travel. The skirt was tied up to reveal a pair of rolled-up muddy leggings, not unlike what Kai was wearing.

Kai was ten steps away. This was a dream. Or he had walked into a lingering web of intentions and was now trapped in a chimera. The familiar line of the jaw, the angle of the head . . .

Then the person glanced up. He yelped, scattered his papers and scrambled back. The Blessed lamp flared brighter, taking away any doubt. Kai said, "Dahin?"

THE PAST:
THE BECOMING

. . . says the lands of the Far South were captured much the way the Arik was, through assassination and manipulation. There the Hierarchs raised a generation of soldiers who believed it was their destiny to conquer and destroy the rest of the world, that they would one day receive lands in the east and west and north for their own. Whether that promise would have been kept or not, no one knows.

. . . how many of the southern legions had doubts. Accounts say the Hierarchs were vicious in rooting out dissension in the ranks. Many surviving legionaries escaped when they had the chance, to the independent cities that rose out of the shattered lands along the northeastern coasts; others tried to return to the South. Many settled with the other refugees and live throughout the north and east, farming or fishing or trading, as they were once promised by their masters.

—*The East Falls*, Weranan, historian of Seidel-arik

Kai and Ziede ran down the processional corridor back toward the Cageling Demon Court. Kai found moving easier if he just tried not to think about what his body was doing; his legs still felt too long and being almost as tall as Ziede made him dizzy.

When they reached the walkway, the court was shrouded in perpetual rain again. Kai didn't step to the railing to look inside. If there were any living demons in there, they had voluntarily returned, and he didn't want to see it. They made their way over the stiffening mortal bodies on the walkway and back to the door to the intention chamber.

As they climbed the stairs to the upper level, the air was increasingly close and humid. The basin was filled with water again, with no sign of Ziede's struggle to block it except for puddles on the floor and damp splashes high on the stone walls. Kai wasn't sure that Ziede's idea would help, but as she had pointed out, it was worth a brief stop on the way to certain death to find out.

He circled the basin, running his hand along the edge and below. They had searched unsuccessfully for the controlling design here before, but Ziede's theory was that now that Kai had Talamines' memories, he might be able to identify the intention that made the rain. "You think using it will confuse the Hierarch," Kai had said, back in the Temple Halls. "They'll think 'what are these idiots trying to do' and while they're distracted—"

"No." Ziede had tapped her nails on her belt. "I think water disappears into the air, so this intention must create water, or rather draw it from somewhere, to keep the Cageling Court saturated."

"Or they just carry buckets up to refill the basin," Kai had pointed out.

Ziede's expression had not indicated appreciation of that insight. She said, "Humor me, Kai."

Salatel and her soldiers had wanted to follow them but Kai had sent them ahead to inform Bashasa of their plan, such as it was. Kai was surprised Salatel had listened to him. Turning to run his hands over the rougher stone of the wall behind the basin, he said as much to Ziede.

She said, "Bashasa told them they were your personal guard now. To follow your orders."

Kai was so taken aback by that, he turned to stare at her. Her expression was enigmatic and he asked, "When did this happen?"

"When you were unconscious, after we realized you'd taken that body," Ziede explained. She poked him in the shoulder and he turned back to the wall to keep searching. She continued, "He didn't want anyone to kill you thinking you were an expositor. He also didn't want to hamper you if you woke up and decided to do something else miraculous, so making them your personal guard, subject to your orders, solved both problems." She frowned a little. "I didn't trust him at first, not at all. I'm still not sure how far I can trust him, and given our current circumstances I doubt we'll live long enough to find out. But he is a more sensible person than I took him for."

Kai didn't understand. Bashasa had saved him from the Cageling Court, but the only reason Kai had been chosen was for his small size, so Bashasa's sister's body could take his place. It wasn't as if Bashasa should feel responsible for him. "He was drunk when we left the Hostage Courts."

"I know, but he got over it quickly."

"Yes, but . . ." Kai stopped, staring at the wall, and forgot what he meant to say. He had seen something, like a character in an unfamiliar alphabet, etched onto one of the blocks. He couldn't see it now, but he was sure it was in the middle of the wall, just opposite the center of the basin. He knew he had looked there the first time they searched, but he had a different body's vision now. An expositor's vision.

He tried holding a hand over one eye, and caught a flash of pale light. He turned slowly away from the wall. There it was, at the very edge of his sight. The block had writing on it, a circular character from a language Talamines recognized but Kai didn't know how to read.

"What do you see?" Ziede asked softly.

"A word, or a sign." He looked around, then stepped to one of the damp patches on the wall and with a finger sketched the character. "You can't see it on the block?"

"No, to my eyes nothing's there." Ziede stepped close. "I don't know what this is. Did Talamines?"

"He'd seen it before, but he can't read it." If Kai turned his head the right way, he could keep the word in sight. The substance used to draw it was pale, the lines a little smeared. It was a liquid that wasn't ink. At least not the kind of ink the Saredi or borderlanders made, or like the ink Bashasa had used to draw his maps. *Like liquid light,* he thought. Is this what an intention looked like? Or not an intention, but a marker for an intention. A written design?

Ziede was intrigued. "I've heard that there's a language from the Hierarchs' homeland that no one can read."

"I thought Imperial was the Hierarchs' language." Kai prodded the mortar around the marked block, wondering if they could remove it.

"No, Imperial comes from Sun-Ar, which is supposedly the first land the Hierarchs conquered after they left their own." Ziede poked at the mortar too. "Well, we can't get it out. Even if we could find a chisel or a pick we don't have time—"

An impulse made Kai put his hand on the word. He felt something cold attach to the skin of his palm. He drew his hand away from the block and the pale substance came with it, holding the shape of the intention, though it didn't look at all the same. Looking at it from this angle was like the difference between a drawing of an object and the object itself.

"Now I can see it," Ziede whispered.

That same impulse made Kai carefully cup his hand to hold the intention, and bring it toward his chest.

"Kai, don't—" Ziede began urgently.

Kai's hand seemed to snap the last few inches and flatten to the front of his silk tunic. He felt the intention sink through his skin and sit atop his breastbone, a cold weight like mud from the bottom of a mountain river.

He looked at Ziede. Her expression was incredulous, bordering on horrified. Kai wasn't thrilled with what had just happened either, but they needed a way to move the intention. She said, "Will that come out?"

"Probably? Maybe?" Kai bit his lip. "I don't want to try until we get to where we want to put it."

"Kai." Ziede reached up to rub her face, apparently remembered her already ruined makeup, and planted her hands on her hips instead. "Could you manage not to find any more unique ways to destroy yourself until after we find this Hierarch? I don't really care to die alone."

"Well, I'll try." It wasn't like Kai could make any promises right now.

———⚬⚬⚬———

They followed Salatel's map away from the court, switching from one wide corridor to another, then climbing a ramp upward to a new level. The decoration was richer up here, the walls set with marble panels that looked like ocean waves of black overtaking an icy shore. They heard shouting in the distance and saw a few mortals in the corridors, but no one tried to stop them. All were fleeing, and while most ignored them, a few stopped to ask Ziede for help. Others called to them, urging them to run, too. Kai was still wearing Bashasa's blue brocade coat and kept his face averted so he could pass as a mortal. He still had Talamines' veil but hesitated to put it on; he thought it would make him look like an expositor. Ziede just directed the mortals away from the area where they knew Bashasa was fighting with the legionaries and told them to keep going.

They came to a place where the walls and ceiling of the corridor dropped away and it turned into a bridge across a narrow man-made canyon of stone. Above them smooth white walls stretched up to an opening that allowed a brief glimpse of cloudy sky and daylight. A few levels below, mortals ran along the paving, all heading the same direction.

"This must be one of the ways out," Ziede said as they crossed quickly over the bridge.

Kai said, "At least someone's getting out alive." Across the bridge and back inside, the corridor turned into a gallery along a series of small garden courts, each one luxuriant with flowering plants, very different from the untended gardens in the Hostage Courts. A flicker of images from Talamines' memory said they were getting closer. "You could leave, too." With Ziede's power, it would be easy for her to float down to the floor of the open corridor and join the mortals moving toward freedom.

"And do what, sail back to Khalin to sit alone in the empty burned-out shell of my cloister?" Ziede threw him a grim glance. "Why don't you go?"

Kai felt a surge of bitterness so intense it nearly choked him. "Where? Even if there's any Saredi clans left, they won't take me in like this. I'm not Enna anymore."

"Does the body you're in matter so much? You're still a demon." Then she shook her head. "I'm sorry, I won't ask again."

It mattered. All the mortals in Kentdessa who might have accepted him anyway were dead. Or at least—and this thought was like a shard of rock in his heart—he would never know if they would have rejected him the way the demons had.

The next turn took them through a gallery that ran along a small court of tall fir trees. Kai didn't hear any fighting, but something in Talamines' memory sparked, and he said, "Wait, we're close. We can cut through here."

There were no stairs. Ziede swung over the balustrade and floated down. Kai climbed the nearest pillar, finding handholds in between the rough stone blocks. He was cautious about dropping the last few paces, not sure of this new body yet. But Talamines had been young and strong, and Kai still seemed to have the demonic properties that had protected Enna's flesh, at least if his resistance to Arn-Nefa's attack was anything to go by.

They made their way through the potted trees toward an archway. Kai nearly jumped out of his skin when a figure stepped into view, and Ziede's hands snapped up reflexively.

It was an Arike soldier, and fortunately Ziede caught herself before the summoned air spirit did anything more than ruffle the woman's ringleted hair. "This way," the soldier whispered in accented Imperial. "Just through there."

Kai heard voices, whispers, and the shuffle of movement. They followed the soldier's directions across the corridor and into a wide high-ceilinged room, crowded with Arike soldiers and other mortals. Kai saw Salatel first, then realized she stood next to Bashasa, who was studying a map. As if he had sensed their entrance, Bashasa looked up and met his gaze with startled delight. "There you are!" he said, managing to keep his voice low. The whole crowd turned to stare at them and Kai's hackles went up. But Bashasa said, "Quick, quick, come here! You have a plan?"

The soldiers parted for them, Salatel elbowing a mortal who didn't step aside quickly enough. Kai followed Ziede, suddenly uncertain. Every eye in the room seemed to be on him, the demon in the stolen mortal body. He was the same height as Bashasa now, which just reminded him how much had changed. Ziede said, "Salatel told you we think we know where the Hierarch is?"

"Yes." Waving the map, Bashasa turned to point. Past three broad archways, the bulk of the Arike soldiers and other armed mortals gathered in front of a large set of barred doors. "If we're reading this right, the court on the other side of that wall is the one from your vision. It's called the Sanctuary Court. The room where we think the Hierarch is hiding is on the level just above the gallery, on the far side."

Kai thought Bashasa was optimistic with that choice of the word *hiding* rather than *waiting*. He asked, "Do you know why they haven't overrun you yet?"

"It's clear that they're waiting for their second garrison to come through here." Bashasa pointed at the map again. "We've sealed those doors off too, of course, but with our forces split"—he shrugged—"we won't last much longer."

Kai wondered if the mortals found Bashasa's ability to not sound particularly concerned about anything to be terrifying rather than reassuring. They all seemed very dubious. One said, "You believe this can work?" They were a large figure, with very dark skin and long heavy braids, dressed in rich blue-green robes over a silver-gray caftan painted with cranes and other waterbirds, now liberally dotted with blood.

Bashasa waved a hand and introduced them. "This is Tescai-lin, Light of the Hundred Coronels of Enalin." As an afterthought, he indicated the two other Arike in brocaded coats standing nearby. "Oh, and that is Hiranan, First Daughter of the Prince-heir of Seidel-arik, and Vrim, Second Son of the Prince-heir of Descar-arik." Hiranan was an older woman, her expression grim, leaning on a carved and polished crutch. Vrim was Bashasa's age and seemed skeptical.

Tescai-lin still watched Kai, and he realized they had actually meant the "you believe this can work" question for him. He said, "I can do some damage, slow them down, give more people time to leave."

Bashasa clapped Kai on the shoulder. Some of the other mortals flinched and stared, though Tescai-Lin just looked thoughtful. Bashasa said, "It's the best we can hope for!"

Kai just wanted to get this over with. He pulled off the coat Bashasa had loaned him and handed it to Salatel, leaving him in Talamines' black tunic and skirt. "How do I get to the Sanctuary Court from here?"

Behind him a familiar voice said, "I'll take you."

Kai turned. It was Tahren.

"Still alive, I see," Ziede said. It was probably meant to be a joke but something about it didn't hit right. Ziede sounded too relieved to be cynical.

Tahren just lifted a brow, then said to Kai, "You got taller."

Kai was eye level with Tahren's chin. He said, "I know, I'm not sure how it happened," and thought, *Speaking of jokes that aren't funny.* "Let's go."

As he started to turn away, Bashasa stopped him with a hand on his arm. Now his brow was creased with worry. "Fourth Prince." He hesitated, and Kai wondered what he was going to say. No one was expecting Kai to be successful, including Kai. No one was expecting to survive this battle. The Saredi had never been much for speaking empty platitudes, like some of the lesser borderlander leaders. Then Bashasa squeezed his arm and said, "Make them pay for it."

The surge of emotion caught Kai by surprise. He wasn't even sure what he was feeling. This was the whole point, wasn't it, to make the Hierarchs pay for what they had taken. To hurt them on the way down, so someone would know it wasn't impossible. He just said, "They'll pay," and followed Tahren.

⚬⚬⚬

Tahren led them back through the fir tree court and up and around via an unobtrusive stairwell. The door had been barred and a young Arike soldier left to guard it, which was a prudent precaution, since the legionaries obviously knew exactly where Bashasa's forces had gathered. "You don't have to come," Kai told Ziede, as they climbed the narrow stairs. He had realized she hadn't followed just to say goodbye away from the watching mortals. "I'll have to go in alone anyway."

"I may be able to do something . . ." She didn't finish that sentence, which was probably going to end: *if this doesn't work at all and they kill you before you get near the Hierarch.* She asked Tahren, "Do you know if your brother got out?"

Tahren was in front, her back a straight line of tension. "One of Bashasa's soldiers said Dahin and the others left for the nearest way out as planned." Kai thought that would be it; Tahren was not exactly a talker. Then she added, "I don't know if the city is any safer than the palace."

Ziede said, "So many people have fled already. They'll have crowds to conceal themselves in, and no one will be thinking about anything except getting away. Bashasa's people will know what to do." She added wryly, "They must be quick-thinking and competent if they've lasted this long with him."

Kai thought of Salatel, taking her orders to become the personal guard of a demon apparently without protest. He said, "And they're loyal."

He didn't think Tahren would respond, but she glanced briefly back with a small smile. She didn't seem much reassured, but maybe she appreciated the effort.

Tahren paused at the top of the stair and listened. Kai could hear distant movement, quiet voices. Then Tahren led them across a corridor and through a little maze of empty rooms, past doorways where Kai glimpsed marble floors and hangings of heavy, richly colored fabrics. The decor would be better suited to a cooler, dryer climate, like the high-altitude holds in the eastern borderlander mountains. The dampness in this air probably ruined the fabric, but everyone here seemed to be too rich to care. He knew where in the Halls they were now, from the map if not Talamines' memories. They were circumventing the area around the court Bashasa had pointed out to come at it from another direction. The voices of what must be legionaries were getting louder as they drew closer. He stopped Tahren and said, "I can find it from here."

Tahren's expression was grim, but she pointed to her own eyes and said, "Don't forget."

Kai pulled out Talamines' black veil and tried to put it on. Ziede stepped up, took it and adjusted it, so it hung over the upper part of his face without interfering with the pins in his hair. Finished, she stepped back and let her breath out. "I'd tell you to be careful, but . . ."

Kai looked at her through the black film of the veil. "You could say 'be violent' instead."

Tahren, who Kai was beginning to suspect had a very dry sense of humor, patted his shoulder and said, "Be violent."

———⦿———

Following Talamines' sparks of recognition, Kai found his way to the entrance of a broad corridor. As soon as he stepped into it, he saw a cluster of legionaries guarding a heavy gold-chased door at the end. He squelched the impulse to flinch and duck back through the door, managed not to self-consciously adjust his veil again, and made himself walk deliberately toward them.

The wall behind the legionaries was more heavily built, the blocks larger and more weathered than those in the other passages and rooms Kai had just navigated. He had known he was getting closer when he passed a broad ramp that led down a level and heard the murmur and movement of a large number of people, probably legionaries and loyal Hierarch followers waiting for the orders to break down the barred doors and overrun Bashasa's rebels.

The legionaries ahead were all taller than Talamines, their shoulders broad under their fine leather and sculpted metal armor. They all had pale skin and light eyes, like the islanders from the far south who had traded with the Erathi sometimes. As Kai approached, no one shouted or ran forward to attack him. But since he was walking toward them like a fool, maybe they were lazily waiting for him to get within range.

But when he stopped, easily within short spear–reach, the one with the officer's tail made a formal salute and said, "Expositor, this way." Another opened the left side of the heavy door for him. When he passed through, the left slipped after him, moving ahead to lead the way.

Kai's jumping nerves made his skin tingle as the corridor opened into a gallery along an open court. A partial glass roof stretched over it, and a strong scent of green plants and dampness rode the breeze. It sparked what was left of Talamines' memory again, and Kai knew the archway they were moving toward led to the Hierarchs' private quarters, the most heavily guarded sanctum of the huge rambling Summer Halls.

There were legionaries everywhere. Kai found himself dropping his gaze to the floor again. There were no stray weeds growing between these polished paving stones. The water intention burned cold in his chest.

They passed through another cluster of legionaries, another guarded door at the end of the gallery, and then another. The floor was made of marble slabs now, white mottled with red streaks. They walked between long narrow pools, shallow and clear. Too shallow for the intention, Kai thought. The idea was to flood this court and distract and delay the legionaries; he didn't want to dramatically sacrifice himself only to do nothing more than make the floors wet.

The air was still damp but cooler, tinged with a scent that was clean and sweet. He managed to drag his eyes up enough to see legionaries stationed along the walls. Square columns were sheathed in gold plates and etched with figures picked out in red and black enamel. It was rich and strange and different from anything else he had seen in this place. Maybe this was the way the Hierarchs lived in their homeland, wherever that was.

Kai's life had been hanging from a thread since he had been captured, and it seemed inevitable that he was going to be ripped out of his body and set adrift in the mortal world. He probably deserved it, for stealing Talamines' body, expositor or not. He tried to stop thinking about it, focus instead on the faint breeze from ahead, the scent of stone and water and flower perfume.

They passed through an archway and Kai stopped when his guide did. The veil obscured much of his vision and he couldn't risk a look around. He had a sense of a large space, sound echoing off a high ceiling, and the lap of water that sounded promisingly deeper than the shallow pools in the corridor.

The people here were speaking softly, pausing to stare at Kai. The legionary who had led him in was making some kind of bow and Kai realized he had no idea how expositors greeted Hierarchs. Pure panic jolted through his brain and he almost grabbed for the water intention.

But that jolt must have stirred Talamines' memory because he found his body bending from the waist, his hands coming up cupped together as if offering something, then he straightened up and forced himself to lift his head.

With the veil he still couldn't take in much of the chamber, just that it was big and curving, with more of the brightly enameled gold on the walls. A breeze and daylight came from somewhere to the right, probably windows high in the wall, open to the court outside. The curved pool took up well over half the room. That should work, if Kai could get to it fast enough.

Barely ten long paces away, the Hierarch sat on a cushioned couch atop a low platform. This one was a small figure dressed in gold robes, with fish-pale skin and long silver-gray hair, and softer features than the one Bashasa had killed in the Temple Halls. Other mortals sat at the Hierarch's feet or on cushioned stools, all dressed in richly colored coats or robes and jeweled veils. Three of them Talamines' memory identified as lesser expositors. Like Cantenios, the expositor Kai had killed in the Hostage Courts, before he had any idea how far Bashasa's suicidal plan was going to take him. Standing beside the platform like a statue was an expositor like Talamines, a still shape in a gold coat and veils, there to be this Hierarch's focus for the Well.

The tall figure pacing away from the pool was the Hierarch's Voice Raihankana. Then Kai registered the much smaller person sitting on a pillow on the floor, between two standing legionaries. He didn't need Talamines' memories to recognize him; it was Dahin.

Tahren's young brother had a darkening bruise on one cheek, his light-colored tunic was torn and pulled off one shoulder. His bare toes peeked out under the hem of his pants. He looked frightened, and sick, and very alone.

Raihankana turned and said, "Where have you been, Talamines? We feared you dead." He wore a long tunic and skirt in a shade darker than bloodred, his coat covered in black brocade. He didn't wear a veil but a delicate gold diadem held back his dark curling hair.

Kai said, "I was outside the Temple Halls." Talamines' voice came out rough and thick. Something felt wrong, and he prodded Talamines' memory and belatedly added, "Hierarch's Voice." Kai had intended to sacrifice himself but sacrificing Dahin was something else. Had the rest of Bashasa's household been dragged here or had they been killed outside the Summer Halls? Or had Dahin left them to find Tahren?

"What were you—" Raihankana began, then stiffened. His voice changed, taking on a higher register, as he said, "Where is our sibling?"

So when they called Raihankana a Hierarch's Voice it wasn't just a ceremonial office. The Hierarch had actually taken control of his body. Kai could feel the power rising in the room. Like a cold draft tinged with the bitter bite of the wind that followed with the Hierarchs' Well, like a low deep tone on the edge of his hearing, like something pushing on the inside of his eyes. It was a mix of sound and scent and sensation, as if he lacked the right sensory organ to interpret it. To Talamines, it had been all that was left for him, but to Kai it was alien and wrong.

Kai wondered if Hierarchs could inhabit expositors like that, what would happen if this Hierarch tried to control him that way. He decided never finding out was better.

And then Kai had a wonderful, terrible idea. He said, "My master is concealed near the Temple Halls. My master sent me for the Lesser Blessed child."

Dahin's head jerked up, new fear in his eyes. There was a startled, speculative murmur among the other courtiers.

Through Raihankana, the Hierarch said, "For what purpose?"

Good question, Kai thought, but fortunately his frantic racing thoughts were just a little ahead of the Hierarch's. "The Immortal Marshall said she would betray the rebels if her sibling was returned."

There was confusion and betrayal in Dahin's gaze now, as if he didn't think Tahren would do that. Kai had no idea if Tahren would do it or not and didn't care, as long as the Hierarch believed she would. If they would let him walk out with Dahin, Kai still needed to drop the intention in water. The larger pool in this chamber would be best for causing confusion, but maybe the fountains in the court outside would work after all. It was risky, less effective than what Kai had originally intended to do, but if he could get Dahin out . . .

One of the mortals said, "It's unnecessary, Master. Once the Stios garrison arrives, we can trap the rebels between us."

Had Bashasa planned for that? Kai thought Bashasa hadn't believed their rebellion would last any longer than the Temple Halls attack, so maybe not.

Another mortal started to say, "But Master, the—"

Raihankana held up a hand and the mortals went silent. He paced slowly toward Kai.

Kai held himself motionless, barely breathing, trying to imitate the statue-like stillness of the gold-clad expositor. This didn't feel like a normal interaction between a group of people making plans, even a group like this. *The Hierarch doesn't believe you,* he thought. He shouldn't have tried to get Dahin out. *Idiot.* He should have remembered the burning remnants of Kentdessa Saredi and known that no one was getting out.

Raihankana stopped barely a pace away and met Kai's gaze through the veil. In the Hierarch's voice, Raihankana said, "You should not have left our sibling's side."

Since his first attempt to make up a clever story had gone so wrong, Kai didn't try again. He told himself that if Raihankana could somehow see through the veil, all these expositors and legionaries would already be attacking him. He said, "My master sent me." His voice sounded raspy with nerves and he managed not to wince.

Raihankana turned away then, but Kai didn't let himself relax. In his own voice, Raihankana said, "It may be worth it. The Lesser Blessed is meant for the Well, he can be taken back from the Immortal Marshall later."

Something in Raihankana's tone told Kai he was the one making up a story now. *He knows, they know,* Kai thought. It felt like ice trickling down from the top of his skull through his veins. *They may not know what or how, but they know Talamines is not in this room.*

Raihankana paced toward the Hierarch. And Kai sensed a shift in the flow of power, something burning and discordant. It drifted up from the gold-clad expositor like heat from a banked fire.

Tahren had helped him in the Cageling Demon Court and he wanted to help Dahin for her. But at least if they both died here, Dahin would never be taken by the Well.

As Raihankana stepped past the gold expositor, Kai lunged forward. He made it two steps before something struck him in the back, hard enough to stagger him sideways. He cried out, shocked as deep agony tore through his side; it hurt so much more in this body than it ever had in Enna's. He knew someone must have stabbed him in the back, that Raihankana must have signaled a legionary standing behind him. Kai tried to straighten up, felt something pull at his flesh. Hard metal scraped against his ribs. He choked on a scream as the blade was withdrawn.

Raihankana turned back toward him, saying, "Now, before you die, you'll tell us—" And Kai stopped listening, because pain meant power now, the power to use the only intention he had learned from Talamines' memories. He lifted his hand and called fire.

The air in front of Kai sparked into flame, a ball of smoke and fire that roared across the platform. Heat bloomed against Kai's face and mortals scattered, screamed. Raihankana staggered back, and Kai lost his view of the Hierarch in the smoke.

It wouldn't last, Kai had only moments to take advantage of the distraction. He slammed into the expositor, shoved a hand under the gold veil and grabbed his face. Kai felt a gasp against his hand as he ripped away at the expositor's life. It gave Kai the instant he needed to drag the dagger out of his belt and stab him just below the sternum. He knew the expositor would resist him at least as hard as Cantenios; he had no time for a lengthy battle. The expositor went limp under his hand and Kai shoved away. A cursebreaker swung through the air he had occupied and hit the dying expositor instead.

Kai spun, dropped the legionary next to Dahin with a hand to the bare flesh of his arm. He grabbed Dahin by the tunic and ran for the pool.

The rim was under his feet just as the world went black. Then he slammed face-first into water. Sputtering, floundering, he still had a death grip on Dahin's tunic; he must have been struck a glancing blow with a cursebreaker but it had only knocked him out for an instant.

On the platform, mortals shouted and scrambled away from the fading fire cloud, but the surviving expositors recovered fast. Kai felt the pressure in his head grow as they drew power from the Well to attack. His feet weren't touching the bottom and this was terrifying. But he pulled the intention out of his chest and slapped it down on the water, and pushed all the life and pain he had left into it.

It would have been both fatal and embarrassing if the intention only caused a little fountain of water, or made a gentle rain fall. But Ziede thought there must be a good reason it had been on the wall behind the Cageling Court's water source, and not in the basin itself. And what was left of Talamines had been certain she was right.

A deluge roared up from the pool and the level dropped so abruptly Kai thumped down onto the bottom, suddenly sitting in knee-high water. Throat burning, he coughed his lungs clear and clawed the veil off his face. Dahin huddled next to him, drenched and wide-eyed. Around them the water was a rippling wall, rising up through the chamber like a boiling pot, roaring like a storm. Somewhere nearby mortals screamed. Kai remembered there was still a Hierarch in here and a few expositors, though hopefully they were busy not drowning. In a croak, he asked Dahin, "Can you swim?"

"Uh." Dahin managed a nod. "Yes."

"Good, because I can't." Kai struggled to his feet, pulling Dahin with him. "We need to get to a window." He knew there were openings in the far wall, which he could dimly make out through the translucent rippling mass. The water still rose toward the ceiling and once it got there it might flood the narrow column of air that had formed around the intention.

"Yes, but—Who are you?" Dahin said worriedly, sloshing toward the water wall with Kai. "Why are you helping me?"

Oh right, Kai had forgotten to mention that part. He was almost as bad at that as Bashasa. He pointed at his eyes. "Dahin, it's me, Kaiisteron. I'm in this expositor's body now."

"Oh!" Dahin stared, then gasped a strangled laugh. "I didn't know you could do that! You came to rescue me?"

"No, I came to distract and maybe drown the Hierarch," Kai told him. He poked at the rippling wall, and was relieved it was no harder than sticking his hand in a running stream. "We didn't know you were here, and your sister is going to be upset."

"She's going to be furious," Dahin admitted. He took a firm hold of Kai's wrist. "Hold your breath."

Kai didn't need to breathe as much as a mortal but he didn't want any more water inside his body than there already was. He clamped his jaw shut and winced as Dahin pulled him into the liquid wall.

His feet left the floor as they were both shoved upward by the force driving the water. Dahin had grabbed Kai by the arm on his wounded side, and being tugged along hurt, but they had to keep going.

Kai knew about swimming in theory, he had seen mortals do it, and tried to kick and wave his free arm to help Dahin push them along. The water was cloudy with foam but shapes moved in it, other flailing bodies to avoid. The current flowing out through the archway nearly caught them and Kai helped Dahin wrestle away from it.

They bumped painfully into a wall, scraped against the figured gold as they shoved upward. Kai's head broke the surface next to Dahin, who gasped and coughed. Kai didn't know what powers or abilities Dahin had as a Lesser Blessed, but being underwater without breathing for long periods wasn't one of them. He scrabbled on the wall, then hooked his fingers on a carved ornament shaped like a mountain range and wrapped his other arm around Dahin's shoulders. Dahin clung to him and Kai managed to pull them both up to get a look around the chamber.

Bodies bobbed in the rising water, none of them recognizably the Hierarch, though the one in red might actually be Raihankana. Kai had to make certain. He couldn't waste this opportunity. He looked up and had his first good view of the ceiling. It was crisscrossed by heavy wooden beams, and each met this wall a short distance above a window. On the far side of the room was a balcony, still above the rising water and obscured by the spraying geysers. Kai thought he saw something there, a shift of bright color that might be moving bodies.

Dahin stared in fascination at the enamel figures on the wall in a way that seemed strange, considering everything else that was going on. Kai hoped the water hadn't turned his brain or something. He said, "Come on," and pulled them along toward the bright daylight of the nearest window.

It was more than wide enough for both of them, open to the court outside. Kai struggled up onto the stone sill, resisting the pull of the water pouring out into the court below. A legionary's corpse floated up next to them and Dahin frantically kicked at it. "Wait," Kai hissed. He couldn't drain life in the water and needed another weapon. As he leaned down to grab a stray arm, Dahin shuddered and looked away. Kai pulled it close enough to grab the long knife out of the sheath at its back, then pushed it into the swirling current. He tucked the knife into his belt and twisted around to look out the window.

"How far down is it?" Dahin gasped.

The court had two levels of galleries and a glass half dome stretching over it. The drop would have been too far for a mortal, except for the water already filling the space, trapped by what must be locked doors on the lowest level. It was fairly clear, swirling with leaves and other debris from the flooded planting beds. He said, "Don't look," but Dahin heaved himself up on the sill, looked down, and made a dismayed noise.

"Next time I tell you don't look, don't look," Kai said, annoyed. "Just take a deep breath, and when you come up, swim for that gallery." He grabbed Dahin's arm. "Keep going in that direction."

Dahin nodded and squeezed his eyes shut, muttering, "The Well of Thosaren blesses us, the Well of Thosaren protects us, the Well of Thosaren—Wait, aren't you coming with me?" Then he shrieked as Kai toppled him out of the window.

Kai waited until he saw Dahin surface, splutter, and flail. He twisted around, evidently searching for Kai, then looked up and waved urgently. Kai pointed emphatically toward the opposite gallery. Splashing indecisively, Dahin pushed away a floating branch, then finally gave up and swam for the gallery. Kai pushed up into a standing position, balancing on the ledge as he turned his back to the window. Then he crouched and leapt for the beam overhead.

He caught it, fingers digging for purchase on the smooth wood before he could drag himself up onto it. Talamines' long arms and legs were unexpectedly helpful. He climbed along it rapidly, knowing he didn't have much time.

As he neared the balcony he saw a legionary officer on his feet and three figures half collapsed behind the railed balustrade. Two wore veils caught in the ornaments in their hair, which would have told Kai they were expositors even without the whisper of power. The last was someone short in stature, wearing gold robes, wet white hair plastered to their skull. The Hierarch.

Kai dropped to his belly and crawled along the beam, hoping that for mortal eyes he faded into the shadows. Between his sopping wet clothes and hair, dragging himself along like this wasn't easy; he missed the sinuous body of his original form, another thing he would never experience again.

The legionary strode off through the door at the back of the balcony. One expositor leaned over the Hierarch. Kai pulled himself up into a crouch, drew the drowned legionary's long knife, and leapt.

He landed on the expositor's back and whipped the blade across his throat. As he fell forward Kai shoved off him and lunged for the second expositor. He drove the knife up under the man's chin. The force of it knocked the expositor against the stone railing and the cold power of his hurriedly drawn intention dissipated harmlessly into the damp air. Kai pulled the knife out and grabbed a handful of his skirt, upending him over the rail. He splashed into the roiling water, blood spreading as he struggled weakly. Kai turned.

The Hierarch crawled toward the door. Kai felt that stir of power again, sluggish like cold mud, but a wave of it could still drown him. He lunged forward and drove the knife through the Hierarch's back.

Kai stood over the Hierarch, aware now that terror pounded through his veins along with Talamines' blood. He watched the struggle to breathe, the hands that clawed at the marble floor, the gradual sinking as the last breath left the lungs. Bashasa had killed a Hierarch and Kai still hadn't believed it was possible. But under all that power, they were just flesh.

From the corridor, there was an echoing crash of stone, then distant, frantic shouting. Kai realized his feet were cold and looked down to see water creeping up his ankles. It was pouring in from down the corridor now, onto the balcony. "Oh. Uh-oh," he muttered aloud. Was the water just . . . not going to stop?

He yanked the knife free and used it to saw the Hierarch's head off. Between the rush of water and a knife not designed for the purpose, it took forever. He used the dead expositor's veil to hastily wrap it up and tie it to his belt.

Kai climbed onto the railing and jumped for the beam again. Water poured out the windows in waterfall torrents. He scrambled along the beam and across the chamber, then had to drop down into the water to get to the windowsill. Fighting to hold on against the flow, he saw the open court outside filling up, the treetops sinking under the surface. At least there was no sign of Dahin floating dead anywhere.

As he braced himself to jump, another crash and a roar made him turn. A wall of water slammed toward him, carrying chunks of stone, wood, and corpses. Kai launched himself backward out the window.

TWELVE

Dahin stared, more affronted than frightened. "Who are you? What—" He squinted into the dark.

"It's me." Kai felt cold. He didn't know what this meant, Dahin being here in secret, in the flooded ruin of the Summer Halls. "It's Kai." Dahin couldn't possibly recognize him; he was in a different body, his eyes concealed by the body-stealing ghoul's, wearing clothes the worse for days of travel on a rotted river barge.

"Ridiculous. You don't even look like—Wait, are you implying that you're Kaiisteron in a different body? You're not even a demon." Dahin peered at him. Kai was certain he had an Immortal Blessed weapon nearby. There were a few different tools near his hand, nothing Kai recognized. Dahin was dangerous in a completely different way than any Witch or expositor. "Even in mortal bodies, demons' eyes—"

"I borrowed these, from a body-stealing ghoul." What Ramad said about Dahin meeting with an official of Nient-arik went through his head.

"Well, that's disgusting." Dahin hesitated, regarding him with wary skepticism. "If you're really Kai, tell me something only you know."

Distracted by unwilling suspicion, Kai said absently, "Your great-aunt Kavinen thinks your nine-volume history of the Hierarchs war was a boring waste of time."

Dahin let out a breath that was half laugh, half gasp of outrage. "Yes, but she never said it to my face. You scared—I almost shit myself, Kai!" Dahin pushed to his feet and demanded, "What happened to you?"

Kai shook his head a little. He fought the urge to pretend like nothing was wrong, to fall into their old relationship. He had to know the truth. He stepped to the edge of the tarp. "Dahin, first tell me why you're here."

Suddenly evasive, Dahin dropped his gaze. "I'm working on something." He made an airy gesture at his camp, and turned to collect his scattered papers. "Are my sister and Ziede here, too? What are you doing? You're going to tell me why you're in a different body, right? Who is—was this person?"

Kai struggled with doubt. The obvious reluctance to say what he was doing was typical; Dahin had always been secretive about his work. Kai couldn't afford to be careless, but he was certain that if Dahin had really betrayed them, he would do a better job of it than this. "How long have you been here?"

Tucking the papers into a waxed leather case, Dahin looked up at him again, frowning. "A month, a little more. You smell like a dead turtle; were you in the canal mud? How did you get here? Why are you looking at me like that?" His eyes narrowed. "What's wrong? What's happened?"

Someone was going to have to break and answer a question. Kai picked the least revealing one. "I had to revivify a rotting river barge to get here, parts of it were still oozing." Ziede was impatient in his head, demanding to know what he had found. With her just outside the ruined building, he let her hear through his ears, so he wouldn't have to explain. He didn't want to be suspicious of Dahin, but he needed a second opinion. "Why didn't you tell us you were coming here?"

Dahin shifted uneasily, brushed some dirt off the case and set it aside. "I just . . . didn't want to be disturbed." When he was younger, he had always had an open face, had never been reluctant to show his true emotions while everyone else around him went to pains to conceal theirs. Now he looked guarded and guilty, but not the kind of guilty that said *I have betrayed my family and friends.* He huffed in exasperation. "I knew what Tahren would say if she knew I was here! Now can you tell me what happened to you? Did your old body die? I didn't think that was possible."

Kai felt his heart unclench just a little, despite himself. It was just so good to see Dahin again. "We were caught, Ziede and I. They put us in an underwater tomb. We've been there for most of the year. We only escaped days ago."

Dahin's head jerked up as he met Kai's gaze. His face went through shock, dismay, horror. "Where's Ziede? Is she all right?" He plopped down and patted the tarp in front of him. "Kai, sit down."

Kai should have been braced for an attack, but he just felt tired suddenly. And if Dahin was the one plotting against them, maybe it was time to give up. He sat down on the tarp. It was thick and waxed to stay dry, but slipping a little against the muck underneath it. "Ziede's here. Dahin, we don't know where Tahren is. The last we heard of her, she was looking for you."

Dahin had stopped trying to distract Kai and was all attention now. His hands had gone limp, his brow furrowed. It had been rare in recent years to get Dahin's full attention, but Kai had it now. Almost plaintively, Dahin said, "But . . . She must be . . . No one could touch her."

Kai shook his head. "Ziede can't find her pearl. We were told she didn't go to Benais-arik for the coalition renewal. She's not at Avagantrum. They haven't seen her since she left to look for you."

"She can't be hurt," Dahin protested.

Dahin had always believed his sister could do anything, even when they quarreled. Especially when they quarreled. "Whoever took us has Immortal Blessed helping them," Kai said. "The expositor who came after us when we escaped had an Immortal Blessed ship."

Shadows stirred across the dark space, but Kai sensed Ziede. A moment later she drifted in through an archway in the back wall and stepped down onto the grimy floor. Air rushed past as her wind-devils dispersed, carrying a scent of clean river breeze. Her voice raw, she said, "Dahin, do you know where she is?"

Dahin shook his head, bordering on distraught. "No, no, Ziede, I haven't seen her since I left Avagantrum. I didn't know she was looking for me. Honestly, I've been avoiding her. I just wanted—" As Ziede approached, Dahin held out a hand to her. Then he caught himself. "Uh, who's that?"

Ramad followed Ziede, stepping into range of the lamp, a closed expression on his face. Kai said, "That's Ramad, a Rising World vanguarder. He's helping us."

"Dahin, listen to me. We're not just taking a tour of the places Kai's destroyed, hoping to find her." Ziede knelt on the tarp and took Dahin's hand, and started to tell him what had happened from the beginning. Waking in the tomb when the water receded, Menlas, going to the fire islands to speak to Grandmother, then Aclines and Saadrin. Kai found himself watching Ramad's face, the frown lines at the corners of his eyes. He was studying Dahin carefully, as if looking for signs of guilt. It made Kai's hackles rise, even though he still had suspicions of his own that he couldn't quite banish.

By the time Ziede finished, Dahin was less agitated and more angry, but it was his angry thinking face. "Stios was definitely a trap. Even if Saadrin didn't set it, by the time you got there, they would have been waiting for you." He turned to Kai. "You're here for a finding stone. The one Cantenios had."

"Yes," Kai admitted. It was a relief not to have to explain. He had forgotten how quick Dahin was. "No one else knows about that one."

Dahin nodded. "I've been diving. I can help you find it." He pushed to his feet again and started shoving things into his bag.

⸺◦∞◦⸺

Ziede took Ramad into the air again, and Kai and Dahin used Dahin's small boat. As Kai rowed across the murky foul water,

Dahin spread a map drawn in smudged lead and covered with scribbled notes across his knees. Before they had left his camp, he had packed away all his supplies into a small copper-bound chest, and sealed it with an Immortal Blessed sigil. He had tucked all the papers into a bag with some clanking objects that were probably more Immortal Blessed devices. Ramad and Ziede had already gone outside again, and Kai said, "I've never seen you use so many of their tools."

Dahin had shrugged. "It's the only option I had."

Now he instructed Kai, "Bear a little to the left. There's an Immortal Blessed supplication tower about two courts over. Not that there was much supplicating going on, but the Hierarchs had it so when they used their finding stones to whistle up some Immortal Marshalls, there was somewhere to land the rafts. The top is still above water and I'm afraid that's the closest spot for diving." Dahin squinted up at the sky, judging the light. "I haven't tried to get into any of the Hostage Courts. I've mostly been concentrating on the Hierarchs' quarters."

Kai dug the oars in, following the directions. "But what are you looking for? Why are you here?"

Dahin frowned down at his map. "You're suspicious of me."

Kai could have denied it. He knew enough of Dahin's weak spots to make him feel like a traitor for even suggesting Kai might not have complete faith in him. But Dahin knew all Kai's weak spots, too. A war between them would lead to nothing but scorched earth.

Or at least Kai knew the old Dahin's weak spots, but then the old Dahin would never have come to this haunted place and stayed for so long, alone. Kai gave in and said honestly, "I don't want to be. But someone drowned me in Benais-arik and buried me and Ziede in an underwater tomb. Bashat had to know about it. A lot of people at court had to know about it."

Dahin winced. "I almost lost you both and Tahren and had no idea." He shook his head. "I'm sorry. I suppose I should have told you what I was doing, or left word somewhere. But . . ."

"But you didn't, because you thought we'd argue with you. Or tell Tahren, who would argue with you," Kai finished.

"Well, it sounds childish when you put it like that." Dahin sighed, and shrugged, as if committing himself to a course he wasn't sure he wanted to traverse. "I don't know if you remember, but we saw a map engraved on the wall of that court, the one where the Hierarchs lived."

Kai shook his head, baffled. He had no idea what Dahin was talking about. "What court? When?"

"It was when you killed the expositor and put the Cageling Demon Court intention in the water, and we swam to the wall of the room and were drowning," Dahin clarified hopefully.

He was talking about a mortal lifetime ago, the day they had all escaped this place. "I remember there were walls," Kai said. He remembered the sharp fear, the flimsy fabric of the veil that was his only protection against discovery, the desperation.

"Good enough." Dahin directed Kai to go further left. Kai glanced over his shoulder to orient himself to the supplication tower. There were only three fan-shaped landing balconies for Immortal Blessed ascension rafts, one jutting out from each level still above water. Ziede and Ramad had already flown to the lowest, the only one facing this direction. The rounded edge was a bare pace or so above the surface and Ziede stood there, studying the dark water. Kai was still sharing his vision and hearing with her, and he could feel her nervous energy at the fringe of his thoughts. Ramad watched Kai and Dahin, his gaze worried.

Dahin continued, "The map had beautifully made enamels, the colors were so bright. At first I thought, well, they're just gloating over all the land they've stolen, aren't they. The cities they destroyed, the people they've killed. But the Summer Halls was one of the only permanent places the Hierarchs actually built for themselves, and certainly the largest. The stone and a lot of the material came from the Sendrinnian temple complex that used to stand here. It was huge, and that little section off the main canal where the city is now is the only part that was left of it. The Hierarchs killed all the Sendrinnians and took all the temples down stone by stone, and built the Summer Halls out of it. They dug the moats, and used all the displaced dirt to build the earthworks. This place looked exactly the way the Hierarchs wanted it to." He rubbed his hands on his cotton skirt. "It took me a long time to find out all that. It's hard to research the past when almost everyone who saw it happen is dead, and their books left to rot in their empty cities."

Kai rowed more slowly. He thought that he had known, or assumed, that the Hierarchs had built the earthwork. It was a lot like the temporary earthwork forts they had built in the grass-plains, except on a much larger scale. He hadn't known, or had never thought about, the fact that the Hierarchs had built the Summer Halls. Now that he did, he saw Dahin's point. "I don't remember any other enamels on the walls. Or maps, or any other decoration like that." The Hierarchs had clearly not wasted much time on the Hostage Courts, but in the Temple Halls and the Hierarchs' court there had been marble and fine materials and fabric hangings, and then the hall of trophies.

The Saredi had carved images in wood and bone and painted the canvas of their great tents; the Arike loved large detailed paintings, especially of groups of people at festivals or battles, scenes that told stories, as big as possible; the Erathi put fish and shells and wind symbols on everything; the Enalin drew natural vistas and trees and the complex characters of their beautiful written language. Even the Immortal Blessed had their favorite art, mostly carvings of their Patriarchs and their sun symbols. But all the Hierarchs' art seemed to be in their clothes or the arrangements of their stolen goods. "So the map was special to the Hierarchs."

"Exactly. I know you were chained up in that horrible court

so you didn't see as much of this place. I saw quite a bit before Tahren hid me with Bashasa, and there was nothing like that map anywhere I went. So it was special, and private." Dahin's mouth twisted and he looked over the drowned ruin. "I think it was something from their home. A symbol of it. The way back to it."

Kai still didn't understand. "We know they came from the Capstone of the World."

"The Capstone of the World is a pretty big place, Kai." Dahin snorted. "We think it was somewhere near Sun-Ar, right? Because that's the language we now call Old Imperial, the language the Hierarchs used. But after the war, Enalin explorers went to Sun-Ar, and found no one, nothing left alive. It's a place of cold desert plains and rock formations. They grew gardens inside caves, and kept herds of wild sheep. The Sun-Ar used to have moving cities of tent-huts and special palaces for temples and seasonal gatherings carved out of the cliffs and the standing rocks. They're empty now. The Hierarchs killed them all."

Kai said, "That's not unusual, they killed everybody." It wasn't quite true, though sometimes it felt like it. "Almost everybody."

"But I think they killed the Sun-Ar because they had contact with the Hierarchs before they became the Hierarchs," Dahin said. His voice was intense, his gaze dark and serious. "There were some Sun-Ar in the Hostage Courts. Bashasa tried to get in to see them once, but they were more closely guarded than anyone else, no one was allowed to see or talk to them. I found out the legionaries were ordered to kill them all once the escape started. The Hierarchs didn't want to risk any of them getting out with us."

Caught up in the picture Dahin was painting, Kai had stopped rowing, though he wasn't sure when. Their boat drifted, pushed by the rot-tinged breeze. He said, "I think I saw them. In the furthest court. Small people, light brown, with straight hair?"

Dahin nodded, his mouth set in a thin line. "We don't know where the Hierarchs came from, Kai. Not even the Immortal Blessed know. They came down from the south, from the top of the world, and destroyed everything in their path. They could still be up there. They could come again." He frowned. "Why are you looking at me like that?"

"Because I'm shitting terrified." Cold prickles ran down Kai's spine.

"I don't think it'll happen anytime soon, like tomorrow." Dahin backtracked, clearly trying to be reassuring. "Or really, I don't know that it'll happen at all." He looked away at the drowned ruin, the water lapping the filth-encrusted stone. "But I just have to know, Kai. I have to be sure." He added plaintively, "Do you understand?"

Kai understood down to his bones. "Why were you in Nient-arik?"

"When? Oh, before I came here?" Dahin explained readily, "Their archive has copies of Prince-heir Hiranan's journals and maps, from when she was here. It was quicker than going all the way out to Seidel-arik for them. Why?"

"We were looking for you and someone said you'd been there." Kai fumbled for the oars and got them moving again. "You could have told us, Dahin."

Dahin sighed. "I have a lot of unformed thoughts, still. I wanted to wait until I could make a more coherent case."

That was perfectly coherent and damningly persuasive, Ziede said in Kai's head. *The little idiot wanted to produce his evidence on a copper platter like a gift.*

People would panic, if they thought the Hierarchs could come back. Children like Sanja might think they were just old shadow-stories, meant to terrify, but there were so many more mortals and Witches still walking around who knew they had been horribly real, who understood the legacy of devastation in the empty cities and towns. And the Rising World remembered its origins, no matter how far it had drifted from Bashasa's original vision. *Dahin wasn't afraid of us, he was afraid of everyone else,* Kai thought to Ziede.

No one at court now listens to him the way Bashasa did, Ziede added. *He didn't want to be ridiculed.*

Dahin was saying, "But you realize now why I need to see what's on the rest of the map. It's been going slowly. It's huge, it covers the whole wall, and it's been eaten away with this mossy weed growth. I have to clean it off carefully, so I don't dislodge any of the enamels. And I can only stay underwater so long, even with my tools. But I'm making progress."

The hull of the boat bumped against the tiles as they reached the landing platform. Ramad caught the rope Dahin tossed him as Kai climbed out. Helping Kai tie the boat off to the fretwork in the low rail, Ramad said quietly, "Are you all right?"

"Fine," Kai said, sparing him what was probably an unconvincing smile. As Dahin hauled his bag out, he added, "Just catching up with an old friend." He didn't expect Ramad to believe him, and he wasn't entirely sure why he didn't just tell him. If Dahin's theory was right, they would have to tell everyone, and the Rising World would be first, even if Bashat still wanted to kill them. But for now this was between Kai, Ziede, and Dahin.

The balcony on the level above was halfway around the structure, facing away to the west, and the one above it another half turn, facing south. The figured metal door that had closed off the entrance into the tower from this balcony had rusted permanently open. Kai stepped inside, but it was just an empty room with a curved wall shielding a stairwell. The stone steps spiraled up to the two higher levels and down into the dark water that filled the lower part of the tower. Time and weather had eaten away at the stone and crumbled the door sills.

Out on the balcony, Dahin checked his map and surveyed the

water with resignation. "Now, that's what I was afraid of. That's where Bashasa's court was, under that weed mat."

The heavy black mass of what might be plant material was an irregular shape, a thickening in the dark water that blended in so well it was hard to tell how far it stretched under the surface. Dubious, Kai said, "Are you sure it's just weeds?"

"Well, the bits I've seen look like weeds from underneath, but I'm not going to guarantee it," Dahin admitted.

"We can't cut through it?" Ramad asked. He seemed to know he wasn't being told everything but was gamely trying to participate anyway.

"I'm assuming if we tried, we would get trapped in it and drown," Dahin told him. "I didn't try, since I was here alone with no one to cut me out if I got stuck. Especially after I saw how far these mats extend down. There's one in the court outside the room I'm exploring and I've just been lucky it doesn't seem to want to grow inside. It needs light, I suppose." He nudged Kai with an elbow. "Do you remember the glass roof on the Temple Halls? It's absolutely choked with it in there."

Ziede hissed and buried her face in her hands. "You could have died here, Dahin, and we'd never have known. When Tahren finds out, she's going to murder you. I'm going to help her."

By *murder* Ziede meant "stare disapprovingly while lecturing" but Kai knew that wouldn't do any good. It would just make Dahin more stubborn and convinced that he was right to hide his plans. He pulled Dahin into a quick one-armed hug. "Next time you want to do something like this, come and get me. I won't ask questions, or if I do, you don't have to answer me until you're ready."

"Well, all right, then," Dahin mumbled, and Kai knew that was the best they could expect for now. Dahin stepped away, having reached his limit for physical affection. "But I think the best way is to go down here, where it's clear, and for Kai to make his way through the corridors to the court."

Kai kept his expression under control, despite the sick tension settling in his chest. He had known he would have to do this, the whole plan depended on it, but now that the moment was here, it was so much harder than he had expected. Every nerve in his body itched at the idea of sinking voluntarily under that dark water. But there was no way Dahin would be able to stay down long enough to reach the court and search for the stone. He busied himself pulling his hair back and tightening the cord that held it.

Ziede frowned dubiously at Kai, then at the mat. "I'll be going as well."

"That's probably for the best, it'll be safer with two," Dahin said, brisk and at least pretending to be oblivious. "You'll be making some kind of air bubble, correct?" He rummaged in his bag and pulled out a copper-colored artifact, like a narrow mesh box, with a little living star at its heart. "Kai, you can use this."

Kai shied away from the Immortal Blessed device. "I can go without breathing a long time—"

"Not long enough," Dahin corrected. "And if you run out of air you can't just pop up to the surface once you're under that weed mat. And Ziede, you'll need a weight."

"I can make the air in the bottom heavier." Ziede tapped her lip thoughtfully, considering the problem. "For a while, anyway."

Kai started to unlace his skirt. Originally he had assumed he would be able to dive from the surface directly down into the court where he had killed Cantenios. This was so much more complicated than the short trip he had taken with the shell-whale. He told Ziede, "If you float up into the mat, you could die."

"Well, I know that, Kai." Ziede tightened the scarf that bound up her hair.

Ramad began, "I should come with—"

"No. We need someone to stay up here with Dahin," Kai said. He dropped his cotton skirt, leaving him in leggings and the belted wrap tunic. He kept the telescoping rod in the inner pocket, since it could be useful if they had to dislodge any debris. Reluctantly he took the device that Dahin was shoving at him. From the leather strap he guessed it was supposed to go on his chest.

"Because someone might happen by?" Ramad snapped. "I don't think Lesser Blessed Dahin Stargard needs my protection."

"No, it's upside down. Here, let me." Dahin took the device back and turned it into the right position. As he buckled the strap, his gaze went past Kai to Ramad, dark and deliberate. "And you're right about that, vanguarder."

Ramad let out his breath, visibly regaining control of himself. He said quietly, "You either trust me or you don't, Kai."

It was Kai's turn to snap. "Do you want the answer to that right now? Ow, Dahin, what are you doing?"

Dahin was trying to force something like a spiky cuff around his ear. "This way we'll be able to hear each other if you need help." He held up a lump of what looked like clay. "And you need to stick this in your nose. Try not to swallow any of the water. It has odd properties, like preserving the corpses. And it's also full of things like olive and nut oil and animal fat, from the lamps and kitchens and things."

"It isn't about trust, Ramad." Ziede took up the argument while Kai was distracted, in a voice that made it clear this was her final answer. She accepted another ear cuff from Dahin, with a wince of disgust. "It's not possible. It will be difficult enough with just me and Kai."

Trying not to look at the water, Kai got the ear cuff into position, wincing as the spike was apparently supposed to jab into the back of his ear. The air device on his chest was oddly heavy for its size and pulling on his neck. "Why does everything Immortal Blessed have to hurt?"

"I ask myself that all the time." Dahin adjusted the chest thing and did something to the mesh part that made it glow a little brighter. "That will help you see once you're in the water. Just press here to adjust it, and here to control the weight, when you want to go down, or come back up to the surface. Ziede can use this light." He handed her a flat disk with a crystal inset. He stepped back. "You'd better go. Are you both ready?"

In answer, Ziede spun air into a dome, a miniature whirlwind that pulled at her tunic and pants. The wind-devils couldn't go underwater, but she could contain the well of air around her for a limited time.

Kai looked past her to Ramad, who said, "I apologize. Just . . . take care."

Kai wanted to be exasperated, but somehow he wasn't. "It'll be fine," he said. Before he could think too hard about what he was about to do, he shoved the clay up his nose and stepped off the roof.

He plunged into the cold water and managed not to gasp in a mouthful. He pressed the part of the chest device that controlled the weight, and it pulled him gently downward.

The water darkened until it was broken only by the Immortal Blessed lamp. Panic bubbled up and he suppressed the urge to rip the straps off; down was the way he needed to go, the device was only doing what he had told it to. His lungs seemed to have air in them though he wasn't breathing; it was very different from just holding his breath. He was very glad for the clay in his nose because the slimy sense of the water against his lips and skin was bad enough.

Ziede drifted down beside him until her bubble of air bumped against the dark shape of a balustrade. The hand light Dahin had given her glowed and her clothes swirled like she was caught in a miniature storm. Kai managed to move his arms in a way that pulled him through the water to give her room.

Through the pearl, and a heartbeat later in a whisper from the ear cuff, Ziede said, *We didn't account for Kai's nonexistent ability to swim.*

Hah, all we need to do is walk. Kai half bent, half curved downward, to direct his chest lamp toward the bottom. He and Ziede were still sinking, glimpses of their surroundings caught in the edge of the shaft of light: drifts of weedy moss, a piece of another balustrade, a giant clawed hand that turned out to be a petrified tree. They should be dropping to an open court but he couldn't see the bottom yet.

In his ear, Dahin whispered, "Kai, are you sleeping with that man? I can count the number of times Bashasa spoke to you that sharply on the fingers of one hand. If half of them were missing."

That wasn't true. Kai and Bashasa had argued, just not where anyone else could see. Bashasa had had a keen awareness of Kai's often uncertain position among the Arike and the Rising World alliance, and he had done nothing to make it more difficult. To some Kai had been the link to the Witches who were so vital to defeating the Hierarchs. To others, just a weird and particularly dangerous hanger-on. Kai guessed the spiky thing would act like a pearl and thought toward Dahin, *Are you saying this where he can hear you?*

"No, of course not. These work mind to mind." Dahin's voice changed from a whisper to a loud echo, like he was shouting into a bone funnel. "Is everything all right so far? Good." Back in the soft whisper, he added, "That was me talking aloud. I don't want him to know how this really works. Anyway—"

Ziede interrupted, *We can sort this later, when we're not so concerned with drowning.*

Kai saw a solid mass below and stuck his arms out to slow his downward motion. The paving of the court was covered in something discolored and oozy that looked nothing like creek or riverbed mud. As he landed, it drifted up around his bare feet in a low cloud. Ziede's bubble drifted to a halt just above the disturbed surface. *So here we are again,* she said wryly.

Kai's memory of how easy it was to get lost in here was only too vivid. And that had been in daylight, when he could actually see past a narrow band of Immortal Blessed light. With the wall at their back, he at least knew which direction to start in.

Ziede moved ahead into the court. *It's this way. I think.*

Kai followed her. She had spent far more time in this maze of courts and corridors than he had. He would like to banish the whole time from his memory, except that this was where he had met them all. Ziede, Tahren, Dahin, Salatel and Arsha and Telare, Nirana, Hartel, Cerala. Bashasa.

I don't want to be here, it hurts too much, he thought, and felt a thread of sympathy from Ziede. Dahin, picking up something from the ear device, said, "Are you all right?"

Still fine, Kai told him. *Just memories.*

Despite trying to move carefully, they stirred up mud and filth from the buried paving. In the cloud of muck, Kai didn't see the archway out of the court until Ziede made an "oof" noise as her bubble bumped into the wall. She turned, caught in his light, her tunic and the ends of her scarf drifting a little, buoyed by the air around her. She found the opening and they swam and floated through, then lost what little light made it down from the surface of the murky water. It was much colder now and Kai was glad they hadn't let Ramad come; it was bad enough for him and Ziede but a mortal wouldn't have lasted long, and might have been made ill even from limited exposure to whatever was in this foul oily soup.

Even with Dahin's Immortal Blessed devices, Kai would never have managed this without Ziede. Her memory of this place was obviously clearer than his, but then she had spent more time here, risked everything to be here, helping Bashasa plan. He concentrated on following her, his light catching walls, wide doorways, broad windows. Well under the weed mat now, the dark outside the range of their lights was absolute. At the least the water was so poisonous it wasn't full of snakes or gar.

"Still there?" Dahin said in his ear, with the echo in his voice that told Kai he was speaking aloud. "Everything all right?"

It's fine, Kai replied. *If you like dark and hostile.*

Ziede added, *It's not that much worse than when we were here the first time.*

"It's funny because I know you're not joking," Dahin replied.

Then something about the water changed. Kai wasn't sure if it was something audible, or a sensation through his wet clothes and frozen skin. He turned, sweeping his light around, and realized the wall they had been following was gone. Then he caught sight of something dark and skeletal—Another dead tree, preserved in the water like a bug in resin. Then another, and another. They were in the open court close to the entrance to Bashasa's hostage quarters.

Kai, don't fall behind, Ziede said. *We're almost there.*

They passed through two archways and then finally into an enclosed corridor. It didn't get any lighter when they came out into a larger space. Kai's lamp shone on a fountain, the outlines of what had been planting beds, a familiar doorway. The scene was coming back to him, the phantom shapes buried under the rot resolving into the place he remembered. This was the open fountain court where Kai had killed Cantenios. *Ziede, you're brilliant. I couldn't have found the way here.*

I'm surprised I remembered it so well, she admitted, floating above the fountain. *I thought I'd done such a good job of banishing the whole thing from my mind.*

Kai made his way to the fountain. *His body was about here.* Desiccated when Kai drained his life, held down by heavy fabric and leather and metal ornaments, he didn't think it would have floated or drifted far. He moved cautiously, leaning down toward the ground. This made his feet lift up so his whole body was tilting down. The weight thing built into the Immortal Blessed breathing device seemed to center on his midsection. It was strange and awkward but let him reach the ground with his hands without his feet disturbing the thick layer covering the paving stones.

He felt carefully along through the slimy muck, until he found something that felt lumpy, like bones buried under mud. Exactly like bones buried under mud. Even moving so slowly, a cloud of debris rose up toward his face. He spread his hands, searching for the finding stone by feel. Bones emerged from the mud, metal ornaments, a wrist cuff, a jeweled pin for a veil. He moved further out, circling all around the body.

Dahin's voice said sharply, "Kai, remember to breathe. The device won't work if you don't breathe."

It's not here. Kai's heart sank all the way down into the murk. *I can't find it.*

Ziede's voice was calm in a way she only sounded when something was going horribly wrong. *He would have dropped it, wouldn't he? If he was holding it in his hand.*

In the background, in that odd echo, Kai heard Dahin say to Ramad, "They can't find it."

Kai circled further out from Cantenios' body, kneading his way through the mud. Ziede crouched on the bottom of her bubble, as close to the ground as she could get, directing her light on his hands. *He didn't throw it,* Kai muttered in frustration. *Could someone have taken it?*

"The water might have moved it when it flowed into the court," Dahin said. "Or . . . one of us, one of the Arike might have accidentally kicked it. I remember being terrified and everyone running around like we were all on fire."

He was right. Kai swallowed past the taste of foul mud in his throat. *We'll have to search the court, the fountain, maybe the adjoining rooms.* If it wasn't nearby, there was no way they would have enough air.

They were so close to having what they needed to find Tahren. It was maddening for Kai and had to be worse for Ziede. But she kept her calm expression, her brow furrowed as she thought it over. *I have an idea,* she said. *We need to clear the muck off the paving.*

Can you do that and keep your air bubble? Kai asked her. He was intensely aware of the heavy mat above their heads. If Ziede started to drown, sheer terror might give him enough power for an intention to drive a hole through it to the surface, but he would just rather not have to.

Hmm, no, unfortunately. Sitting on her heels, Ziede floated in her bubble, one finger pressed to her lip, dark eyes narrowed in consideration.

Dahin added, "I don't have anything to do that. All the work I've been doing is on the wall, and it's better to remove the residue in small patches."

Ziede nodded to herself. *If I go back to the surface, I could make a wind violent enough to move the water under the weed mat and stir all this up. You'd just need to keep the mud up away from the floor.*

Kai started to chew on his lower lip in thought and remembered at the last moment to keep his mouth tightly shut. It would have to be an intention; it was impossible to draw a cantrip down here under water. And everything was tainted by the influence of the Hierarchs' Well, and the residue from the water intention that Kai had misused to cause the flood. Whatever he did, it would have to be a pure intention. Something not much different from the push he had been thinking of to break a hole through the mat. *We'll try it,* he said.

I'll go up, she told him. *Just be careful. Once you find it, if you're not sure of the way out, I'll come back and get you.*

I'll be fine, Kai told her. *Hurry, so we can get this over with.* Ziede turned in her bubble and glided out, moving faster now that she was certain of the way.

Through the echoing earpiece, Dahin was explaining the plan to Ramad. Kai let his feet rest on the fountain rim and prepared the intention, assembling a design that would use the water motion Ziede would provide to lift the muck gently upward.

Through her pearl, he felt the moment of relief when Ziede got past the mat and was able to surface. "I can't see you," Dahin said.

I'm closer to the Temple Halls, Ziede reported. *I need a little distance from the target.*

Kai stopped listening to them, needing all his concentration to make the design as gentle as possible. If he got this wrong, it would make it impossible to see anything in here. Finally, he said, *I've got it. Whenever you're ready.*

Ziede whispered, *Now, Kai.* The wind must have risen abruptly; he heard Dahin's startled exclamation through the earpiece. "I forgot what that's like," Dahin commented.

The mud stirred right before Kai felt the current. The force of it shoved him back against the wall. The sediment and debris lifted up from the floor, flowing away into the open doorways or washing up and out over the high walls. More flowed in from the corridor entrance. Kai hadn't eaten anyone's life for days, and had no reserve of power. He was going to have to do this the hard way. He braced himself and opened his mouth.

Panic, a choking sensation, and a truly horrible taste gave him all the pain he needed for the intention. The muck and the force of flowing water froze in place, then pushed upward out of Kai's light, toward the darkness overhead and the mat.

Kai had to swallow the mouthful of water. Wrestling his stomach for control was hard, but the hot flush of nausea passed. He bent all the way down and used his light to scan the now clear paving. Rechecking the places he had already searched, he went over the remains of the body, the rim and inside of the fountain, the nearest planting beds. He expanded his range, using the squares of the paving stones to keep track of his progress.

Then in the doorway on the west side, Kai's light caught a mud-covered lump, trapped against the raised edge of the sill. He pounced, the weight of the water slowing the motion to a crawl, but his hand closed around the lump. He felt the shape of the obsidian disk under the grime. It was cold—colder than the water that had filled this dark cavern for so long. *Dahin, Ziede,* Kai said, relief making his heart pound. He had been so afraid they wouldn't find it, that somehow it would be gone, so afraid of failing Ziede, losing Tahren. *It's here. I have it.*

There was no answer. Kai went still, realizing how long it had been since one of them had spoken, and how odd, how uncharacteristic that they had both been so silent. He touched Ziede's heart pearl.

No answer.

THE PAST:
THE EXODUS

The Tescai-Lin of the Enalin is mistakenly thought of as a ruler, but the title translates roughly in Arike to "Great Sage." The Tescai-Lin is a moral authority and advisor to the myriad holders of governance in the territories of Enalin, who are themselves chosen by acclaim. The Enalin are often long-lived, not unlike Witchkind, but are not immortal. Not much has been shared as to the selection of the Tescai-Lin, whether the person may be born to the position or chosen in some way. Howsomever, they are a figure of primary importance to the Enalin character.

—Journey Through the Lands of Enal and Old Nibet,
by A Wandering Songseller

Kai hit the water back first and plunged under the surface. Thrashing, tangled in sharp branches, he realized he had blundered into a tree drowned by the flood. He kicked his way free and surfaced, coughing and sputtering.

The windows above gushed waterfalls. Kai managed to flail and paddle toward the far end, the gallery Dahin had swum to. The walkway was well under now, the water lapping the bottom of the windows. Kai climbed through one and dropped down into a broad corridor with a stream running along the floor. He shoved to his feet and started toward where he had left Ziede and Tahren, the direction he hoped Dahin had taken.

Shouting and the clash of weapons led him to the broad stairs where the legionaries had waited to attack Bashasa and the other hostages. At the bottom of the steps, the barred doors were knocked off their hinges and there was fighting in the big hall just beyond. It sounded as if it was moving away. *Well, it's a short-cut,* Kai thought, and went down the stairs.

By the time he got down to the hall and started across, the fighting had shifted to another corridor. The stone-tiled floor was littered with legionary bodies and stained with blood and viscera, so he supposed things were going well. He went toward the court on the far side.

As soon as he stepped out into the wan daylight, strange mortals ran toward him, all dressed in light-colored caftans and robes, all armed with short spears. Kai backed toward the doorway and dropped into a defensive crouch. A sudden shout halted the attackers. A large person in blue-green and silver shouldered through and Kai recognized Tescai-Lin, the Enalin Light. In Imperial, they said, "Leave off. This is Bashasa's demon." The others backed away immediately. Tescai-Lin added, "I take it you were successful."

Kai straightened up and shoved his dripping hair back. "The other Hierarch's dead." He untied the veil from his belt and dumped the head on the floor at Tescai-Lin's feet.

For a long heartbeat, the Light just stared down at it, their expression blank except for a tightening around the mouth. The other Enalin leaned forward to see, their faces showing amazement, consternation, disbelief. Uncertain suddenly, Kai realized this head could be any random mortal killed in the palace. He should have brought more proof, somehow, though he had no idea what that would be. He said, "I don't know how to prove it's a Hierarch. I—"

"No, I recognize her." Tescai-Lin's voice was cold. "It's the one that came to Water Mountain. You agree, cousin?"

The younger person standing at his elbow nodded gravely. "You are correct, cousin."

Kai let out a relieved breath. So he didn't have to prove himself.

About this, at least. "We need to leave, I don't know when the flood will stop. And I need to find the Immortal Marshall Tahren Stargard. Her brother, Dahin, is around here somewhere."

Tescai-Lin glanced at the water now rushing into the court from the hall. "It has to stop at some point."

"I wouldn't count on that. It's a powerful intention and I don't know how it works." Kai's legs felt weak and he just wanted to lie down. He was beginning to think his new body didn't work as well as Enna's, that there was some trick to being a demon in a mortal body that he had never been told. Or maybe it was just that Enna had been resigned to leaving her body in natural death, but Talamines hadn't and fought to hold on.

Tescai-Lin lifted their brows; the effect was interesting because the hair had been shaved away and replaced with tiny gold studs. They said, "Find something to carry the head. The Arike should be this way."

⸎

Following Tescai-Lin's broad back, his wet clothing leaving a dripping trail, Kai saw they were going back toward the Temple Halls. The head was in a silk bag that one of the Enalin had handed Kai. Apparently it was normally for carrying a sacred something that didn't translate into Imperial.

They passed, or were passed by, groups of mortals running to get away, but saw no legionaries. Though they did see discarded legionary weapons, armor, and clothing strewn along the corridor. Kai couldn't understand it. Were the expositors making the legionaries' bodies invisible but somehow not their armor? Was something eating them? He said finally, "Why are the legionaries taking off their clothes?"

Walking beside him, Tescai-Lin's young cousin explained, "Because we have won."

Won what? Kai almost said. Then realized they meant the battle. That seemed impossible. They hadn't done this to win. Just to cover the escape of Bashasa's people and Dahin, to show that the Hierarchs weren't untouchable. That part they had accomplished, he and Bashasa had touched both Hierarchs; the head still dripping through the bag proved that. "But—"

They had just turned into the processional avenue of trophies and tributes that led toward the Temple Halls, when a shout interrupted him. "You're alive!"

Someone ducked past Tescai-Lin and Kai barely had time to brace before Dahin threw himself into his arms.

Kai hadn't been hugged like this by anyone since the day of the Hierarchs' Great Working, since the Saredi had been broken and burned. He almost forgot how to respond. Fortunately, before he gave into the impulse to weep like a baby, Dahin let go to drag him toward the archway into the Temple Halls. Ziede and Tahren stood there with Bashasa and a crowd of Arike and other mortals. Still dragging him, Dahin told them, "He stabbed an expositor and threw me out a window!"

Tescai-Lin followed, and said, "Show them."

Delighted, Bashasa called out, "Fourth Prince, you've returned!"

Ziede started toward him, saying, "Kai, we thought you were—"

Kai said, "Dahin, wait," and freed his arm so he could pull the head out of the bag.

Dahin said, "What's that?" and everyone grew suddenly quiet, the babble of voices in the corridor dying away.

Kai held up the head by the hair.

Ziede stopped, her eyes wide. Beside her, Tahren let out a long breath.

Bashasa stepped forward, growing awe and elation in his expression. Someone behind him said, "That's the one from the Halls . . ."

"No." Tahren pitched her flat voice to carry. "That's the other one."

Tescai-Lin said, "I confirm that. I recognize her, as does my cousin."

Bashasa hadn't seemed to hear. He reached Kai, his gaze locked on the Hierarch's head. He breathed, "How?"

Kai shrugged a little helplessly. "When the intention from the Cageling Court filled the room with water suddenly, everything was confused. I saw I had a chance at her, if I went back." It hadn't been anything clever, just luck. Plus a combination of being fast and vicious, but he didn't want to say that in front of all these mortals. Too many already thought demons were monstrous creatures.

Bashasa took the head from Kai's unsteady grip and held it up. He turned to face the others. "The second Hierarch is dead. The legionaries have run from us. The Summer Halls belong to us."

Kai remembered he hadn't delivered the most important information. He leaned close to Bashasa and whispered, "The water intention is flooding everywhere. I don't know if it'll stop. It's so far underwater by now no one could reach it to make it stop."

"But we must leave this place where we were held against our will, and make our plans elsewhere," Bashasa continued without hesitation. "The Fourth Prince has unleashed a powerful working which will leave it flooded, and confuse any pursuit. It will also prevent the other Hierarchs from retaking the Summer Halls, at least for a time. Spread the word to all who will listen, make sure the Hostage Courts and slave cells are empty, that none are left behind. Everyone must flee!"

The mortals seemed uncertain or stricken or disbelieving. But Tescai-Lin said, "We will search the northern Hostage Courts on our way to gather the rest of our people. Before we leave, I would speak with you again, Bashasa Arike Heir."

"And I you, Light. We will meet outside in the leaving court," Bashasa said. Tescai-Lin strode away with their followers in their wake and Bashasa added, "Hiranan, you will search the south with Vrim?"

"I will," the older Prince-heir said, gathering a number of Arike soldiers around her with a wave. "We'll see you outside."

The rest of the mortals in the chamber began to move purposefully or to scatter in panic. Bashasa turned back and Kai held out the bag for the head, and said, "That was quick thinking. Sorry about the flood."

"Do not apologize." Bashasa tucked the flap of the bag over the dead Hierarch's face. He handed it back to Kai, grim now. "There is no way we could hold this place, and no rational reason to; having an excuse to leave immediately will keep us moving and acting together, for a time at least." His serious gaze met Kai's for a heartbeat, then Bashasa looked down. "What you have done . . . I cannot . . ."

Ziede stepped forward and squeezed Kai's arm. "Kai, you found Dahin; Tahren was both pleased and furious."

"I was not furious," Tahren said, only a step behind her, holding Dahin firmly by the wrist. "Prince-heir, Ziede Daiyahah has offered to take charge of the removal of the wounded in the Temple Halls. I will help her."

"Very good. Take Arava and her cadre with you," Bashasa said briskly, motioning to one of his soldiers. He lowered his voice. "That other matter—only if you can do so safely. I won't risk a life for it."

"I understand," Tahren said. Ziede strode purposefully away but Tahren focused on Kai. "I owe you my brother's life."

"I wasn't going to leave him there," Kai said, too overwhelmed to even think of how to be polite in this situation. In the grassplains it was assumed you would take care of others, if you had any chance to. And the underearth didn't have wars the way mortals did, slaughtering whole cities. Not that he could claim to belong to either of those places anymore.

Tahren didn't seem to care. She nodded and turned to go. Dahin, towed behind her, began, "Can I go with—"

"No," Tahren said firmly.

Bashasa clapped Kai on the shoulder. "Can you check the eastern Hostage Courts with your cadre? I must secure our transport away from here."

"All right." Kai tied the bag to his belt. "What's a cadre?"

⚬⚬⚬

It turned out a cadre was the Imperial word for a personal guard. Salatel and the Arike who Bashasa had assigned to make sure nobody killed Kai while he was unconscious were actually now his cadre.

Salatel knew only a little more of the layout of the Summer Halls than Kai did, but she knew where the eastern Hostage Courts were. She also still had the coat Bashasa had given him. Kai pulled it on over his still damp clothes to hopefully signal he wasn't an expositor and that no one should stab him in the back.

When they found the gate into the eastern Hostage Courts, Kai could now see the intention to alert expositors woven into the stone. He stopped and lifted a hand in the Saredi scout sign for caution, before remembering the people following him didn't know it. But the idea must have gotten across, because Salatel and the others stopped immediately. Kai eased forward and drew the intention off the stone, partly to see if he could. It came to his fingers as a stretchy web of shifting light. Kai discarded it to the side, and it turned dark and faded into the paving. "That's probably meant to alert someone who might already be dead, but . . ." He shouldn't be telling them he had only the vaguest idea what he was doing; he was so tired he was starting to ramble. Though Salatel and these Arike had been there when everything happened, they knew he wasn't a real expositor. He didn't want to be a real expositor, no matter how intriguing Ziede seemed to find the idea.

But Salatel said, "Better to be cautious, Fourth Prince. This horrible place is full of things we don't understand."

She was right about that. Kai checked for more prosaic traps, then led the way inside.

In the first few courts, they found only confused mortals who needed to be pointed toward the way out, or who were so frightened or shocked that they needed to be told it was all right to leave. The Arike shooed them out and made sure they were heading in the right direction.

In the last court, they found bodies.

The first was in the corridor bordering the entrance court, sprawled and bloody near a broken tray of dirty crockery. Obviously caught by surprise, the others only had time to try to hide, huddling in corners in sleeping rooms or behind baskets in a storeroom. Some had tried to fight, using anything to hand as a makeshift weapon. The Arike spread out to search for survivors, and Kai checked all the bodies he found, hoping for a sign of life. But they were all cold and already going stiff, so they must have been killed not long after everything had started.

By a dry fountain in the central court, Kai crouched beside the body of an elderly person, with gray streaked hair and a lined face, now slack and still, blood dried around the gaping stab wound in their chest. "Why these people? Why not the people in the other courts?" he said as the soldiers returned and gathered around him. The dead were small in stature, the tallest handspans shorter than Enna had been, and most were slender and small-boned, with fine features. Their skin was a light bronze, their hair shades of brown and very straight and soft. They had small, skillfully drawn tattoos all along the edges of their hairlines, in bright colors, symbols or words in a language Kai had never seen.

"The others left first?" one of the soldiers suggested, in heavily accented Imperial. She added, "No one to kill?"

Salatel looked doubtful. "The other courts hadn't been searched, the ones who stayed behind weren't disturbed. Legionaries coming to kill wouldn't let anyone live."

Kai had to agree, the legionaries had never gone into the courts where there were survivors. "Maybe they started here and were called away to try to stop us from getting to the last Hierarch." Shaking his head, he pushed to his feet as the last soldiers reappeared. "Nothing?"

"No, Fourth Prince," one replied. She gestured back toward the empty doorways, dismayed. "They are so small, we searched anywhere they might hide. But so did the legionaries."

Kai rubbed his forehead. He hadn't seen mortals like this before. Maybe the legionaries had chosen to kill them because they were different.

"Fourth Prince, Salatel," someone said, and Kai turned to see a soldier pointing at the arched doorway that led into the court. A trickle of water ran in, following the gap between the paving stones. She added, "It's coming through the corridor from the big hall."

"Right." Kai watched the water find the grooves in the paving. "We need to go."

⁂

By the time they made it through the maze of courts and found a wide columned corridor Salatel recognized as leading to the way out, the water was knee-deep. The oil lamps along the enclosed corridors flickered on the rising water. Kai would have felt more panic, but it was muted from exhaustion.

It was a relief to make a turn into a larger passageway, and see the end where a broad set of stairs led up into open daylight. Kai sloshed forward with Salatel and the others, glad they weren't going to drown in here after all.

As they drew closer, the stairwell looked more and more like a man-made gorge, the walls carved with half pillars, sloping up a long distance, far longer than climbing to the top of Kentdessa Saredi. A few groups of mortals climbed ahead, the last about halfway to the top. The steps were covered with damp footprints and the occasional lost shoe or veil or discarded bag.

As Kai heaved waterlogged legs up onto the first step, he

said, "We're not underground, are we? Are the Halls in a—" He couldn't remember the Imperial word for canyon. "A hole?"

"Yes, Fourth Prince," Salatel said, pausing to wring the water out of her long tunic. "You didn't see when you came here?"

"I was in a bag," Kai told her. And too sick and half-conscious to remember the feeling of being carried down into the earth. "I couldn't see anything."

They started the climb and Kai could tell the soldiers were drooping with fatigue. It had been hours since they had a chance to eat or to even stop moving for a few moments. Kai knew he had more endurance than a mortal and he was worn down, aching in his knees and back. Talamines hadn't been that much older than Enna but even ten full changes of the seasons was a lot for a mortal. But no one complained; the water was rising and they didn't have time to stop.

Finally they dragged themselves up the last few steps. A cloudy gray sky and an unfettered wind scented with recent rain and green earth greeted them. They emerged onto a stone walkway and Kai saw that all the buildings of the massive city-fortress had been surrounded by a high earthen wall. Kai would never have believed a single mortal-built structure could be so large, if he hadn't spent hours running around in it. The scale was hard to take in. He turned, getting his bearings for the first time since he had been captured.

The top of the Summer Halls was an expanse of pitched glass rooftops like transparent mountain slopes and the square openings of terraced courts like canyons. A nearby tower had large balconies standing out at alternating levels, each facing a different direction. The balconies were shaped like spreading fans, or maybe the caps of oyster mushrooms. *For Immortal Blessed craft,* Kai realized. It made the back of his neck itch, knowing more might show up at any moment. Would Tahren fight her own people for them? Or would she even have a choice, once they knew she had helped kill two Hierarchs.

Around the curve to the east was another stairwell exit, a trickle of mortals emerging up onto the walkway that circled the rim. They staggered around in relief, and then hurried toward the nearest path down the outer slope. That was near the spot where he and Ziede had crossed over the canyon-like corridor full of fleeing people.

Two soldiers had sunk down to sit on the top step. Salatel checked the others, gripping their shoulders and patting their faces. Kai went to the edge of the walkway to look outward. Three waterways matched the curve of the earthwork, the outermost one joined with a broad canal that led away to the east. A small city lay next to the canal, with clusters of low stone buildings interspersed with wooden compounds and houses topped with tall narrow spires, with trees and gardens, walkways and wide paths for wagons.

Salatel came to his side. "Fourth Prince, we should go. The Prince-heir Bashasa will be waiting."

Kai just nodded. He didn't think the soldiers would appreciate any attempt to help them, particularly from him, so he waited while they got each other to their feet. Then he took another breath of the fresh wind and followed as Salatel led the way toward the nearest stairs down the outside of the earthwork.

The steps cut back and forth through the slope, made of the same white stone as the rim. It was easier going down, and the earthwork wall was thickly planted with tall grasses, so at least there was something soft to land on if anyone fell. Kai asked, "Who did the Hierarchs take this place from?"

"I don't know, Fourth Prince," Salatel said. Most of her attention was ahead, where the bottom of the slope was coming into view as the stairs wound down. There was a large walled semicircular court, now crowded with fleeing mortals. The court of leaving that Bashasa had mentioned. "This land is called the Sana-sarcofa, I don't know who lived here."

"They say it was Witches," a soldier behind them said. Kai

turned to look at her and she shrugged wearily. "But they say that about a lot of places."

"I don't think Witches build places like this," Kai said. It was nothing like what he had seen in the borderlands.

"The servers said the Hierarchs built it," another soldier volunteered. There were mild noises of disbelief and disagreement. "They did say it," she protested.

As they climbed further down, Kai saw the court had a tall archway cut into the earthwork wall, out of which riding animals, even the giant wallwalkers, and every kind of wheeled contraption poured in a steady stream. The place was a chaos of people, all leaving or preparing to leave.

On the far side was a large pool, a harbor, with barges and sailing boats emerging from another stone arch built into the earthwork wall. Every form of transport was rapidly filling with people. A high stone wall enclosed the outer side of the court, but its heavy iron gates and railed portcullis led onto a wide bridge. The watergates protecting the harbor were open to the inner moat.

As Kai and the cadre reached the floor of the court, Salatel stopped to get her bearings. Kai took the opportunity to pull his veil back on, tugging it down just enough to shield his eyes.

Salatel stood on her tiptoes to see over the crowd. A soldier caught her sleeve and pointed. "There he is," Salatel said, relieved. "This way, Fourth Prince."

She plunged into the crowd and Kai plunged after her, but only a few steps in it was almost too much. Too many frightened people, too much noise, too much like a battle. Kai fought the impulse to make a break for the bridge. After all this, the sight of an open path to freedom was too tempting. But with a practiced mix of apology and aggression, Salatel shouldered through the crowd and suddenly Bashasa was there.

"Fourth Prince!" Bashasa greeted Kai with pleasure and pulled him in, putting a confident arm around his shoulder. "Fourth Prince, can you speak for the demons?"

"No," Kai said. At least it was an easy question. Those gathered around were Tescai-Lin, the Arike Prince-heirs Hiranan and Vrim, and others he had seen with Bashasa outside the Temple Halls. Ziede, Tahren, and Dahin weren't here and he couldn't spot them in the crowd.

"Ah, the Fourth Prince cannot speak for the demons," Bashasa told the group as if this was the answer he expected. "But this is a matter that can be taken up later, as the demons freed from the Cageling Court will surely not be fighting for the Hierarchs."

"What?" Kai didn't understand.

Bashasa squeezed his shoulder. "Yes, before this day, demons taken from the Cageling Court were brought to the battles in Palm and the Belith Straits. They were forced somehow, obviously." He turned to the mortals again. "The Fourth Prince was imprisoned in the Cageling Court himself and did not know this."

Kai reeled, shocked cold, barely aware of Tescai-Lin asking a question, someone else answering, a clamor of objections. That was what the Hierarchs had done with the demons removed from the court. *Against their will,* Kai thought, a sick knot settling in his chest. It had to be against their will. Demons tortured to the point where they would agree to fight for the mortals who had cut off their connection to the underearth, who had killed their mortal families and burned the clan tents. He didn't want it to be true.

An Arike soldier appeared out of the crowd and caught Bashasa's eye. "Trenal, are they here?" At her nod, he told the group, "We must go. I'll send my messages from Benais-arik and yours will find me there."

Another mortal, a tall person with the pale coloring of the archipelagoes, said, "You can't really believe we have a hope of succeeding."

Bashasa's grip on Kai tightened. "I don't give up hope," he said, his voice suddenly flat.

Into the startled pause, Tescai-Lin said warmly, "I shall count on that."

Bashasa recovered instantly, and smiled. "You can."

Tescai-Lin inclined their head, and turned away. As the others gave Bashasa their farewells and promises, Kai spotted Ziede, Tahren, Dahin, and a scatter of Arike soldiers crossing the court. Tahren carried something wrapped up in what looked like a wall hanging . . . It was a body, Bashasa's sister's body, retrieved from the Cageling Demon Court.

Bashasa had Kai's wrist and was tugging him away. Kai let himself be towed. It wasn't like he had anywhere else to go. Bashasa said, "We know messengers were sent toward Stios. They will be carrying word to the legionaries stationed there, and any patrols on the road. Everyone must be gone before they arrive!"

"Won't they expect us to leave and move to cut us off?" Kai tried to get his mind back on what they were doing now, and not on how many captured demons might be fighting for the Hierarchs, and what would happen to the others from the Cageling Court who had refused to follow Bashasa. What would happen to Arn-Nefa.

Kai hadn't gone far enough into the Temple Halls to see if any of them had still been there. Surely they would have left as soon as possible, well ahead of most of the mortals.

"When the messengers left, this was only a little rebellion among the hostages." Bashasa tossed the words over his shoulder. "They will be coming here to help secure the place, and will not be expecting"—he waved his free hand toward the earthwork—"that! If we move fast enough, they will lose their chance to intercept us." They passed wagons and coaches and horses that were being hastily loaded with supplies, past people streaming out the gate on foot.

He was probably right. Even if there were escaping legionaries or servant-nobles among the fleeing crowd, they would be far behind the initial messengers.

Kai hoped he was right.

They headed for the boats but then Kai realized that Bashasa had angled away from the harbor toward the wallwalkers.

The beasts were easily four times the height of a tall mortal, shaggy dark fur hanging down over the tough, lizard-like hide on their long legs and clawed feet. Their rodent-like heads narrowed to a long snout that belied how wide their mouths could open. Each was hung with nets and harnesses holding cargo carriers, like giant versions of saddle bags. Atop their backs were wide, partially enclosed palanquins, with awnings and curtains catching the wind.

Bashasa headed straight for one. Kai recognized the Arike standing around it from the Hostage Courts. Those were Bashasa's dependents, the ones Dahin had been supposed to accompany. Preparing to get onto a wallwalker.

Kai planted his feet. Bashasa jolted to a halt and turned to him, startled. "What is it, Fourth Prince?"

Kai said, firmly, "I'm not getting near that thing."

Salatel and the cadre milled around them, confused, and Bashasa waved them on toward the beast. "I've looked at the maps, and this is the fastest way. We must be there as soon as possible!"

The Arike and others boarded the wallwalkers, some climbing up the side on the cargo nets, others using an ornate wooden scaffold with a spiral stair that let them step directly into the top palanquin. There were other riding places, small compartments attached to the harness and hanging lower on the creature's sides, that soldiers scrambled up into. Kai said, "Have all you mortals lost your minds?"

Bashasa let go of Kai and planted his hands on his hips. "What exactly is your objection?"

"They eat people." Just being this close to it made things in his chest do something fluttery and unpleasant. The air in the court was suddenly hot and thin, like being back in that bag again.

Bashasa countered, "They eat grass and vegetables."

"One almost ate me at the Erathi border." Among the things that would destroy a demon was being chewed up by large teeth and deposited in a giant stomach.

Bashasa said reasonably, "That was war. You probably provoked it."

Ziede, Tahren, Dahin, and the Arike with them were boarding a second wallwalker, following behind a straggling group of mortals, many injured, some being carried up the scaffold. The last of the soldiers climbed the nets. Ziede shouted across to him, "Kai, just get on the damn thing!"

"No!" Kai shouted back.

Bashasa's brow furrowed in dismay. "A demon is not afraid of a beast, no matter how big. What are you afraid of, Kai?" He lifted his brows. "Is this how you were brought here?"

Kai hadn't known until just this moment. So much of what had happened between being captured and imprisoned in the Cageling Demon Court was a blur. He almost bit through his lip to keep the words in, but maybe if Bashasa knew, he would stop asking. "I didn't know. It's the smell."

Bashasa moved toward him and Kai dropped back a step. Bashasa held up his hands. "Kai, you cannot stay here. You will be killed. Either by someone who sees what you are and panics, or by the escaped legionaries who will be hiding near here hoping for revenge."

Kai shook his head. He knew he wasn't being rational but he couldn't make himself stop. "I'm not staying here. I'm just not leaving on that. I'll walk."

Bashasa eased forward a step, somehow meeting Kai's gaze as though the veil wasn't there. He lowered his voice. "I need your help in Benais-arik, Kai. We two, we have slain Hierarchs. And by some miracle, we live to speak about it. We can do so much more than I thought possible." Kai knew how persuasive Bashasa could be, but having the whole force of that personality turned on him at once was heady. It was like a Witch using their will. Maybe there was Witch somewhere in Bashasa's ancestry. That shouldn't affect Kai, but whatever Bashasa was doing was working.

Kai looked around at the rapidly emptying court. Some mortals fled in barely controlled panic, but so many others were departing in orderly groups. Another pack of wallwalkers already strode away down the bridge. Behind them a train of open wagons and roofed carriages rolled out the main gate, followed by stragglers in small wheeled carts or on horseback. The other Arike Prince-heirs climbed onto a third wallwalker. Tescai-lin's people had boarded a barge and led a flotilla of boats out the watergate into the canal. They weren't escaping, they were purposeful. Kai remembered what that was like. Did he want to be purposeful again?

As if Bashasa read that thought, he stepped close and took Kai's hand. He had never been afraid to touch Kai. He had thought it was overconfidence, but maybe it was just a way to show trust. Bashasa said, "If you cannot bear it, there is time to leave with others. The Enalin would welcome you, I think. Do you have anywhere you wish to go, Kai?"

"No." Just burn scars in an open plain. A place where everyone who would welcome him was dead. Kai took a deep breath and felt the knot of panic in his chest break apart. "No. I don't have anywhere else to go."

Kai followed Bashasa up the side of the beast, climbing on a set of narrow stairs woven into the harness netting. Salatel and the cadre had waited for them, standing beside the creature's horribly large clawed foot. Bashasa had waved them on, and most boarded the smaller compartments that hung from the beast's side while Salatel climbed to the top. Kai didn't know if he should follow the cadre but the smell here was choking and overwhelming. He had to stop and hang off the stairs so he could cough into his arm. Bashasa paused to wait for him, peering down worriedly, until Kai managed to keep climbing.

A little half door opened into the covered palanquin at the

top and Kai squeezed inside after Bashasa, then pressed himself against the rail. The long compartment was already stuffed with mortals, all the way to the curtained back wall. They overflowed the padded benches along the sides and huddled on the floor. A mix of Arike, servers, dependents, some wearing brocade like Bashasa. All were disheveled, and many had injuries. A number were clearly from other places, refugees taking the chance to travel to Benais-arik because they had no place to go, just like Kai. Some had young children or babies tucked in next to them. The back of the palanquin had been turned into a miniature infirmary, with mortals huddling over prone bodies and passing around bandages and water flasks.

Salatel slipped past Kai and stepped across to join the two soldiers at Bashasa's side. With nowhere else to go, Kai claimed his spot by wedging himself in between the supports and cables securing this corner of the awning.

An Arike, dressed like a woman in wide pants and long tunic under a torn gold and blue brocade coat, said, "Bashasa, what's this? You have an expositor prisoner?" Her expression was appalled. She seemed the same age as Bashasa, the curls of her dark hair held back by jeweled pins. She sat on the bench near the front, with a younger Arike man standing beside her.

Kai's veil had fallen over his face during the climb and he hadn't pulled it back. He had agreed to cooperate with Bashasa, and he had no idea if that was going to involve concealing his identity or not. He didn't really care one way or the other; he felt like he was still in the rising water filling the Summer Halls, adrift and slowly sinking below the surface.

Bashasa was leaning over the bow of the palanquin having a shouted conversation with whoever controlled the beast. Kai had glimpsed a little cabin just behind the head, which was apparently where the drivers were. At least it couldn't turn around and eat them from that angle. Bashasa turned back to the woman to say, "No, of course not." He waved a hand toward Kai. "This is Kaiisteron, Prince of the Fourth House of the underearth. Fourth Prince, this is my cousin Lahshar and her son Dasara."

Kai pulled the veil off and shoved it into his belt, since there was no point in it anymore. Lahshar recoiled and Dasara glared. Others reacted with gasps or fear. But most of the mortals just watched, or went on with their own anxious conversations. Kai didn't recognize them, but they seemed to recognize him, probably from the fighting in the Temple Halls. Lahshar said pointedly, "Bashasa, are you mad?"

"Cousin, we both know the answer to that." Bashasa leaned over the side again and shouted, "Tell them to get on that one with Arava! Yes, that one! Hurry! We're going now!"

The world lurched and Kai clung to the cables. *Quake,* he thought, the terrifying phenomenon from the mountains on the far east of the grassplains, when the land shook and changed itself in a wrenching way utterly unlike the smooth transitions of the underearth. A heartbeat later he realized the wallwalker had taken a step and was now turning toward the open gate and the bridge causeway. This was going to be even worse than he thought, and he had already thought it would be awful.

Another lurching step and Salatel and another soldier grabbed the back of Bashasa's tunic to keep him from falling out. Kai gripped the cables even tighter and was just glad he wasn't the only one who had yelped.

Lahshar stood, swaying on her feet as if used to the motion. Her jaw was set. "Bashasa, just who have you made alliances with?"

"A great many people, I admit." Bashasa straightened up and leaned out to see behind them. He waved urgently at someone and the nearest soldier ducked to avoid being hit in the head.

Kai caught a flash of gold at the edge of his vision but it was only Ziede, landing on the bow of the palanquin with a breeze that fluttered clothing and stirred hair. She leaned down under the awning and said, "Vasha said she knows we're camping at the far side of the river in case we get separated but she wants to know where exactly and what river." She frowned at Kai. "Kai, are you all right? You look like you're going to vomit."

They were past the gate now and moving along the bridge. The pace was more even, but it was the stench, and the nervous crawl in Kai's spine. He wound himself tighter into the cables and said, "I'm fine."

Bashasa told his cousin Lahshar, "We will speak of this later, in private." He stepped over toward Ziede, digging a map out of his tunic.

On the far bank of the tree-lined canal the city passed by, with low stone buildings and wooden spires, bright-colored awnings along wide streets. The wind held the tinge of woodsmoke and heated metal and incense. Figures moved in the streets and Kai wondered if they had come here with the Hierarchs. Or if they were prisoners, too, held here to help supply the Summer Halls. Or if this had been their land before the Hierarchs came. If they had to run before the other legions arrived, was there anywhere to go. Was there anywhere for anybody to go?

By the time Bashasa and Ziede settled the question of the meeting point, they had reached the end of the bridge and turned away from the city, down a high road leading across marshy paddies and terraced fields. Ziede stepped back into the air, headed to her wallwalker. Bashasa leaned over to Kai. "We're past the choke point now." He kept his voice low. "Even if the legionaries arrived at this moment, they couldn't block our escape."

Kai felt his heart unclench a little. He hadn't known about the choke point, he didn't know any details of Bashasa's new plans. He was still half expecting to die with everyone here in some sudden cataclysm; that had been the goal of the original plan. Bashasa squeezed his shoulder and said, "You should rest. Many unexpected things have happened today." His mouth quirked. "I know that is a vast understatement."

Kai half snorted, half laughed. It was only funny because he was so, so tired, and maybe about to faint. He said, "I'm going to sit down." There was just enough room on the floor in between the little door and the cable anchor. He wedged himself in and let himself go as the wallwalker rocked like a ship in a storm.

THIRTEEN

Kai kept his snarl of rage internal. He shoved the finding stone into the lining of his belt and pushed away from the wall, half swimming, half running through the now still water. He held the intention, knowing if he let it release the mud and debris suspended above the court, it would explode into a watery tornado he would never find his way out of.

Could it be Ramad? No, even a distracted Dahin was too suspicious to let Ramad get the better of him. Let alone Ziede. Besides, she had surfaced nearer to the Temple Halls. She hadn't gone to the supplication tower where the other two were waiting.

No, they had a worse problem than Ramad could cause by suddenly turning on them.

Kai reached the tree-lined court where the suspended muck swirled in the branches. He found the archway out into the corridor, then finally let the intention drop. The suspended debris billowed loose in the current. His shaft of light showed the court instantly clogged with muck, like a solid wall of mud, blotting out the paving, the skeletal trees.

Kai turned away hurriedly and pressed his chest device to lighten his weight. He swam down the corridor, awkward but fast, and focused on tracing the location of Ziede's pearl.

His earpiece made a weird rustling noise and Kai stopped, put a hand against the nearest slimy stone to steady himself. It sounded like the speaking device was being jostled in a bag or—Or held in someone's hand. Then Ramad's voice, distant and echoing, said, "He told you, the person down there is just a Lesser Blessed servant, there's no reason to send hunters after—" The earpiece crackled and cut off abruptly.

So. It really wasn't Ramad who had attacked them. Kai didn't want to admit how much of a weight that lifted off his heart. *You're a fool*, he told himself, since Ziede wasn't here to say it.

It would have been better if Ramad had managed to work in the identity of just who was up there, but he had gotten the most urgent information across. Kai had a feeling he knew what *hunters* meant.

He put his hand over the light on his chest device the way Dahin had demonstrated. After a few heartbeats, the glow died away, leaving him in complete darkness. He made himself fix all his attention on Ziede's pearl.

It was ahead, toward the east, and up toward the surface. Fingers on the wall to keep himself pointed in the right direction, Kai plowed on through the dark. Finally a dim light ahead marked an opening to a court that must be free of the choking weed mat.

The glow moved.

Kai swallowed a snarl, hastily paddling backward. There was still no answer from Ziede's pearl and this wasn't the cool light of an Immortal Blessed lamp. His fumbling hand found an opening and he swung inside it, pushed on his chest device until its weight decreased and let him move up to the top of the doorway. He clung to the stone frame and curled his body up.

The light came down the corridor, moving erratically as whoever approached bounced or swam along the floor. The glow passed the doorway and Kai risked sticking his head out just enough to see.

Swimming away down the corridor was an expositor's amalgam. Dull gray flames burned just above its head: an intention for heatless light. It was big and blocky, muscles standing out on a torso that from the wedge shape and the ridge of the spine was more animal than human. Its three arms had far too many joints and the double claws of shellfish instead of hands. It flailed awk-wardly, like it was unfamiliar with moving through water, but was so physically strong the strangeness didn't slow it down.

Kai waited until the erratic flame vanished into the dark. He slipped around the doorway and bobbed up to the curved ceiling, then used it to pull himself forward down the hall.

A faint lightening in the water led him to the end of the corri-dor and into a larger room, with a row of windows outlined against the dark; the water beyond was daylit. Being able to see even a little was a relief and he wriggled through a window and groped his way past the roof of a balustrade. The heavy shadow of the weed mat extended only a short distance into the open water of this court. Ziede's pearl told him she was close.

Ziede wasn't wrong, Kai's swimming ability was not exactly practiced, but he slapped the device to lighten it again and shot upward until his head broke the surface. Even the gray daylight was too bright, dazzling his vision. He squinted, eyes watering. The long peak of a glass roof, mottled black and green with mold, blocked his view of the supplication tower. He twisted around, and saw her.

The building he had just exited had a top floor balcony high enough to break the surface. Another amalgam gripped Ziede's arms, dragging her up over the low stone fretwork wall. Her body was limp, her legs still in the water, the light cotton fabric of her clothes caught with bits of weed, her scarf gone and her braids loose and dripping as the creature pulled her up. This amalgam was smaller, more like it had started out with some unfortunate mortal's body, but it had no head.

Kai's mind went white with rage and he thrashed his way toward them. The amalgam sensed his approach and jerked upright. Its skin was fish-belly pale, dotted with scales from whatever other poor creature had gone into its making. Three random human eyes and four ears had been jammed into the stump of its neck and collarbone. Focused on its task, knowing it was out of his reach, it dragged Ziede out of the water just as Kai reached the balcony wall. Kai couldn't drain the false life of an amalgam and there was no time for an intention. He pulled the collapsed telescoping rod out of his tunic's inside pocket, grabbed the carving on the wall for leverage, and triggered it.

The rod shot out and Kai had a heartbeat to be glad he had pointed the stupid thing in the right direction. The point pierced the amalgam's shoulder, razored edges widening the wound. It dropped Ziede onto the floor of the balcony and flailed soundlessly at Kai. Trying to jerk backward and free itself just jammed the rod in tighter.

Kai let go and dragged himself up onto the wall. It clawed at him, hampered as the rod caught against the balcony rail. Kai leaned on the rod to keep it wedged in place and ducked under the reaching hands. He managed to get one hand on its foot, which was mostly human with some kind of hoof melded in where the heel should be. He felt for the designs that kept it whole and animated. Fingers grazed his head as it forced its pierced body further down the rod, but the angled razors must be catching on bone. Kai focused on threading his way into the animating intention and not the fact that he was in a bad position and had moments before this thing tore him apart.

A hand gripped his hair just as he found the heart of the design and shattered it. The amalgam fell apart, legs, torso, arms thumping down on the wet stone. Shoving pieces aside, Kai scrambled for Ziede.

He gently took her shoulders and caught her lolling head. His hands were shaking. If she was dead, he was going to kill everybody he could catch.

Her body was still warm except for the natural chill of the water. The skin on her forehead and right cheek was abraded, maybe from a fall onto stone. She wasn't breathing. An instant later he felt her life and a lump closed his throat in pure relief.

He took a deep breath and looked for an intention, sensing one immediately. Something to cause stasis, sent from a distance. She must have been standing on one of these rooftops to call the wind, stirring the current for him, and had been hit by surprise. From the air, maybe? From behind? She had tumbled into the water and the stasis had kept her from drowning. He rolled her half over, supporting her on his lap, and felt her back. There it was, an intention buried just under her right shoulder blade. He felt for the shape of the design and gently pulled. It came reluctantly out of her flesh as a dull red glow, just a slight thickening of the air in Kai's palm. He put it on his own chest, mostly because he needed to get it out of his hand so he could take care of Ziede.

She gasped in a breath but didn't wake. It had been a strong intention; it would take her some time to come fully out of it. He listened to her heart and lungs to make sure she was well and then struggled upright to pull her through the balcony door into the filthy room beyond. He didn't want her near the water so he carried her up the steps to an interior gallery and set her back against the half wall. It wouldn't be comfortable but it would keep her upright, away from the water. Just in case the worse came to worst, he took the finding stone and tucked it under the extra scarf she had wrapped around her wrist. His hands were still shaking.

Kai stood and forced himself to take a deep breath. The air device had stopped working at some point, and he had been breathing through his mouth. He didn't want to take the nose plugs out, knowing he had to go under again. He stepped outside and pulled the rod out of the amalgam's torso, and slid the weapon back down into its compact form. Tucking it away again, he climbed over the wall and dropped back into the water.

He stuck his head under just long enough to make sure the other amalgam wasn't lurking down below him anywhere, then paddled toward the glass roof peak on the opposite side of the court. He banged his knee encountering the submerged slope, then eased upward and flattened his body to keep his silhouette as low as possible. His hair had come loose from its tie and it was full of drifting mossy weed bits, which made his skin crawl like he was covered with slimy ants, but it would help him look like flotsam from a distance.

As he neared the roof peak, Kai heard voices, the words blurred as the sound traveled over the water. Gritting his teeth, he lifted up just enough to see over the verdigris-covered ridge.

An Immortal Blessed ascension raft had landed on the topmost balcony of the supplication tower. Bigger than their river barge, it was a bright gleaming copper color, shaped like the fan of a gingko leaf with the edges curled up. The steering column was visible in the point of the fan with the low curve of a curtained dome shelter behind it. Someone moved on board, a flash of white and yellow, but he couldn't tell how many people were up there or who they were.

On the lowest balcony, just above the water, Dahin huddled, his head down. Kai couldn't tell if he was unconscious or trapped by another stasis intention. Ramad stood in front of him, hands held out as if asking for calm or trying to placate the people facing them.

At least two expositors, or one expositor and an apprentice, Kai thought. Their dark coloring might be Arike, it was hard to tell at this distance. They were dressed in coats and divided skirts, in practical grays and blacks, not the gleam of finery. There were four mortals wearing light chestplate armor and carrying bladed weapons. They scattered across the balcony, all watching the water, alert for attack. Behind them an Immortal Blessed paced back and forth like an angry leopard. The white tunic, pants, and gold tabard were what all Immortal Blessed wore when out in the world, but his light-colored hair hung past his shoulders, meaning he was male. It was rare to see Immortal Blessed men; they were too important to deal with mortals and Witches and other lesser creatures. One other person stood at the edge of the platform facing out toward the water, a veiled figure wearing dark clothing. It might be another expositor, it might be an enslaved familiar.

Whatever Ramad was saying wasn't what anyone wanted to hear. The Immortal Blessed turned abruptly and hit him across the face. Kai flinched; the blow staggered Ramad and he barely caught himself with one hand and a knee on the ground. The Immortal Blessed gestured and the guards moved swiftly forward to drag Ramad up and take hold of Dahin. They hauled them inside the tower.

Kai sank back down, biting his lower lip. This was going to be tricky. The only point in his favor was that these people had arrived in the Immortal Blessed ascension raft, probably the same one that had tracked Saadrin to the ship at Orintukk. It meant that they hadn't come through the harbor and that Tenes and Sanja were probably still safe. He hoped.

Kai slipped down fully into the water and pushed off the roof. He needed to get to Dahin and Ramad. If they thought to try, the expositors who had created the amalgams might be able to tell that one had been dispersed. He needed them to be thinking about something else. He needed a distraction.

Once clear of the submerged roof, he pressed his chest device and sunk down to the floor of the court. The breathing part started to work again as soon as he was all the way under, which was one less complication. And he had an idea.

Cantrips wouldn't work in water, so it would have to be another intention. He propelled himself across the court to the first-floor balustrade and pulled the light off his chest device. Holding on to a pillar to keep from drifting away, he pushed it to turn it back on. Immortal Blessed devices weren't inclined to allow manipulation by other forms of power, but then he wouldn't actually be changing the working that controlled the device. Tapping and twisting at it, he found the right combination to make it shine brighter and to narrow the shaft of its beam.

Kai quickly assembled a design. It was an old one, useful during the war, and he was counting on the fact that this new generation of expositors wouldn't recognize it, at least in this form.

Once it was ready, Kai hesitated, wincing. He had to open his mouth again for enough pain to fill his own well in order to power the intention long enough to make this plan work. He knew now just how bad the water was, which made it that much more effective.

He briefly wrestled his instinctive self-preservation down and opened and closed his mouth. He gagged, choked, his stomach tried to heave. He cupped his hands around the Immortal Blessed light, fed the pain into his design, and set it loose.

The intention wreathed around the light and created thick bands of shadow, solid enough to temporarily block the glow and make it fluctuate wildly.

Kai took deep breaths through the air device and thought, *That was even worse than the first time.* He set the light and its intention loose. It rolled and bounced along the paved court, stirring up muck, headed for the corridor Kai had used to get here. It would make for two courts over, where the mat was spotty, and then move up toward the surface. With his distraction on its way, he had enough pain left in his well for two more designs. He built them and attached their nascent forms to his chest next to the one he had removed from Ziede. Then he turned to swim awkwardly across the court toward the dark shape of an archway.

Without the Blessed light, he had to grope his way through the next building. Just enough light fell down through the water to see the shapes of outside doors or windows.

It gave him time to think about the thing that set like a weight in his belly. Someone had not only known Kai and Ziede were coming here, but had known exactly what they meant to find, and where it was. The second amalgam had been heading right toward the Arike Hostage Courts.

Kai had thought everyone else who had been in that court, who had known about Cantenios, was dead. He had been certain of it. So had Ziede. They had both been certain enough to risk all their lives on it.

Guided by the faint light from the windows into the next court, Kai floated up through a stairwell, meaning to make his way around to a vantage point on the far side of the supplication tower. But the next doorway led into a room with oddly mottled light coming from above and he realized it was another glass roof, not as coated with mold as the others.

Kai lightened his chest device and swam upward, breaking the surface under the roof. At the first breath of air, his stomach almost turned over. He forced it down ruthlessly; he needed that pain.

Eyes watering from the unpleasant effort, he looked around. The glass peak overhead was discolored, coated with something oily, glinting with a sickly hue in the wan light. But panes were broken out along the eaves just above the surface. He paddled to the jagged opening and got a view of the tower.

He shook the water out of his ears to hear shouted voices. Two Lesser Blessed were out on the lowest balcony now, and the ascension raft docked two levels above looked empty. His light and shadow intention had made its way to the open court where Kai had aimed it and someone had spotted the light shining intermittently up through the clouded water. It was meant to look like Kai was down there possibly wrestling with an amalgam, or searching something. Whatever the invaders assumed, it was having the desired effect. The Immortal Blessed made a sharp gesture. The expositors argued, and it was hard to tell if they were disagreeing over who wanted to go or who didn't, but the Immortal Blessed cut it off again. One expositor and two bodyguards went to climb into Dahin's boat.

The other expositor and the veiled figure that Kai thought

might be a familiar stayed where they were, at the edge of the balcony. Kai hissed out a breath. It would have to do.

He sunk down below the surface again.

———— ∞ ————

Kai entered the supplication tower through a doorway in the lowest level, far below the landing platforms. In the dim light falling down from the surface, the frame glittered with the still bright sun signs of Immortal Blessed metal, both decoration and warning. With no windows in the lower levels, it was completely dark inside. Navigating by feel, he swam into the circular stairwell, lightened his chest device, and started up.

He swam in upward circles in utter blackness for so long it felt like the season must have changed, that he would emerge from the water into icy rain or a windstorm. When his head suddenly broke the surface it was a shock. Dazzled by light, Kai froze, silently cursing himself for moving too fast. But no one came running to see what the splash was.

He blinked until his eyes adjusted. Light stone walls were streaked with the usual creeping mottled growth, and the last few steps stopped at a slime-covered landing. The gray light came from the opposite side of the shaft, where it must be open to the room with the outside door to the first balcony. Around the curve, the stairs continued up.

Kai eased out of the water, careful not to splash, and on his hands and knees climbed the steps onto the landing. Breathing through his mouth sounded so loud; he pulled out his nose plug and shoved it into his tunic. Then he carefully plucked the first of the intentions he had constructed off his chest. He set it carefully on the water where it lapped against the steps, a rippling black spot of deep shadow.

If the expositor who had been out on the platform or his familiar came in here, they would see it, but Kai needed it centered on the tower. He couldn't let it loose outside where the wind might drift it closer to Ziede's position. He fed the design just enough pain from his well for it to send tendrils through the water to join with his other intention, the shadow band wrapped around the Immortal Blessed light. It was currently rolling under the weed mat over the Hostage Courts, luring the other expositor and the two bodyguards further and further away from the tower. He had a little time until the two designs managed to find and join each other.

Kai edged further onto the landing and heard a low voice. He went still again, wincing, but there were no shouts of alarm. He crawled around the central stone shaft until he could see the open doorway and a little of the weathered room beyond. Outside air only a little less dank drifted in. Another voice spoke, still too low to make out the words. There was no movement, no sign or sound of Dahin and Ramad on this level. If either was in any state approaching consciousness, they would be talking. Kai slid past the door and climbed the steps in a low crouch.

At the next turn, it was easier to tell that the voices came from the highest level, where the Immortal Blessed ascension raft was docked. Kai stopped just at the point where the words were clear enough to understand.

"You are lying." That was the Immortal Blessed, speaking Old Imperial with the usual tone of superiority. "Your kind always lie."

"I am not lying." And that was Ramad, his voice a little thick, probably from the blow to the face. It eased the tight anxiety in Kai's chest a little. At least Ramad lived, now he really needed to hear Dahin.

Kai crept up the steps to the landing and slid on his belly, moving near silently, pressed to the mucky stone. There was a story among the Vidraiaen that he could turn into a snake; it was too bad it wasn't true, it would come in handy right now. He eased forward until he could just see through the doorway.

The room took up the whole interior of the tower top, high enough to be mostly free of mud and mold. In the outer wall, a short flight of steps led to a doorway open to the landing balcony, but it allowed him only a glimpse of the gleaming side of the ascension raft. Kai risked another wriggle forward until he could see the whole room.

Ramad stood back against the wall, Dahin collapsed at his feet. Dahin at least was conscious, blinking up blearily at the Immortal Blessed man. His tunic was torn at the chest where he had been dragged by it. His bag lay nearby, a few leather folders open and scattered around. Ramad's nose bled and his hair had come loose. Just from the way he was standing, it was clear he had taken hits to his ribs and stomach.

The Immortal Blessed faced Ramad, one of the expositor's bodyguards standing back to flank him, and seethed with frustration. Kai could smell it just as strongly as the fear wafting off the mortal guard. There was no sign of the two Lesser Blessed Kai had spotted earlier.

Stubborn and persistent as ever, Ramad said, "You can kill us both but it won't change the facts."

The Immortal Blessed was unimpressed. "Facts? Lie to me again, then. We know you came here for a Hierarch's finding stone. Tell me where it is."

"There's no finding stone here." It was a gasp from Dahin. He sounded weak, hurt. He made a noise half sob and half laugh. "I was only looking at a map. I hate you people, I hate you all."

Ramad didn't waver. "Safreses and Kinlat were taken prisoner and have told everything they know. Aclines is dead. The Imperial renewal has passed, and even without Tahren Stargard, the treaty with the Immortal Blessed will not be altered. If you harm Kaiisteron or Ziede Daiyahah, Bashat bar Calis will take revenge with all the power he has. There is no point in any of this anymore. You should board your craft and leave." He added deliberately, "I don't recommend you go to Nient-arik."

Ah, Kai thought, *there it is.*

The Immortal Blessed was impatient. "No one knows of my involvement. Stop this ridiculous delay and tell me where the finding stone is."

"Why do you even want it, Faharin?" Dahin demanded from the floor. "How many other Immortal Blessed are wrapped up in your stupid useless conspiracy? Are you afraid of the Rising World tracking them down or the Immortal Marshalls?"

Ramad pressed his lips together. "Dahin."

"Oh come on, you were never going to get anywhere by being reasonable with these people, they're like children with giant egos—" Dahin cut off with a gasp as the Immortal Blessed leaned down to backhand him.

The Immortal Blessed Faharin grated out the words, "Little apostate, you talk of conspiracies like you know more than you should."

Kai grimaced. The intention he had left on the water was a cold shiver through his nerve endings as its tendrils crept through the weed mat, nearly to the shadow-band. He needed that distraction. But it was risky to wait, with Dahin's death wish in play. Kai pushed himself up, just enough to catch Dahin's eye. Ramad, focused on Faharin, didn't see him.

Draining an Immortal Blessed able to resist wasn't easy, it was far more difficult than draining a powerful expositor. But Kai had planned for that. Sort of planned. Mostly planned. A lot was going to depend on Faharin's reaction.

Dahin's throat worked as he swallowed, the only indication that he had seen Kai. He glared up at Faharin. "What does it matter, you're going to kill us anyway," he said, his voice scratchy with pain.

Immortal Blessed never liked to be argued with. "Quiet, you foolish child. You have only yourself to blame for—"

"Where is my sister?" Dahin's voice rose in fury. "You Hierarch's ass-licker, what did you do to her?"

Either it was a good distraction attempt or Dahin was done soliciting information from Faharin. Kai felt the two intentions connect and weave their designs together. Hoping the expositor in Dahin's boat was close enough to get the full effect, he emptied almost the whole well of his pain into the incipient intention floating on the water two levels below. It was hard not to hold back more for self-defense, but this would need almost everything he had left. Then he let go.

A whoosh-thump echoed up the stairwell, then horrified screams. Kai shoved to his feet as heat and the stench of burning waterweed flowed up the shaft. Faharin and the bodyguard whirled toward the stairwell. Kai lunged forward.

The small intention he had readied was already primed with pain; he plucked it off his shoulder and flung it at the guard. He didn't have a chance to see it land. Faharin moved so fast that before Kai took another step a Blessed blade stabbed through his chest.

It felt like a punch at first, the real pain still just terrible potential, like a poisonous flower about to unfold. Kai let his momentum and his weight carry him forward and forced another full inch of Blessed metal through his breastbone. He was close enough to see the white blond beard stubble above the man's upper lip. Faharin's expression was calm and condescending, just a slight twist of distaste to his perfect mouth. Kai scraped the last intention off his chest, stretched forward, and slapped it down on the man's wrist.

This was the powerful intention that had stunned Ziede, already charged by the expositor who had cast it. It hadn't been meant for an Immortal Blessed so there was a chance it wouldn't work.

But Faharin froze for a long indrawn breath while Kai's heart's blood soaked his tunic and tearing agony seized his chest. Darkness crept in at the edge of his vision. Then the man's face went slack and he started to slump.

Kai tried to pull free but the blade was wedged in too far. It dragged him down, abrading his sliced flesh. He fell to his knees as Faharin collapsed in a heavy heap. Kai's head reeled, new power rushed into him but with the Blessed blade jammed into his heart, there was nothing he could do with it.

Someone shoved the unconscious man aside and hands gripped his shoulders. Ramad crouched in front of him, staring in wide-eyed horror. "Kai," he whispered.

Past Ramad, the mortal guard lay sprawled on the floor, insensible from the weaker intention. Dahin scrambled around gathering his scattered papers and folders, jamming them back into the bag. "Just pull it out!" Dahin snarled. "Don't you know anything?"

Kai echoed, "Pull it out," but it was an almost voiceless rasp.

"Are you certain?" Ramad sounded sick. He must be even more injured than he looked, Kai would have to deal with it later.

"Yes!" Dahin shoved to his feet, slinging his bag over his back. "Just do it!"

"Yes," Kai whispered.

Ramad swallowed with difficulty. His face set, he gripped the hilt and pulled it free.

The relief was almost as shocking as the pain. Kai gasped a huge breath and clapped his hands over the already closing wound. He bent over, wrestling the rush of power generated by his own agony under control as his damaged body struggled to repair itself. The pain flowed to his well until it buzzed through his skin like a lightning strike. His vision went black, his stomach wanted to turn itself inside out. He couldn't remember why a well of his own pain had ever seemed like a good idea. Expositors were maniacs. Cantrips were easier, being a demon was easier. Being dead was easier, but he had never been able to let that happen.

As the first overwhelming wave passed, Kai's lungs reinflated. His heart stammered to a start again. He sat up, squinted at the light, and wheezed, "That's better. Ramad, thank you."

Ramad's mouth dropped open. Dahin swooped down to grab the blade out of his hand, stepped to the stunned Faharin, and stabbed it down through his heart.

"Dahin!" Kai's damaged lungs were still regrowing and his voice came out in a squawk. "What did you—"

"The Marshalls would kill him anyway!" Dahin snapped, wrenching the weapon around, widening the wound to make certain the man was dead.

Ramad clutched Kai's arm, looking from him to Dahin and back in bewilderment. It was too late now; destroying the heart with Blessed metal was a sure way to kill even an Immortal Marshall. If they had taken the man prisoner, Ramad could have hauled him off to Benais-arik to disclose the rest of the Blessed conspirators. Kai said helplessly, "If you were going to just kill him, I could have drained him."

"I can't think of everything!" Dahin yanked the weapon free and stormed up the steps and out to the ascension raft. "Oh shitting great, Aunt Saadrin's here! They've got her tied up in the cabin!"

"Don't stab her!" Kai yelled, half falling over, trying to get his legs under him. Sharp pain shot through his knees. Ramad took a gasping breath and seemed to snap out of his daze. He shouldered Kai's arm and hauled him to his feet. Together, they staggered up the steps and out onto the platform.

The heat and the stench of burning muck choked the air. Clouds of dark smoke obscured the platforms below and the sunken rooftops around them. Through the haze, sheets of fire rolled across the weed mat, more smoke billowing up.

"How did—What did—You set the water on fire?" Ramad sounded overcome, as if this was just too much. Kai wondered if that blow to the head had done something worse than break his nose. They might be able to get Dahin to help him, once they got out of here. "There was that much oil in it?"

"They're intentions, they don't need fuel to burn," Kai told him. It certainly helped things along, but it wasn't necessary. "It looks worse than it is." Only the water around the tower and between it and the other intention was actually on fire, not the whole of the Summer Halls. Though from here at the top of the supplication tower it was hard to tell.

Ramad seemed to shake off his shock. "How long will it burn?" He helped Kai to the ascension raft, where a small gate stood open in the side. The interior was big enough to fit a dozen or more people, the floor curving up to form benches along the rails. White curtains were pulled away from the door of the domed cabin in the back, revealing a couple of cushioned couches and Saadrin half sprawled back against the wall. Her wrists and ankles were secured with gold metal bonds and something like a small plate had been fixed over her mouth, preventing her from talking. She was conscious, her eyes narrowed in fury.

"How long will it burn?" Dahin laughed. He stuffed his bag into a cubby in the cabin, ignoring his aunt. "How long has this place been flooded?"

"I know what I'm doing now, Dahin," Kai snapped. He hated it when Dahin got like this. His legs were still shaking but he pulled away from Ramad. "It'll stop in a few hours." He felt a tentative touch from Ziede's pearl and asked her, *Are you all right?* Her answer was a grumble. If she was conscious enough to be grumpy, she was going to be all right. He leaned back against the rail, relieved. "We need to go. And do not stab your aunt!"

"Fine, all right, fine." Dahin dropped the Blessed blade and turned to the steering column. "I'll get us out of here."

"We have to find Ziede Daiyahah." Ramad told Kai, "She was knocked out somehow, before we saw the raft."

"I found her, she's just woken." Kai focused on yelling through Ziede's pearl until she answered more coherently. *Meet us down in the harbor,* he told her, when he was sure she understood. *Be cautious.* The smoke was too thick for easy flying and he had no idea how many bodyguards and expositors had survived. With their luck, most of them. *We're on an Immortal Blessed ascension raft.*

How did you—Never mind. She sounded fully alert finally. *I'm going now.*

"She'll meet us in the harbor," Kai said.

Dahin nodded, distracted as he wrestled with the steering column, trying to make it respond to him. Kai winced as the Well of Thosaren flowed through the raft. The alien power was too close, abrading his nerve endings, like an itch deep in his throat.

The deck pushed against his feet as the raft lifted off the platform. It dipped toward the top of the tower, then rotated away. "I'm out of practice," Dahin muttered.

Ramad stumbled and grabbed the rail. Wisely, he didn't comment on Dahin's steering ability. "They can track this craft, correct?"

A cloud of suffocating smoke enveloped the raft and cut off any answers. Then they were out into open air, gray sky overhead, the raft pointed toward the edge of the Summer Halls earthwork. Kai coughed and wiped his mouth on his sleeve. Ramad's expression was pinched; he wouldn't be the first mortal to vomit on an ascension raft. Kai said, "When there's time, Dahin should be able to stop any Blessed from finding the raft." Then he made eye contact with the inhabitant of the cabin, who was glaring furiously. "Oh, and there's Saadrin." She had no reason to help the Blessed who had taken her prisoner. Surely this would make her easier to reason with. "We should—"

Something jolted the raft and a dark shape vaulted the rail. It slammed Ramad aside and he bounced off the bench and landed on the deck. It was the second amalgam, the big one made of both mortal and animal parts, with too many arms and shellfish claws instead of hands.

The raft rocked with its unexpected weight as it surged toward Dahin. Kai flung himself at it, struck the hard-shell plate protecting its chest. That startled more than hurt it, but it gave Dahin a heartbeat to swing the raft around. The amalgam wobbled backward and Kai shoved with the half-formed thought of sending it over the side. The biggest clawed arm swung toward him and the blow knocked him back into the rail.

Kai thumped down onto the deck, winded, his head ringing. His right eye had gone dark and fluid ran down his face. He clawed at it, trying to see, and something squishy came away in his hand. His stupid ghoul eye had come loose. He threw it away and looked up. The amalgam stood over him, claw lifted for another blow. There was no time for a cantrip, no time for an intention.

Ramad suddenly wrapped his arms around the clawed limb and wrenched it backward. The raft rocked again and dropped, Dahin cursing frantically. Metal screeched as the hull scraped solid ground; they were over the edge of the earthwork and sliding down the slope. The amalgam twisted toward Ramad and grabbed at his head with another claw. Kai pulled the telescoping rod out of his tunic and used the deck's tilt to lunge forward and slide into the creature's legs. He jammed the rod up into a gap in its carapace and triggered it.

The amalgam couldn't roar without a mouth but it dropped Ramad. The extended end of the rod pierced its carapace and it leaned down to claw for Kai with all its arms. He jammed the rod in harder and twisted.

Ramad fell to the deck beside Kai, scrabbling for something. Then he shoved upright, the Immortal Blessed blade that Dahin had discarded in his hand. It went through the amalgam's shell-covered chest like a knife through water.

Kai flung an arm over his head as the amalgam collapsed into component parts. Ramad staggered, breathing hard and bracing himself on his knees. Kai shoved amalgam limbs and a section of torso off himself and stumbled upright. His left eye had also gone dark. When something shoved him from that side, he thought it was Dahin.

Then the intention hit him.

It was meant to tangle, to freeze his limbs. Kai's hip hit the curved metal bench just before the deck slammed into the side of his head. Cold power burned through the damp cotton of his tunic and into his skin. Dahin shouted, high-pitched and furious. Everything was blurry confusion, but a step away from Kai's outstretched hand, Ramad sprawled on the deck again. More booted and sandaled feet stood in the raft than there had been a heartbeat ago, way too many. Then everything went dark.

FOURTEEN

The intention wrapped Kai in a web of cold, froze his blood, traced every vein in his body, and set a block of ice in his newly repaired heart. Around him were shouts and movement, but he turned all his focus inward.

He used the lingering pain from his torn flesh to unravel the design and drag its claws out of him, piece by chilly piece. His sense of Ziede returned and her fear filled his head, mixed with his own. She could tell something had happened to him but not what it was, and he couldn't form the words yet to explain.

When Kai drove the ice out of his eyes, everything was blurry and half-dark, the gray sky obscured by weird shadows. He recognized Ramad, upside down and leaning over him. Kai was lying down, possibly on the bench below the raft's rail, and he was pretty certain it was Ramad's thigh under his head. Ramad squeezed his shoulder and breathed the word, "Careful."

Right, they had been caught, someone was listening to them. There was an extremely powerful expositor nearby and that was very, very bad. Kai's head hurt, his chest and back felt like he had been stepped on by a wallwalker and maybe ground into the dirt a little. He tried to move and Ramad gripped his shoulders to help him sit up.

Someone, speaking in Old Imperial with a Blessed accent, said, "You told us it would keep him unconscious."

Kai's vision was still blurry and shadowed. The raft was not moving and there were a lot of unfriendly people in it. *Oh, the other stupid ghoul eye,* Kai thought in exasperation. He pulled it out and flicked it away. Someone made a horrified exclamation of disgust, and next to him, Dahin muttered, "Ugh, Kai."

He blinked and wiped at his eyes and the blurry scene resolved into clarity. It was worse than he thought.

The two Lesser Blessed. The bodyguards who had been on the lower platform, some bearing charred clothing and burns on their arms and legs. One was tossing amalgam limbs over the raft's rail. The expositor with the veiled familiar was also aboard. The raft was at an angle but not a steep one, so it must be on the upper slope of the earthwork, maybe jammed on top of some brush. A smokey haze hung in the air, so the Summer Halls were still burning.

To Kai's right, Dahin crouched on the bench, bleeding from a cut on the head, his teeth bared with the expression of a thwarted predator. Kai said silently to Ziede, *They've got us, stay hidden*. He let her see through his eyes and felt her groan of dismay.

The razored rod and the Immortal Blessed blade were nowhere to be seen, but one of the Blessed cradled a weapon that was far more deadly. It looked like the stock of an Enalin crossbow, but drew on the Well of Thosaren to cast a debilitating force onto anyone within a short range. If it was turned on a mortal long enough it would kill. During the war, Kai and the other Witches had never found an intention or cantrip that could stop it. The range was limited, but that didn't help when they were cornered in this raft.

The Lesser Blessed gazed at Kai in disgust and the mortal guards were wary and horrified, though that was probably about the discarded eye. Would it be the Lesser Blessed or the expositor in charge now, the expositor who had gotten Kai with that powerful intention . . . No.

Kai took in the way the veiled familiar stood, the set of their shoulders. The way the expositor's dark eyes were empty, trained not on Kai but past him, into the distance. The intention had been so strong, so effective, reaching down into the parts of Kai that were still of the underearth, even after all this time. No expositor had ever been able to do that before, not like this.

He didn't know how, he didn't know who, but he had a terrible feeling . . . *Kai,* Ziede whispered in his head. Tangled in his emotions, she knew what he was thinking. *It could be a Witch.*

It's not a Witch, he told her. *It should be impossible, I don't understand.*

His gaze on the veiled figure, Kai said, "So who do you think gets eaten first, when all this goes wrong?"

One Lesser Blessed grimaced, and a shiver of tension went through the guards.

It's not a Witch, Ziede agreed.

The veiled person stepped forward and knelt to be at eye level with Kai. Hands lifted to draw the dark gauze back. Their eyes were like his, whiteless, matte black.

It was still a shock, no matter how he had prepared himself, how certain his impossible hunch was correct.

Kai didn't recognize the face, but then, they wouldn't recognize his face, either. Their features were regular, lips thin, skin a light archipelago brown, dark hair braided tightly back under the cap of the veil. The body under the dark coat, tunic, and skirts seemed far too thin. In a light, even voice, they said, "I know you came here on the canal. I saw you arrive."

Kai didn't let the spike of dread show on his face. They knew about Tenes and Sanja. They would have sent guards and expositors after them. "Because you followed us, or you just know me so well?" he said, then told Ziede silently, *You can't help us, you need to take the others and go.*

I'm not leaving you, she replied. He sensed she was in motion, in the air and already far down the slope toward the harbor.

"I think I never knew you at all," they said, calm on the surface, a quiver of fire underneath. "I thought you were a child, an innocent, easily falling into mortal corruption. But you knew exactly what you were doing."

Kai was aware that Dahin had gone still, eyes wide. Ramad said softly, "Kai, who is this?"

Kai's throat was dry. "This is a demon in a mortal body, who came here before the Hierarchs closed the passage to the underearth." Unexpected anger made his voice thick. "But surely not one I've ever met, since leaving your gifted mortal body and taking another is such a terrible crime. Even when it's an accident that let a mortal prince kill a Hierarch."

They tilted their head, smiling faintly, eyes narrowing in old disdain. "I will never believe that was an accident, Kai-Enna."

It was the way she said the name that wasn't his any longer that sparked recognition. "Arn-Nefa. You were going off to die because fighting the Hierarchs was pointless." Kai leaned forward. He wanted to bite her throat out. "You left us there. You left me there."

A Lesser Blessed shifted, impatient or uneasy, and said, "Aren't you going to restrain him? We have Blessed chains." There was something about her that suggested youth, the way the yellow and white silk tabard fit her lanky body.

Arn-Nefa didn't turn to look at her. "Chain him yourself."

Kai told the Lesser Blessed, "Go ahead." He held out his wrists. "Just come over here." Arn-Nefa wasn't yielding to sentiment; she had tried to drain him once before and it hadn't worked. He knew he couldn't drain her, either. Demons weren't meant to fight each other in the mortal world, using the power they only gained when they left the underearth.

The Lesser Blessed's lip curled. There was obviously no confusion about who Kai was, and both Blessed knew the Well weapon was the best way to keep him under control.

"Make him give you the finding stone, Expositor Arnsterath," the other Lesser Blessed spoke up. He was older, hair long but tied back to show his lower status. "The Immortal Patriarch wants it, to keep it out of the hands of these abominations. And he'll want it even more, now that you've let the honored Faharin be killed."

Dahin snorted bitter laughter. "An Immortal Patriarch is behind this conspiracy? That should have been obvious." He asked Arn-Nefa, "Regret picking the Blessed for allies yet? In case anyone needs to know"—he gestured to the two Lesser Blessed—"these are Narrein and Shiren, long known for clinging to Faharin's tabard like the little shitballs they are. Their duty is undoubtedly to keep an eye on him for the rest of the conspiracy since he's so full of himself his brain doesn't work. Oh, pardon, was full of himself, because he's dead now."

Narrein's expression turned colder and Shiren hissed, "Shut your blaspheming mouth, you Witch-lover."

Dahin laughed again. "What? Witch-lover? Is that all you could come up with? With everything I've done?"

"They think you're an expositor?" Kai asked Arn-Nefa, mostly to distract everyone from Dahin. He was afraid the grimly offended Narrein would tell him to calm down, which would be like throwing distilled palm liquor onto a bonfire. "They don't know what you are?"

"They know," she assured him. She tilted her head to the expositor standing behind her and to one side, watching her flank. Arn-Nefa had turned an expositor into a familiar, which was unexpectedly horrifying. He was a young Arike, tightly curling hair confined by a gold fillet, his expression still blank, uninterested. Around his neck was a leather cord, whatever pendant hung from it tucked under the fine material of his dark blue tunic. And Kai had to stop thinking of her as Arn-Nefa; Nefa and any trace of the Kanavesi Saredi were long gone.

Ramad had obviously been trying to calculate a less fatal way out of this. He said, "As I told the Immortal Blessed Faharin, the Rising World knows about the Nient-arik conspiracy. Harming us will not help you. The finding stone will go to the Rising World to be handed to the Immortal Marshalls." He added, "You should leave now, while you can. Find a place of safety."

"They can't go," Dahin said, with a good deal of satisfaction.

"For one thing, they're too stupid. For the other, they've lost their protector Faharin. The Patriarch they're working for will throw them to the Marshalls to save himself at the first opportunity."

Ramad's expression tightened. Kai knew what he was thinking and also wished there was a way to make Dahin shut up. But unfortunately Dahin was right, Ramad's attempts to be reasonable wouldn't work.

Arnsterath flicked some drifting ash from her sleeve, as if none of this mattered to her.

Narrein said, "All we want is the finding stone. We can come to an arrangement."

He's lying, Kai thought to Ziede. *They came here because they don't want any witnesses.* This conspiracy of Blessed had gone against the Patriarchs who supported Bashat and Benais-arik and they knew the penalty they would face. *Take the stone, get Tahren, and come back for us together.*

No, Kai. By the time we come back, there's no telling what that self-righteous shit will have done to you. He got a hint of the harbor cave around her, dank and quiet, Tenes' anxious presence.

Angry and frustrated, Shiren said, "Make him give you the finding stone, or we'll kill the vanguarder."

Arnsterath didn't react, still with that faint smile that hid so much hate. "He doesn't have it. Ziede Daiyahah has it."

Kai's eyes widened, he couldn't help it. He had a terrible feeling . . .

Shiren was suspicious. "You said your other creature had found her and she didn't have it."

"She has it now." Arnsterath pushed to her feet. "He must have found it and left it with her."

Kai set his jaw. Arnsterath could hear the pearl. "How?" the word came out in a near snarl. Ramad and Dahin both watched him in confusion.

Arnsterath slipped a folded square of silk out of her sleeve, and held it up. It was stained with the faintest drop of rust-brown, vanishing under the shifting darkness of an intention even as he watched. She said, "A Witch should be more careful with their blood."

Shit, Ziede whispered, *shit, shitting*—Her voice cut off as she withdrew from Kai's thoughts and sealed her mind away. On the ship's deck at Orintukk, she had done the finding cantrip with spit and blood. A drop must have fallen unnoticed to the deck, but only a demon could have sniffed it out; a mortal expositor would never have found it. That was how Arnsterath had known they were coming here, feeling the pull of that blood like a lodestone. And at close range, with the power well formed by the Summer Halls, it had let her hear Ziede's pearl.

Narrein said, "Where?"

The person who had been Arn-Nefa a lifetime ago smiled. "She's down in the harbor."

With Shiren still holding the Well weapon, Lesser Blessed Narrein took the steering column and the ascension raft lifted up. As it rotated, Kai caught a last glance of the Summer Halls. Through the roiling smoke, the flicker of flames sheeted over the weed mats. His intention wouldn't catch the stone, even the parts sticking up above the surface, but sparks skittered across a glass roof, searching for plant matter to burn. He turned back to Arnsterath. "Where did you go?"

It wasn't a private conversation: Dahin and Ramad were on either side of him, they faced the guards and Shiren, all obviously listening, as well as the expositor turned familiar, who seemed to have been left with as much free will as a root vegetable.

But Arnsterath didn't seem to care. She leaned against the rail, watching Kai with a dispassionate but complete attention, as if no one else mattered. At the question, her smooth brow wrinkled slightly. "Where did I go when there was nowhere left? Why didn't I put down my mortal body and drift into nothing, you mean?"

"That too." Kai couldn't help adding, "You were all so sure fighting for the mortals was useless."

"Maybe I should have stayed with you," she said, talking about the Temple Halls, all those years ago. "But then you wouldn't have been the only one. The heroic Arike Prince-heir's pet demon. The Witch King."

Kai sensed Ramad's riveted attention. He was past caring about that. If they all died, then at least Ramad would have a few of the answers his historian's heart craved. "You took an expositor's body." *After what you said to me, after you left me.*

She said, "I did what I had to do."

Dahin snorted. "Enjoy it, Kai. It's the biggest 'I told you so' in known history."

Shiren cast a contemptuous glance at him. "It's no surprise to find you here, apostate. Stories of your corruption are legendary."

"Eat shit," Dahin told her.

Shiren's jaw went tight. "If I told the guards to beat you—"

"It would be a mistake," Kai said, flat and calm. Shiren had the Well weapon, but he could tell from the tightness in her shoulders she knew it was the only thing keeping this from turning into a bloodbath that even the Lesser Blessed wouldn't survive.

The guards avoided his gaze, looking at the deck or toward Narrein. They probably belonged to the expositors who had been sent by the Nient-arik conspirators; at least two had died in the fire intention and Kai wasn't sure if others had been sent after Tenes and Sanja. Shiren glanced at Arnsterath, as if expecting her to intervene. Arnsterath didn't react at all.

The raft slowed and came around above the last set of rock-cut steps down to the harbor plaza. The canal flowed sluggishly through the waterweed growing in the broken stone blocks where the bridge had once stood. Ramad tried again. "You should go.

Cut your losses. The Nient-arik will certainly offer you no help." This was clearly aimed at the Lesser Blessed.

At the steering column, Narrein said sourly, "You're so certain of that, are you?"

"If you aren't, you must not know the Nient-arik very well," Ramad said, with clear irony. "This is hardly their first attempt to take over the governance of the Rising World."

The raft circled down into the enclosed court. It landed with a jolt and a thunk near the edge of the canal basin. No movement anywhere, no sound but a breeze through the rushes, no evidence of Ziede, Sanja, or Tenes. The big doors into both the stable and the harbor caves were still closed.

Shiren's brow furrowed as she scanned the court. She demanded, "Where is the Witch? Did they take the stone and flee?"

"She's here," Arnsterath said, and jerked her chin toward the stable archway.

Kai twisted to look. Three sprawled bodies, crumpled just inside the shaded corner of the arch. Two mortal guards and a figure in an Enalin-style caftan. Not unexpected, though it was hard to tell at this distance if it had been Tenes or Ziede who killed them. Dahin sat up straight to see what everyone was looking at and laughed.

Arnsterath added, "She won't leave without Kaiisteron." Her voice was as even as ever, but there was something dark under the tone, an edge of some emotion Kai couldn't identify.

Shiren's mouth hardened, and Narrein turned even more saturnine. Arnsterath made a gesture, tugging at an intention. Before Kai could tense, her familiar turned and vaulted out of the raft. He walked toward the closed stable doors.

He moved fluidly, not at all like a person with no will of his own. The connection between an expositor and a familiar was something Kai had never understood, except for the little he needed to know to break it. Arnsterath must be able to give him commands that he was compelled to follow; she didn't seem distracted, as she might if she was controlling his movements. "Where did you get your friend?" Kai asked.

"A gift, from the Nient-arik. His name is Viar." Arnsterath kept her gaze on the stable arch. Viar paced toward it slowly, sometimes stopping to scuff at the stained paving, searching for designs or cantrips laid as traps. "Of course, they meant to give me to him. It didn't turn out as they planned."

"He'll get the doors open?" Shiren asked, her voice tight with tension.

"He'll try." Arnsterath eyed her. "You could help him."

Shiren and Narrein exchanged a guarded look. Narrein told her, "You stay here. If the demon moves, use the weapon. Kill the apostate, if you have to."

Dahin hissed out an annoyed breath. Narrein turned to leave the raft, motioning the guards to follow him. He added, "Make yourself useful, vanguarder."

Ramad glanced at Kai, brows lifted. Everything depended on Ziede and Tenes, but it was better to have Ramad away from Arnsterath. Kai nodded once.

Ramad stood, clearly suppressing a wince, and moved like his ribs hurt. He followed the reluctant guards off the raft, trailed by Narrein.

Viar had found no traps on the paving and had reached the heavy metal doors. They filled the large space of the archway, the metal streaked with verdigris, partly eaten away along the bottom. Narrein said something to the mortal guards, who hung back to wait as Viar examined the doors carefully and checked the locking mechanism in the center.

Kai wanted very badly to warn Ziede, even with Arnsterath listening in. But she and Tenes were obviously planning something. Arnsterath was still a demon and Tenes' blossom cantrip would only mildly inconvenience her, if Tenes could even get close enough to cast it. Arnsterath obviously knew Ziede would have a plan and was confident she could counter whatever it was. Kai was afraid that between her abilities and Shiren's Well weapon, she was right.

The door wasn't yielding. Narrein had taken something metallic out of his tabard, some Immortal Blessed tool, and stepped forward to use it on the lock.

The only thing Kai could do without getting Dahin killed was distract Arnsterath. He shifted, just enough to get her to look at him again. "Where were you? All this time."

Her gaze went abstract, as if she had to work to remember. "I left with the others, I don't know what they did. I didn't care. I was going home."

After all this time, it was still maddening. "To die uselessly in the grasslands."

"Yes." She said, "But there were legionaries, called to assemble here. I couldn't get past them, I had to follow where the road led. I took an expositor's body. Like you did. I used the Well of the Hierarchs to fight. Like you did."

Dahin's head turned, consternation in the slant of his brow, trying to meet Kai's gaze.

Kai said, "I never used the Well. Never." He managed not to say, *Then I really would have been an abomination.* She knew what she was doing to him.

Across the court, Narrein stepped back and gestured. The mortal guards and Ramad reluctantly went closer to try to haul the doors open.

Kai had to keep Arnsterath talking. "Why are you with the Nient-arik conspirators?"

"They freed me. I'd been imprisoned." She frowned a little at the memory, her smooth brow furrowed again. "I'd tried to go south, but I was found by the Nahar. I fought for them, until . . . they wanted to be rid of me."

It took Kai a baffled moment to recall the name. The Nahar had been the family who had colluded with the Hierarchs to hand Nient-arik over without resistance. With so many years of hindsight, Kai thought now that it had probably seemed the best way to survive a terrible situation. But at the time, to the other Arike and the coalition, it was the ultimate perfidy.

The Nahar had eventually gone down in a struggle with the other Nient heirs, the Reharan branch of the family. All this had been more than sixty years ago, during the war and right after. Kai didn't know if he believed Arnsterath. If he even wanted to understand. But he said, "The Nahar have been gone since the war. How long were you imprisoned?"

Arnsterath shook her head a little, as if time was too difficult to comprehend. Or as if she was distracted by whatever communication she was receiving from Viar. The door wouldn't budge and Narrein was using the Immortal Blessed tool to cut through or do something to the lock. Kai still had no sense of Ziede. Then Arnsterath said, "Until these Nient-arik let me out."

That was a shock. Kai knew his expression was revealing too much. "You don't mean . . ."

Arnsterath's smile returned. She enjoyed his consternation. "Seven Cold Winds ago, they let me out. I don't remember what they call the winter here."

So at least fifty odd years by Arike reckoning, imprisoned.

At a shout from the archway, Dahin twisted around, alarmed. A gap had grown between the doors, not quite enough for one guard to slip through. Kai looked to Ramad, who stood at the edge of the group of mortals. His expression held poorly suppressed alarm.

Narrein listened to someone speaking from inside the stable. Then he turned and called to Shiren, "Be wary. A mortal servant is coming out with a message."

Kai had no idea what Ziede and Tenes were planning, but clearly they needed more time. He said, "She's just a mortal child."

"We won't kill children," Shiren said, with a prim air of decision.

Arnsterath's mouth quirked in amusement, a painfully familiar expression. "Lesser Blessed, don't pretend you care."

"You are too used to living among mortal savages," Shiren said.

Dahin said sourly, "Yes, Immortal savages are so much better."

Shiren gritted her teeth. "Demon, you should tell the apostate—"

Kai was so sick of Immortal Blessed right now. He said deliberately, "You're the ones who made him this way, not us."

Shiren glared, but just then Sanja slipped out between the gap in the doors.

She glanced around with obvious fear. A little too obvious; Kai had seen Sanja afraid and this wasn't what it looked like. She didn't seem like she had been hurt; her tunic and pants were mussed and stained, but that was from their boat trip, and probably from moving around in the filthy deserted harbor and stables. She spoke in a tone too low to hear.

Narrein listened, then turned to the raft. "Bring the demon and the apostate here."

"What about Saadrin?" Kai said. It was a last-ditch effort to get some help or at least distraction from that quarter.

Shiren glanced back into the cabin where Saadrin was still bound and furious. She didn't looked pleased to be reminded of their other captive. "She will stay where she is." Shiren motioned sharply with the Well weapon.

Arnsterath didn't do anything so obvious as shrug, but she tilted her head, indicating Kai should go. As Kai stood, he took Dahin's hand and tugged him along. They stepped out of the raft and went toward the archway.

Once they were in earshot, Shiren said, "Stop there."

Sanja kept her eyes downcast, giving the impression she was afraid to look at anyone. Narrein said, "Go on, child, speak."

Addressing the paving stones, Sanja said, "My master the Witch says she will trade the finding stone for the lives of her companions, if you will first let her use it to locate and release Tahren Stargard." She added, "She asks Kaiisteron to please cooperate, and to remember how we left the Summer Halls together."

Kai's thoughts raced. Cooperate. Not try to stop what was happening, let Ziede—and Tenes and Sanja?—handle it. *How we left the Summer Halls together. On a wallwalker? With Bashasa? Ziede and Tahren went separately with Dahin, I came out with Salatel and the cadre . . .* That made no sense; he was missing her meaning.

Frustrated, Shiren said, "We can't possibly trust her. We must have the finding stone now."

Gaze still downcast, Sanja sniffed, on the verge of tears. "I can only tell you what she said. Tahren Stargard is her wife, she has to rescue her."

Narrein said, "We will free the Fallen once she gives us the finding stone."

That was obviously a lie. Kai didn't need to see the flicker in Shiren's expression to know that. Arnsterath watched Sanja with concentration. Her gaze flicked once to Viar, checking to make sure he was still alert for traps.

Was Ziede working on a windstorm, inside the stables? The air was still. She and Tenes might be constructing some destructive cantrip, but Arnsterath could counter it with intentions she probably had already prepared. Viar would be carrying intentions for her as well. An expositor familiar would be so much handier for that than a Witch familiar.

With what Ziede had seen on the raft before she had to seal her mind from Kai, she would know that. And Arnsterath would know she knew it. Unless Tenes had thought of something unexpected. Something that couldn't be countered.

Tenes' affinity was with ground spirits, not much use at sea or on the canals. But here, it would be different. Did Arnsterath know much about Tenes? Would Aclines have wanted himself or his familiar to be anywhere near a powerful demon? He certainly wouldn't have shared any information with her.

Sanja hadn't responded, and Narrein added, "Go and tell her, she must give us the finding stone first."

"Oh." Sanja lifted her gaze. Her eyes were wide and she did something with her shoulders and the angle of her head that took at least two years off her already slight age. Even distracted, Kai was impressed. "I . . . But . . . she's my master, she doesn't . . ."

"Go back and tell her what we've said." Narrein was impatient. "Once she gives us the finding stone, Tahren Stargard will be freed."

Sanja's mouth trembled and a tear trickled down her cheek. "I'm afraid, if I go back and tell her you said no, she'll hurt me."

Shiren's lips thinned, but she said without heat, "Child, she sent you to negotiate, just go and tell her—"

Sanja's eyes welled with tears. "She told me to stay out here. I'm afraid. Please—"

Ziede needs Sanja out here. Because of what's going to happen inside, Kai thought. Ziede had sent Sanja out here because it was less dangerous for her than what she and Tenes were doing in there.

"Child—" Narrein tried again.

"Blessed lady, please save me!" Sanja had identified Shiren as the one most likely to give in to sentiment, the easiest mark. She took a few stumbling steps forward, holding out empty hands, and then dropped to her knees. It brought her closer to Kai. "Please!"

Kai felt a faint vibration in the paving. Arnsterath lifted her head, alert suddenly. Kai took a step forward and her suspicious attention shot back to him. The Lesser Blessed tensed, watching him warily. He said, "Ziede isn't known for being reasonable. And she can't possibly trust you."

Shiren's chin went up in disdain. "Unlike mortals and apostates, we do not lie—"

Dahin snorted and stumbled sideways into Kai. "Don't lie, hah! You were part of a conspiracy to take over the Rising World! I'm sorry, that involved lying."

Ramad contributed, "And the capture of a cohort and an officer's cadre."

They had both clearly gotten the message to stall.

"That too," Dahin agreed. "And why anyone would believe you—"

The earth pulsed beneath Kai's feet. The air changed, the omnipresent odor of the canal overwhelmed by something that smelled more like Gad-dazara, like the aftermath of a thunderstorm. That was when Kai knew what Ziede meant. How we left the Summer Halls together. *Running from a flood.*

Arnsterath didn't turn toward him. Her arm shot out but Kai lunged forward. The design she flung skimmed past the edge of his senses as it missed him.

He snatched up Sanja and threw her to Ramad. Shiren fired her Well weapon but Dahin stepped into the way, shielding Kai from all but the fringe of the effect. Arnsterath's hand filled with another intention, guards turned toward them, Dahin started to collapse, Kai sensed an intention from Viar.

A roar sounded from inside the stables. The metal doors burst open and a gray-green wall of water fell out with the force of a collapsing mountain.

Kai didn't have time to think, just act. As Dahin went down from the force of the Well weapon, Kai grabbed his coat. Then the torrent hit like a flung boulder.

At the first touch of the water, Kai's Blessed breathing device kicked back on but it didn't help the weight and force of the flood. He concentrated on keeping his hand clamped on Dahin's coat and his mouth closed. He wished he had kept the stupid nose plug on.

They tumbled over something rocky and painful, then slammed against a metal railing. The blow would have been stunning for a mortal; Kai knew he had to get to Ramad and Sanja quickly. He pulled Dahin closer, wrapped an arm around his chest, and dragged himself up on the metal rails.

They broke the surface. To Kai's relief, Dahin started to spit up water and cough, struggling weakly. He grabbed onto a rail and gasped, "Didn't we do this before?"

"This time we meant to do it," Kai said. The flood had carried them all the way across the court to the closed outer gate where the bridge had once been. They had fetched up against the rusted bars of the portcullis.

The torrent poured out through the wide open watergate into the canal almost as rapidly as its unabated rush out of the stable archway. The harbor doors still held, concentrating the initial force of the water; they must be jammed on the inside with the remains of docks and broken boats.

Kai couldn't spot Ramad and Sanja in the confusion of bobbing bodies and churning water. The ascension raft spun as it floated with the swirling current. It was too buoyant to overturn, though if it kept to its current course, it would sweep out through the watergate. It should come right past them. But as it whirled around, Kai saw Arnsterath was in it, her clothes dripping as she leaned over the rail. She was trying to help her familiar Viar aboard as he clung to the edge of the raft. She must have run for it as soon as she realized the trap, and ordered Viar to come to her.

Dahin snarled, "We need that raft."

"Get ready." Kai let go of him and swung higher up on the gate, bracing his feet on the crossrail.

Dahin struggled up after him. "Don't worry about me, just go."

As the raft spun nearer, Kai jumped.

He landed on the deck. Behind him, there was a yelp as Dahin hit the side. Arnsterath yanked Viar into the raft, dropped him, and whirled toward Kai.

But Kai hadn't charged at her.

Viar slumped on the deck, battered by the flood. The gold fillet in his hair might be the token that held the powerful intention that enslaved his mind and body to Arnsterath. But he had lost his coat and the pendant cord around his throat now lay on top of his tunic instead of concealed inside it. The pendant was an old wooden pin, carved into the emblem of the Kanavesi Saredi plainswolf.

Kai dove for Viar instead of Arnsterath. He grabbed the Kanavesi pin and crushed the light wood in his fist. *If I'm wrong about this* . . . He just hoped that Ziede and Tenes would be able to find Ramad and Sanja.

Viar jerked away. He looked up, eyes wide open, aware, and furious.

An intention struck Kai's shoulder, scorched through his sleeve as a burning coal ground into his skin. He staggered back, fighting to dig its tendrils out of him, and fell backward against the bench.

But Viar lunged toward Arnsterath. He plucked intentions off his chest, the ones she had given him to carry, and flung them at her. She scrabbled backward, her hand flailed as she managed to cast an intention at Viar. He reeled, but was too enraged and too desperate to stop. He tackled her and they grappled. With every touch he transferred her own intentions to her, while she pushed others back onto him.

Kai couldn't stand. He had to get this intention out of his body before it went to his heart. Whether Viar or Arnsterath won, the survivor would go after Kai and he would end up dead or a familiar. Then Dahin dragged himself over the raft's side, hit the deck, and crawled rapidly into the cabin.

Kai doubled over as more fire shot through his veins. He focused inward and the extra burst of pain and desperation let him grip the design. He clawed it out of his bicep and it dissipated as it left his flesh.

Saadrin tore out of the cabin, prying the metal gag off her mouth.

Arnsterath and Viar slammed back toward the rail, still struggling. Saadrin's expression was beyond fury, but she hesitated, obviously aware of the cloud of intentions around the demon and the expositor. She looked at Kai. His throat was nearly closed from the heat that had raged through his body but he managed a pushing gesture.

Saadrin nodded grimly and strode forward. The two hit the rail again and grappled, Viar's back to Saadrin. She grabbed his ankles and lifted and shoved, all in one motion. He cried out and Arnsterath snarled. Both tumbled over the side into the flood.

Dahin staggered across to the steering column and wrenched at it. The raft shot upward out of the water. Kai collapsed on the bench. He just hoped Saadrin wouldn't decide to throw him off, too. He pulled himself up on the rail, frantic, then spotted Ramad and Sanja.

They perched on the earthwork to the side of the harbor entrance, both drenched but above the rushing water. Sanja must have been able to give Ramad enough warning to get them away from the main force of the torrent, and they had climbed to safety. Kai pointed, and croaked, "There!"

Dahin said, "I see them! Aunt Saadrin, for the shitting Well's sake, get down! You're a giant target!"

"Don't swear at me, child!" But Saadrin ducked. Dahin wheeled the raft and it jolted sideways. Kai sensed a half-formed design narrowly miss them. He touched Ziede's pearl: *Ziede, come out, we have the raft. Arnsterath is in the water with her familiar.*

Coming, she sent back. It was so good to hear her voice. Kai wanted to laugh but his throat hurt too much.

The earthwork loomed up. Dahin nearly slammed the raft into the slope, brush scratching against the Blessed metal. Kai tried to get up to help, but Sanja tumbled over the rail and Ramad swung in beside her. As Dahin took the raft up and toward the canal, Kai croaked, "Stay down."

Sanja sunk to the floor, shivering but grinning. Ramad ducked but made it across the raft to where Kai huddled on the bench. "Are you all right?" he asked. "Where is—"

Ziede dropped down into the raft, an unconscious Tenes in her arms. Kai slid to the floor so Ziede could deposit Tenes in his lap. Both were soaking wet and Tenes had mud ground into her arms up to her elbows.

The raft shot away toward the east. Kai knew they were passing over the concentric moats, following the old route over the destroyed bridge and past the deserted city. This time Kai, gently patting Tenes' face to revive her, didn't bother to look back at the Summer Halls.

Dahin laughed, loud and free and without any bitterness at all. "Where to now?"

Saadrin stood up from her crouch near the steering column. There were bloodstains on the light yellow of her tabard, and a fading bruise still discolored the right side of her face. She must have fought the Immortal Blessed Faharin, and probably Narrein and Shiren, too. She said, "Is anyone going to tell me what in the name of Holy Thosaren that was all about? Some mortal conspiracy?"

Ziede didn't bother to answer. She took the finding stone out of her tunic and said, "We're going to find Tahren now."

Sanja sat up on her knees and leaned against the bench beside Ziede. "Can you make it work? Does it need special magic?"

"Anyone can make it work," Kai told her, not looking up from Tenes. "That's what made it so dangerous to the Immortal Blessed."

"They used these stones to keep us under control," Saadrin said. It was so unexpected, even Dahin turned to look at her. "The Hierarchs. I lied to you, there are none kept at the Conventiculum. We thought they were all destroyed. I had no idea one still existed. It would have given Faharin and the Patriarch he served a great deal of power to have that."

"I know you lied," Ziede said. She studied the stone with a frown. Kai sensed another alien itch on the edge of his awareness, a different sort of irritation than the ascension raft. "You can have it when I'm done. Dahin, keep to the east."

"Yes, no one wants to find you now, we just wish you'd all go away," Dahin told Saadrin.

Saadrin didn't answer, watching him with a mix of worry and confusion. Kai would have to try to talk to Dahin, but first he had to take care of Tenes. He thought of Bashasa and felt a deep pulse of loss again; Bashasa had always seemed able to do a hundred things at once; calm the frightened, negotiate with the angry, make plans, strategize. They were all sitting here in sopping wet clothes with no food or water and Kai didn't even know if there was anything useful on this ridiculous raft.

And he couldn't help but feel there had been a solution within reach. If the Lesser Blessed had agreed to let Ziede take the stone to find Tahren. If sixty years ago he had thought to search for Arnsterath or any of the other lost demons.

Ramad tried to wipe his face with his wet sleeve. "Did you actually breach the inner wall of the Summer Halls? Tunnel through the earthwork? How was it done?"

Sanja was pleased to explain. "When you left, we started exploring. Mostly in that big stable next to where the boats used to be. It kept going back into the side of the hill, all these rooms, but they were empty except for trash. We got to a place in the very far back with a stone wall, but it was wet. Tenes said she didn't think this place would last too many more years, that something had gone wrong on the other side and the water was going to push through eventually. I mean, I didn't understand some of the words she was using, so she had to kind of act it out, but that was basically it.

"Then we heard those people—they must have been searching the docks while we were way in the back—and Tenes made them vomit flowers. We were going to go up and try to warn you but then Ziede came, and Tenes said she could get the dirt spirits to make the holes behind the leaky wall bigger."

Tenes blinked, gasped, and gripped Kai's arm. He said, "It worked, you're with us."

Her brow furrowed, but the frantic confusion in her gaze subsided to relief and her grip on his arm relaxed.

"Still east, Ziede?" Dahin asked.

"Yes." She sounded odd, and Kai looked up to see her frowning at the stone.

Dahin laughed. "It would be ironic if we were heading toward Benais-arik! To be going to the same place that Bashasa took us when we escaped from here the first time."

"Yes," Ziede said grimly, meeting Kai's gaze. "That would be ironic."

THE PAST:
THE JOURNEY

The Prince-heirs of the Arike city-states were always drawn from powerful families, inheritors of a martial tradition that had been fading . . . Scions of these families could be risen to the status of ruling Prince-heir through a combination of approval by a council of artisans and tradesman, support among the other contending families, and acclaim by the city's population. Candidates had to be well-known, active in good works and the business of their city, and successful Prince-heirs would serve for a term of some years. This system was much open to manipulation, and competition among the eligible families could be intense, but violence was rare and not well-regarded . . .

. . . after wholesale slaughter in the Arkai, the Hierarchs decided that the Arik's command of trade routes and their artisans and farmers were more useful alive than dead. At least for a time.

—Journal of Hiranan Desal, late Prince-heir of Seidel-arik

Kai woke, cramped and sweaty. The sudden cessation of motion had jolted him out of sleep like a kick to his ribs. It was night, lit only by starlight and a half moon, and he was curled up on the wooden floor, still crammed in against the bow. Sleepy voices, complaints, groans of pain sounded from the rest of the palanquin. He registered that it was Bashasa who was moving around. "What happened?"

"We've crossed the river," Bashasa said, silhouetted against the night sky as he reached for the cables. "We mean to make camp, but we have to destroy the bridge so the legionaries who will inevitably pursue us will have to cross further downriver."

"Do we have time? How far behind us are they?" Kai levered himself up. His clothes had dried everywhere except where the fabric had been pressed between his body and the floor of the palanquin, and his side was unpleasantly damp. He kept blinking, waiting for his dark vision to adjust. Then realized it might not.

He was in the wrong body and he had killed one Hierarch and helped kill a second and it hadn't fixed anything. Kentdessa was still dead and he would never be Saredi again. He wanted to curl up like a wounded animal but that wouldn't fix anything either. But even with all that, he felt better than he had before getting on the wallwalker.

"Ziede has been scouting, and has seen no pursuit as yet." Bashasa started to step over Kai. "Which means we were right and the legionaries in Stios went first to the Summer Halls, having no better orders."

A lot of people had been sleeping on the floor and were now waking in confusion, and there was no room to move. Kai grabbed Bashasa's leg, guessing that if he didn't then Bashasa would be out of the palanquin and he would have to chase him to get answers. "How are you going to destroy the bridge?"

Bashasa wriggled to get free. "I have no idea! I doubt anyone among us has firepowder. I'll have to consult with the others."

Kai held on, letting Bashasa drag him into a sitting position as he tried to get to the palanquin's door. "Is the bridge made out of wood?"

Bashasa stopped, then leaned down to peer at him. Salatel bumped into his back. She was maneuvering around, trying to kick the other soldiers awake without hitting anybody else. Bashasa said, "Parts of it. What are you thinking, Fourth Prince?"

"That it needs those parts to keep from falling down," Kai said.

Kai was far more motivated to get down from the wallwalker than to climb it, and once he managed to unfold his cramped legs he swung easily down the netted side. Bashasa took the little stairs. Salatel followed as other soldiers spilled out from the lower compartments, and they all reached the ground at the same time.

The wallwalkers had stopped in a field with sparse grass and gravelly soil, stands of tall trees that were just dark shapes outlined against the night sky. Night birds twittered and swooped overhead, disturbed by the arrival of three wallwalkers and a lot of exhausted mortals. The smell of water and river mud was heavy in the cool air. Kai's night vision was a little better out here, but then the roof of the palanquin wasn't blocking the moonlight. This might be as good as it would get. The ability to see in the dark could be a part of his demonic nature that had been left behind with Enna.

Bashasa spun around, getting his bearings in the dark. "This way!" Salatel and the soldiers hurried after him as he strode off toward the line of trees.

Kai followed. As they came around behind the wallwalker, he tripped on a broad square stone. This was the road, then. He grimaced, flexing his abraded foot. This was going to take getting used to.

The group followed the road back toward the river and the rush of water. More figures waited at the gap between the trees and he recognized Tahren's tall figure, the moonlight glinting off her hair. The river was a broad expanse of darkness flecked with silver. A number of voices were arguing in Arike, almost drowning out a chorus of frogs in the rushes. Ziede's voice, pitched to carry, demanded in Imperial, "Do we know what we're doing?"

In the sudden silence, Bashasa said, "The Fourth Prince has a thought."

Ahead, where the road met the edge of the bank, the bridge slanted up, a wide shadow across the gleaming band of water. It stood high on stone pilings, but there was no arch or railings, just a flat surface of wood. Kai had seen a number of bridges in the fighting in Erathi and the borderlands, and he admitted he had been thinking of something either more decorative or more makeshift. Certainly nothing this solid and clearly meant to be permanent. Even then, the older demons had been the ones tasked with destroying bridges.

Kai walked to the edge of the ramp and leaned down to feel wooden boards and metal bolts. Bashasa had said there was no firepowder. He raised his voice to ask, "Does anyone know about this bridge? Or bridges like this? The most vulnerable point?"

"The combines?" an Arike voice suggested.

Kai didn't know what a combine was. He said, "Come and show me."

This was not going to be as simple as Kai hoped. Someone had to run and get lamps for them to see by as the knowledgeable Arike soldier, Nirana, kept trying to describe the way the combine supported the bridge. But none of the Arike had the vocabulary in Imperial to let Kai understand. They quickly established that no one nearby had paper or anything to draw with, and that making a human diagram with the other soldiers was useless, no matter how many times Nirana held out her arms and tried to get Hartel to stick her head between them while saying, "Like this." Kai gave up and told them, "I'm just going to climb under there and look."

By this point Bashasa had sent a cadre of scouts across the bridge to keep an eye on the road, and then he, Tahren, Ziede, and the others had all gone off to hopefully do something else to keep the legionaries from finding them. Kai was left with Salatel and her cadre and Dahin, who had given up trying to make suggestions and was now sitting on the edge of the bridge dangling his legs. "Tell me if I can do anything," he said around a yawn.

Kai took off his coat and skirt to make the climb easier. Even though he was still fully dressed in his tunic and leggings, this apparently scandalized the soldiers, who all quickly looked away or turned their backs. Ignoring all the offended murmuring, he climbed over the edge of the bridge down to the maze of stone pilings and wooden supports underneath. Hartel leaned over to hand him a clay ball lamp with a wire hanger, and he set it carefully on the end of a beam.

Crouching on a cross brace, he saw what Nirana had been trying to describe. The supports fit together so that if the end of one collapsed, the beam would shift and might fall. She had kept saying it was like a chair, but the Saredi didn't use this kind of construction. Or chairs.

Kai stretched to put his hand on the end of the beam and felt for a trickle of life. It had worked on a leaf; it should work on a piece of wood. They both came from trees, which were obviously alive.

But the only life left was impossibly faint and distant, like a dim memory too faded to recall except by its absence.

Kai groaned under his breath. He had been hoping for one dramatic masterstroke that would take down the whole bridge and maybe make him feel better about his continued existence.

Ziede had said he was an expositor as well as a demon now.

He concentrated on the fire intention Talamines knew, drawing on the pain still in this body, the bottomless well the Cageling Demon Court had left in his own mind. The flame sparked on his palm, just like it had in the Temple Halls. He tried to press it against the beam. The flame winked out, leaving the wood unmarked.

Kai bit his lip. *This is going to be tricky.*

He passed the lamp to Hartel, then climbed back up, saying, "The word isn't *combine*, it's *join*." But running footsteps came from the other end of the bridge and voices called out in Arike. Kai swung up onto the bridge to see the soldiers confronting a person. Young, short, with tangled dark hair and amber skin, dressed in rough practical cotton, a long wrap tunic over leggings. They might be another refugee from the Summer Halls, but Kai was certain the wallwalkers had been moving too fast for anyone on foot to keep up.

Her voice low, Hartel said, "Fourth Prince, the scouts didn't see him coming." She sounded troubled. "He says he's a refugee."

Dahin was on his feet, asking the person, "Wouldn't you rather go along the river? It's not safe to follow us, the legionaries will be looking for us."

"My elder said we cross tonight," the person said in halting Imperial. They were sweating and dusty, their broad brow creased in worry. "We have to. There's been a message in the water."

Dahin and Salatel looked confused. "A message?" Dahin repeated.

Kai said, "What's this?"

The person turned toward him. Kai had lost his veil somewhere on the floor of the palanquin, and braced himself for the reaction he was beginning to get accustomed to, the startled fear or repulsion. But the person gasped a little in something like relief and said, "Please, the wagon is broken. The others are coming on foot. Just give them time to cross."

Salatel glanced at Kai, and he realized she was asking his permission. Was he actually in charge of the bridge now? Whose brilliant idea was that? Probably Bashasa's. Kai told her, "It's going to take me some time to destroy the bridge."

Salatel considered. "You ran here?" she asked the person. "Your people can't be far behind you."

"No, I . . ." They hesitated, uncertain. Then glanced at Kai. Their hands moved in Witchspeak: *I swift-traveled.*

Kai hadn't seen a Witch other than Ziede since the clan tents had burned. *You're all Witches?* he signed back.

More Arike were coming up the bridge from the camp, but Kai's attention was on the person's hands. *Not all, a few. We were trapped in this region when our ship was destroyed and have been hiding in the empty lands. Our elder read the stream water and said the*

Summer Halls were dead. They told us to follow this road east to meet the future. Please wait?

We'll wait, Kai signed. *Can you tell me how long it will take your people to get here?*

Their hands moved in a Witchspeak sign that Kai had to convert into Imperial reckoning. More Arike had just arrived, soldiers and a few others. Salatel stepped aside for Bashasa's cousin Dasara. "What is this?" Dasara asked.

Kai told him, "We need to wait for the rest of their people to catch up and cross. A few hours."

Dasara made a sharp gesture. "No. Destroy the bridge now."

Kai hissed out a breath, and did not grab Dasara by the face and drain his life. This stupid young mortal was related to Bashasa by blood, he couldn't just kill him. Bashasa was using Kai for his own ends, but he had been kind about it so far. And it would start a fight between Kai and all the Arike, which he would lose, and it wouldn't help Ziede or Tahren or Dahin or any of the other desperate people fleeing for their lives.

And the last thing Kai could afford to do right now was show any weakness, including admitting that he wasn't sure he could destroy the bridge at all.

Salatel's expression had gone blank, and her cadre were uneasy or wary, dreading and anticipating the next few moments. Dahin took a step backward, then another, then turned and pelted down the bridge back toward the soldiers on guard there. Probably he was going for Tahren, to help stop Kai if he started killing Arike.

Kai hadn't responded immediately and Dasara was mulish and impatient. He said, "You heard me!"

Kai had heard him all right. He said, "Why?"

Dasara had obviously been prepared for a response, but that wasn't it. He opened his mouth, then managed, "Why what?"

"Why not wait? You don't think Witches can help us fight?" Kai planted his hands on his hips, trying to look in control of the situation and not like he was stalling while frantically trying to think of a way out that didn't involve a pointless battle.

Dasara made a sharp gesture, his expression thunderous. "There's no time."

This was firmer ground. "Bashasa said there is time. Ziede's been scouting from the air, the legionaries aren't coming yet."

Someone in the back said something in Arike. Kai made out Dasara's name and the Imperial word for demon.

Dasara ignored them, stepping closer. "Who do you think you are?"

It would have been more daunting, if Kai wasn't sure now that Dasara had no more idea what he was doing than Kai did. He was just a princeling who had seen a moment of potential weakness and wanted to exploit it. Kai made himself smile. "The only one who can destroy the bridge."

Dasara's jaw went tight and he leaned forward. Kai had no idea what would happen next and he was fairly sure Dasara didn't either.

"Dasara!" Bashasa jogged up the bridge, followed by a scatter of his soldiers and Dahin. The other Arike hastily cleared a path for him. "Dasara, this is not complicated. I'm sending Arava back with a wallwalker to bring these Witches more quickly. The Fourth Prince will wait until they cross before he destroys the bridge."

Dasara rounded on him. "You're going to get us all caught." He sounded flustered, but even more determined, which made Kai wonder if he really was that stupid. Anyone with any sense would have been glad of the chance to back out of this standoff.

Bashasa stopped a few steps away. "I am not arguing with you, Dasara. I need your cadre to help guard the perimeter, go and see to it." His voice was firm, as calm and affable as ever. He turned to clap Dahin on the shoulder. "Your sister would like you to stop looking for trouble. Perhaps you can help Okosh put up a tent."

Dahin was startled. "Oh, but I've never done that before."

"Time to learn." Bashasa gave him a gentle push to get him started back down the bridge. Dahin went, but he was walking backward, still watching the confrontation.

Dasara hadn't moved and Kai thought he could see an edge of calculation in his expression. Sounding more sure of himself, Dasara said, "I don't agree, cousin. I think you're being reckless and you could get us killed."

With a sinking feeling, Kai thought, *Oh, now this is about forcing a confrontation with Bashasa.* He hesitated, caught between distracting attention back to himself and not knowing if that would just be playing into Dasara's hands.

Then Bashasa turned back and met Dasara's gaze. Kai watched the personable, slightly dizzy Bashasa, the man who changed tactics to get around every roadblock as swiftly as a startled lizard, disappear as his expression went flat. Bashasa said, "Is that what you think, Dasara?" His voice was gentle and even, as if this was a serious question that he really wanted the answer to. "And what should you do about it?"

Something passed through the soldiers, the others watching, even those who had come with Dasara; their tension leaked away and they were quiet and waiting. Whatever happened next wouldn't be up to them.

Dasara lifted his chin, but what came out was, "I have to report to Mother."

It would have been funny, but everyone here had too much sense of self-preservation to laugh. Bashasa's gaze brightened and he said, "Of course!" He clapped Dasara on the shoulder and somehow turned him around and got him pointed in the right direction. "Keep her apprised! I'll be back in a moment."

Dasara strode away down the bridge, his followers splitting off to hurry in his wake.

Bashasa clapped his hands and turned to Kai. He looked slightly over Kai's head, avoiding his gaze. "Fourth Prince! Is all well here?"

Kai wasn't going to ruin this by voicing his doubts. "It's fine. Uh, I know how to destroy the bridge, but it's going to take some time."

Bashasa nodded sharply, still not making eye contact. He was flushed a little and Kai got the sudden impression that he was embarrassed by the altercation with Dasara. Embarrassed to have to show just how much raw steel lay under his affable exterior. "Can the Witch speak Imperial? Someone must guide Arava to the stragglers so she can carry them here."

The Witch had taken cover behind Kai. He nudged them back out toward Bashasa. "Yes, they can."

"Good, good." Bashasa motioned to the Witch. "Come on, come with me. We will get a wallwalker to go back for your people."

The Witch looked at Kai, who signed, *You can trust him.* He was surprised how readily the words came. He did trust Bashasa. It was unexpected, and a little frightening.

The Witch gestured, *Thank you,* and added a sign Kai didn't recognize. They followed Bashasa, who was already jogging back down the bridge.

Kai, Salatel, and the cadre were left standing in the circle of lamplight, the flow of water below the only sound.

Salatel said, "Please put your clothes back on, Fourth Prince. At least—" She gestured and Hartel held out his skirt.

Kai sighed, and wrestled it back on. At least it seemed to make the soldiers happy. He told Salatel, "It's good we have to wait. I need to make an intention, and . . . that's going to take a while." The water intention had been all other expositors' work, and the flame intention was apparently the first thing they taught baby expositors. Kai was going to have to search Talamines' memories, and that wasn't going to be easy. He sat down on the side of the bridge, one of the pillar supports at his back. "Just leave someone here in case I need help and everyone else can get some sleep," Kai told Salatel and the rest of the cadre.

He expected her to take the order without argument; she had

been doing everything else he had told her to do so far. Salatel said, "No, Fourth Prince. We are your cadre, we guard you."

That just seemed a waste of their time. "If Bashasa's wrong and the legionaries arrive, there's not enough of you."

Salatel lifted her brows. From the other soldiers' expressions, he had just said something naive. Salatel said, "It isn't the legionaries we are guarding you from."

Ah, Kai thought. After the confrontation with Dasara, he should have thought of that. He didn't want to have to kill any Arike, it would upset Bashasa's plans. He said, "Right. Do what you think best."

Salatel was placing her soldiers in guard positions when the wallwalker went past. In the lamplight, most of it was invisible, just clawed feet and giant furred legs striding back the way they had come. Kai tucked himself up beside the pillar, though there was plenty of clearance on the wide bridge. He had until the wallwalker came back to do this. He took a deep breath, and sank down into darkness.

Kai didn't want to grasp at the first possible solution only to realize later there was a much better way. But sorting through fading, elusive memories that weren't yours was confusing and exhausting. He came out of his trance twice, just to breathe and remember that he was a living being, that this was still him, even if this wasn't the body he had been born with or the body he had been gifted. The first time Salatel and Cerala were watching him worriedly, and he asked, "What?"

Salatel pressed her lips together. Cerala said, "Your face looks like it hurts."

That . . . wasn't a surprise. The training the conscripted expositors had received had not been kind, even seeing it in these fitful, deteriorating images.

The second time, the soldiers stood further back, and someone had set a wooden water flask near his hand. He drank some water, rubbed a handful on his face, and went back in.

He wanted something like the water intention, already devised and ready to go, except maybe including a way to stop it when it had fulfilled its purpose so it didn't try to burn both banks of the river and the fields and the entire world. But the fragments of memory he could dredge up told him how intentions were constructed, how to devise a new one. He pushed harder; what he needed was the little flame intention, but with heat, with combustion, and larger, but still confined to a specific object.

The bridge vibrated under him and he opened his eyes with a jolt. A wallwalker appeared out of the darkness on the far side. As Kai shoved to his feet, Salatel stepped to his side. "It's Arava returning, Fourth Prince. The scouts on the other side signaled."

"Good." Kai felt sweat soak the back of his tunic, an ache in one knee. The night had advanced, they were running out of time. "Call the scouts back, anybody else who went over there."

The beast strode by, its long legs making nothing of the distance. Kai caught glimpses of faces looking down from the palanquin, catching the lamps the Arike had set along the bridge. A small hand waved, and Kai waved back.

It had occurred to him that he could ask the Witches for help. But he knew their abilities tended to be tied to specific spirits, like Ziede's control over air. But if he had to ask someone else to do this, then Dasara and the other Arike would know Bashasa's demon was powerless. Kai wasn't worried that they would kill him; if he didn't want to die, he would walk away into the dark now and the Arike would never catch him.

He wanted to do this. To personally teach the Hierarchs another lesson in destruction.

After the wallwalker passed, Salatel walked into the center of the bridge and lifted a lamp, moving it in a quick pattern.

More lamps sparked in the darkness on the far side of the river:

scouts passing the signal back. Not long after, Arike soldiers trotted toward them across the bridge.

Kai paced, wiping his hands on his skirt, until the last scouts ran past and Salatel said, "That's all, Fourth Prince."

Kai took a deep breath and stepped to the center of the bridge. "All of you get back."

Salatel frowned but waved the rest of the cadre to obey. Kai waited until they retreated. He crouched down and put his hands on a broad plank. It felt as solid as rock. He pulled the pain out of Talamines' body, his death at Kai's hands, his weak memories of his conscription and training, but it wasn't enough. He hissed out a breath. There was no avoiding this. He held out a hand. "I need a knife."

A quiet step on the bridge and Salatel was there. She put the hilt of a knife in his hand. It was a short, practical blade meant for a tool, not a weapon. She probably thought he needed to cut something with it. Well, he did. Kai pulled the closure of his tunic down, and before he could think about it too much, drove the blade into his chest.

The next part was almost harder. He took a grating breath and yanked it out. He heard Salatel gasp as he arched forward, curling over the pain. He slammed his free hand down on the plank and put all the pain into the fire intention.

For a heartbeat nothing happened. The wound was closing, a little spray of blood dripping from the knife. Then just under Kai's hand, the dark wood glowed cherry red.

That's not enough, he thought. But then the red glow turned black and crumbled at the edges and started to spread.

It touched the hem of Kai's skirt and the fabric started to smolder. Sense caught up to him and he shoved to his feet, stumbling backward. Salatel caught his arm to steady him. The glow spread further. Flames suddenly leapt up from below, from the heavy supports. Kai said, "Run. Run!" and he and Salatel pelted toward the end of the bridge.

He didn't slow until they were all the way down the ramp, until it was the stone of the road under their feet instead of wood. The rest of the cadre, the scouts, and a scatter of other soldiers waited there, holding lamps, wide-eyed and shocked. Obviously thinking of the flooded Summer Halls, Salatel asked worriedly, "Will it stop?"

"Uh, probably." Kai looked back at the leaping flames, the red flowing like water over the wood. He had limited the design to just the center part of the bridge. Or at least he thought he had. And he wished he had taken the time to search Talamines' mind for water intentions. Just a little water intention. He wondered if the Cageling Demon Court's intention would overflow the earthwork and flood the whole world. Or what would have happened if he had dropped it in a river instead of a pool in an enclosed space. Probably it didn't work like that, or the Hierarchs would have used it to flood whole valleys somewhere. But maybe they had done it somewhere, what did Kai know.

A tremendous crack made him flinch. Something gave way in the bridge's undercarriage and the middle part slumped sideways as beams detached from a stone piling. A soldier muttered something gleeful in Arike. Kai glanced at Salatel. She watched him with a tense, worried expression. He guessed his demeanor was not engendering confidence. She said, "Should we warn the camp?"

That wasn't a bad idea. The fire still spread from plank to plank with that inexorable liquid intensity. "It might . . ." Kai began.

With another loud crack more beams gave way, and the fiery center section toppled sideways and crashed into the water.

Kai darted forward into the shallows, brushing past the reeds to see. With sparks and steam, the planks and cracked beams sank into the water. The fire on the two still-standing sections winked out abruptly. With a certainty that came from Talamines, he knew that once disconnected from the placement of the initial design, the fire had lost its fury and power. But it had worked: large pieces of the middle part of the bridge floated down the river, and the gap between the two surviving sections was too wide for a fast-moving legionary force to repair on their own. They would need engineers, scaffolds, material. It would slow them down.

Kai reached up to rub his face and winced; his chest and right arm hurt, were going to hurt all night, probably. He still felt the ache in his back from the spear wound yesterday.

He turned and sloshed his way back up the bank to where the cadre was expressing relief by talking loudly in Arike and slapping each other on the back. They quieted when Salatel asked, "Fourth Prince, why did you stab yourself?"

Kai might as well tell them. "I'm not an expositor. I don't want to be one. Using the Hierarchs' Well would make me . . . like them. I use pain instead. My pain." They were all staring at him and he didn't want to see what was in Salatel's gaze, horror or worse, sympathy; it was too much. "Let's go tell Bashasa it's done."

Salatel turned to take the lead and they walked down the road. The scouts dispersed, taking up positions along the river to keep watch.

Some lamps had gone down with the bridge, but Nirana and Telare had grabbed a couple, enough to light the way to the camp and the wallwalkers. The scent of woodsmoke mingled with something that might be seared onion made Kai's stomach cramp. He had the bad feeling this body was going to need feeding more often than Enna's had.

He hoped someone was watching Bashasa's back.

The chorus of insects had started up again. Different insects than the grassplains or the hilly borderlands, a familiar-not-familiar song. They left the stone-paved road for the field, the tall grass catching in Kai's skirts. A little distance away the wallwalkers loomed in the dark, sleeping while standing up, breathing like wind-filled caverns. Three large tents had been erected, the same sort of tall domed structures that were used in the temporary earthwork forts the legionaries built. Dim lamplight shone through the dark canvas. From the smell of smoke and cooking, fires had been built but kept low and concealed to prevent the light from being seen at a distance. Salatel explained, "These wallwalkers were loaded for a Hierarch High Noble to take somewhere. So there were tents, and bedding and food."

Kai could hardly tell one mortal from another in this light, but none of the shapes wandering around in the dark was absurdly tall. "Do you know where Ziede and Tahren—the Immortal Marshall—and her brother are?"

Salatel called softly to someone in Arike, then reported, "Either scouting, or in the perimeter guard. The young Lesser Blessed was told to stay with our dependents, I think." They headed for the tent at the end, where a lamp shone on two unfamiliar Arike soldiers standing on either side of the flap door. Their sashes were in elaborate folds, their tunics had more embroidery and trim than Bashasa's soldiers. Behind Kai, Arsha muttered something critical and Cerala shushed her.

Salatel stopped when she reached them and said, "The Fourth Prince needs to report to Prince-heir Bashasa." One guard replied in Arike. The tone was aggressive in a way that made Kai want to bare his teeth. Her voice flat, Salatel said, "Speak Imperial or stand aside now."

The second guard said, "They don't want to be disturbed." There was a hint of satisfaction in her voice that said this wasn't a misunderstanding of orders.

Kai saw the tendons in the back of Salatel's neck stand out with tension. She said, "Prince-heir Bashasa wanted the Fourth Prince to report when he was finished."

Neither guard moved. The first curled her lip and added, "We don't take orders from whatever that is."

They were pushing again, like Dasara. Kai might have no standing among the Arike but Salatel did and this was an insult to all of Bashasa's people. He stepped up beside Salatel and in

Arike said, "Move." It was an easy word to pick up; people had been shouting it at each other constantly over the past day.

One guard's eyes widened and the other twitched her hand toward her belt weapon. Kai took a step forward well into their reach, making it clear he wasn't afraid of them. He could get into the tent whether they liked it or not, but the trick was to make them let him. In Imperial he added, "Stabbing me won't stop me, but it will make me angry."

Salatel stepped forward to stand at his side again. Now her voice was relaxed and easy, but laced with contempt. "Don't be stupid. Prince-heir Bashasa wants our report. What do you think will happen if you deny the Fourth Prince and he has to fight you? Who will take the brunt of that?"

The first guard, the one who had started it, broke and stepped aside. She looked away, staring off into the dark. The other hesitated, flustered, then grimaced and said, "Go ahead."

Salatel moved first, shouldering her out of the way, and lifted the tent flap for Kai.

He stepped inside to a large lamplit space, sectioned off from the rest of the tent with dark-colored curtains and gauzy drapes. It gave him an unexpected chill; the richness and colors of the fabric were like the room where he had found Raihankana and the Hierarch. But voices speaking Arike sounded from behind a curtain, an agitated argument. Kai pitched his voice to carry and said, "Bashasa, are you in here?"

The argument cut off abruptly and Bashasa lurched out of a curtained doorway. "Fourth Prince! I heard you were successful!"

He didn't look well. His skin had gone sallow, and his gaze was bleary. He stumbled and Kai stepped forward and caught him, one of Bashasa's arms going across his shoulders. A soldier who had been with Bashasa on the wallwalker burst out of the curtained doorway behind him, then stood there helpless as Bashasa leaned his weight on Kai.

Worried, Kai asked, "Are you all right?" Bashasa must have been awake through the whole long ride here, while Kai and many of the others had managed to sleep.

"I'm fine," Bashasa assured him, mumbling into Kai's hair.

"You don't seem fine," Kai argued, as the curtain was shoved aside and Prince-heir Lahshar stepped out, her face set with distaste. In the room behind her a carpet and seating cushions had been put down, and there were metal plates and cups and the remains of a meal on a round tray. Sitting around it was Dasara and a few other Arike nobles that Kai hadn't met. None of them looked happy.

Lahshar demanded, "What is he doing here?"

She was obviously talking about Kai but not to him, implying he wasn't important enough to speak to her. But that was her problem, not Kai's. He said, "Bashasa wanted to know when the bridge was down."

She grimaced. "Get out."

Bashasa's head jerked up, his voice suddenly hard. "Do not give orders to my allies, Lahshar. You have the diplomatic gift of an angry goat."

She didn't like that. She bared her teeth in a way that reminded Kai of the Overlord of the Fourth House. "Do not insult me in front of servants, cousin."

Bashasa countered, "Oh, don't make me fight you with words, cousin. It will get out of hand, as once started I lose the will to stop. You should retire." He made an airy gesture with his free hand that almost caught his soldier in the face. "I should retire."

That was the most rational thing Bashasa had said yet. Kai asked the soldier, "Where is he supposed to sleep?"

She pointed toward another section of draped brocade and Kai hauled Bashasa in that direction. Salatel hastily stepped forward to lift the curtain for them.

Inside was a room with a hanging lamp and a padded bedroll,

so thick it was almost knee-high. Kai suspected the space was intended to be much more lavish if it was meant for a Hierarch's servant and his attendants, but the Arike obviously had only unpacked the bare minimum of the tent's accoutrements. There was also a finely carved wooden case with some maps piled atop it and a leather pack, and the same long wrapped bundle that Kai had seen Tahren carrying before they left. Bashasa's sister's body.

He steered Bashasa toward the bedroll, but Bashasa stumbled and Kai half collapsed trying to help him sit down. Releasing Kai, Bashasa flopped over backward. "Ah, thank you, Fourth Prince." He sounded exhausted.

"You can call me Kai, remember." He supposed he should get up, but his skirt was caught under Bashasa's leg. And the bedroll was just as comfortable as it looked, sinking down under his weight.

Obviously disturbed, Salatel yanked the curtain back into place, and in a low voice asked Bashasa's soldier, "Trenal, where is the rest of his personal cadre?"

Trenal nodded toward the map case. "Prince-heir Bashasa came in here to study his maps and plan our route, and Prince-heir Lahshar sent the cadre away." Trenal appeared to be trying to communicate something else to Salatel via facial expressions. "I was busy bringing in the Prince-heir's things for the night and she neglected to order me to go with them." She threw a worried look at Bashasa. "He said it was all right."

"And so it was all right," Bashasa contributed, flopping one arm around.

Salatel's jaw tightened. Kai had little to no idea how the Arike did things but even he got that ordering Bashasa's cadre away from him was against the rules. As well as being a terrible idea under these circumstances. He said, "Is he safe here?"

"You are all worrying needlessly." Bashasa sat up on an elbow.

His still somewhat bleary gaze fell on Kai. "Sister Witch has been scouting, up in the air. Did you know she could fly? I knew she could float, I didn't know she could fly. It involves communion with some sort of air or wind creatures."

"That's how Witches work," Kai told him. He couldn't tell if Bashasa had actually been drugged, or if he had had some of that horrible rancid fruit liquor while nearly too tired to stand up and it had affected him badly. "Why don't you go to sleep?"

"No, I have to wait for her to return with her intelligence," Bashasa protested, sounding more alert. "I have to know if the route to the southeast is clear. The Immortal Blessed did not go with her." He sat up a little more. "Do Immortal Blessed fly like birds? I know they can travel swiftly."

"I don't think they fly, not on their own," Kai said. Part of his attention was on Salatel and Trenal, who both looked less tense. Kai suspected that like with the bridge, he had somehow been put in charge. Since he had absolutely no authority over Lahshar or Dasara and no idea whether even Salatel's cadre would support him if it came down to a fight between Arike nobles, this was not ideal. Though it was still better than being in the Cageling Demon Court. "It's something to do with the Well where they get their power."

"Ahh, I see." Bashasa frowned at Kai, and reached out to touch the collar of his tunic. "This blood wasn't here before."

"It was from the intention that destroyed the bridge." Their faces were close, and Kai could smell the mortal blood and wall-walker musk ground into their clothes. He tried to remember the last time someone had been this close to him. Since he had gotten Adeni killed, maybe. He didn't think his Saredi family had drawn away from him. But maybe he had drawn away from them. "You should sleep until Ziede comes back."

Bashasa seemed to realize they were very close, too. He drew back. "No, I need to hear what she—"

"If she finds anything that might change your plans, I'll wake you. Or she'll wake you." Kai added, "You honestly think Ziede won't drag you out of bed if she needs to tell you something?"

Bashasa smiled. "That . . . is a good point." He flopped back on the bed. "I think you are right, Fourth Prince. Kai."

Kai didn't move, and Salatel and Trenal kept still. After only a few moments, Bashasa's breathing deepened into sleep.

Softly, Salatel asked Trenal, "Where are his servers?"

Trenal winced in anticipation of Salatel's reaction. "Prince-heir Lahshar sent them to the tent with the other dependents, to rest."

While Salatel seethed, Kai asked, "Did he eat or drink anything?"

"Yes, a little, that I saw," Trenal said. Proving she knew exactly what he was asking, she added, "But it was not poisoned, it came from the supplies stored on the beast. I brought it myself, and the others ate, too."

Voices sounded from the front of the tent, Lahshar and someone else. Salatel tensed again, her mouth set in a grim line. Trenal shifted uneasily.

The curtain swung open and Salatel stepped aside for Hiranan. The elder Prince-heir leaned on her crutch, surveying the scene. She looked tired, the lines around her mouth and eyes more deeply drawn. Lahshar stood behind her, glaring at Kai with thin-lipped outrage.

Standing would mean wrestling Bashasa off his skirt and then possibly sliding off the too-soft bedroll to the floor, so Kai didn't. Hiranan's expression seemed dubiously amused. Bashasa's breathing had roughened into a soft snore. Kai said, unnecessarily, "He's asleep." One of Bashasa's hands twitched but he didn't wake.

"So it seems," Hiranan said, dry-voiced. She asked Salatel, "Did Bashasa send for him?"

Salatel's posture stiffened and she flicked a hard look at Lahshar. "Fourth Prince Kaiisteron of the underearth was to give a report to Prince-heir Bashasa about the destruction of the bridge, but he judged Prince-heir Bashasa needed rest first, and the Prince-heir agreed, and we helped him to bed. I am chief of the Fourth Prince's cadre, as seconded by Prince-heir Bashasa."

Hiranan raised her brows. "I see."

Some subtle shift in tone seemed to occur that Kai couldn't interpret. Salatel had been offended on Kai's behalf and also her own, but he wasn't sure how. But Hiranan spoke to him directly, "My sentries reported the bridge was dealt with. That was your work?"

Before Kai could answer, Lahshar interrupted, "Hiranan, I told you I—"

"Lahshar, I'm receiving a report." Hiranan's voice was even but she didn't seem pleased.

Kai said, "I was able to burn the middle section. Any legionaries that come here can repair it, but not quickly, and likely they'll have to wait for the right equipment and supplies. I meant to look at Bashasa's maps, but he fell asleep before I could ask him. Is it true there's no other crossing nearby?" If there was another bridge within reach, it would be wise to take it down, too, even if it meant getting Kai on a wallwalker to get there.

Hiranan said, "No, Bashasa chose our route well, there is no other crossing for some distance. The Hierarchs destroyed the other bridges along this river when they originally took this area. You've bought us time for our escape." She tilted her head, a trace of amusement in her expression. "Well, I'll say goodnight, Fourth Prince. I'll speak to Bashasa in the dawn before we leave."

She stepped back through the curtain, saying pointedly, "Come, Lahshar."

Kai waited until their steps and voices retreated, Lahshar's raised in protest. They were speaking Arike, so he couldn't understand. He asked Salatel, "Can we trust her?" It might have been more accurate to ask *can I trust her* but it was very late and Kai knew he was not exactly equipped for political maneuvering among these strange people.

Salatel let out a relieved breath, her shoulders slumping a little. "I don't know," she admitted, and it made him trust her more. "The Prince-heir will know when he wakes." She added more grimly, "And I'll find his cadre and servers and ask for them to return here and assign shifts for his care."

"I'll wait with him until they get here." No one questioned Kai's ability to keep Bashasa safe, which was gratifying. And if Kai waited longer to move then Bashasa was more likely to sleep through the effort to extract his skirt. He also didn't have anywhere to specifically go, though he could probably find a patch of relatively soft grass to curl up on. It was something he had done frequently in Enna's body, though he knew by now that Talamines wasn't as limber. "Can you and the cadre rest now?"

Salatel nodded. "Yes, Fourth Prince. We'll assign shifts also. Is there anything you need?"

"Can someone drag the maps over here?"

Salatel made a formal gesture, bowing over her folded hands. "As you order, Fourth Prince," while Trenal carried over the map chest.

As they slipped out through the curtain, Kai pulled the chest closer and took out the maps on top. He was hampered by not being able to read Arike, or even recognize the characters that made up the alphabet. It was all little sticklike markings, not like Saredi or Erathi or Imperial at all. But the map on top had the river, the road, and the bridge, and he recognized Bashasa's work in some roughly drawn additions to the elegant inked lines.

Kai traced their route back to the Summer Halls on the other loose maps. Since the major points were depicted with little drawings there was no mistaking the image of the pitched rooftops buried in the earthwork, the canals circling it. Kai couldn't believe they had gotten out of there. He couldn't believe he was sitting here on a soft bedroll with a snoring Arike Prince-heir beside him. Maybe he was still in the Cageling Demon Court, and wild dreams were what happened when your flesh rotted away and you drifted free with no path to the underearth to draw you back. Trying to push that image aside, he pulled out another map that seemed to show the territory to the southeast.

He had been hearing voices occasionally from the front of the tent, Salatel and then Trenal, and a few others. Then he heard Ziede. Kai said, hopefully not loud enough to wake Bashasa, "Ziede, in here."

Bashasa snorted, but didn't wake. Ziede swept the curtain aside, took in the scene, and raised her brows. She said softly, "He's asleep?"

"Yes. Is his cadre back on guard out there?" Kai asked her. She had scrubbed all her makeup off, and looked oddly vulnerable. And tired.

"Yes." Her brow knit and she let the curtain fall behind her. "Why? Was there a problem?"

"Lahshar ordered them away."

Ziede was annoyed. "It would be nice if they waited until we had actually completed our escape to start stabbing each other in the back."

Kai wanted to laugh but he didn't want to wake Bashasa. "When was the last time something nice happened?" Ziede didn't deign to answer the rhetorical question with anything but a grimace. He asked her, "Did you find anything?"

"There's some movement to the south, but it's not coming this way. I'll go back up at dawn before we leave and check again." She added, "That was good work with the bridge. Did you have any trouble stopping the spread of the flames?"

Kai should probably lie, but he didn't have the heart for it. "There was a moment when I was terrified it would burn the trees and fields and the camp . . . Ziede, what if it had?"

Ziede's wince deepened. "We need to get a handle on this." She gestured to him.

"How?"

She shook her head slowly, but said, "I'll have to teach you some limitation cantrips. You might be able to combine them with whatever it is you do to use an expositor's gifts without drawing on the Hierarchs' Well." She frowned critically at Kai, then Bashasa. "Are you all right?"

"Sure." Kai fished out the map that had their route on it. "Have you seen this?"

"Not specifically." Ziede sat down on the carpet at Kai's feet, her expression turning wry when she saw the problem. She sat up on her knees and tugged gently at Kai's trapped skirt. "What are you looking at?"

"Don't wake him," he cautioned her. "I was trying to find Benais-arik, but I can't figure out what some of these symbols mean." Kai shifted to give Ziede room as she pushed the bedding down and managed to ease his skirt loose. She slid her hands under the top layer of stuffing-filled padding and held it still as Kai slipped off to the floor with a thump. "Thanks."

"Which symbols?" she said as she took the map. "These? It's the Arike word for—Hmm, it's *desolation* in Imperial, though that's not quite right. It's how they mark empty cities."

"Empty? Dead cities? Destroyed by the Hierarchs?" Kai took the map back. No wonder Bashasa was so confident they wouldn't be cut off.

"Yes." Ziede turned the map. "Here's Benais-arik, at the edge of this more populated area. The Arike city-states didn't do so badly during the invasion, but that's because they were taken over or infiltrated. They didn't resist, in most places."

Frowning, Kai turned back to the larger map, the one where the whole area of the Arike city-states was smaller than his closed fist. The Erathi had said that refugees fleeing by boat claimed the Hierarchs had conquered and destroyed the whole of the south and the east. This was the first time Kai had any idea what the scale of that looked like. There were more *desolation* marks than whole cities here. And just because the city was still on the map only meant it had temporarily survived its capture.

Did the destruction spread all the way south, up to the top of the world?

Kai didn't understand what they were even doing here. He looked up at Ziede. "What does Bashasa want? I know he's building an alliance, but his own cousins don't want it. And . . ." He gestured helplessly at the map. "What's the point?"

"The point is the Hierarchs aren't finished. There are plenty of us left for them to kill," Ziede said with quiet intensity. "And there's every indication that they will keep going." She hesitated, and admitted, "We stop them, or die."

Kai leaned back against the bed. He supposed Bashasa still wanted what he had said he wanted in the Summer Halls: to hurt the Hierarchs in any way possible. His gaze fell on the wrapped bundle by the tent wall. There was no odor, but then he knew they had used witchwork to preserve the body. "That's his sister?"

"Yes." Ziede folded the discarded maps and put them away. "Yours—Enna's—is still packed on the wallwalker."

Kai stared. He couldn't have been more startled if Ziede had slapped him. He managed, "Did they take all the Arike dead?"

"No. They had to leave them behind." She nodded toward the wrapped bundle. "The soldiers knew he meant to take his sister's body. Part of his new plan is to show the Arike leaders in Benais-arik that the Hierarchs killed a Prince-heir hostage. Everyone knows the Hierarchs' treaties are worthless, but this is proof, dramatic proof. And he'll need to show them how she was killed." She met Kai's gaze. "He didn't tell anyone else he was taking Enna's body. He asked Tahren to bring her."

The bundle Kai had seen Tahren carry out of the Halls had been Enna and not Bashasa's sister. "Do they think they can do something with her? With Enna?" Mortals outside the grasslands thought all kinds of strange things about demons. He didn't want Enna cut up for useless protective amulets.

But Ziede shook her head. "He said he thought you wouldn't want her underwater."

Kai stared at Ziede until her mouth quirked wryly, then he stared at Bashasa's sleeping face.

Ziede said, "Do Saredi bury their dead?"

Kai shook his head slowly. "Pyres, on the flats above the river, so the fire wouldn't spread." It wasn't possible here; there was too much grass, and he didn't want to use an intention. He had managed not to burn the camp and kill everyone once tonight, he didn't want to trust his luck again. "I can't risk that."

Ziede looked regretful. "No. But you could do a Witch burial. I saw a ruined wall near here when I was scouting, and outlines of foundations."

"For a cairn?" At her nod, Kai pushed his hair back, and managed not to startle at the different texture. "Would you help me?"

They found the spot to the south of camp, on the far side of a copse of tall trees. The breeze was up and it was cooler now, the half moon peering out from behind the clouds again, gleaming silver on the tall grasses, turning the trees into dark outlines against the sky. Kai could just make out the tumbled stone wall Ziede had seen from the air. It had once enclosed some wooden buildings that had collapsed and rotted away in the weather. The Hierarchs had come through here and destroyed the bridge once before; they would have destroyed everything around it, too.

They had retrieved Enna's body from the other wallwalker's cargo net, and Kai had borrowed a shovel used to make the pits for the campfires. Now he waited while Ziede walked back and forth across the ruined dwelling, her head tilted as she listened to the air. She stopped and said, "Here. This is where the hearth was." Kai started to dig while Ziede carried over rocks from the wall.

Kai had left Bashasa's coat in the tent and tied up his skirts to keep them out of the damp earth, and wound his hair into a bun with Talamines' pins. He was finding Arike clothing comfortable but impractical. He said to Ziede, "I thought you hated Immortal Marshalls."

"I do." She dumped a rock to one side of the hole and went back for another.

Kai shoveled more dirt. "Then what's going on with you and Tahren?"

"Nothing"—Ziede put on her intimidating voice—"is going on."

Kai grinned to himself. "She's very tall. The Saredi always thought broad shoulders were very attractive—Hey!" Kai scrambled away, shaking out the double handful of dirt Ziede had just dumped down his back.

Not long after that, Kai sensed someone watching them. When they left the tents, Salatel had been asleep, and Cerala and Hartel had been easier to order to stay behind to help guard Bashasa. Kai had strongly implied they were going off to do Witch's work that was both important and dangerous.

Moving casually, Kai dumped one last shovel of dirt and stepped out of the shallow trench, pretending to stretch his back so he could look over the field without being obvious. But the figure standing some distance away was tall, broad-shouldered, and pale, the moonlight catching on short light-colored hair. Tahren was standing knee-deep in the grass, hands on her hips, watching.

Kai let his held breath out in relief and said, "Ziede."

She dropped a rock beside the growing pile. Dusting her hands, she looked up. She demanded immediately, "What are you doing lurking there?"

Tahren walked through the high grass, drawing close enough so Kai could see her furrowed brow. She said, "I assume this is all normal."

Kai supposed digging a grave in the middle of the night might seem strange. He told her, "We're burying me."

Tahren's frown deepened. "What . . . Permanently?"

"The old me, Enna," Kai clarified. He couldn't help it, he

snorted a laugh. "No, I was going to get in the hole and let Ziede cover me up."

"Tempting as the prospect might seem," Ziede said, and Kai folded over laughing. Possibly he was losing what was left of his composure. He thumped down onto the pile of dirt and buried his face in his hands, laughing until he felt tears on Talamines' face. He managed to look up at Ziede, who had slumped down to sit on the remains of the rock wall and was still chuckling quietly to herself.

Tahren took all this in silently, then said, "I think you need help."

Ziede waved a hand. "I can see why it might appear so."

"No, I mean . . ." Tahren hesitated. "May I help?"

Ziede started to speak, then turned and looked at Tahren quizzically. "Kai?" she said softly.

Lying in the dirt, Kai wiped his face. Whatever was happening, it felt more weighty than a simple offer to help dig a grave. He said, "It's fine. I, uh . . ." He thought of Tahren plucking the bolts out of his back in the Cageling Demon Court, and finished, "I trust Tahren Stargard. To help."

Ziede still watched Tahren, who returned her gaze steadily. "I'm startled to realize, so do I." She held out her hand and Tahren took it. "In that case, you may join us."

FIFTEEN

As the ascension raft fled the Summer Halls and flew over the plains, it was clear the finding stone was leading them toward the Benais-arik city-state's territory.

"If the stone keeps on this course, she's most likely somewhere on the old border into the Arik," Ziede said quietly. She sat cross-legged on the deck, the finding stone in her lap, a map from Dahin's bag spread in front of her. "The Kagala, probably."

Next to Ziede, Kai leaned over to look at the map. He felt a tickle of unease. The forts had been built generations before the Hierarchs came, back when the Arike city-states had fought and raided each other. During the war, Bashasa had used them mostly as distractions; after the war, they had temporarily housed refugees. Years later they had fallen into disuse. But after their first escape from the Summer Halls, Bashasa had led the rebels to the Kagala, expecting to leave some of the refugees at the town there, and then resupply at the fort for the final journey into the capital of Benais-arik. Kai said, "Does that seem . . ." He wasn't sure what it seemed like.

"Like a looming presentiment of some sort of disaster?" Ziede said, her voice dry and tense. "It could be a coincidence. All those forts have been deserted for years, and this one borders Nient-arik territory, but is technically part of Benais-arik, which makes for a level of plausible deniability if Tahren was found there."

Kai sat back, not reassured. Omens were always tricky and hard to interpret and mostly useless, except to point to in hindsight. There had apparently been omens among the borderlanders before the first Hierarch attack on Erathi, but no one had recognized them at the time. This was more likely a coincidence.

But it still felt strange, to be retracing that journey again, from the Summer Halls to the Kagala.

The rest of the raft's occupants were quiet. The sun had come out as they flew and their clothes and hair had dried but they were all disheveled and bruised and weary. Tenes had revived enough to fall into a normal sleep, and was in the small cabin with Sanja curled up next to her. Saadrin had apparently seen enough of that cabin and sat near the steering column, watching Dahin with a frown, while Dahin studiously ignored her. Ramad was on the opposite side, leaning on the railing to look down at the ground below. Kai barely remembered the first time he had flown with Ziede, but recalled enough to know how fascinating it was to see the world unroll below you from a height like this.

After they had gotten the raft pointed in the right direction, Ziede had explained that Tenes had called earth spirits to exploit the weakness at the back of the stable cavern, to tunnel through it and cause the flood. "And it gave way quite spectacularly. But we caught the edge when I tried to fly us away." She had added with a grimace, "It didn't work quite how I imagined."

Nothing had worked the way Kai had imagined, but they got here in the end. Ziede had also apologized for losing a drop of her blood on the Immortal Blessed ship. Kai was over the frustration of that lapse by now, and had told her it didn't matter. At least whatever intention Arnsterath had used to read Ziede's pearl had seemed to consume the blood, so it couldn't be used again. "Hopefully she doesn't have any more," Dahin had pointed out, not helpfully.

Now Ziede let out her breath in a frustrated huff. "I don't care where we're going, if it's an omen or not, I just want to get there."

Kai said, "We'll be there soon. No more waiting." The raft was making short work of the journey, much faster than canal boats or wallwalkers.

She looked at him. Under all the tension, her face was drawn and weary. But she said, "That must have been a shock, to see another Saredi demon again."

Kai didn't want to talk about this, but the roil of conflicting emotions felt like it was boiling his brain. "Demons don't get shock."

"I'm absolutely sure they do," Ziede countered. "Was she in the Temple Halls with us?"

Ramad had turned toward them, listening with his brow furrowed. The bruises along the side of his face had darkened and looked painful. Kai shifted uncomfortably and leaned back on the bench. "Yes. I think you spoke to her, after I killed Talamines and—" He made a vague gesture to his body. "All that. Before Bashasa left to look for the other Hierarch. She was in the body of an older man."

Ziede's brow knit in consternation. "The one who tried to attack you later?"

Kai let out his breath. That was the moment he had really understood that even if he survived to leave the Summer Halls, nothing would ever be the same. "I didn't think anybody saw that."

"I saw. It seemed . . . better not to comment on it, at the time." Ziede touched the finding stone again to check their course, something that had turned into a nervous twitch in the last few hours. "Were you close, before that?"

"She was older, as a demon and as a Saredi. She was always there." He looked at Ramad, who was carefully keeping his expression neutral, and actually barely breathing, unwilling to disturb this view into the past. It should have been invasive and irritating but it wasn't. Ramad's interest in the real history of this time was a true calling, and maybe Kai owed him this.

"She was imprisoned for decades, Ziede. The whole time we've been living our lives, she was . . ." Kai shook his head impatiently. "We weren't close. I don't even know why—" He didn't finish the sentence, even silently.

"Even if you two had never met before, she was a Saredi demon whom you had just saved from the Cageling Court," Ziede said inexorably. "But she knew you, she was older, she had a responsibility toward you. She should have been the one watching over you instead of a Witch and an Arike Prince-heir you had known for less than a day. You would have watched over her, taken care of her, if she had been the one hurt." Her gaze flicked past him to Ramad, and she added silently, *It was the first time someone betrayed you.*

Kai buried his face in his hands. *It's too much right now,* he told her. She squeezed his arm, and didn't press it.

Kai looked up at a rustle from the steering column. Dahin was checking the map he had tucked into his tunic. As if he needed to, as if he hadn't crossed this territory over and over again in the last sixty years, as if he wasn't an expert mapmaker. "We're coming up on a traders' post at that junction where the two major eastern canals meet the new trade road. You want me to swing wide around it?"

"No." Kai knew the outpost he meant. "Ziede, we need to stop. Just for a little."

Sanja poked her head out of the cabin. "Please? I have to pee."

"I have to pee, too," Dahin contributed. "Though someone will have to stay with the raft to make sure Aunt Saadrin doesn't steal it."

Saadrin was apparently too weary with Dahin at this point to even get angry. With exasperation, she said, "I am under kin-right and Obligation." She had admitted earlier, not even grudgingly, that Dahin and Kai had saved her life. Dahin was covered by kin-right, but she owed Kai for it, and just saving his life in return wasn't enough to wipe out the debt. To the Immortal Blessed, her life was worth far more than a demon, two Witches, and a couple of mortals.

Ramad must know the outpost, too, and was probably calculating whether he could send a messenger to the cohort post that was down the canal from it. He asked, "Will there be time to buy food?"

Ziede knew what Kai wanted to do, and he watched her wrestle her impatience. "Everyone has to hurry," she said finally, and added meaningfully to Kai, "Don't drag it out."

They were passing over low hills covered with yellow grasses and tiny bright flowers when Kai spotted the first canal. Water trees dotted the shallows, tall with spreading canopies and cages of roots that stood above the surface. Not long after, they saw the woodsmoke of the outpost rising in the distance, and the second intersecting canal that curved toward it.

As they drew closer, Dahin guided the raft down, avoiding the broad stone-paved road that wound through the fields. Stands of tall flowering trees, vividly pink and white against the faded grass, decorated the hilltops, a sign that they had been cultivated at one time by a vanished town or farm. When they were close enough, Dahin set the raft down on the far side of a low rise, within easy walking distance of the outpost but out of its immediate view. People had probably seen them land, but no one was going to come running to see what an Immortal Blessed ascension raft was doing here.

Tenes, still a little groggy, wanted to stay behind. Ziede took Sanja with her toward the outpost, and Saadrin left the raft to stand dramatically a little distance away, so Dahin would feel comfortable leaving it unattended.

Kai got out, knowing Ramad would follow him. Dry grass crackled underfoot, but the breeze was cool and kept the gnats at bay. They walked up the rise to stand in the trees, surrounded by bright fallen petals, with a view of the canals and the busy market. The wooden structures were built atop old stone pilings in a curve, extending out into the basin where the two canals met. Under the shade of the tall water trees, mortals wandered past shops, traders with wares under brightly colored portable awnings, vendors serving food out of steaming cauldrons and clay ovens. Many boats and barges were docked along the pilings, with wagons and even a few wallwalkers in the stables and corrals just off the road. The scent of the flowering trees mingled with grilled meat and garlic and woodsmoke, and the distant sound of voices traveled on the breeze. Kai spotted Ziede moving with brisk efficiency toward the food sellers, Sanja skipping after her. The place was so well-populated, it might be on its way to becoming a city not so many years from now. It eased a tension in the back of his neck, looking at this sign of vibrant life in the countryside. They might be retracing their steps, but the Summer Halls was in the past; this was the new world.

Ramad folded his arms. "This is going to make an interesting report for Bashat bar Calis and the Imperial council."

It was an invitation to talk, and Kai took it. He said, "I think I owe you the answer to a question."

"Do you?" Ramad shook his head, and said wryly, "You've told me so much. It's very generous of you. I know these are often painful subjects and my quest for knowledge has sometimes been . . . thoughtless at best."

"Ask while you have the chance," Kai said.

"Very well." Ramad hesitated. "What happened to Lesser Blessed Dahin?" From his pained expression, he was clearly reviewing some of the details of their escape. "The way he killed that Immortal Blessed . . ."

This wasn't a pleasant memory either, but Kai said, "During the war, he was on a mission for Bashasa and he was caught by the Immortal Marshalls who supported the Hierarchs. His family didn't help him. He wasn't expected back soon and it took us too long to realize he was missing, and then too long to find him." It was why Dahin wouldn't let Kai give him a pearl. He couldn't stand the thought of anyone with that kind of access to his mind. "He doesn't blame Tahren, he knows she would never hurt him. But she's also . . . one of them."

Ramad took that in gravely. "Everyone who survived that time bore scars. Bears scars." He turned to face Kai. "There's something I should—"

Kai didn't want to hear it. He had put this off long enough. Ramad thought the warm threads of unspoken connection between them were still there. It was time to cut them. "I know you're Bashat's agent."

Ramad was too experienced to be caught out like that. He smiled a little. "I'm his vanguarder."

Kai pressed on. "You knew about the conspiracy. You and Bashat." He couldn't help adding, "I'd given up on Bashat, but I'd hoped you didn't know."

Ramad's face went still. He obviously had no idea how much Kai knew, and it had caught him utterly by surprise. "Kai . . . That was the Nient-arik, and some overly ambitious Immortal Blessed. Surely what just happened to us is proof that I am not working for them."

The lie by omission made this a little easier. "You didn't have to work for them. All you had to do was not stop them." Kai let the painful irony show in his smile. "It got Tahren, Ziede, and me out of the way during the Imperial coalition renewal. Bashat knew we thought he and Benais-arik had too much power, that I didn't support the idea of a Rising World empire. He couldn't take the chance that Tahren would speak against him when she renewed the Immortal Blessed treaty. So he let the conspirators take us. Then at the Imperial renewal, he exposed the conspiracy. The council agreed to continue the Blessed treaty without Tahren since her nonappearance was involuntary. Bashat was able to get rid of the dissidents and paint Nient-arik as a nest of traitors, so they lost their influence in the Rising World. The Immortal Blessed will come out of this weaker, now that the council knows they have dissension among their Patriarchs."

Kai saw the moment that Ramad understood it was time to give up the pretense. Some part of him seemed to relax, as if the deception was a weight he had just put down. "Bashat did send me to find Tahren Stargard, and you. He would have ordered your release—"

Kai had to admire the effort. "Don't make it worse."

"I'm not—" Ramad pressed his lips together, visibly regaining control, considering his next words. "I apologize for my part in this. When I agreed to it, I didn't know you."

That was unexpected, and sharp like a little stab with a very thin knife. Ramad had apparently never fooled himself into thinking this wasn't a betrayal. Kai said, "Very good. Now tell me if it was Bashat who poisoned me, or if he just let it happen."

"He poisoned you. He knew what the Nient-arik planned wouldn't work. He—We let them think you had been betrayed by a traitor inside Benais House."

Kai had to laugh at that one, though it came out harsher than he intended. "I was betrayed by a traitor inside Benais House."

Ramad looked away, a hard line to his jaw. "The Rising World needed the Imperial renewal. We couldn't let you talk the Enalin into refusing their agreement—"

Ramad had been clever, Bashat had been ruthless. It was almost a pity to tell them it had been pointless, because Kai had betrayed them first. "I talked the Enalin into that five years ago."

Ramad turned to face him, brow furrowed. He didn't understand. Then abruptly he did. The breath caught in his throat.

Kai shrugged. "It took two years of discussion." All the Enalin provinces were individually governed and they selected their own leaders by agreement among the populations. It was a complicated system, but at least more organized than how the Witches did it. "I had to talk to all their leaders, then they had to agree among themselves." It was unexpectedly hard to look at Ramad's dawning comprehension, so Kai turned toward the outpost again. "Before we reached the Summer Halls, I got a message from the Enalin ambassador to Benais-arik. Enalin withdrew its support of Benais-arik and Bashat as planned, after he exposed the conspirators, and the Imperial renewal failed. The Rising World is no longer an empire, it's a coalition of free allies again. The council will divide up Benais-arik's responsibilities, and they even gave Bashat a seat, so he shouldn't be too disappointed that he won't rule as Emperor." Kai wasn't nearly as calm as he knew he sounded. "Benais-arik could go to war with Enalin about it, but Enalin has too much support. The rest of the coalition would turn on Benais-arik for disrupting the peace."

"Five years," Ramad echoed, his voice dry as dust. "So I betrayed you . . . Bashat betrayed you for nothing."

Kai was still angry, but it was so wrapped up in hurt, at anger at himself for daring to believe that Ramad didn't know. "That's why those two Lesser Blessed were so afraid of losing the finding stone." Their plan for Nient-arik to be named capital of the Rising World had failed, and the Immortal Blessed would still be held by the coalition treaty. The Immortal Marshalls would be ordered to hunt down any Blessed who had participated in the conspiracy and an old Hierarchs' finding stone would have made short work of that. "I wasn't sure that you were part of it, until you tried to get Faharin to let us go, when you told him it was too late." Ramad had thought the Imperial renewal had succeeded, that there was no reason to keep Kai and Ziede from returning. Kai had to add, "It was always too late." He could look at Ramad now, and turned to meet his gaze. "You forgot what I am."

Ramad huffed a breath that was almost a laugh. "An immortal demon prince."

"No," Kai said pointedly. "Bashasa's immortal demon prince." Down below, Ziede and Sanja emerged from the chaos of the market, both carrying bundles, and started up the dirt track that would lead them back to the raft. "I'll give you one more answer. The words Bashasa spoke to me before he died were 'Don't let everything we fought for be for nothing.'" Ramad's expression was turning stricken. Kai pressed on. "He never wanted an empire to replace the Hierarchs. He wanted everything to go back to the way it was before they came. I can't give him that, but I can give him this." Kai stepped back, looking away. "You can tell Bashat, all we want is to be left alone."

"He's not mad for power," Ramad said abruptly. "That's not what this was about. He knew about the schism in the Immortal Blessed, that there was a Patriarch who wanted to end the treaty. He thought it was only the beginning, that the coalition would fracture under the pressure. He thought it had a better chance of survival if Benais-arik stayed in control."

Kai started down the hill. He wasn't going to argue. If the coalition fractured and alliances shifted or re-formed in different ways, that was just the way things were. Kai had learned to live with it; Bashat could too.

Ramad didn't try to follow, still standing under the flowering trees. Kai waited at the raft as Ziede and Sanja made their way through the field and he followed them back aboard.

Ziede set down a large bamboo container and squeezed Kai's shoulder. One of Sanja's burdens was a palm leaf basket filled with stuffed fried pastries. The smell of spices and chickpea and eggplant made Kai's stomach rumble, despite everything. Tenes emerged from the cabin, wide awake now.

Dahin was ready at the steering column, shoving honey dates into his mouth. Saadrin eyed him from her seat on the bench. "You're polluting your body," she told him repressively.

"I've been eating Blessed travel rations for months, my body is desperate for pollution," Dahin told her, his too-sharp gaze on Kai. "Ramad not coming along?"

"He can get a boat to a cohort post from here." Kai closed the raft's gate. "Let's go."

⁃⁃⁃⸙⁃⁃⁃

The Kagala stood alone in a rocky, dusty plain, the trading route it had once guarded fallen out of use. A canal ran toward the structure, but it had been dammed at some point and was now dry, filled only at its lowest points by rainwater. It ended in an empty basin that had been a circular high-walled harbor, connected to the main body of the fort by a high curving bridge.

The fort itself was typical Arike military architecture: round towers topped by cupolas, with slanted outer walls plain and polished smooth, and inner walls figured with scenes from legends and martial stories. The paint on the carving was faded but still showing hints of bright greens, blues, reds.

The land on the far side of the canal had once held a trading town, but the round wooden structures and compounds had long since collapsed and fallen into the dusty fields. Only the stone foundations remained.

At the edge of the desert, they had stopped briefly again to refill the water containers underneath the benches in the cabin, but Kai didn't want to stay in this area any longer than they absolutely had to. He didn't think Ramad had been lying about not knowing where Tahren was, since the renegade Immortal Blessed involved in the Nient-arik conspiracy would have brought her here. But Bashat might have, and simply not told his vanguarder. Those Immortal Blessed had thought that their conspiracy had cleverly avoided Rising World scrutiny, and instead they had played right into its hands.

The fortress looked deserted, and there were no tracks in the dusty pathways leading toward the gates. "There wouldn't be a Well-source here," Saadrin said, standing in the raft with her arms folded. "It's too isolated to be reached quickly in any other way."

"Except the way we're flying in," Dahin said. "Thank you for your wisdom, Aunt."

Kai, sitting on the bench, leaned his forehead against the rail and said, "Dahin, I am begging you." Ziede stood like a brittle statue, all nerves, and the last thing they needed was an argument.

"I know, I know, sorry." Dahin wiped his face distractedly. "I can't—It's hard not to, sometimes. Sorry, everyone." That was as close as he could evidently get to an apology to Saadrin. With more sensitivity to the situation than Kai had expected, she said nothing.

Dahin guided the raft slowly over the inner walls. Inside was a large courtyard on three stepped levels, each one carved deeper into the earth, with the lowest below the surface. The stables, the water well, the food storage were down there, taking advantage of the cool underground. This side of the inner walls was honeycombed with windows so the chambers built inside could catch the breeze. Across from the gate, on the balcony where the commander of the fort would stand to give announcements, the platform and the stone chair still stood.

"Should I land?" Dahin studied the scene. "It doesn't look like there's any—" Just as figures emerged from an arched gateway onto the second level of the courtyard. Kai ducked and pushed Sanja off the bench. Ziede crouched with a grimace of irritation. Tenes, already seated on the deck, flinched in alarm.

Dahin swore. "That's a Lesser Blessed." He had crouched a little behind the steering column, head turned to shield his face from view.

Saadrin was the only one who hadn't moved. "It's Vrenren," she said, with the air of a shopper being presented with an inadequate selection of melons. "Third cousin to Narrein and Shiren. There are mortals with him."

"Why are they just walking out like idiots?" Dahin hissed.

"Because we're in an Immortal Blessed flying thing?" Sanja pointed out. "Maybe they think we're them."

"Right, right." Dahin made a throwaway gesture. "So we can use that to our advantage. Maybe I can lure them out and we can land on them. Or—"

Kai had an idea. Vrenren obviously knew Saadrin, but hadn't taken alarm at seeing her. He might not know who else was involved in the Immortal Blessed side of the conspiracy. Surely he wouldn't believe Dahin was involved, but from a distance, with his hair tied back, Dahin could be mistaken for a woman Lesser Blessed. If Dahin kept his face concealed, they had an excellent chance for a deception. Kai sat up a little and said, "Immortal Marshall Saadrin, would you like to pay your debt to me?"

———⊂∞∞⊃———

Dahin brought the raft down on the top platform just inside the sealed front gate. Using Old Imperial, Saadrin called out, "Stay where you are. I'll come to you."

With the others crouched in the cabin and Dahin concealing his face by pretending to fiddle with the steering column, she reached down and lifted an apparently unconscious Kai.

Slung head down over her shoulder, Kai tried to stay limp. He had underestimated how uncomfortably bony her shoulder blade would be. She strode across the platform; every step jabbed Kai in the stomach. He regretted the two fried pastries he had eaten earlier.

This was an exercise in trust for both of them. He had to trust Saadrin wouldn't betray him just because she could; she had to trust he wouldn't drain her life just because he could.

A voice called back to her, echoing against the stone and too garbled to make out. Saadrin, using the commanding tone of the Immortal Marshall, had no trouble making herself heard. "I've got the demon," she told them. "Faharin sent me here. We need to hurry."

The jolting as she went down the ramp to the lower platform was worse. Kai was supposed to be deeply unconscious and didn't even have the relief of groaning. He kept his eyes shut but felt the temperature drop as Saadrin walked under the overhang of the inner wall. The air was dank, promising a still-working water source somewhere nearby. She said, "Take me to the cells, hurry."

The voice that was presumably Vrenren said, "Faharin sent you? I didn't realize you were—How did you get the demon?" He sounded startled, but not as if this was an utterly unbelievable event. He had obviously had a lot more confidence in Faharin than anyone else Kai had encountered.

Saadrin's impatience was probably not a performance. "We'll speak later! I can't risk this creature waking. The others won't be able to track him once he's in the cell."

The mortal guards murmured nervously, and Vrenren said, "Of course, Blessed Marshall, this way."

They walked into the cool shadow, sand-dusted stone grating under their feet, leaving the heat in the courtyard behind. They took a turn into a dimmer space, past window-shafts of daylight that glowed through Kai's closed eyelids. Then they stopped and Vrenren said, "Here, get that one open."

Over the movement of the guards, Saadrin asked, "This is where the Fallen is imprisoned?" Kai winced internally. Her voice sounded stilted, but maybe Vrenren was too off-balance to notice anything wrong. Or maybe this was just how Saadrin often sounded.

"No, hers is there," Vrenren said, hurried. "There are seven cells altogether. The Patriarch thought they would all be useful, once the Nient mortals take the Rising World and free us from the treaty. He said there would be plenty of apostates to—"

Kai tapped Saadrin's arm and she dumped him off her shoulder. Kai twisted to land on his feet. They were in a junction in a broad corridor, daylight falling in through high windows just below the curved ceiling. Large square doorways lined the walls, rooms that had once been civilian quarters; now they had new heavy ironbound doors installed.

Saadrin had lost her Blessed blade somewhere between her capture at Orintukk and the Summer Halls. She backhanded the nearest mortal and snatched his sickle sword as he started to go down. She jerked her head toward the doorway to Kai's left. Then she went for the horrified Vrenren.

One brave or uninformed mortal guard grabbed Kai and got his life drained. Others bolted, frantically shouting the alarm. Steel clashed as Saadrin and Vrenren fought. His Blessed blade sliced strips off her mortal sword, but it didn't seem to be helping him much as Saadrin drove him down the corridor with sheer strength and confident aggression. There might be other Immortal Blessed here and Kai needed to hurry.

He had the cantrip that opened the Witch cells, given to him by Grandmother days ago, what felt like months ago. He stepped to the door Saadrin had indicated and began to mark it onto the ironbound wood. The blocks around the door didn't match the warm sand-colored stone of the rest of the corridor; they were darker, smoother, blended through with red veins. Kai felt an alien cold radiating from them, something that ate the heat right out of his blood. He set his jaw and concentrated on the cantrip, trying not to think about what Tahren had gone through. It had to be terrible in there.

The mortals who had fled stumbled back into view at the far end of the corridor, one choking on flowers, the others still yelling for reinforcements. A breeze stirred Kai's hair where no breeze could be; Ziede and Tenes were coming. More frantic shouting echoed from the direction Saadrin had driven Vrenren.

Kai finished the cantrip and fed a little of that last unlucky mortal's life into it. The door cracked and started to open under his hand.

It slammed backward on its hinges so hard, Kai nearly screamed. Tahren stood there, dressed in a filthy tunic and pants, still taller than him even in his new body. Her hands gripped his shoulders. She stared down at him, her brow knit in confusion. "A demon?" Her voice cracked as if she hadn't used it in far too long.

"It's me," Kai managed. "Tahren—"

It's Kai, Ziede's pearl echoed, as she spoke to him and Tahren together. *Get up here, there are more idiot Lesser Blessed! And don't kill your aunt Saadrin, she's helping us!*

Tahren's expression cleared. She yanked Kai forward, kissed him on the forehead, released him, and strode down the corridor.

Kai stumbled, laughing with relief, and followed her.

THE PAST:
THE BEGINNING

None of us understood that the future hung by a thread that day. We had most of us resolved by then that we would have no future.

—Letter found in the Benais-arik archives, attributed to Bashasa Calis, but the identification is in dispute

Kai managed a few hours sleep in the outer room of Bashasa's tent, and woke well before dawn with Salatel and the others when Bashasa popped back to consciousness and swept everyone into motion again. Considering how divided the Arike seemed to be, the one thing everyone could agree on was getting out of here as quickly as possible. In the dim gray light before the sun broke the horizon, the camp was just flattened grass and a few buried fire pits and they were ready to leave.

Bashasa had ordered everyone to take the same places they had yesterday so there wouldn't be confusion. In the scramble of helping the cadre reload the tent and the other supplies, Kai ended up with the map case slung over his shoulder. His stomach roiled at the idea of climbing the wallwalker again, but having something important he needed to carry somehow made it a little easier to force himself up the side in Salatel's wake. He wanted to be here, or rather he wanted to be here more than he wanted to be dead or a drifting spirit, so he was going to make himself cooperative and unobtrusive. Which was harder now since he was tall and gangly instead of neat and compact like Enna.

As Kai climbed over the rail into the palanquin, Bashasa was already aboard. He hung on the rope supporting the canopy and leaned dangerously far over the side to shout, "Arava, are you all in there? Tell them to lead, we'll follow!"

The predawn air was very still, the birds and insects silent, disturbed by the whirlwind of activity. The only sounds in the dark were the wallwalkers' deep breathing and the soft worried voices of the passengers. There was no sign of the Witches; either they had moved on last night or mixed in with the other refugees.

A small oil lamp lit the palanquin, revealing all the anxious faces and nervous bodies crowding onto the benches and helping the wounded settle on the floor. Most of the servers and non-Arike refugees had ended up further forward. Lahshar and Dasara and their dependents had moved toward the back, though they seemed far less confident than they had last night. Lahshar fidgeted with a long scarf and Dasara kept twisting around to peer outside, back toward the river, still just a black void in the dark. He didn't even spare Kai a glare.

Last night, after the long strange day, maybe their escape hadn't felt quite real to them; now they were on the run again and all their scheming meant nothing if a legion caught them.

Lamps in the other palanquins winked out one by one as the wallwalkers started to move. Bashasa dragged himself back inside and turned to them. "Ah, Salatel and Fourth Prince! Are you the last? And you have the maps, excellent."

Kai shoved the map case into the cubby in the prow of the palanquin and took up his square of floorspace. Judging by yesterday, he would probably end up sleeping curled around the cable support again but right now he was wide awake. Bashasa gestured to Trenal to snuff out the light and the wallwalker lurched into motion.

Salatel and Trenal settled down along the rail, Trenal leaning her head on Salatel's shoulder. Surely the creature's motion hadn't been this rough yesterday. Kai didn't know what was worse, looking inward toward the swaying palanquin or out into the predawn shadows. No, away from the inside of the palanquin was definitely better. He wriggled up onto the rail so he could face front and wrapped his arm more firmly around the support.

Leaning against the prow, Bashasa said worriedly, "Careful, Fourth Prince! You don't want to fall out."

Kai could have said something fatalistic like he did want to fall out, but it would just upset Bashasa who was busy trying to keep them all alive. So he only said, "I won't fall."

The wallwalkers followed the old stone road, moving swiftly. As the sun started to break the horizon, they were coming out of the river flat and into tree-covered hills. Kai had been wrestling with what to say, wishing the circumstances were more private. But all the others near them seemed to be dozing or wrapped in their own concerns. A small child was a babbling distraction somewhere in the middle of the palanquin. Finally Kai just said, "Thank you for Enna."

"Ah," Bashasa said. For a moment it seemed like there would be nothing else, then he added, "Sister Witch said you put her to rest last night?"

"Yes. I just . . ." Kai cleared his throat, suddenly feeling as awkward as if he had never been in a human body before. "There were so many others that were left behind."

Bashasa still looked out over the rising ground. "I understand what happened to you is not . . . usual, even for one of your kind and lineage." He shook his head a little. "It seemed inappropriate to leave her."

Kai tried not to wriggle uncomfortably. Saredi weren't this direct about things like feelings and gratitude. "I'm glad you were able to bring your sister."

"Now, that was selfish, though I tell myself it was necessary. I will tell the assembly in Benais-arik that I brought her to prove the Hierarchs violated our treaty—such as it was—by allowing their minions to murder her and remain unpunished." His expression was calm as he looked out over the dark landscape, but Kai felt that calm was skin-deep. "But the truth is . . . my sister was the last of my close family. Our mother was poisoned not long after the Hierarchs arrived. Our father—who was an artist—went with his sister and my maternal cousin to a negotiation, during which they all disappeared. The Hierarch's Voice for the city-states said they never arrived. Some remains were found but of course there was no sign of how they died. Thus my family was whittled away bit by bit."

"Do you think your people will listen?" Kai asked. Just based on his limited experience with the Arike here, he had doubts.

"Well, that is the question fate rests on." Bashasa sighed. "When the Hierarchs no longer need our mines and our farms and artisans, they mean to slaughter all of us that are left." His expression held a weariness that went beyond the last few days. "But those who were pushed into power by the Hierarchs like to pretend they will somehow be the exception. That the methods the Hierarchs have used on the rest of the known world will somehow not be used on us." Bashasa shifted against the rail to face Kai. "Did the Saredi know anything of war, before the Hierarchs?"

"Grandmother was at war with the underearth, until she made the treaty." Kai had to think back to Aunt Laniaa's history lessons; the memory of sitting around the big fire at night and listening to her stories squeezed his heart painfully. He forced his way past it and added, "And there were skirmishes between the borderlanders, sometimes. But the Witches arbitrate for them. Used to arbitrate."

"Your grandmother led a war against the underearth?" Bashasa said, distracted. "How?"

"It wasn't easy, that's why she made the treaty," Kai said. "And it was ten—eleven mortal generations ago, I wasn't born then."

Bashasa looked intrigued, like he wanted to ask more questions, but went back to the subject. "This part of the world had also been peaceful for generations, before the Hierarchs. The seven city-states of the Arik hadn't fought each other since my great-grandmother was a child. The Enalin had not gone to war in living memory. All across the Arkai, the Sana-sarcofa, the archi-pelagoes, the coasts of the sea people, and beyond. Skirmishes, or defense against bandits, or old martial traditions. The Hierarchs came without provocation, without reason, that anyone knows. But for these past terrible years, they taught us to fight. I hope they taught us to work together."

Kai leaned his head against the palanquin's support and con-sidered Bashasa. "You really think we're going to survive this."

"Ah." Bashasa tossed him a quick grin. "If we do, I have plans."

For the last two days, the plain grew dryer and more rocky, the grass and scrub trees more sparse. But Bashasa's route let them intersect with and then follow along beside a canal, so there was plenty of water for the wallwalkers, and brief bathing and clothes-washing opportunities for the passengers when they stopped at night to rest the beasts.

Kai had time to figure out the vagaries of his new body. With most of the scented oil washed out of his hair, it had turned into a frizzy mass, and he was using Talamines' emerald pins and a knotted cord borrowed from Salatel to keep it under control. Some other things were the same, others were worse. Besides the loss of much of his night vision, he got tired more easily, had to eat more. When he felt pain it was sharper, more immediate. That helped with his ability to create intentions, but he still had to dig the knowledge out of Talamines' brain. It took forever and the intentions Talamines had been taught were not very helpful for their current situation.

It was midafternoon on a clear blue day when they saw the town, and then the stone fort on the rocky rise above it.

The canal ran between the fort and the town, ending in a boat basin below the fort with a high bridge over it. Irrigation water channeled from the canal fed lush green fields and orchards. The town was mostly one- or two-story wooden buildings painted sun-faded colors, with tile roofs, and an open paved plaza in the center. Big awnings and a few trees lined and shaded the streets and the stalls of a market, and canal boats were drawn up along the docks. People were already coming out to stare at the wall-walkers. Probably out of fear, thinking there were Hierarch nobles aboard.

"Prince-heir, the banner," Trenal said suddenly. She stood at Bashasa's elbow, and Kai glanced back to see her eyes were wide.

"I see it." Bashasa's expression was thoughtful rather than grim, but then Kai wasn't sure Bashasa had looked grim when he had been leading a charge against a Hierarch. "Dasara, get your mother."

Dasara had been loitering to the front of the palanquin, maybe having recognized the terrain and that they were drawing near the town where Bashasa meant to pick up supplies. The past couple of days, several of the wounded had recovered enough to sit up, which meant there was more room for moving around the palanquin. Dasara leaned forward to peer out, jerked back with alarm, then turned to push toward the back.

"The banner?" Kai asked. There were three long colorful banners, not unlike the one that Bashasa had liberated from the hall of trophies, hanging from a horizontal bar above the fort's gate. Salatel and Trenal both gave him worried grimaces.

Bashasa said, "The banner of our cousin, Karanis. The usurper the Hierarchs handed Benais-arik to. It shows that he is in residence here, instead of the capital." He scratched his chin, where beard stubble had appeared because his soldiers had forgotten to remind him to shave this morning. "This could be difficult."

Lahshar shouldered her way through the crowd and elbowed Kai aside to stand next to Bashasa. She stared at the banners as if hoping everyone else was wrong, and then hissed something in

Arike. Bashasa and Salatel and the others had been teaching Kai the Arike language, but he didn't know that word yet. He had seen enough of Lahshar at this point to know he would never like her, but she was at least as tough as a Saredi captain. Seeing her so dismayed was unnerving.

"Yes," Bashasa agreed, speaking in Imperial. He glanced at Lahshar's stricken expression and said, "Cousin, you knew this would come to pass sooner or later."

"Yes, but—" She bit the words back. "How did that puckered ass know we were coming? There hasn't been time!"

Tahren swung up onto the palanquin's rail beside Kai, and he managed not to twitch. She was the only one who could climb down from one wallwalker, run to catch up with another, and climb it while it was in motion. The first time it had been twilight and when she popped up out of nowhere it had startled Kai so badly he had almost punched her in the face. She said, "The legion that came to relieve the Summer Halls must have used Immortal Blessed to carry messages ahead of us."

Bashasa nodded agreement. "There is a source for the Well of Thosaren at Benais-arik. The puckered ass—I like that, Lahshar, it's apt—thought we might travel here and came to meet us."

"But what are we going to do?" Lahshar demanded, an edge of despair in her voice. Kai was wondering that too, but thought it was typical of how Bashasa's cousins were so obstructive right up until it was time for him to think of something to save their lives.

Because it was obvious this was the end.

Bashasa said, "We will stop in the town, and let everyone disembark. I'll continue on with my cadre and speak to Karanis."

Kai watched Trenal's shoulders relax, as her fear settled into determination. The soldiers here had always planned to die defending Bashasa, even before he had decided on his impossible plan to fight. That had been Kai's plan, too, more or less. He said, "I'll go with you."

Bashasa turned to him, and smiled. He looked pleased and fond, as if they were planning to do something fun. "Thank you, Fourth Prince."

———— ✦ ————

They brought the wallwalkers into the town plaza, instead of the stables outside it, the better to give the refugees a chance to conceal themselves among the population. Kai thought they might be attacked immediately, but the Arike seemed confident in the people who lived here.

When Kai climbed down after Bashasa and the soldiers, the leader of the town was already greeting them, speaking rapidly in Arike. Salatel translated, "Karanis arrived at dawn today with word of our escape. She says they will hide everyone they can. There may be traitors in the town but there are already many refugees here and our people can blend in with them."

The breeze played with the fringed awnings at the edge of the dusty plaza, water chuckled in the big fountain. The smell of woodsmoke and sizzling olive oil and garlic came from a nearby cookhouse. Other mortals gathered, fearful and staring, some already mixing with the wallwalkers' passengers as they climbed down. There was a steady murmur of dismay, of wonder. The Arike, both the townspeople and the refugees, kept coming up to clasp Bashasa's hand, like a ritual. Kai felt a little sick. The last real Prince-heir of Benais-arik, going to his death. What would it have been like if the Kentdessa Saredi could have said goodbye to their last captain, or to Grandmother? Bashasa allowed the touches and handclasps, continuing his urgent conversation with the town leader while distractedly nodding to each person who came to him. "No one ever came back from the Summer Halls before," Kai said in realization.

Salatel nodded grimly. "At least they will remember us."

By the time the other Prince-heirs and soldiers were all gathered, the town leader had ordered horses to be brought. "They don't want Bashasa to walk into the fort like a criminal," Salatel explained.

Kai watched it like a story being acted out, mostly in languages he didn't know, though Salatel translated when she could. The other Prince-heirs, Hiranan, Vrim, Asara, and Stamash were coming with them, bringing their cadres. So was Lahshar, though she ordered Dasara to stay behind. He argued violently, began to cry, and she told two of her cadre to drag him away and keep him from following. Others were coming too, servers, dependents, some who weren't Arike. Tahren tried to make Dahin stay behind, but he became so agitated she finally hugged him and agreed. Bashasa tried to tell Ziede to leave but she said pointedly, "We started this together, we'll finish it together."

There were only enough horses for the Prince-heirs and higher-ranking soldiers. Bashasa asked for Tahren to be given one, as courtesy to an Immortal Marshall, and Ziede swung up to ride behind her. These horses were a breed Kai hadn't seen before, sandy-colored and tall, with long legs and pads on their feet instead of hooves, teeth a little too sharp and eyes a little too beady. But when they brought one for him, it shied like a normal horse. Kai told them, "Horses don't like demons. Salatel, you take it." She protested, but Bashasa was suddenly there. His mount snuffled in protest at the proximity but Bashasa was apparently too good a rider to let it further express its dislike. He leaned down and held out his hand. "Fourth Prince?"

Kai swung up behind him. With the cadres and others walking, they rode toward the bridge.

The outer walls slanted back, the stone polished to reflect the sun. The inner walls were painted with bright colors and carved with images of savage battles where the warriors had elaborate and implausible armor. Soldiers watched them from the little cupolas atop the many round towers.

The inner gates of the fort made clanking noises. Gears

turning as the heavy doors were cranked open. Kai leaned on Bashasa's sturdy back because why not, and thought, *This is fine. I'm tired.* He had gotten more vengeance than he could have ever hoped for, and a chance to put Enna's body to rest, even if it was far from her home.

"She said 'escape,'" Bashasa said thoughtfully.

"What?"

"The town leader. Our escape," Bashasa clarified. "Implying that we slipped away from a place that was still intact."

Kai understood then. Escape, not rebellion. Either Karanis hadn't been told the full story or he was keeping it from the other Arike. "How can that help?"

"Eh." Bashasa shrugged. "It's given me an idea."

They rode through the gates, the shadow of the heavy walls and pillars falling across them like bars. Inside was a broad stone plaza, looked down on by walls honeycombed with windows and balconies. A ramp dropped down to a lower plaza, then to another even lower, like a giant's version of a step well. Most of the fort's soldiers were assembled on those two lower levels, watching them. More mortals watched from the windows or lined the balconies.

They wore legionaries' armor and gear, but they were all various shades of brown, their dark hair in loose or tight curls, and few looked happy to be here. Only those with officers' tails were the paler-skinned mortals from the south, from wherever the Hierarchs bred their followers. Conscripts from Arike and the surrounding areas, then. And all those Kai could see were dressed as men in tied split skirts. Kai had figured out by now that Arike soldiers were traditionally women, and Arike women wore pants; had the Hierarchs killed the whole garrison and conscripted men to replace them, or made the captured soldiers change their gender? Another reason they didn't look happy to be here.

Opposite their position, high in the far wall, was a large shaded gallery where a group of brightly dressed mortals and legionary officers stood. Only one was sitting down, on a carved stone chair on a raised platform like the Hierarch in the water court. But he didn't look like a Hierarch, he looked like an Arike in a very elaborate brocaded coat, like the one Bashasa wore. That had to be Karanis.

It was disturbingly quiet, just the banners snapping in the breeze, and the occasional grumbling noise from the horses.

"He's arranged this like a stage," Bashasa said, thoughtful and without a trace of nerves in his voice. As resigned as Kai was, his heart was pounding in every pulse point. "Which means something is about to happen."

This was already a massive trap, there was no way they could escape. But Karanis would know Bashasa, and Bashasa was never more dangerous than when he was talking. Kai's gaze snapped to the balconies, tracking potential lines of sight, just as Tahren shouted, "Crossbow!"

Kai grabbed Bashasa's waist and swung him around, putting his own back toward the most likely direction of attack. He felt the thump below his right shoulder just as they tumbled off the horse. It danced sideways, snarling, blocking more potential shooters. Kai stayed in a protective crouch over Bashasa. He could smell someone's fear sweat, feel the gritty stone underfoot, the rise and fall of Bashasa's chest as he tried to get his breathing under control. Tahren and the soldiers moved around them, re-forming to better shield them from the balcony vantage points.

Someone tapped his shoulder to let him know they were protected. He straightened up with a wince and let Bashasa stand. Kai looked down at the bloody bolthead sticking out of his upper chest. He didn't want to pull it out; it was wedged in deep and he couldn't afford to lose the use of one arm right now, even for the short time it would take him to recover.

Bashasa gripped his shoulders, brow furrowed in concern. "Fourth Prince, this grows more disturbing every time it happens."

"It's fine," Kai said, absently dusting off Bashasa's coat. "What's your plan?"

"There's a plan?" Lahshar muttered from nearby.

Hiranan had taken charge of the Arike while Bashasa was distracted. She leaned on her crutch, her free hand lifted to tell the soldiers to hold their positions. Her cadre leader stood in front of her, blocking the line of sight from the balconies. Hiranan was outwardly calm, but sweat dampened her gray-streaked curls to her brow. She said, "Is there a plan, Bashasa?"

"Yes." Bashasa pulled a folded square of fabric out of his coat. "Step aside."

Trenal and Salatel signaled the other soldiers and Hiranan gestured to her cadre. The group parted and Kai walked forward with Bashasa, out to the front of the platform. A watchful Tahren moved to flank them. Ziede was to Kai's left, the soldiers and Prince-heirs in a loose formation behind them. Every nerve-ending on Kai's body was alert; whatever this was depended on his ability to block the next attempt on Bashasa.

As they stepped forward, the silence broke. Murmurs, gasps ran through the assembled conscripts. It made Kai think Karanis had not told his people who was arriving. Even the mortals on the throne platform reacted with shock. Bashasa lived and he was standing next to someone apparently unaffected by a crossbow bolt jammed through their chest; both must be startling.

From the gallery, Karanis said, "Bashasa Calis." His voice was deep, sounding hollow in the large space, some trick of the way the walls were shaped helping it carry. In Imperial, he continued, "You have violated the treaty with the Honored High Hierarchs and endangered all our people—"

Bashasa shook out the fabric, the torn banner he had taken from the trophy hall. He held it up, let the sudden wind catch and unfurl it. Kai was certain Ziede was responsible for that wind; it wasn't disturbing the other banners hanging above the gallery.

The murmur this time took on an edge. Dahin, suddenly at

Kai's elbow, whispered, "That's the banner of Suneai-arik, the city that the Hierarchs completely destroyed."

Kai nudged him back as Tahren whispered, "Dahin, get back here."

Bashasa pitched his voice to carry. "We left the Hostage Courts and marched through the Summer Halls, leaving ruin behind us. We fought the Hierarchs there. We won."

Kai felt Ziede's command of the wind change, as she altered the air movement to make sure Bashasa was heard. He continued, "I took this from their wall of trophies, where they hung the stolen treasures of a hundred lands and the bones of the brave who fought them, disgraced and despoiled like animals. I ripped this banner from their wall and we redeemed the blood of our murdered kin in Hierarchs' flesh. Cousin, show them."

Trenal passed Salatel her short spear and pulled the bag open. Lahshar hesitated, then her expression turned grimly determined. She stepped forward, dragged both heads out of the bag and held them high. Even Kai understood the politics of that; Lahshar and Bashasa were from rival branches in their family, and they had just shown they were united in this.

"This is a lie." Karanis shoved to his feet. His voice held an edge of panic, also clearly audible. "The dispatch from the High Shield of the Hierarchs—"

"It is no lie." Bashasa roared the words and still managed to sound calm and controlled. "I joined with the Prince-heirs of our imprisoned cities, with allies from Enalin, Ilveri, Grale, Nibet, and many others. All have risen to fight. An Immortal Marshall joins us, a Witch Sister of the Khalin Islands, and a powerful demon prince of the Fourth House of the underearth. Others will follow in our wake. We left the Summer Halls a ruin where the bodies of legionaries and Hierarch nobles rot in floodwater." He took another step forward. "Karanis, you took this duty because you love our people and wish to protect them. Now it is time to fight for them. Join with us—"

Bashasa had given the usurper a way out, and he should have taken it.

Movement on the gallery warned Kai before Tahren could speak. He stepped in front of Bashasa and lifted his arms. Three bolts thunked into his back. One passed under his arm and struck Trenal in the leg. She fell back with a low grunt of pain as Nirana caught her.

The crowd had gone silent again. Cerala helped Nirana pull Trenal back between the horses. Kai took a deep breath, meeting Bashasa's worried gaze. Pain reverberated through Talamines' body but if he faltered, they might be done for. Bashasa had claimed the support of an unstoppable demon prince, and Kai had to make that true. Karanis was surely too smart to let Bashasa talk his way out of anything less. Kai released the pent breath, made his face neutral, and turned around.

He stepped to the side, revealing Bashasa again, unhurt, his demon prince apparently unaffected by the bolts. Bashasa raised his voice again and said, "I call on you all, join us."

Karanis yelled, "Kill them!" and the crowd erupted.

<hr />

The sun had shifted toward twilight and the day's heat had broken by the time Kai climbed up to the viewing gallery where Bashasa was working. In the courtyard below, conscripts hurried back and forth along with the cadres, but Kai honestly wasn't sure what everyone was doing. Once the crossbow bolts had been extracted from his chest and back, he had spent the last couple of hours helping Prince-heir Hiranan and Salatel question the few surviving legionary officers and the two Hierarch servant-nobles. Karanis himself had been one of the first to die. A server standing at the back of the viewing gallery had stabbed him from behind with a meat knife.

Bashasa had thrown his coat over the stone seat and sat on the platform below it, where he could spread out his maps and notes and writing implements. A few members of his cadre were stationed around the platform, to guard him and run messages. There was a flask of water and cups nearby, but someone was going to have to make Bashasa stop and eat soon.

"What news, Fourth Prince?" Bashasa said, without looking up.

Kai took a seat on the dusty stone beside him. He did have a report to give, but it wasn't urgent. "How is Trenal?" The other cadre members had only scrapes and bruises at best. Most of the fighting had been over by the time they got off the platform.

"She will recover, the doctors say," Bashasa assured him. "But she is forbidden to walk for now, at least without a crutch."

That was good to hear. Kai absently brushed at a bloodstain on his skirt. He had had a chance to change clothes, but kept the tunic with the crossbow bolt tears, to make a point for anyone who had any doubts. He had a question and there probably wouldn't be a better time to ask it. "That was the plan? You were just going to talk?"

"Yes." Bashasa glanced up to grin at him. "But before I realized Karanis had been lied to and was woefully unprepared, I had no idea what to say."

"He could have accused you of selfishly endangering all the Arike." Kai tried to recall the exact words. If he was going to be Bashasa's . . . whatever he was, he wanted to make sure he understood everything that had happened. "He started to, didn't he?"

"He did. I would have replied that the Hierarchs had no intention of fulfilling their treaties, that they would slaughter us all eventually so they could settle our land unimpeded, but I have said this before, to not much effect." Bashasa looked down over the courtyard. On the lowest platform, a group of Arike conscripts were singing and doing some kind of ring dance. Others lit the lamps that hung along the walls, anticipating the oncoming night. Kai spotted Tahren, following Ziede along an upper gallery with Dahin trailing behind. "There seemed no other option then." Bashasa turned back to his map. "He could also have offered deals to the other Prince-heirs and played us off each other." A thought struck him, and he turned to Kai. "But you made him too afraid to think. That was very well done, Kai. And then he ordered an attack that made it clear he was afraid for the people to hear me speak." Bashasa shrugged. "Of course nothing is guaranteed. We could all die tomorrow! But until then, we work."

Kai nodded. "Did you know the conscripts would turn on him?"

Bashasa waggled one hand, then reached for his pen again. "I knew any Arike conscripts would not have been treated well, and would not be pleased to turn on their own people." He lifted his brows as he made a note. "It was certainly worth a try."

Kai watched Bashasa write, as the shadows lengthened over the court. He was well aware he didn't have a tenth of Bashasa's self-control. He said finally, "I don't know if I can do what you want me to do, Bashasa. If I can stay calm and always think ahead, like you do. I'm so angry, I could burn the world."

Bashasa didn't seem concerned. "Unfortunately, someone else has already burned it. We need to unburn it." He looked up, his expression serious. "Will you help me do that, Kai?"

Kai had already made that decision. "Yes." He stood up, dusted off his skirt, and added, "You need to eat something. I can tell you what we got out of the prisoners, and Hiranan wants to talk to you after that." He held out his hand.

"Ah," Bashasa said, smiling up at him as he took it. "Then let us go and do that."

SIXTEEN

Kai sat in the dusty stone chair on the viewing platform overlooking the Kagala's courtyard. Tahren and Saadrin had made quick work of the rest of the Lesser Blessed and the mortal Nient-arik in the fort. Saadrin had even managed to keep Vrenren alive to act as a witness when she returned to the Blessed Lands. Tahren and Ziede were having a reunion in the guardroom just below this gallery, and Kai had sealed off his connection to Ziede's pearl to give them privacy. Tenes and Sanja were sitting in the shade near the raft, swinging their feet and talking in Witchspeak.

There was still a lot to do. Get to a place where they could find transport, so they could return the ascension raft to Saadrin and she could carry away her prisoner. They would have to come back here to dismantle the Witch cells and hide them where Bashat and the Rising World couldn't find them. Maybe Grandmother would have some ideas about that. Worry about Arnsterath. That was the one he had no idea what to do about.

It was too much at the moment; Kai was just going to sit here for now.

Dahin wandered up the gallery and plopped down on the step at his feet. "Did you talk to Tahren?" Kai asked him. Dahin had sobbed with relief when he saw her. Kai thought it was a good sign.

Dahin's brow creased in what might be concern. "She said it was like being asleep, and having dreams she couldn't remember." He didn't look up at Kai. "Do you believe her? Is she lying to make me—make us feel better about not finding her sooner."

It was certainly a Tahren thing to do. But Kai didn't think so.

Tahren hadn't been maddened when she came out, just confused. Like Kai and Ziede had been, when they had woken in the tomb. All the horror of the situation had been in retrospect. "I believe her. The cells were made a long time ago by borderlanders. They had no reason to be cruel."

Dahin absorbed that information in silence. Early night birds flew over the fort walls, hunting flying insects. "So, what should we do with this place?" he asked finally. "Burn it down? I assume a flood isn't likely. The rock looks worn away down there, Tenes could probably knock down a wall or two and start a collapse."

"I like this place," Kai said, then was a little surprised to realize he wasn't being ironic. "Despite everything. It should stay."

Dahin swiveled around to look up at him. He eyed Kai for a moment and evidently decided he was serious. "Then as long as we don't have to live here, it should stay."

Kai met Dahin's gaze, and said, "Come back to Avagantrum with us."

"Ah." Dahin smiled and looked out toward the court again. "Are you trying to impose your will on me?"

"Yes, Dahin, that's what I'm doing, can't you tell?" Kai leaned back in the stone seat. He was going to leave it at that; more persuasion would just give Dahin reasons to say no.

Footsteps sounded from the far side of the gallery, then Ziede and Tahren emerged from the door there. They were holding hands, Ziede towing Tahren along, Tahren content to follow where Ziede led.

Kai pushed up from the chair. "Are you ready to go?" he asked them.

Dahin stood. "I'll tell Aunt Saadrin to put what's-his-name in the raft," he said, and was out the opposite door before Kai could say anything.

But looking after him, Tahren said, "I think he's better." She looked better herself. With the fort's well still working, Ziede had filled a cistern for her to have a bath, and had washed her clothes.

They were still damp, but in the dry heat they wouldn't be for long. Ziede looked relaxed for the first time since they had woken in the tomb, all the tension washed out of her shoulders, the strain from her eyes.

Kai started to turn toward the door to the stairs, but Ziede took his hand instead. A cool breeze swept through the gallery as she called a wind-devil. "Where exactly are we going next?" she asked. "Besides away from here?"

"I don't know yet," Kai admitted. He had meant to ask Dahin for ideas. But the vivid memory of sitting here with Bashasa was all he could think of now. He said, "To find something to unburn."

Tahren flicked a knowing look at him, and Ziede said with decision, "I like that."

And together they stepped into the air.

ACKNOWLEDGMENTS

This book might not exist without my friend Felicia O'Sullivan, who must have read what felt like a hundred drafts of the first 30,000 to 80,000 words with no resolution in sight, and who was encouraging and enthusiastic and helped me figure out what I was trying to do.

This book would not be in your hands without editor Lee Harris, publisher Irene Gallo, jacket designer Christine Foltzer, editorial assistant Matt Rusin, the copyeditors and proofreaders, and the rest of the Tordotcom team, especially Mordicai, Desirae, and Renata.

This book would not be nearly as lovely without cover artist Cynthia Sheppard and map artist Rhys Davies.

And I would not still be writing without my agent, Jennifer Jackson, and Michael Curry.